PRAISE FOR ERIKA ROBUCK

PRAISE FOR *THE LAST ASSIGNMENT*

"In *The Last Assignment*, Erika Robuck brings to life Georgette 'Dickey' Chapelle, a fiercely daring photographer who dedicated her life to capturing history through her lens. In an era when female photographers were often overlooked, Dickey took extraordinary risks—crossing borders in Hungary, confronting communists in Cuba, parachuting into Laos—all in pursuit of one goal: to tell the truth to the American public. Vivid and compelling, rich with historical significance, and sharp-edged like Dickey's own haunting snapshots, *The Last Assignment* offers not only a gripping account of the tumultuous events of the 1960s but also serves as an elegiac anthem for a woman who lived boldly on her own terms and lives on as a legend."

—Weina Dai Randel, *Wall Street Journal* bestselling author of *The Last Rose of Shanghai* and *The Master Jeweler*

"Dickey Chapelle covered the Cold War like no other—risking her life and sacrificing her safety to tell the stories of those fighting for freedom on the front lines. Robuck's sweeping prose gives new depth to this larger-than-life figure whose legacy deserves a place in the pantheon of American heroes. From start to finish, *The Last Assignment* pulls readers into Dickey's heart-pounding narrative of war and peace."

—Lorissa Rinehart, historian and critically acclaimed author of *First to the Front: The Untold Story of Dickey Chapelle, Trailblazing Female War Correspondent*

"*The Last Assignment* exquisitely captures the daring exploits and risks of real-life combat correspondent Georgette 'Dickey' Chapelle in a way that is relatable, heartfelt, and impactful. Erika Robuck is a master of her craft in detailing the lives of real women who have left their mark on history, and this book is no different. Brilliantly researched and written with incredible skill and heart, this story is a testament to the power of Dickey's determination to share the suffering of those in need with the world."

—Madeline Martin, *New York Times* and international bestselling author of *The Booklover's Library*

"Compelling and exhilarating, Erika Robuck's *The Last Assignment* brings to life the extraordinary story of one of war journalism's most daring figures, Georgette 'Dickey' Chapelle, a trail-blazing photojournalist whose determination to bear witness to the brutal realities of war left us with a deeper understanding of the human cost of conflict. I loved learning about this incredible woman."

—Whitney Scharer, bestselling author of *The Age of Light*

"Full of passion, courage, and surprises, Dickey Chapelle is a firecracker of a main character! *The Last Assignment* takes us on a wild ride around the globe with one of the twentieth century's most fascinating photojournalists. I couldn't put this book down."

—Elise Hooper, author of *The Library of Lost Dollhouses*

PRAISE FOR *THE LAST TWELVE MILES*

"What a fun and riveting ride! Erika Robuck has unearthed two real-life Prohibition-Era heroines—one a savvy rumrunner, the other an ambitious codebreaker—and vividly recreated their adventures, including a tension-packed cat-and-mouse game that threatens to destroy them both. *The Last Twelve Miles* so immersed me in the wild and raucous world of the Roaring Twenties that I never wanted it to end—even as I furiously turned the pages to see what would happen next."

—Karen Abbott, *New York Times* bestselling author of *The Ghosts of Eden Park*

"*The Last Twelve Miles* is a richly detailed portrait of two compelling women on opposite sides of the law. Set against the backdrop of the Prohibition Rum Wars, Robuck has brought two real-life figures to the page with heartfelt intimacy and crackling suspense. A fascinating read!"

—Chanel Cleeton, *New York Times* and *USA Today* bestselling author of *The Cuban Heiress*

"Action heroes have nothing on real-life cryptologist Elizebeth Smith Friedman. *The Last Twelve Miles* is a nonstop historical thriller that poises two brilliant women against each other in a deadly game of rumrunning, codebreaking, and murder. Erika Robuck brings this real American hero and real criminal mastermind to vivid life. Knock back a shot and prepare to have this novel knock your socks off. Dazzling!"

—Pamela Klinger-Horn, event coordinator, Valley Bookseller

"In this gripping and devilishly exciting Prohibition-Era novel, *The Last Twelve Miles* effortlessly tells the story of two real and brilliant women, one running illegal booze between Miami, the Bahamas, and Cuba, and the other, a master codebreaker, hot on her trail. Robuck's meticulous research and impeccable characterization shine through in this fierce, feminist, and unforgettable novel."

—Nicola Harrison,
author of *Hotel Laguna*

"Two women, a coast guard special agent and a bootlegger, face off against each other in this Prohibition-Era novel. Their journeys of marriage, motherhood, and career intertwine in this fascinating story based on true events."

—Rae Ann Parker,
bookseller at Parnassus Books

"Move over Al Capone and Eliot Ness! It's time to make space for Elizabeth Friedman and Marie Waite—a captivating pair of badass women on opposite sides of Prohibition law. In her terrific new historical fiction, *The Last Twelve Miles*, Erika Robuck brings you Elizabeth, the brilliant cryptanalyst who breaks code for the U.S. Coast Guard, and Marie, the equally brilliant rumrunner who plies the waters off the coast of Florida. Never has there been a more fascinating set of rivals, and you will find yourself torn over which of them you'd like to see win. Richly drawn characters, a crackerjack plot, and a setting that is equal parts glamorous and deadly make *The Last Twelve Miles* a must-read for 2024."

—Deborah Goodrich Royce,
national bestselling author of *Reef Road*

"*The Last Twelve Miles* is the thrilling story of two extraordinary women on opposite sides of the law but with more in common than they think. Based on a true story, Elizebeth, a meticulous government codebreaker, hunts down Marie, the flamboyant rumrunner who makes and loses fortunes on the waters off the Florida Keys during Prohibition. Both the G-woman and the mobster are also wives and mothers struggling to thrive in men's domains. A breezy and brutal glimpse into the world of Jazz Age gangsters from a fresh angle. Really enjoyable!"

—Anika Scott, international bestselling author of *Sinners of Starlight City*

Historical Fiction by Erika Robuck

The Last Twelve Miles
Receive Me Falling
Hemingway's Girl
Call Me Zelda
Fallen Beauty
The House of Hawthorne
The Invisible Woman
Sisters of Night and Fog

The
LAST
ASSIGNMENT

A Novel of Dickey Chapelle

ERIKA ROBUCK

sourcebooks
landmark

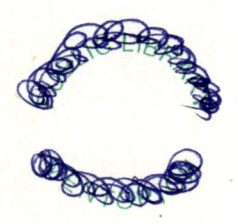

Copyright © 2025 by Erika Robuck
Cover and internal design © 2025 by Sourcebooks
Jacket design by Sarah Brody/Sourcebooks
Jacket images © Phawat/Shutterstock, white snow/Shutterstock, Oliver Denker/Shutterstock

Sourcebooks and the colophon are registered trademarks of Sourcebooks.

All rights reserved. No part of this book may be reproduced in any form or by any electronic or mechanical means including information storage and retrieval systems—except in the case of brief quotations embodied in critical articles or reviews—without permission in writing from its publisher, Sourcebooks.

No part of this book may be used or reproduced in any manner for the purpose of training artificial intelligence technologies or systems.

The characters and events portrayed in this book are fictitious or are used fictitiously. Apart from well-known historical figures, any similarity to real persons, living or dead, is purely coincidental and not intended by the author.

All brand names and product names used in this book are trademarks, registered trademarks, or trade names of their respective holders. Sourcebooks is not associated with any product or vendor in this book.

Published by Sourcebooks Landmark, an imprint of Sourcebooks
1935 Brookdale RD, Naperville, IL 60563-2773
(630) 961-3900
sourcebooks.com

Cataloging-in-Publication Data is on file with the Library of Congress.

Printed and bound in the United States of America.
VP 10 9 8 7 6 5 4 3 2 1

*For Richard Robuck, my father-in-law—a Vietnam veteran—
and Patricia Robuck, my mother-in-law,
with gratitude for their service and love.*

"The wreckage resulting from man's inhumanity to man... was the litany I wrote and the subject I photographed."

—Dickey Chapelle, *What's a Woman Doing Here?*

OCTOBER 1965
MADISON, WISCONSIN

Combat boots with the soil of four continents in their treads pound over the tree-lined walkways of the University of Wisconsin, Madison. Breath coming fast, arms aching with effort, thighs burning, knee protesting, the war correspondent races toward the stairs of the building housing the Wisconsin Historical Society. Crisp wind rushing off Lake Mendota fills her lungs, and the thrill of beating her little nephew and niece—seven and five respectively—puffs her ego, making her euphoric.

"Georgette Dickey Meyer Chapelle takes the lead," she yells over her shoulder, like a horse-race announcer. "Forty-six years old, combat-fatigued, fake knee, smoker's lungs, and all, she triumphs over youth. She laughs in the face of it."

Over the crunch of the first fallen leaves, Dickey hears the shrieks of the children close behind her, followed by the laughter of her brother. Though her arms are laden with a box of files, and her camera-filled field pack bangs against her back, she pulls farther ahead of Hans and Martha. Students part on the walkway before them, faces an equal distribution of amusement and disapproval. The kids grow hysterical, clearly unable to believe their aunt is going to beat them in a footrace while carrying a ten-pound box.

At the grand columned Historical Society building, Dickey takes the stairs two at a time, smashes into the wooden doors with the box, sets it on the landing, and jumps up and down, whooping with joy. Once the kids touch the door, she lifts Martha and swings her around, eliciting giggles. Dickey places her niece on the stairs, ruffles Hans's hair, looks up past the oak tree leaves, golden against the bright blue sky, and takes a deep breath.

Robert walks up behind them—the very picture of the dignified army veteran turned professor—and shakes his head. He's a geology instructor at the university, and his wife, Marion, got her PhD in comparative physiology here while the kids babbled in playpens in her office. The campus is a second home to them, and just blocks from their real home.

"Still got it," Robert says.

"No training like marine training," Dickey replies.

Dickey picks up the file box and they proceed inside. Walking through the neoclassical building, inspired by the Place de la Concord's colonnades, makes Dickey draw up her shoulders, a surge of pride pulsing through her. The face of the undergraduate on work study at the information desk brightens when she sees Dickey and her entourage coming toward her. The young woman hurries out from behind the desk to help. Dickey has been in contact with the Wisconsin Historical Society for months about donating her many boxes of files, photographs, journals, and news clippings to an archive under her well-known name. Her Manhattan apartment can no longer hold the files and Dickey has felt an urge to clean out and to nest, almost the way a pregnant woman does before the birth of her child.

"No need," says Dickey. "Just direct me."

"Through those doors," says the young woman.

Dickey takes the box to a conference room and places it on the table. Her brother, his children, and the young woman follow.

"My photo agent will send the rest," says Dickey. "I wanted to see to these boxes myself."

After Dickey discusses a few more logistics with the young woman, she leaves them. Dickey turns to see Hans and Martha poking through the boxes. Hans lifts a photograph out of one that brings a smile to Dickey's face.

"Who's this?" asks Hans.

"Father Hoa. The priest-soldier I told you about."

"The one who lives in Vietnam?"

"Yes."

"The one who's saving that village you love."

"The one who's trying," Dickey says.

Who tried, she thinks, her smile evaporating.

"Why are you bringing all this here?" asks Martha.

"I've been wondering the same thing," says Robert.

"I told you," says Dickey. "I'm donating my papers so future war correspondents have a road map. So researchers can see how twentieth-century history unfolded from the front lines."

"Isn't this a little premature?" says Robert. "This is the kind of archive people leave in wills."

Dickey and Robert stare across the table at each other for a long moment.

Hans pulls a book from the box. It's a well-worn copy of James Michener's novel *The Bridge at Andau*. There's a bookmark and Hans opens up to the page it holds.

"It's signed, to you," says Hans.

"Yes, by my old friend Jim, who wrote it."

"What's the book about?"

"Remember when I told you about the Hungarian Revolution?" she asks.

"And the prison?" Hans asks, eyes wide.

"Yes, all that. The book is about the revolution. And I'm in it."

"Wow," he says, his voice a whisper.

Martha pulls out a gold medal.

"What's this?" she asks.

Dickey sees the award Fidel Castro gave her for being a "friend of Cuba," reporting on the Cuban Revolution. Her arms have fresh scars from the boat explosion just months ago she got with anti-Castro guerrillas. The halls of her memory echo with Fidel's warning that if she ever returns to Cuba, she had better do so with the marines, because she'll need protecting. He once told her, when she portrayed him favorably, that she had tiger blood in her veins.

"It's an award from an old friend turned enemy," says Dickey. "From Cuba."

"Weren't you kicked out of there?" asks Hans. "Like Hungary?"

"Yes. I'm not allowed back in either country. I'm trying to behave better in Vietnam, but my odds aren't looking good."

Losing interest in the ephemera from Aunt Dickey's world

travels, the kids chase each other around the table. Robert sends them outside to play. Dickey follows, but Robert touches her arm, stopping her. He stares at her, searching her face. She finds she cannot look him in the eye. She turns away, and they walk out together to fetch the rest of the boxes from his car.

Outside the building, they stand at the top of the stairs, looking out over the campus, warm and saturated with autumn colors. Though it's tranquil now, protests over American involvement in Vietnam keep erupting. A gust of wind rattles through the trees, dislodging a wrinkled brown leaf. It floats to the ground to rest in the yellowing grass.

"You're not coming back, are you?" Robert asks.

"I don't think so."

"Dickey," he chokes on her name.

"It's not like that," she says. "I mean, I don't think I'm going to die."

"Beg your pardon, Sis, but you're getting too old for this."

"Did you not just see me beat your children in a footrace, while carrying a box?"

"I don't mean only physically. Seven conflicts, Dickey. Seven wars. One is too much for most people. You keep going back into the belly of the beast. And we all know you act first, think second. You look up to soldiers like we're heroes. We're just men, Dickey. Men who don't always make the right decisions. Sometimes I wonder if you're addicted to conflict."

Dickey's skin grows hot. She feels her tongue ready to lash out at Robert. However, the gentle face of Father Hoa appears in her mind. She thinks of how he tries to win the hearts and minds of his enemies rather than destroy them. She pulls a cigarette out of her pocket and offers one to Robert, which he declines. She takes a few long draws to steady herself.

"When I said I'm not coming back," she says, "I mean Wisconsin will never be my home base. In spite of Aunt Lutie hoping I'll sell my New York apartment and move into the old family house with her."

"We would all love to have you here. At least as a kind of headquarters before you go on your endless missions."

Dickey's anger evaporates. She reaches for Robert's hand.

"Slug," she says using her old nickname for her little brother. "I love you all so much. But you know my contacts in New York and DC are essential to my assignments. And at this point, if I ever set down roots, it would be in South Vietnam. I've fallen in love with it. You'd understand if you could watch the sunset over the rice paddies of the Mekong Delta, while the flute plays, and the kids fish the canals, and the bell on the church rings the all clear every hour. Where a lifetime of birth, death, marriage, war, and worship happen in a day, and the world is in vivid color. I have this dream that your family will visit me there, sometime in the future."

"Sure, I'll pack the kids in a chopper and we'll all parachute into the village under enemy fire the way Aunt Dickey does."

She laughs.

"If I achieve my life's goal," she says, "you'll be able to do just that, minus the enemy fire."

"I thought your life's goal was to always *be first*."

"That was a directive by an editor. A code of female correspondent conduct if you will. My new goal is different."

Hans and Martha's laughter calls her attention. They glide around the lawn with arms outstretched like airplane wings.

Dickey thinks of the endless air shows she dragged Robert to growing up. She thinks of the grainy black-and-white film of her hero Admiral Richard Byrd in his flying missions over Antarctica, and of the rush she gets jumping out of airplanes. Dickey stomps out her cigarette and holds up her hands to frame the scene, thinking of the captions. Children, higher learning, a brisk fall day, a Norman Rockwell vision of freedom and democracy. She pulls her camera out of her field pack, aims, and takes the shot.

"So, what's your goal?" Robert asks.

"My goal is to make the picture to end all wars. And until my last assignment, for them," she says, pointing toward the children, "I'll work to achieve it."

PART ONE
1954–1958

ONE

DECEMBER 1954

New York City

It was a mistake coming here.

Dickey thinks this over and over on the way to the restroom of Bemelmans Bar at the Carlyle Hotel, wobbling in stiletto heels on feet partial to combat boots. She'd excused herself during her mother telling a story to Dickey's husband, Tony, and a recently immigrated German Quaker couple—Ernst and Helga—about Dickey's first date. Dickey's mother told the group, shortly before the boy arrived to pick up young Dickey, the phone rang and a classmate informed Dickey the boy only asked her out because he was dared.

"Chubby little Georgie Lou was a soldier about it," Edna said.

"Marmee, please," Dickey said.

Edna continued. "She squeezed herself into a dress for the first time since childhood, told the boy to take her for a milkshake, and spent the whole time staring into the engine of his car asking how it ran. At least they had that in common."

The inebriated group howled.

Their cackles follow Dickey to the bathroom, joining with those of all the bullies she's endured throughout her life whose cruel laughter echoes, relentless, in the halls of her memory. She has never fit in, anywhere. No one understands her. She barely understands herself. Over time she's created a sort of imaginary shield to protect herself, but that shield is harder to access when teasing comes from those closest to her.

Since Tony met Dickey's parents, years ago, he and Edna aligned themselves over their shared conviction that Dickey couldn't function without either of them. Every time they got together it was as if those two were on one side of a tennis court, Dickey on the other, trying to lob back endless shots fired at her. It was foolish to think her mother's personality might be tempered by widowhood. If anything, the woman has thrown herself into overdrive. Dickey's father was an ally for her, but he died two months ago. The memory of his kind face, his dignified manner, and his encouragement draws forth a lump in Dickey's throat, but she pushes it down. If she starts crying, she might never stop.

The light in the bathroom is unforgiving. It reveals the dark circles under Dickey's blue-green eyes behind her harlequin eyeglasses, the wide dark line of her roots against the brassy bleached blonde Tony wanted her to dye her hair, and the pills on her hunter-green dress. She didn't have time to paint her nails—chewed low on rough, dry hands—and her teeth are stained from the Roma burgundy she drank at home.

Dickey grabs a red hand towel from the stack, scrubs her smile clean, and pinches color into her cheeks. She longs for the tanned skin she had when she'd been onboard the hospital ship, the USS *Samaritan*, in the South Pacific during the Second World War. Her photographs of a marine dying, and resurrected the next day because of a blood transfusion, have been used by the Red Cross ever since and have inspired countless thousands to give blood. It's why she does what she does: to bring about good in the world so desperately lacking it.

How could it be that almost a decade has passed since the war? It was the best time of my life.

In spite of the dangerous circumstances in the Pacific theater, Dickey never felt more alive, more useful, and more purpose-filled. Charmed by her fearlessness under fire, the U.S. Marines, especially, took to her. It was the first time she had felt as if she were part of a group—that she belonged. The men called the feeling the esprit de corps: a camaraderie born from union of mission and heart, especially in battle. She has craved that feeling ever since.

Looking back at her reflection, Dickey sees the happy memories of her beloved marines have brought forth a smile. She looks better already. She has to find a way to get back to them. She gives her hair one more smoothing, tightens her pearl earrings, and takes a deep breath, full of fresh hope. When she arrives back at the bar, however, she stops, and her smile disappears.

The silhouettes of her companions have rearranged themselves. Edna and Ernst are the bookends, with Helga and Tony in the center, Tony's arm resting low around Helga's waist. Dickey's photographic and PR work with the American Friends Service Committee led to the couples' connection. As Tony and Dickey have helped Helga and Ernst acclimate to their new country these past few months, Tony and Helga have become overly familiar. Ernst either has not seen or ignores them, staring moodily at his drink. Dickey's mother, on the other hand, gawks at Tony's arm. It takes an act of will for Dickey to rejoin them. When Edna sees Dickey approach, she frowns.

This wouldn't happen if you'd just stay home and be a wife, Edna's look says.

Dickey feels a roiling in her stomach. Edna has told Dickey many times that her career as a photojournalist is hurting her marriage. The worst thing is, Dickey knows it's true. No, Dickey thinks, the worst thing is what she has been lying to herself about these past months, which is harder to deny under the scrutinizing spotlight of her mother's gaze. It was a mistake inviting Helga and Ernst, but Tony insisted.

Immobilized, Dickey panics. She longs to go back to the time, just an hour ago, when the merry company set out from their apartment on West End Avenue. Dickey's mother traveled from Milwaukee to spend the holidays with them. Tony was in good spirits, playing tour guide around Manhattan for Edna and for the immigrants they had "rescued" from behind Berlin's Iron Curtain. They couldn't wait to reunite Edna with her sisters: Louise—also recently widowed—and Georgette, who'd moved from her artist's flat in Greenwich Village into Louise's luxurious apartment at Sutton Place. In the covered horse-drawn carriage ride across Central Park, as a gentle snow fell, they'd passed ice skaters, loving families, and couples walking arm in arm.

"What an idyllic scene," Dickey said.

"Idyllic," Helga agreed in German-accented English, beaming at Tony.

Shameless, Dickey now thinks, her skin heating with embarrassment at what she's refused to see. The irony of a photojournalist pointing her lens away from the truth is not lost on her.

Today is Tony's fifty-sixth birthday. Dickey is thirty-six. Tony seduced Dickey when she was his nineteen-year-old photography student, desperate to get out from under her mother's suffocating wing. Dickey saw Tony as her savior, and he certainly billed himself that way. Helga is twenty-four. She also sees Tony as her savior. Tony likes young, impressionable, naive women who see him as a savior.

"Dickey."

At the mere sound of the voice of her beloved aunt Georgette, her namesake, Dickey bursts into tears.

"Aunt George!"

In her old aunt's embrace, Dickey inhales the familiar patchouli-and-jasmine-scented Maja Eau de Cologne like it's oxygen. After she hugs Aunt George, Dickey launches herself at Aunt Lutie.

"Goodness," says Aunt Lutie. "You act as if you're just back from Iwo Jima. You've got the same shell-shocked look. We just saw you last week."

"I'm sorry," Dickey says. "I'm so glad you're both here."

She dabs the tears away with her ring fingers, behind her glasses.

Aunt George looks over Dickey's shoulder, narrowing her eyes and nodding grimly. Aunt Lutie, less observant, hurries over to hug her fellow sister widow. The company at the bar stands, welcoming her.

"I see Edna's holding court," says Aunt George.

You've no idea, thinks Dickey.

Since the death of her father, Aunt George is Dickey's only ally. Edna loves her daughter, but she has never understood her, not for one moment. Not from the day her daughter insisted upon being called Dickey, in honor of her hero, explorer Admiral Richard "Dick" Byrd. Not from the day Dickey dropped out of Massachusetts Institute of Technology—one of the first young women admitted there, on full scholarship—to become a pilot, nor when poor eyesight resigned Dickey to her second love: reporting on pilots. Edna could not understand Dickey marrying Tony, a man old enough to be her father, though Tony charmed Edna like he could the shell off a turtle. Edna especially couldn't fathom Dickey wanting to be the first woman photographer in the Pacific theater of war and on Iwo Jima, or wanting to travel through postwar Europe's rubble-framed misery photographing refugees.

Aunt George, on the other hand, has always understood and encouraged Dickey, and her presence is a lifeline. The old woman loops her arm through Dickey's and smiles at her.

"For a pacifist," says Dickey, "Marmee sure knows how to make war."

Growing up, Dickey's parents tried to instill pacifism in their children. Both of their children had disappointed them on that front. Dickey's brother, Robert, joined the U.S. Army, and Dickey has been going to and reporting on war since 1945.

"None of us see ourselves as causing war, do we?" asks Aunt George. "But no need to fret. Your wingman has arrived."

Dickey's booming laugh erupts.

"I love that a sixty-three-year-old divorced bohemian poet uses military terminology to describe herself," Dickey says. "In all seriousness, thank you. Things turned south quickly tonight. Caught me off guard."

"It always does, Dickey," says Aunt George. "But, aside from your tendency to walk into sniper fire, I wouldn't have you any other way. Hopelessly hopeful."

Dickey squeezes her aunt's arm and steels herself for a return to battle.

There's much enthusiasm at Aunt George's arrival, and Dickey decides to dull the sting of her personal life with another of Bemelmans's famous martinis. The bartender knows her well. Dickey, Tony, and their literary agent, Marie Rodell, are frequent guests, along with most of the New York literary scene. Writers love the place named for and decorated by Ludwig Bemelmans, the creator of the charming children's Madeline books. Sometimes he can even be found at his favorite table by the piano player, sketching on napkins for patrons.

The martini soon arrives, with its sidecar. Dickey normally switches to beer after a strong drink, but tonight calls for mindless oblivion.

The volume of Tony's voice, shouting over the piano about how underappreciated his photography is, sobers Dickey. The aunts have left, taking Edna in a taxi back to their place. Dickey had longed to go with them, but now that she's attuned to Helga and Tony, she cannot leave them alone, even with Ernst there. The large young German man sulks. English is proving hard for him, so Dickey is forced to engage him. She's fluent in German because her mother's family left the country at the turn of the century, before the land they loved had cannibalized itself and the world with its war machines. Ernst, however, has shut down completely, and the bartender gives Tony looks dirtier than the martinis they've consumed.

"Time to go," Dickey says, touching Tony's shoulder.

He shakes her off, clipping her glasses with his elbow and knocking them askew.

Dickey rights them and clenches her teeth. She knows this routine well. They went through it last week at the Overseas Press Club, after Tony broke a beer bottle against the bar and threatened another journalist with the jagged remnant of it for calling Tony "Hardy." It was an allusion to Laurel's portly partner in crime, and an apt comparison. Two hundred pounds is a lot on a five-foot-seven frame. At the OPC, Dickey felt compelled to get Tony out, to protect their reputation. Freelancing is hard enough without editors hearing about bad behavior, and it's a very small community. Their peers aren't here, however, so Dickey feels less need to shield Tony.

Helga leans in and whispers in Tony's ear, and his shoulders relax. As his anger subsides, Dickey's grows. She realizes she has been too indulgent with Tony, and it has made him a spoiled man-sized child. It's time to put him in his place.

Dickey picks up her purse, pushes in her chair, and walks to the doorway of the bar. She pauses a moment before leaving and looks over her shoulder. Ernst is almost passed out. Tony and Helga's heads are bent together. They either don't notice or don't care that Dickey has gone.

Have at him. And good riddance.

Even now, it takes an effort of will for Dickey to allow these thoughts. Her mother will be disappointed in her. The dissolution of her marriage will validate everything her mother has been saying for years. Dickey feels that old familiar stomach rumbling, the worry over disappointing her mother.

No. I'm no longer a child, Dickey thinks. *Far from it. So, I won't cater to her or Tony.*

Tony is a womanizer. He spends money they don't have. He's a control freak, an alcoholic, and a liar. Dickey has tried to leave him before, but she's always felt trapped.

Several years ago, before Dickey was assigned by the Quakers to photograph refugees across postwar Europe, a woman sent Dickey a letter claiming to be Tony's lawful wife. The woman said because the divorce he'd tried to get in Mexico didn't count in the United States, Tony was still married to her. Not only that, but he'd also never paid one penny of child support for their then eight-year-old son, Ron. Both the ex-wife and the child were news to Dickey.

In the confrontation that had followed, Tony begged, pleaded, and apologized. It was only because of Dickey's insistence that he agreed to support the child and try to get to know him. Ultimately, Tony paid for Ron's boarding school in New York since Tony's ex didn't feel fit to take care of the boy full-time. Dickey knew she could not—she was almost never home, and she couldn't even keep a houseplant alive. After the situation was as settled as it could be, Dickey decided to leave Tony. That is, until the Quakers informed her that if she wanted to go to Europe, she needed a husband. They would not finance a trip for a woman traveling alone.

Dickey has been with Tony ever since.

Tonight feels different, however. With her father and uncle dead, not only is the swiftness of life apparent, but a new horizon has opened. Dickey knows she has value. She has surpassed her husband in talent, and she wants to go where she chooses, when she chooses, especially where no husband is required. A new assignment that will take her to the next level is what she needs, and she's determined to find it.

Dickey takes a deep breath and feels hope returning. Every

step across the lobby—where glowing Christmas tree lights are reflected in the black marble floors and the large mirrors lining the walls—feels like a step toward freedom. It's so close she can taste it.

TWO

DECEMBER 1954

New York City

Freedom isn't as close as Dickey hoped.

The phone rings her out of the bath. When the lawyer tells her the cost of his services to get her a state annulment, she groans, places the handset on the phone, and covers her face with her hands.

Five hundred dollars.

The Chapelles are broke.

Tony's a gambler, placing big bets on poker games and losing more than he wins. A glutton for fine food, drink, and furnishings, the money he pulls in from photography classes and reselling military surplus gear is spent before it's earned. Dickey's job working for the humanitarian organization CARE International—for whom she's been employed at various times the last seven years as a photographer and now a publicist—barely covers rent and monthlies.

Since they aren't technically, legally married, Dickey could just move on with her life. But she wants a piece of paper—a legal document making null in an official capacity what never was. It will represent true liberation to her, and a clean break, and it will keep him from being able to claim any income from her future assignments. She has to get a better job if she wants to afford it.

Thankful to at least have Tony out of the way at a card game, Dickey crosses the small but opulently decorated living room of their two-bedroom apartment. The souvenirs Tony has lugged home from their world travels make the place look like a curiosity shop. Dickey prefers to travel lightly, to live simply. She'd take a tent over a hotel room any day of the week, as long as it fit her typewriter and her camera.

"And you, Oscar," she says to the stuffed monkey, staring at her from the bed. That well-loved childhood toy has been a rabbit's foot for her all over the world—even hanging from the rearview mirror in the truck in which she and Tony traveled postwar Europe.

Dickey tosses her wet towel on the bedroom floor and dresses in her favorite clothing—military surplus gear consisting of trousers, a utility shirt, combat boots, and a U.S. Marine Corps parka. Dickey's final touch is always her pearl earrings, which she had made when she and Tony were in Tehran. She may prefer dressing like a military man, but she's never without this one feminine accoutrement. The pearls not only remind her of her travels and make her feel pretty but also provide a useful distinction in the field between her and the men she covers.

She picks up the worn rose-colored leather case of the trench knife she keeps on the nightstand next to her side of the bed and pulls out the knife, savoring the familiar sturdy feel of the weapon a wounded marine gave her on Iwo Jima, just before she went to photograph the front. A rush of shame washes over her at the thought of the incident that lost her military accreditation. As it turns out, the armed services mean business when one disobeys direct orders not to go ashore to photograph war action, especially when one is a civilian woman. The pain of the experience makes her skin turn hot and she has to force down the memory.

Dickey places the knife back in its case and on the nightstand. Though crime is on the rise in the city, weapons likely won't be necessary on today's mission, and she's determined to see it through.

She heads back to the living room and—watching the door in case Tony arrives home early, angry, and in further debt—lifts the lid off the hunter-green hassock Aunt Lutie gave them as a house-warming gift. Inside are packs of cards, puzzles, and board games. Dickey quickly removes everything until she gets to the game Tony hates—Monopoly—and lifts the lid. Under the board and mixed with the play money is a secret stash of bills Dickey constantly adds to, in case of emergency.

Today's mission isn't an emergency, but it's something Dickey wants to do, and that's good enough. She slips a twenty in her jacket pocket and stores the game in its place. From the kitchen table, she picks up a pack of Pall Malls and the gold Dunhill lighter that could feed a family in Poland for a month, which Tony got her for her birthday. On her way out, she grabs her combat field pack from the coatrack, pulls it over her shoulders, and locks the door.

Outside, the December air hits her with force, stealing her breath. Ever since visiting postwar Europe, photographing war orphans and refugees behind the Iron Curtain, Dickey has despised the cold. Her mind goes back to that first stop, the Warsaw orphanage run by friars working with the Quakers to feed and care for the human collateral of war. Like the city, the Church of St. Francis looked like a tree that had been felled by a dull axe, new shoots emerging from places where violence had been enacted. The pale gaunt friar who greeted her had paused at the door before taking Dickey into a mess hall.

"Mrs. Chapelle, what you're about to see is going to trouble you greatly."

"Oh, don't you worry about me," she said, waving her hand. "I was in the Pacific theater. I've seen men die. Lots of them."

"Death, fighting for a just cause, can be easier to see than insane orphans."

"*Insane* orphans?"

The Quakers only told me there were plain old regular orphans at this stop, Dickey thought.

"From the Nazis to the Soviet occupation," he said, "what these children have seen would break the strongest adult. These children are the Beatitudes come to life: the poor, the mourning, the meek, the hungry, the thirsty. We care for them as well as we can, but we need help. We need food, clothing, physicians, and psychologists. Adopters. Your photos will help the children by calling people to action."

His words had sobered Dickey. She was forced to admit to herself that she'd seen a free trip to Europe mostly as an adventure. She understood then that it was much more.

"I'm ready," she said with a nod.

He gave her a sad smile, revealing his thought that she could never be ready, but he opened the door anyway.

The odor was ungodly. Though there were no babies, clearly many of the waiflike creatures before her had soiled themselves. A quick scan of the room revealed thirty or so children ranging in age from about three to thirteen years. Some rocked in their seats; some picked at sores; most stared blankly into space, drooling and shivering.

The nuns caring for the orphans nodded gravely when they saw the friar and Dickey. And as the friar had predicted, Dickey learned with the first flash that she was not ready for this.

A shrieking began, screams of sheer terror echoing off the walls. Children crawled under tables, clawing at their ears, howling in a way Dickey had never heard come from human beings.

"I'm so sorry," she cried, her eyes blurred with tears.

"Again," the friar commanded, his mouth grim.

"They're terrified."

"Again."

She didn't understand the order, only that she must obey it.

Flash.

Another howling round of screams arose.

Dickey's hands shook so badly she was glad the camera hung from a neck strap. Otherwise, it would have been shattered on the floor.

"Again," he said, quieter but every bit as insistent.

Flash.

Another round of screams.

"Again. Until I tell you to stop."

Flash.

There were fewer screams. Some of the children crawled out from hiding to look at her.

Over and over, she took pictures, all the while growing in understanding, getting closer because the children let her.

Flash.

Her hands stopped trembling. Her heartbeat grew steadier. Her tears remained. When she finished, the friar thanked her.

"I know that was hard," he said. "But now they're starting to learn. Not every stranger and not every flash of light will bring destruction."

Those photos inspired both Cathedral High School, in New York City, and the Girl Scouts of America to run clothing drives, and continued to be used to bring in donations from refugee exhibits all over the world.

A Salvation Army bell calls Dickey's mind back to the present. She rifles through her jacket and pants pockets until she finds a stack of coins and deposits them with a salute. She'd planned on walking through Central Park before catching the subway to her aunt's apartment, but the biting wind whipping around the buildings drives her underground. It's even colder outside when she emerges from the train by the East River, so she practically runs to her destination.

On the corner of Fifty-First Street and Second Avenue, an old Italian man sells Christmas trees, fresh cut from his place in the Poconos, Regina Farms. Every year since living in New York, Dickey has held her breath, hoping he makes it another Christmas. She's rewarded by his warm smile, so expansive it makes the crinkles around his eyes meet those at his cheeks.

"You're a sight for sore eyes, Mr. Regina," she says.

"Miss Dickey," he says in Italian-accented English.

"How do you remember me every year? You must meet hundreds of people."

"You're unforgettable," he says.

Dickey grins and pats his arm.

"Thank you," she says. "Now, as much as I'd like to browse around, I'm not made for this cold. Do you have anything for a high-ceilinged, fancy joint?"

"Ah, you've moved up in the world? Finally recognized for your great pictures?"

"Ha! No, sirree. I'm surprising my aunt. My uncle just died, and she hasn't been able to bring herself to decorate. My mother is staying with her, and she just lost my papa. They were brothers."

"*Santo cielo!* I'm so sorry, Miss Dickey. I have the perfect thing."

He calls and gestures to his teenaged grandson to fetch the tree, while Dickey grabs tinsel and several packs of lights. The old man tries to wave off Dickey's money.

"That's too generous," she says.

"I insist," says Mr. Regina.

"I insist," she says.

They haggle for a few moments until Dickey agrees to half price on everything. She hugs him, packs the lights and tinsel in her field pack, and hoists the tree on her shoulder.

"At least let my grandson deliver it with you," he says.

Dickey shakes her head and calls over her shoulder, "Don't worry about me. I can keep up with soldiers half my age."

Mr. Regina's laughter follows her down the street.

"You are unforgettable," he calls.

"You are a nincompoop," Dickey says to herself.

Chest tight, she drops the tree on the floor with a thump outside Aunt Lutie's apartment and bangs the knocker. Dickey looks down the hallway, hoping the doors stay closed. The neighbors in an opulent building like this won't appreciate a woman in fatigues making a ruckus.

The door opens and the warmth of the apartment reaches out

and pulls Dickey inside it. The aroma of goulash surrounds Aunt Lutie like a halo.

"Georgie Lou," she says, shaking her head. "What happened to you?"

Still catching her breath, Dickey points to the towering tree bundle leaning next to the door.

"*Mein güte!*" says Aunt Lutie.

Aunt George and Dickey's mother appear behind Aunt Lutie, their faces breaking into smiles when they see Dickey's delivery. They usher her in, taking her field pack while she heaves the tree in the door and over to the windows overlooking the East River.

"You're an angel," says Aunt Lutie.

"You have to have a tree," says Dickey.

"Thank you, sweet girl," Aunt Lutie says, her eyes misting over. "So thoughtful."

"Please tell me you have a stand. I didn't think of that."

"Yes, Aunt George brought a box of old Christmas ornaments and a stand when she moved in with me."

"*Perfecto.*"

The rest of the afternoon and into the night, chain-smoking and eating stew—listening to Bing Crosby and the Andrews Sisters Christmas records from Aunt George's collection—the women decorate the tree. There's so much cheer and laughter that Dickey loses track of time, until the shrill ring of Aunt Lutie's phone reminds her of Tony. Her stomach roils the moment she remembers. She realizes if one's husband calls forth this kind of anxiety, it can't be a good marriage.

Why have I subjected myself to this for so long?

Aunt Lutie's face sobers, and she passes the phone to Dickey.

The shouting and slurring make Tony hard to understand. In the past, she would have tried to placate him and rushed to get home, but one look around the room at all its peace and warmth gives her resolve.

"I'm spending the night here," she says.

Tony begins a tirade, insisting she come home. She hangs up the phone, lights a cigarette, and walks over to the window. All day, the East River has run silver under the slate gray of the cloudy winter sky, but the twilight has turned it purple. Horrid as winter is, Dickey thinks, the colors are extraordinary. Her fingers tingle, longing to photograph it. Better yet, she'd love to fly above it in an airplane.

"Dickey, you should go home to your husband," says Edna.

Dickey looks at her mother rearranging the tinsel Dickey hung.

From the couch, Aunt George mutters something under her breath.

"My husband is drunk and he's angry," says Dickey. "You've never had a husband who got drunk and angry, but let me assure you, it's not something you want to be around."

"Does he get violent with you?" Aunt George asks.

"He hasn't hit me," says Dickey. "Yet. But he gets pushy and loud, and the threat is there."

Aunt George purses her lips, her pale, papery skin flushing.

"You need to leave that man," she says.

"No," says Edna. "Divorce is out of the question. Dickey's reputation will be sunk."

"I'm divorced," says Aunt George. "My reputation suffered no blow."

"You're a poet, Georgette. Greenwich Village isn't like the rest of the world."

"How about seeing a marriage therapist?" says Aunt Lutie. "I read an article about it in one of the women's mags. It's becoming quite the thing."

"I also read those magazines," says Edna. "And every article you see emphasizes that if men are unhappy in marriage, wives need to reflect on what they are doing to contribute to such unhappiness. Just look at yourself, Dickey."

Edna throws her arms toward Dickey and points to her clothing.

"Wearing men's military gear," says Edna. "Competing with your husband for jobs. Traveling all over the country and the world without him. You're gone more than you're at home. What do you expect him to do?"

Every word makes Dickey's face turn redder, burning with shame.

Aunt George erupts in anger. Aunt Lutie joins in the fight. While the sisters argue, Dickey retreats more and more into herself. When she can take it no longer, she stubs out her cigarette and grabs her field pack.

Dickey doesn't want discord, especially at Christmas. She'll do what she can to patch it up, to hold the fragile webbing of what's left of their family together, at least until they're on the other side of the holidays.

She slips out of the apartment unnoticed and heads home.

THREE

MAY 1955

New York City

"I swear," says Aunt George, to Dickey, in the back of the taxi. "The man claims chest pains every time you firm your resolution to leave him."

Tony had a heart attack. It resulted in the installation of a pacemaker and a daily schedule of pills that requires the skill of the Joint Chiefs of Staff to manage. Naturally, this has fallen on Dickey. Tonight, however, she's taking Aunt George to the theater for her birthday. Aunt Lutie is visiting Edna in Milwaukee, and Tony is resting in bed, so it's just Dickey and her favorite person left in the world, and Dickey couldn't be happier.

That night, back at Christmastime when Tony called Dickey at Aunt Lutie's, drunk and angry, and Dickey had gone home, he passed out before she arrived and remembered nothing the next day. The drunken episodes were becoming a regular part of their marriage, however, and with her suspicions about his relationship with Helga, Dickey finally told Tony she was leaving him. He'd broken down, alternating between tears and shouting, then denying the affair and accusing Dickey of being paranoid. Finally—in the midst of his health troubles—he blamed her for breaking his heart. Tony is convincing, especially when he's bedridden. He has a way of widening his eyes and pouting that tugs at Dickey's sympathy.

"I know that with my brain," says Dickey. "My heart is another story. I can't exactly leave him while he's an invalid. He really did have a heart attack."

"Based on his lifestyle, this will be the condition of the rest of his life, which won't be long if he keeps it up. Have you found another job yet?"

"I'm working on it."

"Work harder."

"Aye, aye, Captain," says Dickey, saluting.

"Wingman," says Aunt George, correcting Dickey.

The taxi soon arrives at the New York City Center Theater. Dickey helps Aunt George out, and they sigh under the lights of the marquee on the Moresco-Baroque facade. Dickey feels glamorous in the blue-gray satin A-line cocktail dress and matching hat and gloves her aunts and mother bought her for Christmas and the gold Cartier watch Tony gave her. The evening spring air is fresh and pleasant, and there's an expectant murmuring of the crowd filing in to see the Pulitzer and Tony Award–winning Rodgers and Hammerstein musical, based on James A. Michener's Pulitzer Prize–winning novel, *Tales of the South Pacific*.

"Enough about Tony," says Dickey. "I've been dying to see this show. Did you see Michener's article on Japanese war brides in *Life* magazine?"

"Before you change the subject, one more thing about that husband of yours," says Aunt George. "I'm tired of seeing people treat you poorly. You're a fearless combat correspondent who's taken photographs while being shot at by Japanese snipers, snuck past Soviet guards to go behind the Iron Curtain, and survived a sandstorm in a tent in the Iraqi desert, yet you let the people closest to you walk all over you."

"I know," says Dickey. "I think I'm so used to it from Marmee that it's just carried on in my marriage. Believe me, though, I'm working on it. These things take time and money."

"If I had Lutie's bank account, I'd give you the money in a heartbeat."

"I wouldn't take it from you, Aunt Lutie, or anyone. I need to be able to support myself, and I'm going to start by paying for my own annulment."

"Annulment. You aren't even legally married. Just say you're divorced and move on."

"No, I want a blank slate. Legally and spiritually. Once Tony's health is improved, that is, and I have the money, which I think might be soon."

"Oh?"

"Yes. I might have persuaded CARE to send me—*sans* husband—to Haiti, to cover their humanitarian assistance to villagers in the wake of that awful hurricane. There are programs there in desperate need of American funds."

"And your photographs will bring in those funds. Good girl. Keep going."

Dickey smiles and squeezes her aunt's arm, thankful for her unwavering support.

"I don't know what I'd do without you," Dickey says.

"With the way you look these days, you'll snap up another man in no time. You could be Marilyn Monroe, from *How to Marry a*

Millionaire. You know, I saw her walking her basset hound earlier today. She lives right near Lutie."

Dickey looks in the lobby mirror, touches her freshly bleached hair, and notes her trim figure. From very far away, if one squints, she can see—a little—what Aunt George is saying. Dickey has lost fifteen pounds from her daily two-mile runs through Central Park and the judo classes she's been taking. She started exercising more to get out of the apartment and swiftly realized it made her feel calm and strong, two states necessary for existence in marriage limbo.

"Let me assure you," says Dickey. "Once I'm done with Tony, there will be no other husband. Marriage is not compatible with photojournalism, even when both are in the profession. Especially when both are in the profession."

Aunt George nods, and the women continue through the lobby, their eyes drawn up to the colorful geometric tile designs on the ceiling that cascade down the walls to the floors. The interior of the theater itself continues the neo-Moorish design, with a richness in color that elevates the mood.

From the orchestra's opening note, Dickey places her hands over her heart. The scenery, song, and costumes take her right back to the Pacific during the war, to the best time in her life. She can barely see through her tears. She and Aunt George giggle over the shirtless men and swoon over the love stories, including that between an American marine and a Tonkinese woman. When the musical concludes, the women clap so hard their hands are red and tingly, and they chatter the whole way back to Aunt Lutie's place. Dickey tells the taxi to wait while she escorts Aunt George up to the apartment, and Dickey's face hurts from smiling by the time she gets home.

Dickey gives the driver a generous tip and hums all the way to the apartment. Once she's in the hallway, the music coming through the door from inside her place surprises her. It's after eleven o'clock, and Tony should be resting. He must have gotten into the schnapps. Her spirits are too high to fall, however, so she's still smiling when she opens the door. She's still smiling when she looks around and sees no one in the living room, and still smiling when she goes to the bedroom to tell Tony about the play.

When she gets to the door, however, she freezes in place. There's a flash of breast, a scream from Helga, a pulled-off blanket, and Tony's fat, naked, exposed body. Dickey recoils and slams the bedroom door. The only thing she hears after hurrying to fetch her secret stash of money, her cameras, and her field pack—thankfully loaded with her fatigues and boots from her workout—and rushing out the door is Tony's booming voice.

"I thought you were staying at Lutie's!"

FOUR

JUNE 1955

New York City

Dickey leans against the wall, across from the living room window of her new apartment, at 487 First Avenue, and stares out over Bellevue Hospital at the East River. She takes a long drag from her cigarette and exhales slowly, feeling her shoulders relax for the first time in a month.

Her seventh-floor one-bedroom place is tiny and hot. Even with the mover she hired, she had to do most of the work, and she's covered in bruises, both physical and emotional. Helga had the nerve to leave a letter of apology for Dickey with Tony, and it said—bizarrely— Helga thought Dickey knew and was all right with it. Ernst left Helga, so clearly he also did not know and was not all right with it. Dickey made her aunts promise not to tell her mother, and Dickey doesn't know when she will. In spite of all this, Dickey smiles.

I have a room of my own, she thinks. *Mine alone. For the first time in my life.*

After walking in on Helga and Tony in bed together, Dickey was living with Aunts Lutie and George. In Tony's shame, he agreed to a separation and told Dickey to take whatever she wanted from their apartment until she "came to her senses and came home."

The rent at her new place is only eighty-five dollars a month, and her aunt's apartment is within walking distance. The walls are painted stark white, but Dickey brings color through decor. At the window, her plain wooden desk is set neatly with her typewriter, her journal, a C-ration can she kept as a war souvenir to hold her pencils, and her beloved trench knife. A deep-red Afghan rug, from her Middle East travels, hangs on the wall to the left of the desk, and in the small sitting area to her right, she has one hunter-green leather chair from the pair, the matching hassock from Aunt Lutie, and an end table with framed photos of her loved ones. Her two cameras and photo equipment fill some of the kitchen cabinets, while half the dishes from her marriage fill the rest. Her bedroom has a twin bed, with a cobalt blue Italian damask cover. Her clothing, jewelry, photos, journals, and suitcases are crammed in the closet.

I love it, she thinks, looking around. *Every inch of it.*

After a cold shower, Dickey brushes her wet shoulder-length hair and wraps it in a low bun. She puts on a yellow sleeveless dress and her signature pearl earrings, and hurries to meet her agent. It will be her first meeting alone with Marie. Tony always insisted on accompanying Dickey, not only to make sure she didn't get better placement for her articles and photos than he did but also so he could have control of their business lives. Dickey feels liberated.

Dickey arrives first at the King Cole Bar at the St. Regis Hotel. Marie suggested it, now that ladies are allowed after 4:00 p.m., and it's just steps from Marie's agency on East Fifty-Fifth Street. Dickey sits at the bar, and it takes a full hacking cough to get the bartender's notice, along with the disapproval of the clientele, still all men. Dickey checks her watch and sees it's 3:57 p.m.

"Oops," she says. "Should I step out for three minutes, or can I stay?"

The bartender, with tightly cut salt-and-pepper hair and wire-rimmed spectacles, scowls at her. Dickey is glad it's dark enough to hide the reddening of her cheeks. When a man steps up to the bar, the bartender turns away from her and serves him before coming back to Dickey. She looks at her watch.

"Whew, 4:02. I'll take a Bloody Mary, from its birthplace."

"Here, we call the drink a Red Snapper," the bartender says, voice dripping with contempt. "It's far more dignified than the name you used."

"Yes, we wouldn't want to affront dignity in such a place," she says. She points to the painting behind the bar. "Tell me, what's the secret of the painting?"

Now, the bartender gets red in the face. When he turns his backside to her to mix her drink, she blows a loud raspberry. The old man seated two down from Dickey giggles and holds up his drink. He, too, must know the secret. When rich, prickly John Jacob Astor commissioned Maxfield Parrish to paint his face on King Cole, the artist painted King Cole as Astor passing gas, to make fun of him. All the subjects surrounding him in the painting have wrinkled noses and grimaces.

Dignified, indeed.

Marie arrives twenty minutes late, without apology, and nods at the bartender while she sits. Without a word, he mixes her a martini. He doesn't ask Dickey if she'd like another drink.

"What's this about you leaving Tony?" asks Marie in her thick New York accent.

"How did you hear that?" Dickey asks.

"I called to say I was late, and Tony answered and said you'd lost your mind."

A rush of fury heats Dickey from head to toe.

"If leaving him after walking in on him in flagrante delicto with Helga makes me crazy, so be it."

Marie sighs, but Dickey doesn't sense pity, only exasperation.

"I won't be treated that way," Dickey says.

Marie nods. "I agree. You shouldn't be."

"Then why the sigh?" asks Dickey.

"Because I've been through this, and it's an ugly, wrenching, financially and emotionally draining process, and I just want you—so thoroughly caught up both personally and professionally with Tony—to make sure you've thought this all the way through before you divorce him."

"You sound as if you've been talking to my mother."

"No, I've been talking to divorce lawyers. My own. And I've determined I might hate them more than I hate my ex-husband or any of his conquests."

"So, I should just let Tony do what he wants because it's expensive to get a divorce."

"Many marriages have understandings."

"I won't live that way. I'm on my own for the first time in my life, and I'm content for the first time in my life."

"Money, Dickey. You need money."

"That's why we're here to strategize. I've received a letter from my old marine pal from the war, Sergeant Bob Morrisey. He invited me to train with the marines in California for three months this fall."

"What does that have to do with me?"

"I want you to pitch a photo piece to the biggies: *Life, Look,*

Reader's Digest. A piece on our wonderful marines and the hard work they do to keep us safe."

"Dickey, no one cares."

"I care. You know as well as I do that people care about what we tell them to care about. Since the war, I've had special insight into the esprit de corps, the spirit of camaraderie that unites people, especially soldiers in battle."

"The American people are war-weary. We don't want to read another battle story. We can't look at another soldier. We want happy things. Pretty things. We've discussed this."

"Then I can be the story!"

The bartender clears his throat and frowns at Dickey.

"You?" says Marie.

"They want to train me, a girl reporter. A female will train with marines to be the first of anyone, ever, to learn to cover combat as it happens."

"Dickey, you must stop this obsession with being first. Who put that idea in your head?"

"My editor at Fawcett Publications. Before he sent me to cover the war in the Pacific. He said I had to be first."

"Being first lost you military accreditation."

Dickey feels as if Marie punched her in the stomach. Marie has heard Dickey confess how humiliating it was to be escorted by a U.S. service member at gunpoint to a brig, to be reprimanded by an admiral promising she'd never work for her beloved military in conflict again, having her potentially award-winning film confiscated and censored, and getting shipped home without a chance to say goodbye to the soldiers, nurses, and correspondents she'd grown to love.

Dickey swallows the lump in her throat and continues.

"Women journalists have to be first, or no one cares."

"They still don't care," says Marie.

"I think you're wrong about that," says Dickey, her face flushed, more from shame or anger, she doesn't know. "Besides, I'll be able to show people how war looks—close up, in color. And once readers see the human collateral—their sons fighting, and the women and children and innocent people affected... Don't you understand?"

"No."

"There will be no more war. I will take the picture that ends all wars!"

The bartender again clears his throat.

"Dickey," says Marie, "You're an optimist. To a fault. People could watch war happening on their television sets in real time, in color—women and children blown to smithereens—and guess what? War will continue. As long as men are on this earth, they will try to annihilate each other."

"I don't believe that's true."

"Really? You can't have peace in a Manhattan apartment, and you expect the world to be at peace?"

Dickey groans and puts her face in her hands.

"Doll," says Marie, touching Dickey's arm. "I'm not trying to upset you further. I hope Tony's man-parts putrefy. Truly. But I know I won't be able to sell an article on the marines right now, and I don't want you to waste your time."

Marie's martini arrives, and she takes a long drink from it. Dickey feels parched. The bartender disappears before she can ask for a glass of water.

"Aren't you the one always telling me to write and photograph what I love?" asks Dickey. "And then my love will come through and make it brilliant?"

"No. An agent would never say that. Writers spew that nonsense to make each other feel better. I want you to write and photograph what will make us money."

"Well, I believe it. And I love the marines. And more than that, I feel a calling. There is something coming from both inside and outside me, you know? I'm certain I need to train with them. I don't know for what. I hope not another war. But like you said, we can't stop destroying each other, so it's likely. Marie, I need you to trust me on this."

"I don't, and I'm going on record to tell you, articles like that won't sell. But you do what you want to do. You always do, anyway."

Marie motions for the bartender and asks for the check.

Dickey's shoulders fall. She hoped she and Marie would get a bite to eat together—just two girlfriends, sharing divorce stories over meatballs—but Marie is already standing, pulling on her shawl. Dickey reaches for her pocketbook to offer to split the bill, and Marie waves her off.

"Save your pennies," she says. "You'll need 'em."

July 1955
New York City

Dear Marmee,

Our nation is not the only one who just celebrated independence. I have, too.

From Tony.

I'll spare you the details, but what you noticed at Christmas between Tony and Helga, I walked in on. Far from being devastated, I find more relief with each passing day. I wasn't much more to Tony than a caretaker and whipping boy, and I'm happy to pass that baton along to Helga. She's earned it.

You will probably say, "I told you so," and you are correct. Being an international photojournalist and war correspondent is no place for a wife, nor is it one for a husband. It's a twenty-four-hours-a-day, seven-days-a-week, three-hundred-sixty-five-days-a-year job, and it isn't fair to any spouses or dependents. Thankfully, I have neither and I will never again marry.

My life, however, is about to be full of men. Specifically, the hot toddies known as the U.S. Marines. I soon leave for basic training with the recruits at Test Unit One, Camp Pendleton, California.

I know you will worry. Do not. I am in good hands with my old pals—brother-like types from the war. They eagerly await my coming, and I know fruitful work will grow from this adventure. And don't worry about any sordid affairs. I'm old enough to be the recruits' mother.

Yours,
Georgie Lou

August 1955

Telegram: Marie to Dickey

Marine Corps Piece Rejections: *Saturday Evening Post. Collier's.*

September 1955
New York City

Dearest Dickey, my love, my goofball,

Since I can't get down on one knee before you, consider this my proposal. Officially, formally:

Dickey: Will you marry me?

Please consent. We'll do it right, this time, for real. I think all the trouble has been because, as you said, our marriage was never official. I'm not using that to excuse inexcusable behavior, but I'm a changed and chastened man. There is no one like you, nor could there ever be. You are one in a million. Original. Fearless. Unforgettable.

I want you back, Dickey. I need you. My heart aches and breaks for you.

I had another heart attack. It's not biological, it's emotional. Will you continue to torture me? Come home. You need me. I need you. We are one. Everything will be different. Let me take care of you. Let me support you—whether that's at home or in the farthest corners of the world. Let's be a team again.

I have news: the United Nations wants us. They want to send us all over the globe. They'll pay for the travel and our salaries. We'll be the next photographic lovers' team, the next "Robert Capa"—Endre Friedmann and Gerta Taro. But we'll be smarter than them. We'll keep away from the war front lines and land mines that took those two.

What'll we call ourselves? Tony Dickens? George Chapel?

Let's do it, Dickey. What do you say? Let's do it all.

I love you,
Tony

September 1955

Telegram: Dickey to Tony

No.

September 1955
New York City

You whore.

I should have known.

Helga heard Ernst moved to California. Was this marine training Marie tells me about an elaborate hoax so you and Ernst could bed each other?

Was that what the thousand-dollar bank withdrawal was about?

I know you like young strapping men. How many have you bedded at Pendleton? Are you trying to sleep your way back to conflict accreditation?

Your mother thinks you've gone crazy. Everyone who knows you thinks that.

I want the watch back. That Cartier cost me a fortune.

You can keep my name.

Tony

October 1955
Camp Pendleton, California

Dear Marie,

Enclosed is the article the San Diego Evening Tribune *did on me and my beloved platoon, Company C. This might help your pitches for my own piece. Please, keep trying.*

I haven't felt this alive since the war. I've never felt this valued in my life.

I keep up with nineteen-year-olds in boot camp. I can read maps and use a compass like a pro. I can forward roll to standing and scale walls. I've spent time in airlifts, and the men have almost talked me into learning to parachute. Most important, I have found a family. The marines don't criticize me or tell me I'm crazy. They don't tell me my ideas are harebrained. They don't say a woman shouldn't want to do what I want to do. They accept me. I don't ever want to leave them.

I watch the mail every day for military reaccreditation and the boys all seem to think it's coming. My whole world opens up again if that's so, and I'll be ready for it.

Semper Fi!
Dickey

PS: This is between the two of us. Please stop speaking to Tony about me.

November 1955

Telegram: Dickey to Edna

Sorry you aren't feeling well. I'll visit when training is over.
    Please stop talking to Tony about me.

November 1955

Telegram: Marie to Dickey

Rejections: *Life, Look, Reader's Digest.*

FIVE

NOVEMBER 1955

Camp Pendleton, California

Dickey practically attacks the mail deliveryman, desperate for the letter for which she's been waiting months, if not years. She finally formally applied for reaccreditation for military reporting, and it hasn't yet come.

Dickey's arrest for disobeying orders and going ashore at Iwo Jima was humiliating. They weren't amused about her assertion that she had been obeying her editor's orders to be the first woman somewhere. Losing accreditation was her first taste of the importance of obeying orders in the armed forces. The slap stung her ever since. She wasn't able to cover any actions in Korea because of it, and while she doesn't want future war in any capacity, she also doesn't want to be prevented from accompanying the marines or any other armed forces into conflict because of a youthful indiscretion.

Unfortunately, all she has is yet another letter from Tony. He writes from Europe, where he's on assignment for CARE. This one is full of apologies. He says he's sorry he dashed off such an ugly note. Without her, he can't control his emotions. He doesn't know why he lashes out at the one he longs for. To Dickey's consternation, and in spite of her request, Marie shared the *San Diego Evening Tribune* article about Dickey with Tony.

I'm so proud of you, he wrote.

Old Dickey would have melted at that line. She would have caved. She has craved such words from her loved ones—from anyone—her entire life. Now, however, Dickey doesn't need them. New Dickey has found her strength and purpose through the U.S. Marine Corps, and with it, a piece of her identity. She no longer needs Tony's affirmation. She can now see it for what it is: manipulation. She only exists to him to serve him. She will do so no longer.

"Dickey, jeep's here for you."

She looks up at Sergeant Bob Morrisey, her twenty-nine-year-old marine friend from Iwo Jima, who watched her take pictures from a hill there while she mistook bullets buzzing around her head for insects. When she told him the view was fine, but the bugs were annoying, he informed her Iwo was a dormant volcano, there were no bugs, and she was damned lucky to be alive. They'd been buddies ever since.

Dickey folds the letter and stuffs it in her pocket.

"Can I march with the men instead?" she asks, nodding at the lines of marine recruits who've formed.

Bob smiles, his blue eyes sparkling with amusement. She looks up at him with admiration. In spite of his young age, he has wisdom and maturity that surpass hers. He's also tall, so at just over five feet tall herself, she has to look up at him and just about everyone.

"You can do what you want," says Bob. "You always do anyway."

"Will they have me?" she asks, pointing at the baby marines.

"Soldier," Bob barks, at the nearest recruit, "will you have her?"

"Sir, yes, sir! We've adopted her, sir!"

Grins break out on the smooth, sunburned cheeks around him. Dickey's own cheeks warm with pleasure. The young recruits are dazzled by the woman who has been keeping up with them at every moment of training these past weeks, all while documenting every bootstep of the way. She's been asked out and proposed to daily since she arrived, and they shower her with photos to keep in her wallet. It's been good for her bruised ego and not always easy to refuse. Though she's a sucker for men in uniforms, she has consistently declined their offers. She would never do anything to bring bad publicity to the marines, who have so warmly welcomed her. Especially not before she's been reaccredited.

Dickey steps in between two men, salutes Bob, and is soon marching in formation with Company C. It's the birthday of the U.S. Marines, and they're heading to a parade and celebration. Once there, she breaks off to find the best angle to photograph them. She still doesn't know what she'll do with all these photos, but she knows it was good she took this assignment. From the pain of her father's death and the end of her marriage, this experience has brought healing. In addition, and perhaps more so, Dickey feels to her bones that this training has prepared her for something. She can't wait to find out what that is.

Dickey's eyes light up when she sees Mary Jane, Bob's sweet and very pregnant wife, and her little daughter. The Morrisey family has adopted Dickey, having her over for lunches and dinners and everything in which they take part, and Bob and Mary Jane are so pretty they look like they could be body doubles for Debbie Reynolds and Eddie Fisher. Dickey swings her camera around to her back, crouches down, and holds out her hands to little two-year-old Kathleen, who runs and jumps into Dickey's arms.

"Where's your daddy?" asks Dickey, dancing Kathleen to the drumbeat.

"There!"

Kathleen points her chubby finger in the direction of where her father and his boss, General John McQueen, the commander of the recruitment depot, stand. The men wave when they see them.

"We're all devastated you have to leave us," says Mary Jane, placing her hand on Dickey's back. "Who's going to read adventure stories to little Kathy at bedtime? I'm too tired."

"I would stay forever if I could," says Dickey. "But I'm going to spend Thanksgiving with my mother in Milwaukee. She wrote she isn't feeling well, so I'll be nursing her in whatever ails her."

"I was hoping you could nurse me. I feel like this baby is ready to come any day now."

"I'll come back and visit the moment I can," says Dickey. "I'm an honorary marine now, after all. I can't stay away from my adopted family for too long."

Flags waving, the Santa Ana winds blowing, color on her skin, the band playing, soldiers marching—Dickey feels as if she's been reborn. In a way, she has. She's stronger than she's ever been, and the future is opening wide before her.

At the conclusion of the parade, Bob consults with a young courier. He takes an envelope from him, exchanges a few words, and strides toward Dickey wearing a serious look. Her face and shoulders fall. She hasn't seen a military man coming at her like this since her arrest and has never seen Bob's faces so serious.

"Under arrest again?" she asks, a weak smile on her lips.

Without a word, Bob hands her the envelope.

Dickey takes it, trying to read Bob's face without success.

"Well, without further ado," Dickey says, tearing open the envelope.

Dickey reads as quickly as she can, in her head at first, then out loud, her voice and spirits rising with every passing word.

"For integrity, excellence, and a shared vision, Georgette Meyer Chapelle is officially reaccredited for all military, conflict, and war reporting, effective immediately!"

Dickey looks up at the faces now beaming at her, and whoops. Jumping up and down with joy, she launches herself at Bob, followed by Mary Jane, followed by Kathleen, whom she swings around in circles to the child's delight. Dickey can hardly see through her tears. She didn't realize how much shame she carried since her arrest until now that its heavy weight is lifted.

"I've never been so happy in my life," Dickey says, breathless. "I could kiss all of you."

She plants one on Kathleen's fat cheek. Then Dickey passes the girl back to her mother and proceeds to kiss all of them on all their cheeks. A young marine hurries over and asks for one, and she gives it to him on his lips. He smiles dumbly and staggers away.

"You've made his day," says Bob. "Now, let's get a drink to celebrate."

"I would if I didn't have a plane to catch."

"Then we'll take a rain check," he says. "In all seriousness, earning this back is no small matter, and you should be proud of it and of what you've accomplished here these past few months."

"It will forever live in my heart as a new awakening in my life. I'm a changed woman, for the better. Now, I just need to go and change the world, for the better."

"You will," says Bob. "You've got a bright future ahead, soldier.

And I think we can now all stop thinking of you as a girl reporter. You are a war correspondent. And as much as I don't want to see another war, I know I speak for all of us marines in saying if we have to, we want you at our sides."

SIX

FEBRUARY 1956

New York City

Dickey wipes the steam from her bathroom mirror, regards the haggard woman looking back at her, and promptly wants the steam to return.

"Mr. Cherne," she says aloud, "might I reschedule the job interview? My mother is very ill, and I was on long-distance calls all day yesterday I can't afford with doctors in Wisconsin, discussing what might be done for her mysterious and as yet undiagnosed condition. Further, I was up half the night pretending not to be home while my soon-to-be ex-husband banged at my door brandishing a pistol, telling me he'd shoot the lock if I didn't come out and return the jewelry he'd bought me over the course of our sham of a marriage. Luckily, the old lady across the hall called the police, which made Tony flee. But my day would be best spent seeking how to obtain a restraining order against him. Not that I can afford a lawyer."

Dickey laughs before choking on a sob. She lifts her eyes to the ceiling and thinks, *This is too much at once.* It feels like a prayer, but she hasn't prayed in a very long time, and she isn't sure anyone's on the receiving end anyway.

How swiftly Dickey's life has gone from summer to winter.

After the heaven of California and the marines, the first circle of hell was Thanksgiving in Wisconsin. Dickey came prepared with a practiced speech for her mother about how important it was not to side with Tony during their separation, and could she please refrain from answering Tony's calls and letters? Dickey planned to say that surely her mother didn't intend to betray her only daughter, but that's precisely what it felt like. When Dickey arrived, however, her brother, Robert, and his wife, Marion, answered the door with worried faces.

"Mom's not well," Robert had said. "Not at all."

The rest of the stay was filled with one appointment after another, with Dickey visiting doctors at her mother's side and helping to cook meals, do laundry, and keep clean the very large and very empty family house where Dickey grew up. A once formidable woman, Edna was greatly reduced in size and in personality. *Pale*, *fretful*, and *slight* are words Dickey could never have imagined associating with her mother, yet they became apt. Dickey decided not to burden Edna with her prepared speech about Tony and tried to let go how much her mother's continued contact with him bothered Dickey. She hoped to take up the subject when her mother got better.

If Marmee gets better.

Edna had delayed seeking medical help. The local doctors first said she suffered from indigestion. They told her that while her incessant smoking had some health benefits, including aiding digestion, perhaps she was hyper-aiding it and should cut back a little. They soon acknowledged how alarming her weight loss was and said it might be something more serious. Dickey had called

Aunts Lutie and George about their sister, and they tried to persuade Edna to come stay with them, to seek diagnosis and treatment from a New York doctor.

Aside from the good time Dickey spent with Robert and Marion, it had been a stressful visit. Leaving was hard, but there were bills to be paid, and Edna still wasn't sold on coming to New York.

Upon Dickey's return to the city, winter had arrived with its usual blustery horror, and Tony—back from Europe and entering a new phase of disbelief that Dickey still wouldn't give in to him—had become increasingly abusive and violent. Dickey had resorted to taking her phone off the hook because of his incessant calls and was sure she'd missed assignments because of it. She needed to get a new number.

After experiencing total rejection on her long-form photo essay on the marines, Marie had introduced Dickey to a woman leaving a competitive position in publicity for both the Research Institute of America, RIA, an organization advising businesses how to thrive in spite of government regulation and world disorder, and its humanitarian relief partner, the International Rescue Committee, IRC. The IRC, started during the war by an interdisciplinary group including Albert Einstein, sought to help victims of conflict and terrorism, especially of the totalitarian variety. It was the kind of organization that spoke to Dickey's brain and heart and was an excellent opportunity for steady pay. The woman would help Dickey get an interview. There were forty applicants, however, so Dickey was not holding her breath, especially not in the mental and physical state in which she now found herself.

"A cuppa joe and my worldview will change, Oscar," Dickey says

THE LAST ASSIGNMENT   59

to her stuffed monkey. "You're the only man who's been constant in my life."

She steps into her slippers, pulls on her bathrobe, and pads out to the kitchen to make herself a cup of coffee. After looking out the peephole to make sure Tony isn't waiting to ambush her, Dickey opens the door, grabs the *New York Times*, and quickly closes and locks the door. The aroma of brewing coffee already makes her feel more hopeful. When she sees the photograph on the front page of the Black woman getting her fingerprints taken, Dickey is able to stop thinking of her own problems and instead of those in the world.

"'Negro seamstress Mrs. Rosa Parks,'" Dickey reads aloud, "'indicted for her December refusal to give up her seat on an Alabama bus.'"

Dickey shakes her head, pours her coffee, and returns to her bedroom to dress, with a new sense of gratitude and perspective.

"It only took a look at a photograph in the paper to change my outlook, Oscar," Dickey says. "One photograph. That's all it takes."

The dignified man wearing wide-framed black glasses across from Dickey at the mahogany desk sits in front of an enormous picture window in his seventeenth-floor office overlooking Fifth Avenue. Mr. Leo Cherne is the founder and executive secretary of the RIA, chairman of the IRC, an adviser to presidents, the rebuilder of Japan's economy following the war, and a sculptor, among other accomplishments. Dickey twirls the pearl earring in her right ear, enviously watching him smoke while perusing her application, résumé, and the results of the battery of tests and interviews to which the RIA subjected her. IQ tests, handwriting analysis, Rorschach ink blots. No stone has been left unturned. Dickey can't imagine what little grubs have been unearthed from the dirt.

This job doing research, writing speeches and press releases, hobnobbing with New York City elite, and attending glamorous events is so far above anything Dickey has ever experienced that she knows it won't be hers. She tries, however, to enjoy the moment in such opulent surroundings, in such illustrious company, and resolves to take the confidence she felt just walking the halls to wherever life next leads her.

It's her Rorschach results that captivate Leo. He has them laid out on his desk, regarding both the blots and the accompanying reports. She gets a glimpse of the blob that had reminded her of a linden tree, its leaves blowing in a gentle wind, and closes her eyes imagining such a scene.

"Positive," says Leo. "Over and over again. Positive, soft, hopeful responses. Trees. Mothers. Babies. Sunshine. Strong soldiers ready to help. I've never seen anything like it, especially in one with such high IQ test results. You must have had a charmed life so far."

Dickey can't help but laugh.

"I'm sorry, Mr. Cherne," she says. "I don't mean to laugh. My life has most assuredly not been charmed, but I'm fortunate to have one of those personalities with a childlike capacity for hope. Though others sometimes call it naivete."

"For a woman who has seen war and its aftermath in the dimensions in which you have, your responses denote a great deal of strength. You will be an asset to this organization."

"Excuse me?"

"You're hired."

Dickey starts to leap from her chair but checks herself. Leo is not the hug-around-the-neck type.

"My goodness," she says. "I'm so happy I could kiss you!"

He widens his eyes.

"But I won't," she says, "seeing how enormously unprofessional that would be."

He gives Dickey an awkward smile, then touches a button on his desk. Soon, the door opens and a woman who could be Vivian Vance's sister enters.

"This is Miss Selma Blick," says Leo, standing. "She'll be your assistant."

"My assistant?" asks Dickey, incredulous.

"Oh, yes. With the amount of research and writing you'll be doing for the RIA and the IRC, you'll need all the help you can get. Miss Blick, please show Mrs. Chapelle to her office so she can get to work."

"My office?" says Dickey.

"Your very own," says Leo.

Dickey can restrain herself no longer. She jumps up from her seat, hurries around the desk, gives Leo a hug—which he stiffly returns—and rushes over to shake Miss Blick's hands, pumping them up and down. Miss Blick smiles and leads Dickey out of Leo's office.

As they walk, Dickey has a hard time keeping from crying. There have been so many ups and downs, but getting this job feels like a real gift. From her mother to her husband to her agent, so many of her relationships have led to crippling self-doubt. Though Marie brought this job to Dickey's attention, she got it all on her own. That gives her a great deal of pride and reassurance, and even a boost to her faith.

Maybe God did hear my prayer, she thinks.

Leading Dickey through the office, Miss Blick—a New Yorker to the core—chatters like a goldfinch, pointing out the lounge, the research library, the telegram room, the mail room, the bathroom, and her cubicle, calling out hellos all the way. Dickey responds with enthusiasm and is elated by the greetings of men and women, all around. Nothing, however, prepares her for the joy of her own office.

"Ready?" asks Miss Blick.

Dickey nods.

Miss Blick opens the door, turns on the light, and crosses the room to open the curtains.

"Ta-da," she says.

Dickey gasps. She doesn't know whether to be more thrilled about the modern space—painted chartreuse, with one orange accent wall and coordinated furnishings—the double doors that lead to her own balcony, or the view from her fourteenth-floor office.

"Nice, huh?"

"Miss Blick," Dickey says.

"Call me, Stevie."

"Stevie, I'm afraid I might cry. I'm sorry."

"Don't apologize. You're a breath of fresh air. The last one was an heiress, you know. Complained the office was too small."

"You'll hear no such complaints from me. It's bigger than my apartment."

Stevie laughs and opens the door, and the women walk out onto the terrace, the spring sun a lovely contrast to the chilly air. Dickey marvels at all the sights at which Stevie points. Charles Scribner's

Sons Publisher and Bookseller is next door, Rockefeller Center is one street up, and Saks Fifth Avenue is one hundred and sixty footsteps away from the RIA building's front door.

"One hundred fifty if you lengthen your stride," says Stevie.

Dickey laughs.

"Now, before I leave you to your first research assignment," says Stevie, "which Mr. Cherne has already left on your desk, I have two very important questions. One: Coffee or tea, and how do you take it?"

"Java," says Dickey. "Black as Stalin's heart."

"Copy. Two: How would you like me to address you? Mrs. Chapelle?"

"Not Mrs. Chapelle. That's my hopefully soon-to-be ex-husband's last name, but I'll keep it because it's how I'm known professionally. Please, call me Dickey."

Stevie raises an eyebrow.

"My nickname," says Dickey. "I renamed myself after my hero, explorer pilot Admiral Richard 'Dick' Byrd. I trust you've heard of him?"

"Heard of him? I know him. You probably will too soon."

"What do you mean?"

"He's an honorary chair of the IRC. We do oodles of events together."

At this Dickey bursts into tears. Stevie reaches in her dress pocket and hands Dickey a handkerchief, monogrammed with a *B*. Amid apologies, Dickey wipes her eyes and blows her nose.

"Keep it," says Stevie.

Dickey laughs, and Stevie laughs with her.

"I promise, I won't cry like this every day," says Dickey.

"I wouldn't make that promise until you've seen the workload."

All at once the noon bells of St. Patrick's fill the air, ringing the Angelus. The sun glows bright and beautiful, illuminating the spires. The cirrus clouds are wisps in the sky, like angels' contrails. Dickey feels as if she's at the threshold of something new, a whole new life, purpose, and mission. Dickey closes her eyes, turns her face toward the sun, and feels its warmth in benediction.

March 1956
New York City

Dearest Dickey,

I've enclosed the newspaper announcement of your new job, along with the Cartier watch and the Dunhill lighter. You've done well for yourself, kiddo, and I wish you well. Please take these back as the gifts they were meant to be.

 Ron is very sad we're separated. He loves you more than me, his own father, I think. And he should. You're a gem. He'll visit me for Easter this year, and it would be swell if we could have a family dinner, just the three of us, like old times.

 I know you're moving up in the world and you've probably forgotten the old man who taught you everything you know, but I'd love to take you out to celebrate your new position. Call me and tell me when you're free.

All my love,
Tony

PS: I'm sorry to hear Marmee isn't well. Give her my best.

April 1956
New York City

Dickey,

You led us both on—me and Ron. When you met us, we thought that meant you cared, that you wanted to be a family again. You even pointed out the three buildings on the NY skyline—windows lit up with crosses—and talked about how much hope the future held. Then I get a visit from a police officer about a restraining order. My son has had so little stability in his life, and you have pulled the rug out from under him. You are a heartless bitch.

The guys at the Overseas Press Club were telling me they saw you out with your boss and some coworkers. You were dressed to the nines and having a grand old time. I now know how you got that big-time job. Do you think Cherne's wife would like to know what I suspect? His daughter? I walk right by their fancy Central Park apartment building every day. It would take nothing for me to stop by and tell them what I think.

If you get that restraining order, I'll take that as your sign that you want me to visit Cherne's family.

Got it?

Tony

SEVEN

JULY 1956

New York City

Dickey has learned that she's able to exist on an average of four hours of nightly sleep and thrive on five. She can run three miles in twenty-four minutes and is down to only one pack of cigarettes a day. Combat boots have been swapped out for stilettos, and fatigues for silk dresses. Stevie Blick is the sister Dickey never had, and everyone at the office calls them Lucy and Ethel.

"This job has been a godsend," says Dickey, as she and Stevie walk arm in arm through Grand Central Station. They meet every morning to escort each other through the once-glorious, now-grimy building before heading to the office. The homeless sleep along the halls and ramps, the skylights remain covered in decade-old blackout paint from the war, and the film from cigarette and train smoke obscures the ceiling constellations like storm cloud cover. The criminal element has also increased, so Dickey and Stevie hurry out as quickly as possible, though Dickey swears her marine hand-to-hand combat training could save them from attack.

"I should start carrying my trench knife," says Dickey.

"Sure, that'll go over well at the office, sticking out of your clutch," says Stevie.

"I could get a garter to strap it to, under my skirt. Like one of those OSS lady spies."

"Please, Dickey. You could never be a spy. You get the giggles too easily."

"True, true. And my mouth never stops running."

"And you get starstruck, especially by men in uniform. You have no objectivity when it comes to them."

The women emerge onto Forty-Eighth Street, and a wave of heat hits them.

"Speaking of, I still haven't met Admiral Byrd," says Dickey. "You told me my first day that would happen."

"Didn't you say you already met him?" asks Stevie.

"Once, when I was fifteen years old," says Dickey. "He came to speak in my hometown and forever fueled the fire of my dreams of flight and adventure. I didn't wash my hand for a week after he shook it."

"He's recently back from Antarctica, yes?"

"He is and dashing as ever in the newspaper photo."

"And happily married, alas."

"I'd say. He named a region of Antarctica after his wife: Marie Byrd Land."

"Maybe he'll name one in your honor, once he meets you and sees what a fine job you're doing for the institute."

"Please, the only place I'd ever be honored is *MAD* magazine."

Stevie's laugh sparkles as they enter the lobby of the RIA's office building, take the elevator, and proceed to their respective workspaces. There's a note on Dickey's desk indicating she should report to Leo immediately.

"Oh my," says Dickey.

She shoves a pencil behind her ear, picks up her notebook, and walks out of her office to show Stevie the note.

"I'll have your coffee waiting when you get back," says Stevie. "I've got a bottle of brandy in my desk if we need to spike it to take the edge off."

"Thanks," says Dickey.

The elevator ride to her boss's floor is the longest Dickey has ever known.

In the months since starting the job, her admiration of her genius boss has grown to such proportions that he's become a bit of a superhero to her. Dickey lives in constant terror that she will disappoint Leo, though she has not yet.

When Dickey arrives outside his door, Leo's secretary nods, unsmiling, leads Dickey into the office, announces her, and disappears. Leo looks very small at the large desk with the wall of windows behind him. Dark, billowing clouds race across the sky, threatening a storm. She hears a distant rumble, a growling like a beast coming closer.

Leo nods at the seat across from him and continues to work on whatever it is that's got his attention. Maps are spread over his desk like it's a war room. Dickey has learned, in many ways, it is a Cold War room. It's a room where she's learned about the vast, interconnected web uniting totalitarian governments and their satellites from one end of the globe to the other. Her work with the RIA and IRC has pulled her in and opened her eyes in ways she sometimes regrets, but there's no going back now. She has bitten the apple. One can't unknow what one has learned.

After a few moments, Leo looks up at her.

"Your report was favorably received by Congress," he says.

She exhales and sits back in her chair. She didn't realize she was holding her breath.

"Remarkably so," he continues. "On both sides of the aisle. Your ability to distill hundreds of documents into one succinct presentation was exactly what Washington needed."

"Thank you," she says.

Dickey has spent her first four months working for Leo, vacillating between sickening lows of self-doubt and dizzying heights of confidence, paired with a constant, exhausting cycle of disbelief and gratitude that she—little old Georgie Lou—has not only been able to land a job like this but to keep it.

"It was your help with compiling data on the map on communists' seizure of control of regions with vital materials that best helped illustrate the dangers of leaving Red growth unchecked in any part of the world."

"It was my pleasure," says Dickey. "I've been on photography missions behind the Iron Curtain and seen firsthand the horror of daily life for citizens trapped there. The American people are so comfortable that they need constant reminders."

"They do. And so do our politicians. Measured, thoughtful, clear. Your tone was perfect."

Dickey beams.

"What's my next assignment?" she asks, pulling the pencil out from behind her ear and readying her notebook.

"Scripts. Specifically for television and radio news programs. I need to be able disseminate this information about Soviet influence—from Hungary, to Cuba, to Southeast Asia—that will raise awareness in the American people without causing hysteria. Senator McCarthy has done enough damage with that."

"Yes, sir," she says. "Do you have a list of upcoming programs?"

"I do," he says, passing it to her. "If you haven't already, familiarize yourself with the hosts and audiences. Then provide the questions for the interviews. After that, we'll have Washington look at it for approval."

Dickey tries not to groan. There's nothing that makes her angrier than censorship. Hundreds of her photographs are locked in military archives because government censors deemed them too bloody, too dark, or too revelatory. She's convinced she'd have a National Press Photographers Association Award by now, if her best work from the war and from behind the Iron Curtain wasn't confiscated and gathering dust. In her mind, when it comes to censorship, there's little difference between the U.S. government and totalitarian leaders.

Dickey bites her tongue and nods.

"You are uncharacteristically silent," says Leo, narrowing his gaze at her.

"Forgive me," she says. "I always flinch when it comes to getting Washington's approval on my work. They've got my best under lock and key."

"Ah, I see. Well, I have connections you probably have not had in the past. So don't worry about that."

"What kinds of connections?"

"The kinds of connections that head the agencies that run the world."

"Well, then. Since I trust you, I trust we'll be in good hands."

He nods.

Dickey thanks him and leaves, her mind spinning over what Leo meant. Her suspicion that the RIA and the IRC are connected to intelligence agencies grows by the day, and she must admit the thought gives her a thrill.

Oh, how delighted Aunt George will be to hear about all this.

When Dickey gets back to her office, Stevie is standing inside, practically quivering with excitement.

"I fixed your coffee, but I hope you'll switch to champagne," Stevie says.

"Why?"

"Your lawyer called, and he sounded very happy."

Dickey's eyes widen. She closes the door and hurries over to her desk.

"Should I leave?" Stevie asks.

"Heavens no. I'll need you here either to hug me in celebration or catch me in collapse."

Stevie comes around the desk to stand next to Dickey, wrapping her arm around Dickey's waist.

"I'm ready," says Stevie. "For whatever you've got for me."

Dickey grins, dials the number, and motions for Stevie to listen with her at the earpiece. She's connected after a few rings and struggles to keep her voice steady when she asks for her lawyer.

"Are you sitting?" he asks.

"No."

"Okay, don't say I didn't warn you. I have the ruling of the Supreme Court of the State of New York."

"Don't drag this out. I'm dying over here."

"They have ruled in your favor."

The women scream and cheer, jumping up and down with the

phone between them. A group of men walking by outside pauses and looks through the window on the side of her closed door. She gives them the thumbs-up, much to their confusion, but they return it.

"What does this mean exactly?" asks Dickey.

"It means your marriage has been legally declared null and void because it was never a marriage to begin with. I'll send the papers over by courier. You are free and clear."

"A virgin all over again," she says.

Her lawyer chokes, setting off a coughing fit. Stevie giggles.

"I'll send your big fat check today," says Dickey. "You've earned it. Thank you."

She hangs up and feels the prick of tears.

"I'm crying again," says Dickey.

Stevie gives her friend a hug.

"It's a new day, Dickey," Stevie says.

"It is."

When Stevie leaves Dickey, she walks out to the terrace. The storm still hasn't arrived, but the air is charged. Dickey inhales deeply and is surprised that a feeling of sadness creeps into her consciousness. Fifteen years is a long time to be married to someone, and not all of them were bad. Tony did teach her to be a photographer, which opened the world to her, quite literally, and for that she will be forever grateful. She's certain, however, she was never meant to be a wife or a mother. She is meant to be a photojournalist, to bring the needs of the world to those who can satisfy them.

Dickey has always known that she's not like other people. Never content to sit back, she must always be in the thick of things. She's not fearless, but she has what it takes to keep moving in spite of fear. Growing up, she didn't realize that was a special quality, but she understands more and more the older she gets. Ironically—in spite of her terrible vision—she knows she must be the eyes of those who need to see the pain in the world to make it better, but who aren't willing to go to the ends of the earth themselves. She has resolved to do so, and it will make the world better. She admits to herself, less altruistically, that she hopes to be recognized for it.

For the first time since taking the job here, she acknowledges that she misses photography and travel. She was never meant to sit at a desk. Now untethered from Tony, Dickey longs to sever all lines that keep her in place.

Today is not the day to sever any more connections, however. She will do her work, and do it well, and be thankful that she can start anew.

EIGHT

SEPTEMBER 1956

Milwaukee, Wisconsin

How can Marmee be dead? So soon after Daddy?
Dickey and Robert hold hands at their parents' graves at the family plot. They are adult orphans, bearing the strange knowledge that they are next to go in the natural order, yet they must soldier on.

Dickey scans the landscape. The leaves on two hundred acres of trees in the pastoral Forest Home Cemetery are the greens of marine fatigues, a camouflage of shivering foliage just before the coming autumn change. The color and tranquility of the scene are a comfort to Dickey, as are Robert and Marion, her aunts Lutie and George, so many old friends from the neighborhood, so many who've never left Wisconsin, who fawn all over "world traveler" Dickey in a hero's welcome. Thankfully, Tony—now married to Helga—respected Dickey's directive not to attend. Dickey couldn't have endured his presence. He sent a big bouquet, as did Leo and his wife, Phyllis, and Bob and Mary Jane Morrisey from Camp Pendleton—with whom Dickey stays in regular touch. The thoughtfulness of each warmed Dickey's heart.

"Do you think she's bossing around everyone up there yet, Slug?" Dickey asks.

Robert laughs.

"Of that, we can be certain."

They start the procession back to the cars that will take them to the family home, where they'll eat casseroles and drink the Pabst and Schlitz of the local beer barons, and where they'll tell funny stories until the stories run out, and Dickey will collapse in her childhood bed astonished how time passes so quickly and yet in some ways not at all.

Back at the house in Shorewood where Dickey grew up—where Aunts Lutie and George have indicated they're contemplating moving back, full-time—an army of church women cook, serve, and clean with an order that would put the U.S. military to shame.

"God bless 'em," Dickey says, pointing her cigarette toward the women.

"We need wives," says Marion.

"Hear, hear," says Aunt George.

The women have a good cackle over that one.

A tribe of cousin and neighborhood children race through the living room with play swords, riding wooden stick horses and chasing one another. Dickey stubs out her cigarette and leaps up from the sofa to chase them until Aunt Lutie hollers for them to go out outside to play.

In the backyard, Dickey pounces at the kids over and over, making a big show of pretending to miss and falling on the grass. Once she's out of breath, laughing with them and looking up at the sky, they all decide to lie there awhile and watch for airplanes.

"Do you know I once pulled G's riding along on a seven-thousand-foot nosedive?" Dickey brags. "I blacked out."

The boy nearest her giggles.

"Wanna know the worst part?" she asks.

"What?"

"I peed my pants."

The children laugh, rising to hysterics when Dickey tickles the girl nearest her.

"I'm gonna pee *my* pants!" she yells.

Dickey relents and they return their attention to the sky.

"Miss Dickey," the girl says, once she's got her breath back. "Can you take me with you on your next adventure?"

"Yes, please," says a chorus of young voices.

"I'll ask my boss. He'll probably say no, with all the dangerous fellas behind the Iron Curtain."

"You could smuggle me in your luggage," says a small boy.

Dickey sits up and eyes him.

"You might fit in a combat field pack," she says.

She tries to fold him up like a roly-poly bug, while he laughs and squirms.

Soon, the guests start to leave, so Dickey springs up and helps some of the kids to standing. They brush the grass and leaves from their clothing. She follows the kids to the house, looking up at the sky growing thick with clouds. The wind rises, bringing the sweet, rotting smell of the leaves that have already fallen and a chill from the north. She feels the heavy return of the grief over losing her parents and the death of her marriage. Yet she is untethered—a hot-air balloon released—and that gives her a lift.

Something is coming, she thinks.

She's not sure, however, if that something will be for better or worse.

NINE

OCTOBER 1956

New York City

Dickey and Stevie stare up at the Zipper news ticker in Times Square.

Hungarian Resistance Uprising Drives Out Soviets! Rebels Take Budapest!

They look at each other with wide eyes and hurry to work.

All month the office has been a revolving door of government personnel meetings, and Leo has been in constant contact with his IRC chief in Vienna, Dr. Marcel Faust, about the Hungarian uprising. The Soviets have ruled Hungary since the end of the war—the government swinging from far-right fascist rule to far-left communist rule. The Hungarian Red collaborator police—the AVO—terrorized the population every bit as much as the fascist SS and Gestapo had, and the people would no longer tolerate such repressive conditions.

Hungarian students started with a peaceful protest that quickly turned into a riot. By its end, AVO officers hung dead from trees and lay shot in the streets. The resistance was inspired by a similar uprising in Poland and was encouraged by CIA-backed Radio Free Europe, and the Soviets withdrew more swiftly than anyone could have anticipated. The optimism was cautious, indeed.

As expected, Dickey has a note on her desk to report to Leo, and when she arrives in his office—thick with cigarette smoke and strewn with papers—she sees that he wears the same suit he had on yesterday. His tired eyes light up when she walks in, and he motions for to her to sit, while he continues to speak on the phone.

"With the election next week," Leo says, "You and I both know Eisenhower isn't sending any of our troops for support, regardless of what the agency has led the Hungarians to believe."

The agency, thinks Dickey. *The CIA.*

Radio Free Europe has been encouraging the resistance efforts in its broadcasts to empower the Hungarian people. There are some who argue, however, that the implication of U.S. military support is there.

Leo listens and nods, scribbling on a notepad in unreadable script.

"Yes, as I said," he continues, "I will personally deliver the antibiotics to Budapest tomorrow."

Dickey sits up in her chair.

Mr. Cherne is going to Hungary tomorrow? To deliver medical supplies? To see the uprising firsthand?

Her mind spins. Her photo trigger finger twitches.

"Washington will get the full debrief from me when I get back," he says, "but again, you must communicate to the people, there's no hope of military intervention, at least until after the election."

He's quiet again, frowning.

"I know," Leo says. "But we'll provide humanitarian support wherever possible. That I can promise. I'll see you tomorrow."

He hangs up the phone, exhales, and rubs his eyes.

"I'll go with you," Dickey says.

Leo's eyes widen.

"I'm sorry," she says. "I know that's forward of me. But the American people need to see this. I can take the pictures."

"No," he says.

Dickey feels a stab of anger at her boss for the first time since starting her job.

"You are needed here," he says. "For press releases and media outreach. I'll be in constant contact through diplomatic cables via the telex machine at the U.S. embassy. Upon my return, I want to appear on *Ed Sullivan*, *The Tex and Jinx Show*, *Martha Deane*, and whoever will have me. We need to raise awareness and money for medical care and support for the resistance and civilians."

Dickey removes the pencil from behind her ear and takes notes, but in the back of her mind she's already planning her call to Marie, to pitch *Life* to send her to Hungary. Few people know about what's happening, journalists included. She's determined to get documentation from the front lines.

This is what I've been training for, she thinks.

"Dickey, did you hear me?" Leo asks.

"Awareness and money, resistance and civilians, yes," she says.

"No, I need you to arrange a press conference at Idlewild Airport, tomorrow, sixteen hundred. An executive from Pfizer is going to meet me with seventy-five thousand dollars of donated antibiotics for the wounded freedom fighters and civilians."

She scribbles while Leo presses a button. His secretary appears.

"Call Mrs. Cherne," he says. "I need my suitcase packed with a weekend's worth. Suits, camera, et cetera."

The secretary nods and disappears.

"That's all for now," he says.

THE LAST ASSIGNMENT

"Yes, Marie, right now," says Dickey into the phone to her agent. "Call *Life* and tell them there's a flight tomorrow at four. I might be able to get on it if they'll approve the story and forward me the money to cover hotel and expenses. I have oodles of vacation days to use. I haven't taken off a single day."

Dickey hangs up and bangs out the press release as quickly as she's able. An hour later, she has Stevie send it and puts in her own call to the *New York Times* to alert them. They confirm they'll be at Idlewild Airport to photograph the donation of the antibiotics. Another hour later, Marie calls.

"*Life* said no."

Dickey curses.

"Why?" she asks.

"They said they already have boots on the ground there. And before you ask, so do *Reader's Digest* and *Look*. It's covered, Dickey."

How could I be scooped again?

It's a sickening feeling to always be one step behind. Dickey feels as if she's never at the right place at the right time, even when she thought she was on the inside.

Stevie knocks and peeks in her head.

"You okay?" Stevie asks. "Lots of cursing in here."

"Will I ever be the scooper?" asks Dickey.

"I don't know what that is, but I do know you'll want to return the call from *Ed Sullivan*'s PR director. Also, Jinx called herself. She and Tex are broadcasting from Peacock Alley at the Waldorf Astoria next week and would love to have Mr. Cherne on the show."

"Swell! Thank you."

The rest of Dickey's afternoon is spent making television and radio show plans for the tentative return date of Leo from a war zone, all while battling a deep, gnawing, gut-churning envy of her boss's upcoming travel and every photojournalist—none of whom have been trained the way she has to cover combat—whose boots are already dusty from the rubble of Budapest. It's only when her hands are shaking from too much caffeine and not enough food, and the sun has long set, and Stevie has long gone, and even Leo has left, and the phone has quieted that Dickey is able to stand, stretch, and walk outside to get a breath of fresh, albeit freezing-cold, air.

Again, the bells. Always the bells of St. Patrick's. With all they did to buoy her spirits when she started the job, they now taunt her.

I thought you were sending me on a mission, Dickey thinks, looking at the sky.

She listens, waiting for an answer.

All she gets is the blaring of a taxi horn and a blast of icy wind.

———

The *New York Times* runs the photos of Leo's departure, and the phone rings off the hook the entire time he's gone. As promised, through telex and phone calls, he stays in constant contact, and Dickey is there—along with a slew of reporters—to meet her exhausted boss when he arrives back at Idlewild on November third. Once in the car she ordered for him, he tells the driver to go straight to the office.

"Mr. Cherne, go home to your wife," says Dickey. "Sleep. The world will keep spinning without you."

"I have to brief Washington," says Leo. "My office line is secure, but I can't guarantee the same from my home. And I need to check the telex."

Dickey nods. As much as she can see her boss is exhausted, she admires his commitment to the cause. Also, she knows Mrs. Cherne will understand. Dickey has met Phyllis on several occasions and is all in on what she signed up for, marrying the man she did. Leo cannot operate indefinitely without sleep, however, and he looks like he's lost five pounds, which is a lot for his petite frame.

"Then promise me," Dickey says, "you'll go home and try to steal a few hours of shut-eye after that. You don't have to be at *Ed Sullivan* until seven o'clock tomorrow night."

Leo doesn't answer.

The phone rings when they arrive at the dark, empty office, and as Leo listens, his face turns ashen. He sits heavily, nodding and murmuring, scribbling on a notepad with a shaky hand. When he hangs up, the look he gives Dickey is nothing short of agonized.

Without speaking, he opens his satchel and takes out several rolls of film.

Film, she thinks. *Photos from a war zone, a world away.*

Tingles of excitement electrify her.

He stands and motions for her to join him in a small closet in the rear of the office.

She's about to make a joke about this not being the time for an intimate encounter but suppresses it.

Inside the closet, Leo plugs in a small light box for viewing negatives. Once he sets the negatives and finds what he's searching for, he motions for her to look.

Dickey leans in and is struck by the direct, clear-eyed, beautiful face staring at her. A girl who can't be more than a teenager holds a rifle and walks in a group of armed teenagers. In the next photo, there's a young couple—the man holding a rifle, the woman's arm looped through his, a bandage on her face. Their gazes are also direct, clear-eyed, and hopeful.

"Incredible," says Dickey. "Mere boys and girls—who've grown up indoctrinated by communists in schools—able to see through the lies, rise up, and overthrow the Soviet war machine."

"You are right on all counts, except the last, I'm afraid."

Dickey looks at her boss.

"Dr. Faust in Vienna just called," says Leo. "As my plane taxied out of Austria, one thousand Soviet tanks thundered into Budapest."

Dickey covers her mouth.

"The man in the couple is dead," says Leo. "The Soviets shot him two hours after this picture was taken. His fiancée, Julia Sponga, made it to the Austrian border in the first wave of refugees and told Faust."

"No."

"The girl with the teenaged group of fighters," he continues, "Erika Szeles, is missing and feared dead."

Dickey feels dizzy from the horror of crashing so low after such heights of hope. Yet somehow, her exhausted boss continues. He sets another roll of film on the light box, finds the photo he's looking for, and directs Dickey to look. It's a photograph of a Catholic clergyman.

"Cardinal József Mindszenty," Leo says, "the beloved sixty-four-year-old prelate of Hungary, who had enjoyed his first breath out of communist prison—where he has been tortured for eight years and can barely stand for more than five consecutive minutes—had to be rushed to the American embassy for asylum."

"Mindszenty," says Dickey, finding her voice. "I heard about him while I was in Budapest in 1948, working for Quaker relief services. The communists arrested Mindszenty in 1919. Then the Nazis arrested him during the war for refusing to billet them. He hid Jews."

"I know," says Leo. "And as a Jew, I have great respect for him."

He turns off the light and walks back into his office, Dickey following. He looks down at the maps spread over his desk.

"Thousands of Hungarians have already perished, and Dr. Faust says refugees are fleeing to the Austrian border." Leo removes his glasses, sets them down, and rubs his eyes before looking at Dickey. "We have a humanitarian crisis on our hands."

Dickey's heart races. She feels the call, magnetic, to travel to the most dangerous places in the world to tell the story.

"Let me go," says Dickey. "There has to be money in the budget. Please, send me. The American people need to see. They have to understand."

"I'm going on *Ed Sullivan* tomorrow night. That will help them understand."

"No, they need to see photographs. Like these. Television is fleeting, and not everyone has access. And in homes who do, it's on in the background while dishes are being done and children race through living rooms and telephones ring. Magazines and newspapers stay on kitchen counters and on coffee tables and in doctors' waiting rooms. They get undivided attention. They can be passed from hand to hand. Please, send me."

He puts his glasses back on, studying her, like she's a specimen in a lab he's trying to understand.

"I don't think you comprehend how dangerous it is," he says. "This man is dead. The girl probably is, too."

"I've been fired at by snipers at Iwo Jima. I've been attacked on a hospital ship in the Pacific by kamikaze fighters. And I've talked my way past more than one Soviet checkpoint to go behind the Iron Curtain. You know I'm not afraid. I've trained with the marines, for Pete's sake! I have no husband, no parents, no dependents of any kind. I have nothing to lose."

"You have your life to lose."

"If I lose my life taking photos to help those in desperate need, that's no tragedy. That's triumph. If I don't take my last breath in a battle zone, I haven't lived my vocation."

That was good, she thinks.

He rubs the back of his neck.

"You know I speak German," she continues. "So I'll be able to navigate the region. Please."

Leo walks to the large picture window. Dickey forces herself to remain silent, to give him a chance to think, to see that what she says is true and she's the woman for the job. She twirls her right earring, dying for a cigarette but unwilling to move, to break his concentration. Minutes pass that feel like hours, but then he nods and turns back to her.

"I'll see what I can do," he says.

TEN

NOVEMBER 1956

Somewhere over the Atlantic

Am I on a mission for the CIA? Dickey wonders with glee.

From a wing seat on Pan Am Flight 27, Dickey can't stop grinning, though she knows she looks like a fool and might be mentally casting herself in fairy tales. Since that night in Leo's office, Dickey feels like an arrow released from a bow.

First, the appearances she helped arrange for Leo on *Ed Sullivan* and other programs not only upped her clout but more importantly brought in over four hundred thousand dollars for Hungarian refugees. Dickey has received an outpouring of support for her *New York Journal American* article about women of the uprising, including from Tony, which—try though she does to deny it—fills her with pride. She was also proud of the ten-thousand-person rally, Stop the Massacre, at Madison Square Garden she helped organize to support the Hungarian resistance. Never mind that it nearly became a riot when protestors from within arose demanding U.S. military intervention that—under newly reelected President Eisenhower, now dealing with the Suez Canal crisis—clearly wasn't coming.

The most incredible moment of the last weeks, by far, however, was when Leo sent her to Washington, DC, to meet with a man at a so-called press office, where she was given an expedited passport, a tiny Minox camera with infrared film, and three thousand dollars to get across the Austro-Hungarian border to the resistance, just outside of Budapest. Dickey thinks the man might have been in the CIA, though Leo wouldn't confirm or deny it.

"Three. Thousand. Dollars," Dickey had whispered to Aunt George, just last night, in her hospital room in New York, where she was recovering from a hysterectomy for endometrial cancer. "I think it's from the CIA. And I'm going to rendezvous with General 'Wild Bill' Donovan in Vienna for more instructions. Donovan is the former head of the Office of Strategic Services, the forerunner to the Central Intelligence Agency, and a current IRC chair."

"Dickey! You shouldn't be telling me this," says Aunt George with a grin. "Tell me more."

"*Life* has agreed to be my cover, and I'll technically also be working for the IRC—'We are just a humanitarian organization,' I'm told to say—so all will check out if I get caught. I want to bring my trench knife, but I was told that would not be wise. Humanitarian aid workers aren't supposed to be armed."

"No, but you won't get caught, Dickey. You know how to make yourself invisible."

"Invisible? Hell, I have to work to make myself seen."

"But you are a terrible secret keeper."

"Only with you. I won't tell Aunt Lutie."

"No, she'll worry her head off."

Dickey squeezes Aunt George's hand. It's cold and her skin is paper thin.

"I'm afraid I'm going to worry my head off about you," says Dickey.

"Don't worry about me. My doc says he got it all, and I'll be back at fancy Sutton Place soon enough, being waited on hand and foot by Lutie, ordering her to the mailbox every hour to see if you've sent letters."

In the airplane, Dickey continues to grin, staring out at the endless blue below, thrilling over the dips and drops through strong winds. The many pilots she has worked with over the years have told her not to fear turbulence, that the jet stream is the same as water, full of waves and currents, and airplanes can take quite a beating in them without any trouble. It's what they're made for.

Dickey thinks she is the same. Hard as childhood bullying was, hard as difficult family relationships were, hard as rejection continues to be, all of it has made Dickey strong, resilient, and able to handle adversity.

The voice of Admiral Byrd comes through Dickey's memory from his speech at her high school years ago.

"Watch how flocks of birds rise and fall through the air," Byrd said. "They behave as fish do in the sea because water and air are essentially the same. There is no safer way to travel than through air, and before long, all of you will be flying about, going as far as your imagination will take you."

Dickey lights up a cigarette, pulls a pencil out from behind her ear, and opens her journal. She's kept journals since her teenage years, always imagining a researcher will read them someday. Maybe her audience will be a clever young woman looking for inspiration from one of the first women combat correspondents. Or a biographer writing about award-winning photojournalist Georgette Meyer Chapelle. Or maybe a filmmaker, working on the screenplay of Dickey's life.

"Then I have to keep living," says Dickey.

The man next to her gives her a disapproving look and returns his attention to his copy of *National Geographic*.

"Say," she says, "that issue doesn't happen to be from April of 1953, does it?"

"No."

"That's too bad. If so, you'd be sitting next to someone who wrote an article for it, from a war zone. An insect war zone. The Locust Wars. Ha! I can sign this issue for you if you'd like."

He frowns at her and continues reading.

"Some other time," she says.

She smiles and looks back out the window.

I shouldn't draw attention to myself, anyway, she thinks.

After checking in with the U.S. embassy in Vienna, and flirting with the marines there, Dickey takes a bus to the Hotel Bristol, where the press has set up camp. She's not due at the IRC office to meet with Dr. Faust until tomorrow. A doorman welcomes her, giving her entrance to a gorgeous art deco lobby with a black-and-white geometric tiled floor, black-marble-accented cream-colored walls, rich brown furnishings, and brass light fixtures. She knows her peers will be at the American Bar, but before she joins them, she needs to refresh.

Dickey takes the curved white marble–floored staircase, lined in alternating arched mirrors and windows, up to the third level, to her small though beautifully appointed, brocade-wallpapered room. She throws open the navy velvet curtains and gasps. Across the street, the Vienna opera house glows like a beacon, a waxing gibbous moon hanging over it, bright white in the frosty air.

Dickey pulls her stuffed monkey out of her field pack and sets him on the bed.

"How about this view, Oscar?" she asks. "The aunties will swoon when I describe it."

Dickey leaves her dirty, rumpled travel fatigues in a pile on the floor, nibbles on some airline peanuts to quell her hunger, and draws a bath. Stepping in is heaven, luxuriating in the lavender-scented soap and letting her aching back relax in the scalding water. An hour later, dressed in a hunter-green lapel dress and black pumps, her makeup light but impeccable, harlequin glasses polished, her hair pulled back in a chignon, and wearing her signature pearl earrings, Dickey makes her way downstairs.

The cozy dark-paneled bar is a sea of cigarette smoke and suited men. She recognizes several faces of her peers. Seated in various places around the room are Barrett McGurn of the *Herald Tribune*, Carl Hartman of the Associated Press, and *Time*'s Edward Clarke. When Clarke sees Dickey, he snarls, rolls his eyes, and turns his back to her. Staff writers tend to think freelancers are scum, especially when they are women. She walks right up to him and pats him on the shoulder.

"Good to see you, Eddie," she says. "Bartender, what'll I have?"

"Champagne cocktail," the handsome young man says with a wink, in accented English.

"You read my mind."

Once she has her drink, she leaves a large bill on the bar, which draws Clarke's notice. Ignoring his grumbling about leeches, she scans the room, and tucked in a candlelit corner, seated on a red leather chair, Dickey is delighted to see another woman. Dickey looks at the woman's companion, and it only takes her a moment to recognize Pulitzer Prize–winning author James Michener. The woman must be his wife, a Japanese American scholar and editor at the American Library Association who he married last year in Chicago. Their love story has been all over the press.

I can't wait to write Aunt George about this, thinks Dickey for the millionth time.

She heads over to the Micheners' table, fully prepared to make a fool of herself with her gushing before finding a seat alone somewhere, and is astonished after her introduction to not only be greeted with the warmest smiles she's seen in a long time, but also an invitation to join the couple at the table.

"I'm Mari," says Michener's wife, smiling deeply enough to bring out her dimples and extending her hand to shake Dickey's. "It's so good to have another woman here."

"You read my mind," says Dickey, taking a seat. "My spirits lifted as soon as I saw you. And I won't pretend for one moment that I didn't know exactly who you are, Mr. Michener. I'm a huge admirer of your work."

"Thank you," he says. His sad blue eyes stare out at her from behind wire-framed glasses. "Please, call me Jim."

"Jim," says Dickey, "I recently took my dear Aunt George to see *South Pacific*, and she's going to be beside herself when I write to tell her you're here."

"How about he signs a napkin for her?" says Mari.

"That will take her right over the moon," says Dickey.

Jim scribbles a signature and passes it to Dickey.

"Who are you here for?" he asks.

"*Life*," she says. "And I do PR for the IRC and RIA. You?"

"*Reader's Digest*."

"Oh, I'd love a byline there. It has been a long time."

"I'm happy to put in a good word for you," Jim says in his quiet voice. Everything about the man is placid and makes the air around him so.

"That's a kind offer. Thanks," says Dickey. She turns to Mari. "Are you still with the ALA?"

Mari smiles, clearly pleased to be known for her own work.

"No," says Mari, "I divide my time between managing my husband's business and our philanthropy, freeing him to do the work of writing."

"I couldn't function without her," Jim says, reaching across the table to hold Mari's hand.

He gives his wife such an intimate look of tender gratitude that it causes Dickey's heart to ache and forces her to look away. A touch from Mari on Dickey's arm, however, draws back her attention.

"Have you been to the border yet?" Mari asks.

"No, I've only just arrived," says Dickey. "I'm dying to get there. But I have to meet with the IRC chief before that, and I'm not scheduled to visit the office until tomorrow."

"But you also said you're working for *Life*," says Mari. "Jim's car leaves in two hours. Join him."

Dickey chokes on her drink.

ELEVEN

NOVEMBER 1956

Austria-Hungary Border

Jim Michener and Carl Hartman are tall bookends to Dickey's small form. The three writers stare out through the black night lit by the moon and intermittent bursts of tracer fire, warning shots from patrolling Hungarian communist soldiers hunting refugees. In spite of the frigid temperatures and her numb toes and fingers, Dickey's fatigues cling with sweat to her back and underarms. Her breath is visible in quick puffs. She looks up at the bright stars and constellations and says a silent prayer of gratitude to be here, standing at the edge of the Iron Curtain.

It's close to war and danger, feeling one's heartbeat, listening to one's breath, knowing both could cease at any moment, that one feels most alive.

A transport truck calls her attention, rumbling along a farm cart path to a watchtower, moonlight flashing on Soviet-issued rifles. Dickey and the men crouch low behind a small tangle of evergreen brush, the only cover in the flat fields for miles. Once the truck passes, they stand.

Jim nods in the opposite direction from where the transport heads, and the group steals along the dormant, swamp-bordered grasslands and cornfields. They soon arrive at Einser Canal—a roughly twenty-foot-wide waterway, flowing with jagged chunks of ice, the last perilous obstacle on the border between Austria and Hungary. Ice chunks clinking and groaning on the hypothermic river fill Dickey with dread.

"How?" she whispers.

How can refugees cross this?

Jim nods ahead, and as they move around a bend, Dickey sees two glorious sights. The first is a crude but passable plank bridge. The second, farther in the distance, is a roaring bonfire in front of a farm building. At the bridge, a small cluster of men and women wait—peasants by the look of them—plump, watchful, and eager to help. There are piles of blankets, a steaming cauldron, and baskets presumably filled with provisions. An old woman catches Dickey's eye and breaks into a wide smile, as many teeth missing as present. Dickey returns the smile and feels her eyes prick with tears.

There are many good people in the world. And they are the hope of it.

"Okay if I use the flash here?" she whispers to her companions.

They nod and Dickey pulls her camera around to the front of her. She adjusts the shutter speed and takes a photograph of the welcoming party, the burst of light causing all of them to jump. A groaning sound draws Dickey's attention to the bridge, and she gets her first look at refugees. A young man and woman stumble across the plank bridge. The woman—head covered in a blue scarf—holds a blanket bundle, and the man has his arm around his wife's waist.

Like the Holy Family, fleeing a murderous government. Almost two millennia later.

As Dickey points her camera, a farm woman hurries forward to help, blocking the shot.

Darn.

Dickey knows assistance is more important than photos, however, so she rushes to the group. She goes to the woman's other side, helping the father prop up the mother until she descends the bridge steps. Dickey holds out her arms and reaches for the baby, and the mother passes off the child and collapses. Inside the threadbare blanket, tiny white lips gasp for breath. In spite of the cold, the heat coming off the baby is alarming.

Dickey feels a knot of dread in her stomach. She wants her photograph of this baby to show one who has survived, and time for that might be running out. The Austrian farmers rush forward, with hot tea and brandy, and parcel out how to communicate, landing—to Dickey's relief—on German.

"We made it?" the mother asks.

"You made it."

"Praise God!"

"Take them to the barn."

"I'll take them," says Dickey in German.

Everyone stops and stares at her, her peers wide-eyed and wary, especially Carl, who's Jewish and whose dispatches from Germany as the Nazis fell are hardly a faint memory.

"My parents," Dickey says. "And grandparents. From the old country, long before the days of *You-Know-Who*."

Carl relaxes visibly.

Dickey leads the young family toward the barn, still carrying the baby. She thinks she can photograph them once they're settled and warm. On the way, the mother reaches toward Dickey's arms and adjusts the blanket so it covers the baby's face.

"Our sweet Georgika," the mother says in German. "So sick."

"She's going to be okay," says Dickey, as much to herself as the mother. "You all will."

The father pulls open the door, and the group stops short. Inside the large barn, from one wall to the next, are dozens of men, women, and children huddled together, being tended to by Red Cross workers. In spite of their horrific journeys, they have made it to safety, and their relief is palpable. The refugees shift to make room for the newest family, and when Dickey spots a doctor, she motions for him to come over.

The doctor speaks Magyar—the Hungarian language—so Dickey is shut out of the checkup and diagnosis, but the terror on the parents' faces indicates the seriousness of Georgika's illness.

"*Tüdőgyulladás,*" the doctor says.

The father sees the question in Dickey's eyes.

"*Lungenentzündung,*" he says.

Pneumonia.

Dickey's skin heats with fury. Leo delivered many thousands of dollars' worth of antibiotics to Budapest.

Why don't the people have access to them?

But Dickey knows the answer as soon as the question crosses her mind. No doubt, the medicine is now in communist warehouses, under lock and key, and will only be used for those in power, if they need them.

Dickey places her hand on the weeping mother's shoulder. She looks at the father and lifts the camera, in question. He shakes his head no.

When will I ever learn to ask forgiveness instead of permission?

―――

Dickey and her peers work through the night, escorting refugees across the bridge, greeting them with warm drinks and provisions. They help triage, loading the ill and families with young children onto farmer's carts to take them the final fifty miles to the refugee center in Vienna. Those healthy enough to walk still have a long journey ahead.

Dickey no longer asks to take pictures. She simply snaps, over and over again, dozens of photographs of families, single people, young, and old. At four o'clock in the morning, after receiving two young men, Carl turns to Dickey and Jim, his face in distress.

"Uncle."

They nod, all relieved to give each other permission to rest. They invite the last two young men to cross to squeeze into their car to Vienna. One of the men bursts into tears of relief, but quickly stifles them. In a stroke of good fortune, he and his companion speak passable English. He introduces himself as Ferenc and his friend as Zoltan. Before the uprising, Ferenc was a student at the University of Budapest and Zoltan is a mechanic. After Zoltan saw his wife, Eva, to safety in Vienna, he went back and has been guiding refugees for days, including his friend Ferenc.

"Word of children dying of pneumonia has reached us who remain," says Ferenc. "I'm going to try to get antibiotics, and then I'll return to get my wife, Maria, and our little baby and the children of our friends medicated before they start the journey."

A surge of warmth bursts through Dickey's heart at the courage and sacrifice of these young men. To think of all those antibiotics rotting in a warehouse somewhere fills her with resolve.

"I think I can get some for you," says Dickey.

When they reach Vienna, she'll go straight to the IRC building before the doors open for the morning. She knows Dr. Faust will have supplies, or at least the contacts to provide them. Leo had said they'd kept a load of antibiotics in Vienna for refugee centers.

"That would be a godsend," says Ferenc.

Back in Vienna, in spite of their protests, Dickey insists they leave her at the IRC, in the dark, before they take Ferenc and Zoltan back to the Hotel Bristol. Carl has offered to share his room with the men.

Dickey watches them drive away while she sits on the steps, huddled in her thick coat in the doorway. Once they're out of sight, she tucks her field pack against her side, pulls the hat Aunt Lutie knit down over her eyes, and sleeps.

TWELVE

NOVEMBER 1956

Vienna, Austria

"Dr. Faust cannot see you at this time."

Dirty and exhausted, Dickey leans forward, placing her hands on the wiry middle-aged Austrian secretary's desk.

I hope she can smell me, Dickey thinks.

Based on the grimace on the woman's face, she can.

"You, tell Dr. Faust," says Dickey. "His boss and mine sent me, and Mr. Cherne won't be happy to learn I have been ignored."

Flustered, the secretary pushes back from her desk and heads to the closed office door for the second time.

Dickey pushes a pile of folders aside, sits on the desk, and helps herself to one of the candies in the dish there. She looks around her, taking in the luxurious headquarters of the IRC—the high ceilings, the tall windows, the heavy draperies and carpets, marble and brass everywhere.

"Just a humanitarian organization, my ass," she says under her breath.

The secretary returns, lips pursed.

"Dr. Faust is very sorry, but you must know how terribly busy he is. You have an appointment on the books at two this afternoon, which he will honor, but he cannot meet with you a moment before then."

Dickey groans, stands, and starts to walk away, but the faces of Ferenc and little Georgika and many others flash through her mind. Dickey pivots, strides toward Faust's door, opens it, then slams it on the secretary's protests behind her.

Dr. Marcel Faust sits at his desk, where he talks on the phone in German, scribbling on a pad and looking as exhausted as Dickey does, though cleaner. Dickey thinks Faust will listen when he hears about little Georgika. A refugee himself, Dickey knows he fled his home country of Austria in 1938, when the Nazis invaded, and, after making his way to America, has been helping refugees ever since.

When Faust looks up at her, his frown deepens. She stands, arms crossed, waiting. He must not realize she speaks German, because he does not censor himself.

"I'm sorry," he says. "I've got a filthy woman in man's clothing and pearl earrings who has elbowed her way past my secretary. Typical newshound. Let me throw her a scrap, so I can get rid of her. I'll call you back."

He hangs up.

"*Danke schön*," Dickey says, and continues in German. "Can you throw me some antibiotics with that scrap so I can help a few people?"

His face goes white, and he stammers an apology.

"I don't care about me," she says, switching to English. "I care about baby Georgika, who might have already taken her last shallow breath, because her lungs are infected with preventable, treatable pneumonia. I care about Ferenc Welsch, a young man who risked his life to get here to get antibiotics for his baby—back in Budapest, with his wife, Maria—who can't risk the journey until the baby has medicine. I care about countless others who have crossed the border to freedom only to die in refugee camps. You remember those places, don't you, Marcel? Overcrowded, filthy, desperate barns where simple acts of kindness mean the difference between life and death? Give me as much as can fit in this field pack for me to deliver, and I'll be out of your hair."

"For *you* to deliver?" he asks.

"To give to the men who will deliver it," she says.

"I sincerely hope you aren't thinking of crossing into no-man's-land yourself. Are you aware Budapest is currently being referred to as 'suicide city'?"

Dickey was not aware of this. She makes a mental note.

"I can't support you going there," he continues. "I'm quite sure Mr. Cherne would not either."

"He wouldn't, but there are others with whom I work who have given me a mission I intend to see through. General William Donovan is expected any day now, and he will verify what I have told you. It would be helpful if you could expedite the papers that I'll need in case I'm apprehended, to show I'm here for the IRC."

She sits in the chair across from his desk and folds her arms.

"I'll wait," she says.

She reaches in her pocket, pulls out a crumpled pack of Pall Malls, and lights a cigarette.

Faust gapes at her.

The secretary opens the door and looks from Dr. Faust to Dickey with shock that their meeting has gone on as long as it has. Faust stares at Dickey for a long moment, then nods, almost imperceptibly.

"Please put in for ten pounds of Terramycin for Miss Chapelle," he says, "and give her the paperwork to fill out for a work visa. How long are you staying?"

"I was approved for two weeks," says Dickey.

"Make out the paperwork for three, just in case."

The secretary nods, gives Dickey a look of disapproval, and exits.

Dickey stretches her back to the left and right, getting satisfying cracks in both directions.

"Where can we contact you?" he asks, looking at her with distaste.

"I'm at the Hotel Bristol, but don't worry about that. Just give me what I need, and I'll be on my way."

"None of this will be ready by today, or even tomorrow."

"The babies don't have until tomorrow."

"Miss Chapelle," he says. "I don't think you appreciate the amount of pressure I'm under. The Red Cross is furious that Mr. Cherne and I used their flag for my car to deliver the antibiotics. Rumors that we delivered weapons to the resistance are not helping. I'm overseeing refugee centers that are full to overflowing, trying to parcel out antibiotics here. I have a host of agencies harassing me for intelligence briefings, and I haven't slept since I made the trip to Budapest."

"We can sleep, sir, when we are dead. This is a critical time."

"I understand that, but I'm also not a miracle worker. You have my word that I will expedite everything I can, but I need you to be patient."

"Patience has never been one of my attributes, and it never will be. Especially not when babies are dying."

"And if you continue to sit here and take up my time, more babies will die because I won't be working."

Dickey narrows her eyes and stands.

"The sooner you help me," she says. "The less you will have to interact with me, which I know will make us both happy."

He doesn't reply.

"I'll be back at fourteen hundred today," she says.

"The papers and medicine will not be here at that time, so don't waste your time. I will contact you once we have everything you've requested."

"You better," she says, slamming the door on her way out.

November 19, 1956
Vienna, Hotel Bristol

Dear Aunties George and Lutie,

If you had told me my escort to the Austria-Hungarian border to help and photograph refugees from an uprising would be Pulitzer Prize–winning author James Michener, I would have laughed in your face. Yet here I am, with one of the most gentlemanly men I have ever met, in the company of other gentleman journalists, helping desperate people of goodwill reach safety. I haven't felt this useful since the war. It's an incredible gift to know one is where one is meant to be.

I've enclosed a napkin from the bar at the Hotel Bristol, which Jim's lovely Japanese American wife, Mari, suggested he sign for you. Mari and I have become fast friends, and her story is every bit as interesting as a Michener novel. What that woman and her family endured in internment camps, during the war—under our very own government!—is a crime, but there is nothing pitiable about her. She is strong, willful, and brilliant, and her career both during the war and since is fascinating. I'll fill you in at Christmas.

The city of Vienna is full of music, charm, and beauty. I enjoy Kaffee und Kuchen *every afternoon with the Micheners and I hope to ride the Riesenrad—the world's largest Ferris wheel—while I'm here. Enclosed are early stocking stuffers, two space gun dispensers that shoot out a candy called Pez. Pez was invented by an Austrian and is short for* Pfefferminz, *which you fine German ladies know means 'peppermint.' In addition to peppermint, there are many fruity flavors you'll enjoy. You can duke it out over who gets what.*

Auntie George, I hope you are recovering well. I'll bring you Viennese treats upon my return to make you feel even better.

Auntie Lutie, I want you to know, I'm perfectly safe. Though the Hungarian border guards are Reds, they take pity on the refugees. If they aren't turning a blind eye, they are the worst trackers and shooters on the planet.

All my love,
Dickey

THIRTEEN

NOVEMBER 1956

Vienna, Austria

Not for the first time in her life, Dickey thinks how strange it is that one quickly settles into a routine in situations that are anything but routine.

We humans are nothing if not adaptable, she thinks.

After helping at the border all night, Dickey returns to the hotel for a few hours of daylight sleep and a bath. In the afternoon, she meets the Micheners in the hotel restaurant for *Kaffee und Kuchen*. Afterward, they head to the ballroom, which is serving as a refugee processing center, or to nearby centers scattered throughout Vienna. At the refugee centers, while Mari serves provisions covered by various relief agencies, Dickey and Jim interview displaced Hungarians. Few speak English, but many speak German, so Dickey is able to act as an interpreter. While waiting for antibiotics, Ferenc also helps with those who only speak Magyar.

In the interviews Dickey is struck by the terror and triumph of the escape stories. The luck of the refugees vacillates between people who experience little to no resistance on the journey—practically skipping across the border—to those who barely make it out alive from being chased into ice-crusted swamps by border guard dogs.

Even more striking is the extreme hope and near total lack of bitterness that there has been no outside military support from the United States or any other countries. The Hungarians lament the fact of it but there is little anger. Dickey has never felt so inspired.

"It makes me want to take up arms and fight the Soviets myself," she says.

"Your camera is your weapon," Mari reminds her.

Every night at ten, after interviews and dinner, Dickey and her squad—Jim, Carl, Ferenc, and Zoltan, when he's with them—drive to the border to help Hungarian refugees. With the continued arrival of journalists and relief agencies, a crowd has grown at the bridge. Dickey and her men decide to move to another area where a tree has fallen across the canal and a crude rope line has been installed above it. It's a treacherous crossing, but the strong can make it. When the group reach it, there are already three men there, who raise their arms in greeting.

"Dickey Chapelle," she says, extending her hand to a large white-haired familiar-looking man with delightfully young mischievous blue eyes.

"Donovan," he says.

She holds his hand in her grip and leans toward him, lowering her voice to a whisper.

"Wild Bill?" she asks.

"None other," he says.

"I'm Leo Cherne's assistant," she says, pumping Donovan's hand up and down. "The one with *Life a*nd the IRC."

"Ah, yes," he says. "Good to meet you. I think you'll find things moving along with Dr. Faust by sunup."

She breathes a sign of relief and looks to the bright heavens in thanks. The rest make quick introductions until a sound calls their attention. A lone middle-aged woman—wearing trousers, a wool coat, and a headscarf—gasps as she straddles the fallen tree, clinging to the wobbly rope as she inches her way over the canal to freedom.

Dickey releases Donovan's hand and prepares her camera, while the men hurry toward the bank, whispering encouragement to the woman like coaches cheering on a gymnast. Dickey angles herself, so only the woman is in the frame, and shoots. The flash causes the woman to shriek, and Dickey watches, horrified, as the woman wobbles, loses her balance, and splashes into the icy canal four feet below.

"Jiminy Cricket," says Dickey.

She throws off her camera and races toward the bank, ready to dive in, but the woman has kicked her way to shore, and the group heaves her out. Dickey tears off her long coat and helps the woman out of her soaked jacket to exchange them, whispering apologies in every language she can think of. The woman is so stunned, she doesn't respond. Dickey could cry for causing the poor refugee's near drowning and apparent shock, but that won't help. She asks Jim to pick up her camera while she escorts the woman the half mile to the fire at the farm building.

The peasants are there and see the woman needs dry clothing. She is by no means the first to have gotten soaked by the canal, but she is the first who has because of Dickey. They peel off Dickey's coat and toss it to her before escorting the woman away to change. Mortified, Dickey puts her face in her hands. She feels almost as bad as she did when she scared the Polish orphans with her flash. She feels an arm around her and is surprised to look up and see Donovan smiling down at her.

"Leo told me you were a tornado," he says. "Now I know what he meant."

She again covers her face.

"Come on," he says. "Let's get you back on that horse. But maybe this time wait until they cross to get the shot."

They're the last at the frontier, all the carts and helpers abandoning their posts for sleep. In such illustrious company, Dickey feels awake and also determined to prove she's not a complete idiot.

She scans the landscape, her eyes long adjusted to the darkness of night. An inch of snow covers the land, glowing white under the moon. It is beautiful and brutal, and Dickey thinks, as she did in Poland, that she hates the cold.

Only hot places after this.

Dickey spots a movement—the amorphous form separating into distinct silhouettes as it comes closer. She nudges Donovan, and he and the rest take note of the refugees moving toward them. The shadows are tall and small, revealing what is likely a family. She looks at the tree and rope bridge and wonders how the children will manage.

"Psst," she says. "I'm going to cross to them. To lead them toward the bridge at Andau."

"No," says Carl. "That's not safe. You can see there's been a marked increase in guards."

"But kids can't get across the log," she says. "I'm marine trained, so crossing will be easy for me, and I'm so small, no one will notice my silhouette."

"The odds are good," says Donovan. "If I were you, I'd do it."

She grins at him, expecting nothing less from the former leader of the spies of the OSS.

"I'll just pop in and out of Hungary," she continues. "They'll never know I was there."

"You're already in Hungary," says Ferenc.

"S'cuse me?" Dickey asks.

"We all are. Every night. The border is at that farm building. The bridge is technically still in Hungary. Not Austria."

They all look at each other, surprised. Dickey feels further empowered by this knowledge.

"Then what's a little farther?" she says.

Dickey stands, sets her camera on the ground, and makes her way to the tree. She looks briefly at the water—chunks like icebergs clicking along in the current—but quickly adjusts her gaze forward.

All at once she's engulfed by a memory of her father. When she was a child, he would take his daring daughter to construction sites where he supervised, and would allow Dickey to walk the high beams over great openings.

"There are two rules," he'd say, kneeling down to fasten a hard hat on her. "What's the first?"

"Don't tell Marmee," little Dickey would say.

"And the second?"

"Do not look down."

Do not look down, she tells herself, reaching for the rope.

Suddenly, Carl hisses, "Stop!"

Her eyes return to the horizon, and she sees what appears to be a flashlight, blinking on and off like a beacon. The refugees have also seen and the mass of them moves toward it.

No! she wants to scream.

They've seen this once before. It's a trap. The memory of the cries of the children loaded onto commie trucks haunts Dickey's nightmares. She runs back to the group.

"They're falling for it," she says.

Frantic, she again hurries toward the log crossing, but Carl grabs her arm and drags her back, an easy feat for a man as strong and broad as he is.

"Don't be a damned fool," he says.

"Dickey," says Jim, touching her arm. "You'll get thrown in prison with them. Then there won't be anyone to tell their stories."

"You guys can tell their stories," she says. "I'll only distract the guards. Make noise. Redirect them. Then I'll run. I'm a great runner."

"There's another watchtower not a hundred yards from here," says Carl. "They'll shoot you."

"General Donovan," says Dickey. "Please, tell them. I should try."

"Sorry, Chapelle, circumstances change quickly in the field," he says. "You could burn your network if you get caught. That compromises all of us."

The wailing begins: the screams of women, the shouts of men, the cries of children. Motors rumble away from them, until the only sound left is the quick, labored breathing of the rescue team. Dickey storms off toward the farm building, boiling with rage at the men for holding her back and at herself for listening to them.

Scooped. Dissuaded. Redirected. Told no. It's the refrain of my life, she thinks. *When will I stop asking permission?*

When she reaches the farm building, Donovan—close at her heels—pulls her aside.

"Hey," he says. "You remind me of the finest officer who ever worked for me. Code name Diane. You have every bit of her courage, but you still have a lot to learn about risk and reward."

Dickey thaws under his praise.

"Diane would never put herself in a situation that would compromise her networks," he continues. "Even if you have to let bad men take innocent people, you must never allow yourself to get captured. You know too much. Fascists or communists—they will torture everything you know, and even things that aren't true, right out of you. Do you understand?"

"I do," she says.

"Good. Now, let's go get some shut-eye. We'll return to our posts tomorrow fresher, stronger. Wiser."

FOURTEEN

NOVEMBER 1956

Vienna, Austria

"Bureaucracy will be the death of me," Dickey says, pacing, exhaling cigarette smoke.

She and the Micheners wait in the hotel room for the next German-speaking refugee interview, notebooks and cameras ready. They keep meticulous records for their articles, and Jim has indicated he might write a book about this experience—nonfiction—to stir the hearts and minds of Americans.

"Thanks to General Donovan, Faust sent my visa," she says.

And I unloaded the money to Donovan for his man to get to the Hungarian resistance, she thinks. *What a relief that was.*

"So, I guess I should be glad of that," she continues. "But Ferenc still doesn't have the antibiotics. I might go steal some from the warehouse. I know where it is."

"I think it's more that Faust suspects you'll try to deliver the medicine across the border yourself," says Jim.

"He should be glad for me to do so. He probably wants me to get arrested. He can't stand the sight of me. At least, his secretary can't. She's as formidable as one of the women prison guards we've heard so much about."

The door opens and a young Red Cross nurse escorts a woman into the room who looks to be in her twenties. In spite of the woman's exhaustion, her beauty shines forth. A black kerchief covers her thick brown hair, and her eyes are the deep blue of the Danube River. Though she wears a black wool coat that's too small for her, and the dark circles under her eyes are almost as dark as her coat, she has the bearing of nobility.

Dickey stubs out her cigarette, softens her face, and takes the seat nearest the woman. Mari pours the woman a cup of hot tea, which she takes with gratitude. When she removes her mittens and wraps her hands around the cup, they all notice how mangled her right hand is.

Dickey flicks her gaze up to the woman's but it's too late. She's seen Dickey's horrified stare. The woman smiles sadly, as if she feels bad that Dickey has to witness such disfigurement instead of pity at herself for suffering it.

"The AVO," the woman says in German.

Dickey doesn't have to translate these words. All of the refugees have ghastly stories of the Hungarian secret police organization who could give the Nazi Gestapo a run for their money.

Dickey reaches for the woman's hand. It looks as if it has been crumpled like a tissue—twisted, poorly healed bones wrapped in skin with angry, jagged scars and holes, and missing several fingernails. Dickey runs her finger over some of the new scars. The woman doesn't flinch.

"At the prison, at Fö Street," she says.

This woman is not the first to mention the dreaded communist prison system, and Fö Street is fast becoming the most notorious among it. In Buda, on the residential side of the Danube—and not far from the underground tunnels where Vlad the Impaler had been imprisoned for over a decade—the AVO had taken over a complex from the Nazis, picking up where their predecessors had left off. The place is reportedly five stories of brick and stone, complete with Soviet and Hungarian police offices, military courts, interrogation rooms, solitary confinement cells, and torture cellars. The most repulsive story Dickey has heard in her life came from a refugee who said the guards there fed living prisoners sentenced to death to a "meat grinder."

Dickey shudders at the thought. She releases the woman's hand.

"Why were you imprisoned?" Dickey asks.

"A friend I knew had escaped, and they dragged me in for questioning."

Dickey translates for the Micheners, Jim scribbling the whole time.

"What did they expect you to say?" asks Dickey.

"I don't know. Maybe that she was part of the uprising?"

The woman pulls up the right side of her lips, revealing an area of several missing teeth.

"Before they let me go," she says, "they punched these out."

She points to the hole scars on her hand.

"Cigarette burns."

She touches the mangled fingers.

"A rubber hose, tied, twisted, and pulled until the bones gave way."

The woman before them is serene, pointing out the physical evidence of her torture as if she's giving a presentation at a business meeting.

Dickey's eyes are so wide she knows she must look like an owl. She can't comprehend such courage.

"How are you so peaceful?" Dickey asks.

The woman smiles and pulls the cross necklace out from under her coat.

"God," she says. "And Cardinal Mindszenty."

Until the uprising, the cardinal was imprisoned at the highest security prison on the Pest side of the Danube. He was serving a life sentence handed to him by the communists for subverting them through his teachings.

"His example has been our strength," the woman continues. "He never gave in to the Nazi fascists and now he doesn't give in to the Soviet-led communists. He unites all his suffering with God's for the redemption of souls, even those of his enemies."

"Do you know he's safe now, at the U.S. embassy?" asks Dickey. "He was granted asylum."

Leo Cherne had been there as Budapest fell and had seen Cardinal Mindszenty alive and safe. However, the man was so haggard from the years of imprisonment and unspeakable tortures he had suffered that Leo didn't know if the prelate would survive.

"I do," the woman says. "And my family is safe. We feel as if we had angels on our side, leading us. We passed near a group of border guards, and my father sneezed, and the guards didn't even turn our way."

"It's strange how some of the guards turn a blind eye," says Dickey, "and others are so vicious in their pursuit."

"I think it was the mantle of the Blessed Mother, making us invisible."

"What's that?" asks Dickey.

"When you pray for Mary to cover you with her mantle, she protects you. Which was especially good because the border guards we saw were Soviets."

When Dickey translates this, Jim stops writing and they all stare at the woman.

"It's true," she says. "The Soviets have made it to the border. They're replacing the Hungarian guards, whom they don't trust anymore. If the refugees don't get over here soon, they'll be trapped."

A pit forms in Dickey's stomach. She has to get those antibiotics for Ferenc so he can get his wife and baby.

"My family has been blessed," the woman says. "It's a relief to wear my necklace on the outside of my clothing. God is good."

"God is good," says Jim, through Dickey's translation. "As are you. We are inspired by your story and will make sure the American people hear it. And I assure you, I'll disguise your name, so you don't have to fear being hunted down and harmed by the AVO or the Soviets."

Once Dickey tells the woman, she nods and stands, the group rising with her.

"May I hug you?" asks Dickey.

"Of course," the woman says.

Dickey embraces the woman. When she lets go, the woman walks to the door. She pauses before opening it.

"You may give my real name," she says. "Maria Marothy."

"Are you sure?" Dickey asks. "Most of those we've interviewed have not."

"I'm sure. I want the communists to know who I am, and that I have escaped. They will never again oppress me. Even if they are winning for now, they will not triumph in the end. No matter what they did to my body, they are incapable of destroying my mind or my spirit."

November 25, 1956
Vienna, Hotel Bristol

Dear Aunts George and Lutie,

Happy Thanksgiving! I'm sad I wasn't with you, but we'll be decorating one of Mr. Regina's Christmas trees before we know it, and I'll have many inspiring tales of human endurance to tell. Until then, I hope you gave my favorite American cowboy, Roy Rogers, and his wife, Dale, a wave for me at the Macy's Parade. And I hope you told Santa I've been more nice than naughty this year, so that's something.

There was no turkey here, except me, but the Micheners and I had a fine feast of squab and caviar, and a raucous happy good time and sing along at the bar with my journalist pals. My favorite person right now is General You-Know-Who. In addition to being a great help to me on various fronts, he compared me to his favorite wartime spy, a lady of great courage and sense code-named Diane. I don't have to tell you the comparison was more for courage than sense. When I asked him what my code name should be, our Hungarian guide piped in with, "Ilona, Hungarian Fairy Queen." When I probed further, I learned Ilona is known for being lovely, tiny, and sometimes mischievous. The latter two qualities I certainly share.

I have hugged and kissed this letter twice, once for each of you, and I can't wait to do so in person. I'll likely stay on a week longer than I anticipated, but that will still get me home in time for Christmas.

Until then, all my love,
Ilona

December 1, 1956
Diplomatic Cable: Chapelle to Cherne
Classification: Secret

Subject: Urgent—Antibiotics, Refugees

With your permission, I'd like another week of leave. I've been in company with Gen. Donovan and others at the border each night, and with his help, my side mission is complete. I'm sending a batch of photographic negatives for *Life* back to the States with Donovan and his IRC delegation. Please give these to Miss Blick, to get to my agent.

Faust remains uncommunicative and stingy with antibiotics. I would appreciate if you'd intervene. The sooner he releases the meds to me and my guides, the sooner one of our helpers can get to his wife and baby to bring them safely to Vienna, in good health. This is imperative as reports are in that Soviets have replaced Hungarians at the border and are bearing down. I'm afraid the window of crossing is closing and at a rapid rate.

On that note, our trusted Hungarian guides are Ferenc Welsch and Zoltan Dienes, and Dienes wants to emigrate to the U.S. Can we facilitate that? Once Welsch gets his wife and baby safely to Vienna, he wants to remain in Austria until he and his family can return to Hungary. He has great hopes for the fall of communism. If we can help his family financially, I'm sure he will continue to serve our interests here.

December 4, 1956
Diplomatic Cable: Cherne to Chapelle
Classification: Secret

Subject: Urgent—Antibiotics, Refugees

The meds are ready. Pick up at IRC.

No matter what has been discussed, do *not* go into Hungary yourself. Give the meds to the guides—we will do what we can for them—take a picture and leave the meds in their hands to distribute.

I don't have to remind you that *Life* will not vouch for you, nor will the IRC, if you illegally cross the border. You know we're already in hot water with certain groups for using a Red Cross flag for our car to Budapest. If you are caught crossing, it would bring added complications we cannot undertake and would be a legal nightmare.

With reluctance I approve one more week of leave for you but no more after that. You are to report to RIA in NY on December 10, ready to meet with all appropriate parties for debriefing.

FIFTEEN

DECEMBER 1956

Hungary

Dickey, Ferenc, and Zoltan watch the fog swallow the departing taxi. Once it has disappeared, they head toward the barn, but when they reach it, there is no fire burning there, no crowd of journalists and intelligence officers, and not a peasant in sight. The group exchange wary glances, silently acknowledging the heightened danger. They wait for Dickey's nod and continue toward the bridge.

It's Dickey's sixteenth trip to the border, but her first without her peers. Donovan and his men are back in the States. Jim has a cold, and Carl's alarm at the increase of Soviets at the border has made him cautious. He has ample material to file his stories and is no longer willing to risk another rescue mission.

"We've helped thousands," Carl said, back at the hotel. "That has to be enough."

How can one help "enough" people? she thought.

"It's not enough for me," she said.

Carl narrowed his eyes.

"You're not doing this to be the first woman correspondent to cover the uprising behind enemy lines, are you?"

Am I?

"Absolutely not," she said. "Until my last night here, I'll do all I can to help the Hungarian people."

Seeing how utterly alone they are, Dickey feels a prick of regret. The heavy fog limits visibility, and the cold is especially sharp. Gusts of wind throw falling snow in their faces and steal their breath.

Only hot places after this, she thinks for the millionth time.

Dickey is pulled from her thoughts by running into the back of Ferenc, who's stopped short.

"Sorry," she whispers.

She looks around Ferenc, and her blood feels as if it freezes in her veins. The bridge is gone—hacked to bits, no doubt by the Soviets. The men look back at her.

I could take the pictures now. I could give the men the meds. I don't need to go.

She looks behind her. The taxi is long gone. She can't walk fifty-plus miles back to Vienna, nor does she want to sleep in an empty barn, waiting for a morning ride that might not come, while her friends risk their lives to help refugees. She looks down at her boots, already on Hungarian soil, and is resolved. Dickey meets the men's gazes and nods.

Keep going.

The tiny camera she has taped along her bra pokes her skin. The straps of her field pack dig into her shoulders. Along with various personal items, it's filled with ten pounds of American antibiotics, three Viennese chocolate bars, and three oranges from the Hotel Bristol buffet.

Back at the hotel, as they'd prepared to leave, Ferenc had smiled when he saw her packing provisions for the three of them.

"*Anya*," he'd said. "Mom, in Magyar."

"I thought I was Ilona?" Dickey had said.

"No, you care for us like our *anyas*."

She smiled, knowing she does think of these men as her boys, the way she thinks of her marines. She had cupped Ferenc's dear face in her gloves and kissed him on the forehead. Then she'd pulled aside Mari Michener.

"If I'm not back in a couple days, let the embassy know, will ya?" Dickey said. "And here's my aunt's address. Please have my things sent there. Bill it to me."

"I don't like the sound of this," says Mari. "Why a couple days?"

"I might go farther in," says Dickey. "I feel like Ferenc's family is mine. They're trying to get as many out on this run as possible, since there might not be any more chances, and there are several groups at multiple villages that need antibiotics and guides."

"Your altruism is admirable, but are you sure this is a good idea?"

"I'm sure it's a bad idea," Dickey said. "But that's never stopped me before."

Mari had hugged her and told her she wouldn't sleep a wink until Dickey returned, and the small party had set out on their journey.

Dickey and the men walk to the log-and-rope crossing over the frigid, ice-filled canal. Dickey thinks back to her marine training and feels no worry about any of the physical tasks. It's keeping the bogeyman at bay that will be the work of this night.

Last night, Dickey had a nightmare she hadn't had since her youth about the Pied Piper. It was the Brothers Grimm tale she'd most hated growing up: the horror of a strange man—a real-life bogeyman—luring one hundred thirty German children away from their parents to never again be seen. Her German grandparents told her it was based on a true story and used it as a cautionary tale for their daring granddaughter. It did nothing to quell Dickey's spirit of adventure, but at strange times the looming shadow figure of the bogeyman asserts itself and makes Dickey look over her shoulder.

Pushing all childhood nightmares out of her mind, she finds courage thinking of her hero, Admiral Byrd, braving arctic expeditions. She thinks of Cardinal Mindszenty standing up to both Nazis and commies. She thinks of Maria Marothy and countless refugees. Finally, she thinks of Ferenc's wife and baby daughter. That pushes all dark thoughts away.

The crossing is harder than she anticipated. The log is slick from snow, and the rope is wobbly and dry-rotted, with sharp threads poking through Dickey's gloves like splinters. The weight of the field pack pulls her backward, and by the time she reaches the other bank, she's embarrassed how much she shakes. Zoltan and Ferenc again look to her, and she again nods to proceed.

The sound of the canal is behind her. The fields before them are a foggy wasteland. She hears the clink of ice-encased branches on a twisted, dormant tree. It brings a chill to the back of her neck.

The bogeyman is not real.

She touches where her trench knife usually hangs and feels a stab of regret that she didn't bring it on the trip. She must keep up the cover that she is only on a humanitarian mission, however, and a weapon would not support that story.

The seconds stretch to minutes, then stretch to hours. Zoltan leads, Ferenc and Dickey following in a line. Zoltan has made this journey many times. Dickey trusts him the way she was taught to trust the marine platoon leader, to obey without thinking. There's such ironic freedom in that directive. Her trust in Zoltan and in the mission is so complete that it takes her a moment to understand what he says the second time they pass a storage bin in a dormant cornfield and sink to their shins in a slushy stream.

"We are lost," he says.

It's the second time that night her blood feels as if it turns to ice. The second time she's soaked to her knees. Her first thought is, *I have to get out of this water.* She moves so quickly, she trips, falls forward, and loses her glasses.

Panic sets in. Fatigued, disoriented, blind, she loses her sense, splashing around searching with the men for an eternity until she feels the familiar frames. Relieved beyond measure, she lifts her harlequin glasses out of the slush, dries them on her sleeve, puts them on, and charges forward, taking the lead. It occurs to her that she has less idea where she's going than Zoltan must, followed by the strange thought that she still hasn't met Admiral Byrd, when gunfire bursting forth from a haystack causes her and Ferenc to hit the ground. Zoltan runs.

In the confusion, time slows. The forms rushing toward them are not refugees, they're border guards.

For the third time that night, her blood turns to ice. The language in which they are shouting is not Magyar; it's Russian.

"*Stoi!*"

December 7, 1956
Diplomatic Cable: Faust to Cherne
Classification: Secret

Subject: Urgent—Chapelle MIA

On the night of December 5, Dickey Chapelle crossed the border illegally with two guides and was arrested, along with Ferenc Welsch, by Soviet guards. Guide Zoltan Dienes hid in a canal all night, then found his way to us to make the report, but he is now sick with fever in the hospital.

Mrs. James Michener has been to visit us and to the embassy asking for our help. We have instructed Mr. Michener and all journalists to keep the story quiet. The Micheners leave tomorrow, and they assured us they would stay silent, but they would continue to press us to help Chapelle.

We have calls in to the U.S. State Department and the Hungarian minister, but you of course recognize how improbable it is that we will get any kind of confirmation from Hungary anytime soon.

Please notify Chapelle's next of kin that she is missing, and that we will do everything we can to find her, even in spite of the horrible position in which she has placed us and about which we all warned her.

SIXTEEN

DECEMBER 1956

Buda, Hungary

Using what's left of her broken, jagged, filthy fingernail, Dickey scratches the fourteenth line on the wall of Cell 504, in the Fö Street prison.

At least I still have fingernails, she thinks, followed by a manic laugh.

The hulking guard standing outside her door bangs it with his gun.

No laughing. No talking. No sleeping. No putting your hands inside the bloodstained, stinking blanket. No lights out. No shoelaces because you might hang yourself. No compact mirror because you might slit your wrists. No earrings. No privacy. No hot water. No heat. No meat, except a fatty scrap of bacon on Sundays.

There is an ache, deep in Dickey's left ear. She has a fever. Her pants are loose. She should have gotten her period two days ago, but that hasn't arrived. She has not been raped, so for that she's thankful, but she has been abused in every other manner.

The prisoners are not allowed to sleep long enough to dream. They are screamed and shouted awake around the clock. They are tortured and interrogated every day. In the intervals between torture, there's solitary confinement.

Upon arriving at Fö Street, Dickey and Ferenc were separated. She wonders if he's still alive. There are daily executions—at least, guns are fired daily—and people scream and cry out constantly, so the odds aren't good, especially because he's Hungarian and therefore labeled a traitor.

If Dickey ever gets out of here, she knows the movements of this living-nightmare symphony of the sounds of human suffering will never leave her. Every day on the way to interrogation, she's walked by the hanging nooses—blowing in the frigid winds that howl through the courtyard—and the stains on and under the ropes are fresh. Their pollution is always on top of the snow in spite of the fact that it snows constantly.

Dickey has been threatened with execution every day since she arrived. How she has not yet been killed she doesn't know but thinks it's because she reminds them every day that she's an American and they'll pay if anything happens to her. Each passing day, however, her confidence in the Americans being able to get her out wanes. Aside from the Micheners, Dickey doesn't think anyone cares enough about her to incite a search, and many of those who might suspect she's in prison—Faust, her peers, her boss—likely think she deserves it. In her darker moments, she agrees with them. There are more dark moments than light.

It was in the car ride to the prison that Dickey remembered the camera given to her by the man in Washington, DC, to take pictures of whatever could help them, taped under her bra. If that camera was found, she would be assumed to be a spy and shot on the spot. In a feat of miraculous acrobatics, while the guards had their backs to her, she managed to unstick the camera, slide it in a glove, and toss it out the window while she pretended to ash a cigarette that they allowed her to smoke.

Since her imprisonment in solitary confinement, no matter how many times she has told the daily interrogator she's a journalist and a humanitarian worker delivering antibiotics, they tell her she's a lying spy, and not even a good one.

Am I a spy? If so, I'm not good at it.

They tell her every day that the punishment for spies is execution by firing squad, and tomorrow she will be shot.

"Promise?" she asked her interrogator just this morning.

Dickey was surprised that such a response fell from her mouth. Does she want to die? She's sick in her body from head to toe. She's sick in her spirit. She has embarrassed herself and put her bosses in a bad position. She has put herself in unnecessary danger, and her aunts and Stevie must be beside themselves. Even Tony and Helga will be worried. That gives Dickey sick glee at the thought.

The Judas hatch scrapes open.

Dickey stands from her bed on shaky legs and walks to retrieve lunch: a bowl of lukewarm liquid with a few limp cabbage leaves floating that tastes like dirty dishwater. No bowl is pushed through, however, only a magazine. It's not her usual day watcher. It's a Soviet MP, and he laughs in the hallway, saying her name in the Russian accent that incites terror in her. Dickey's senses work so slowly it takes her blurry vision a moment to focus and tell her brain what she holds.

Life. *December 3, 1956. About a week ago. Or is it two?*

It's folded open to a page with Dickey's picture of a Hungarian family reaching the welcoming group at Andau. Dickey chokes on a sob. To think, she finally has a byline and photo in *Life*.

I only had to get arrested and go to communist prison to get it.

The MP tells her to give him the magazine. It takes a monumental effort to return it. She hoped to keep it. If abuse, torture, starvation, and isolation don't kill her, boredom will. She stares at the opening, waiting for her lunch, but none is passed through, and the window is shut. Soon, her usual guard arrives and tells her because she brought bad publicity to the "good" men of Hungary, she gets no lunch.

Though Dickey feels a little death inside, she keeps her chin up and stares at the Hungarian guard until he looks away first. In spite of that small triumph of power, panic rises in her. Her stomach hurts so badly, and her body is in such a crisis, she knows she must do something or she will die.

At least I don't really want to die, she thinks. *Not yet.*

Dickey closes her eyes and takes deep breaths, trying to sift through her foggy memories to a place she was happiest, to marine basic training in the California sun. She imagines Bob and the men encouraging her, while not allowing her to pity herself.

I must exercise, she thinks.

Dickey opens her eyes, removes the pitiful excuse for a blanket on her wooden slat bed, and lays the blanket on the floor. She starts to sit, to stretch, but the guard screams at her, in German, to put the blanket back on the bed. A fury that trumps every survival instinct she has, rises.

"To hell with the blanket," she says, tossing it back on the bed.

Overcome by recklessness, Dickey does the forward roll she learned in marine training toward the door and comes up glaring through the barred window at her guard's surprised face. Exhilarated, she does the roll away from him. Then back to him again. His face is a mask of bemused disgust. He slams the window closed. Dickey, meanwhile, smiles for the first time since imprisonment. This strange show of her fitness has again made the blood pump in her veins. It's the first time she's felt her blood thaw since the arrest.

I will not let them destroy me.

———

That night, instead of shouting Dickey awake, guards drag her from bed, blindfold her, and lead her down to the courtyard, rough hands tight on each of her arms, and a gun pointed in her back. The blindfold is torn off so hard her head hits the bloodstained wall behind her. Without her glasses on, in the dark, she can only roughly make out the forms of four guards. Suddenly, a searchlight blasts on, and she holds up her hands to shield her eyes.

"You have been found guilty of spying, and you will now be executed," a guard says in English.

Dickey hears multiple guns cocked, and she shakes so violently, she thinks she must look like she's being electrocuted. The guards laugh, while she stands there in a state of terror she thinks will stop her heart before the bullets do. They continue to jeer at her, minutes passing like hours. She fears she has wet herself, but it could be the sweat that pours out of her skin in spite of the cold. She tries to think of a prayer, but her mind doesn't work.

After what feels like an eternity, the searchlight goes off and the blackness that engulfs her makes her wonder, for a moment, if she has been shot and has died. But the rough hand on her arm and the dragging back to her room, the throwing of her on the floor of the cell, and the crash of the metal door remind her she is very much alive, though very much in hell.

SEVENTEEN

DECEMBER 1956

Buda, Hungary

It's Christmas Eve.

Dickey wonders, was it only a year ago at this time that her skin and hair were sun-kissed from marine training in California, and her mother was still alive, and Dickey wasn't wasting away with an infection so deep in her left ear she couldn't hear out of it? Dickey thinks of her thoughtlessly confident letters to her aunts, written just weeks ago, when she said she'd be home in time for Christmas.

Dickey can imagine Dr. Faust looking at her, reprimanding her that only an American who hasn't been hungry a day in her life until the present time, who has all the bravado of an adolescent and the swagger of one who's never had a real day of life-and-death struggle to survive would write such things between trips behind the Iron Curtain.

I'm a reckless fool.

She realizes there will be no Christmas now or maybe for the rest of her life.

Before interrogation this morning, Dickey found a morsel of hope that someone, somewhere in this godless stronghold of Red terror would give the prisoners the Christmas gift of music, fellowship, or extra food. All she got from her interrogator, however, was the brutal reminder that the sentence for entering Hungary illegally is five years, and for spying the sentence is death. She doesn't know if she can survive five more hours, let alone five years. Her only hope is in her countrymen, but that hope shrinks with each passing day.

The door scrapes open, and she stands at attention. Her usual guard moves aside while the guard who marched her to her mock execution motions for her to follow him. One of the other guards from that night points his rifle at her back and keeps it pressed between her shoulder blades.

Dickey was already interrogated today, and lunchtime has passed, so she wonders if her fake trial in commie court is about to commence. The room she's led to is quite different from the usual frigid concrete cell, where the interrogator's ink has a layer of ice he has to clink through with his pen tip. This office has carpet and wallpaper, warm burning lamps, a fire in the fireplace, and a gleaming, polished wooden desk. It has been so long that Dickey has seen a room like this that she almost forgot such places existed. She allows the little lift in her heart to give her an ember of hope.

Maybe there is Christmas at Fö Street.

The man before her is one she's never seen. His silver hair is cut short and neat, and he wears a tailored charcoal-colored suit. He does not look like a communist.

Is he a diplomat? An American?

When he smiles, her spirits sink. His stained, uneven teeth reveal he is not from a country with preventive dentistry, and his Russian-accented German confirms this.

"It must be very hard to be in such a place at Christmas," he says.

She cannot read his intentions, so she remains silent.

"You are so hostile," he says. "One would think a prisoner would do her best to behave."

She stares at him, making her face as blank as she can, while trembling with hatred.

"You broke an international law," he says. "Our imprisonment of you is perfectly legal."

She cannot hold her tongue.

"Is it perfectly legal to torture a woman? To tell her every day that she'll be shot for spying?"

"They should not tell you that you'll be shot."

Her shoulders soften.

"They should tell you that you will be hanged," he says. "That is the punishment for spies."

She stiffens.

"I'm not a spy," she says quietly.

It's true. If she was working with a spy agency, she was being used, and she knows she failed at the small mission she had. She never was cut out for spy work, and she never will be. She wants to stay in this warm, comfortable office as long as she can, however, to thaw her bones as much as possible.

"Even the Soviet border guards will tell you," she says, "Ferenc and I were not armed. We carried only antibiotics. We are humanitarian workers, and I am a journalist. The world needs to know about the refugee crisis. And people deserve medical care."

"There would be no crisis if fascists had not risen up violently against their lawful government."

"Just because one opposes the oppressive rule of communists does not make one a fascist."

"American nonsense," he says.

Dickey forces herself to again go silent. As Jim Michener and she learned from interviewing hundreds of refugees, there are no communist countries, only communist governments. The fact is, Hungarian university students had been raised in a communist system and brainwashed in schools their whole lives, and yet they were still able to see through the lies.

Those in power have swimming pools and full bellies and vacation in fancy places. Those in power destroy everyone who speaks against them. Like Satan, they use a morsel of truth to tempt, then they engulf, enslave, and imprison in lies. They use fear to intimidate and control the actions of those under their thumbs. They also try to control thoughts, but that is where they fail. They cannot control thoughts or faith in God. They cannot stop people from praying. That is the piece they can't get their cold fingers on, and it drives them mad. This thought gives Dickey another burst of hope.

They cannot stop Christmas.

The man opens a drawer and pushes a magazine across the desk toward Dickey. At first, she thinks it's the *Life* that ran her picture, but she sees it's a German magazine. She doesn't care what kind of magazine it is, she's desperate for reading material of any kind. She wonders if it's a gift. She looks up, her face softened by gratitude.

He again gives her his tooth-baring smile, then dismisses her.

Back in her cell, she forces herself to wait to read it. She watches the sun move slowly across the sky and for night to fall. Night is the hardest time. It passes so slowly. The darkness outside engulfs the light of hope kindled during the day. Having a magazine as distraction on this Christmas Eve is more than she could have hoped for.

Maybe they aren't completely soulless, she thinks.

When she can stand waiting no longer, she opens the magazine and reads. She savors the words like meaty morsels, allowing each word to digest in German and then in English. The first are fulfilling, but as the words become sentences, and then paragraphs, the sustenance turns rancid.

It's a Nazi magazine. It tells the story of a female prisoner accused of spying. Minute by minute, in vivid language, the details of the prisoner's abuse, torture, and rape are detailed. Dickey knows she should stop reading, but she's so ravenous for reading material, she can't. Though she's aware that psychological torture is even more dangerous than physical torture, she's powerless to look away. She reads all the way to the bitter end, when the woman is hanged in a snowy courtyard and forgotten forever.

Dickey's ragged breath comes in puffs in the air. She shakes from head to toe. She hears an echo of a memory, her dear Aunt George the night two Christmases ago, when Dickey saw Tony put his arm around Helga, and when Edna had humiliated Dickey with embarrassing childhood stories.

"Things turned south quickly tonight," Dickey had said. "Caught me off guard."

"It always does, Dickey," said Aunt George. "But, aside from your tendency to walk into sniper fire, I wouldn't have you any other way. Hopelessly hopeful."

Dickey feels real danger that her pilot light is going out.

Where are you, God? she thinks.

She hears the howling wind and the distant, agonized scream of a woman.

Is she being raped? Or fed to the meat grinder? Will I be killed in such a brutal way?

Dickey drops the magazine on the floor and covers her ears with her hands, but nothing blocks out the sound. It echoes off the walls and concrete floors. It permeates every solitary cell and seeps through the thin skin and into the marrow of the brittle bones of every prisoner there. A chasm of despair opens in her, and—try as she does to stifle it—she weeps.

There is no Christ here, she thinks. *Only anti-Christs, and they are beating me.*

In her agony, it takes her a moment to realize someone is trying to get her attention.

"Psst. Psst."

She looks through her tears at the barred window. Her usual guard is there, but his dark scowling eyes look softer.

Curiosity impels her to stand and walk to the door. When she reaches it, he opens the hatch and pushes something through to her. It's a small hunter-green book with gold lettering. The words are in German. She looks up at him with uncensored fury.

"I've had enough," she says, through clenched teeth.

He shakes his head. "This, you will like."

She has never before seen him so earnest. She softens her glare and looks back down at the book.

Book of Songs, Poems, by Heinrich Heine.

She opens it and turns the pages. It's well-worn, with selections underlined or bracketed in pencil. Some of the corners are dog-eared. She again feels the sting of tears and looks up at him, smiling. He nods, then pushes another treasure through the hatch. In the usual filthy metal bowl of cabbage water is a pile of rice topped with a hunk of pork on a bone. At this, a cry of joy bursts forth.

"*Danke,*" she says.

He again nods and then turns his back to her.

As she walks back toward her bed with her gifts, she catches his whisper, in English.

"Merry Christmas."

January 13, 1957
Diplomatic Cable: Faust to Cherne
Classification: Secret

Subject: Urgent—Chapelle Location Confirmed

The State Department has confirmation that Dickey Chapelle is being held at the prison at Fö Street, Buda. She is not being charged as a spy, but for crossing the border illegally.

Consul Richard Selby and Ambassador Tom Wailes are working around the clock, under marine guard, from the U.S. embassy in Buda, to get Chapelle a lawyer for her trial, date to be determined.

Through various avenues we're trying to secure a visa for AP reporter Carl Hartman to be present at the proceedings. We suspect the Hungarian government will approve it. After all the hell the Reds' kangaroo court trial for Cardinal Mindszenty brought on them, they'll likely want to redeem themselves on the world stage. Also, because Chapelle is unimportant to them and quite frankly to us, there are some who think they'll use her as a pawn to show their leniency.

We are cautiously hopeful for her return, but until Chapelle is back on Austrian soil, we cannot be fully optimistic.

What you do with her, if you ever get her back on American soil, is up to you. I have an opinion on that I will keep to myself.

EIGHTEEN

JANUARY 1957

Buda, Hungary

"Whispers, whispers, whispers. Lines of poetry. German and English. This they cannot take from me."

Dickey composes poems. She reads them. She translates them. She says them aloud. She memorizes them. Poetry has become her prayer.

The old prayers of childhood and memory are on a path in her mind she cannot access, obscured by a tangle of branches and brush made of hunger, sickness, shame, and regret. Only the words on the page that can be read each day can be understood, can create new pathways of memory through these dark woods in her broken mind until they make a well-worn track. The poems' worlds are those of fairies and woods and moonlight and linden trees. She thinks of the linden tree she saw in the ink blot, that got her the job, that got her to Hungary, that got her to prison.

Did I have a premonition?

The guard who gave her the gifts of meat and poetry no longer stands outside her door. She hopes he was simply transferred elsewhere, but he might be dead if someone found out about the gifts. It's unlikely, however, since she's still been able to hide the book.

His replacement is so young there's not a trace of stubble on his pale, smooth face. He has coal-black hair, piercing blue eyes fringed in long black lashes, and thick red feminine lips. He's strikingly good-looking and mercurial. She thinks of him as a vampire, as the ghost of Vlad himself.

He likes to threaten her with pliers—asking, "Today?"—while staring at her fingernails and leering. At first, this terrified her—calling to mind the image of refugee Maria Marothy's raw red empty nail beds. The fear slowly changed to sickness over the capacity of humans for cruelty. Now, however, all fear and sickness in Dickey have become annoyance and even apathy. If Maria could suffer it, so can Dickey.

Besides, this pubescent guard doesn't have the balls to do it, or he would have done it by now.

As the sun sets on Dickey's sixth week in captivity, the vampire opens the hatch to slide in her dinner. Instead, however, he slides the pliers through and asks, "Today?"

On impulse, Dickey grabs the pliers, clamps her own longest fingernail, and twists it until the skin around it turns white. He looks at her in shock.

"Stop that!" he says, his voice squeaking like a teenager's. "Give me those."

Dickey laughs and throws the pliers, so the tool slides through the hatch and crashes onto the floor outside the cell. He looks with horror down the corridor. His boss will not be happy with him for losing a potential weapon and being humiliated by a prisoner. Especially a woman prisoner. Especially an American woman prisoner. He slams the hatch shut, but she keeps laughing. She hopes he'll hear her throaty, guttural, sick laugh—resulting in a wet coughing fit—in his nightmares.

Once she's through coughing, she sits on her platform bed and lights a cigarette. She inhales slowly, savoring it, and exhales thoughts of gratitude. The five cigarettes she's allotted are the best five moments of her days, and for that she can keep herself from full hatred of the commies. On one thing Dickey and the Reds can agree: smoking is as essential as breathing.

Dickey is only halfway through her cigarette when heavy boots thunder toward her cell. Heart racing, she stands from her platform bed. She tries to remain calm, but her shaking hand betrays her.

After the rattling of the key in the lock, the door to her cell slams open. The cruel AVO guard of the mock execution grabs her cigarette, throws it on the floor, and crushes it with his boot, while two others handcuff Dickey.

Today I die, she thinks.

On the way out, she passes the vampire and the corner of his lip curls into a sneer.

At least, if they kill me, I won't have to look at that face ever again.

Dickey hisses like a cat at him, and he recoils. How she enjoys offending him.

If they kill me, I'll come back to haunt him.

She realizes with a pang that her prized poetry book will be forever lost to her, tucked between the blanket and the cell wall, but it's no matter; she has committed it to memory. Perhaps it will stay hidden until the next prisoner finds it, and it may be a lifeline to him or her.

She's led down the five flights of stairs and to a barred door, its metal scraping over brick as it's opened to a courtyard outside. A blast of cold hits her face and violent shaking takes hold of her.

This is it. The end of me.

The poetry of prayer calms her. The lines speak of peace in death. She thinks a blessing on her old guard, who gave her the book. Then, looks ahead to her execution.

Let it be fast.

They don't lead her to the shooting wall or the hanging ropes, however. They proceed past them to another barred door, another hallway, another scrape of metal, another blast of cold, and a waiting truck. The back door of the vehicle is opened and her eyes land on a sight in the back seat that brings her a burst of joy.

My field pack! Is this not the end of me?

Still handcuffed, she's loaded roughly into the vehicle. The door slams in her face, and the driver pulls away from the prison.

———

In the terror of arrest, with Ferenc—being driven from the holding barn to the prison, while trying to figure out how to rid herself of the camera taped under her bra—Dickey scarcely noticed her surroundings. Now, she's fully awake.

The last hints of twilight illuminate the government buildings and those of Castle Hill. They pass Stalin Square, and her heart lifts to see the empty pedestal where the massive statue of Stalin had been destroyed by Hungarian revolutionaries, just months ago. They have not yet had time to build a monument to Khrushchev, and she hopes they never will. Though the Reds are in power here now, she knows they cannot stifle the flames of the fighting spirit of freedom forever.

Still uncertain whether she will live or die, she's at least glad to have a change of scenery and dares to allow a spark of hope to flicker. Between her colleagues, her friends, her family, her boss, and General Donovan himself, someone has to have gotten word of where she is. She has faith in more than one of them to put the machinery in order to get her out of this hell, even if it has taken far longer than she would have imagined.

At the thought of the worry and strain she has caused her friends and colleagues, dread returns to her stomach. She has put people at risk. She cannot bear to think of their disappointment, fear, and anger. How embarrassing this is. How her aunts must have aged from this. How her reputation will suffer.

No, she thinks. *I'm getting ahead of myself. I might be heading to the firing squad, and then my pictures might finally be worth something.*

She laughs aloud at the thought but stifles it when the driver glares at her from the rearview mirror.

They cross the Danube, into the Pest section of the city, and everything takes on the look of industry and machinery, the embodiment of communism itself. They soon pull up to what is clearly another prison, and Dickey falls back in the seat and closes her eyes.

This is about to get worse, she thinks.

The refugees had told Dickey horror stories of the prison in Pest, where Cardinal Mindszenty was kept, where rooms like standing coffins were solitary cells, where loved ones went in and never came out, except on stretchers.

The doors open, and two female guards with bored faces and huge guns march Dickey and her field pack into the prison, which is smaller but no less imposing than the last. With every step, under the confinement of these women who look like the walking dead, Dickey again feels crushed. She can barely move, but every time she falters, the woman behind her jabs her with her gun. The thought of going to another cell, and being alone for another unknown amount of time, and remaining starved for food and stimulation and human connection calls forth a sob Dickey cannot stifle. She has a savage thought, so foreign to her it steals her breath.

Run. And then, they'll shoot. And it will be over.

The thought is said in the voice of the vampire guard from Fö Street. She can picture his wet red lips whispering in her ear. He is the embodiment of the bogeyman.

"No," Dickey says.

She feels a blow on the back of her head and sees stars.

No, she thinks. *The bogeyman will not talk me into suicide. He will not win.*

Once inside the prison, she's forced down a long hall, lit with low gas lamps spread out far enough to create great shadowy spaces between them. It's so dark, it's hard for her to see, but when the door of Cell 21 is unlocked and opened, and Dickey is pushed through, she's shocked by what she encounters.

There are women. Eight of them. They are smiling at her. They are standing and welcoming her. They are pulling her into their arms.

"Where am I?" she asks in German.

"Trial holding," says a sweet, quiet voice.

Trial? she thinks, her heart soaring. *They've done it. The Americans are going to get me out!*

As the door is slammed shut and locked behind her, she collapses into the arms of one of the women and sobs.

30 JANUARY 1957
NEW YORK HERALD TRIBUNE
CARL HARTMAN

American Freelance Photographer Released from Red Prison

After her December arrest by Soviet guards patrolling the Hungarian border, and seven weeks in a communist prison, American freelance photographer Georgette "Dickey" Meyer Chapelle has been released and landed today at Idlewild Airport. She was charged with illegal border crossing and sentenced to fifty days in prison, which the judge said Chapelle has already served. Concluding sentencing, the judge told Chapelle she is never again allowed into Hungary. Chapelle assured him that would not be hard to obey.

Chapelle's Hungarian co-defendant and border crossing partner, Ferenc Welsch, must serve a total of eight months. The pair testified they were apprehended bearing antibiotics from U.S. relief agencies for Hungarian refugee children suffering from pneumonia, to which Welsch's baby was feared to be vulnerable. As of this filing, Welsch has been returned to prison to serve the remaining time. His family has made it safely to Austria, guided by another after Welsch's arrest, and they wait eagerly for his release.

In addition to Chapelle's aunts, a group from the Overseas Press Club was at Idlewild to welcome her. Notably absent was a representative of *Life* magazine, for whom she took photographs, and Chapelle's boss—chief of the Research Institute of America and chair of the International Rescue Committee, Leo Cherne—who cosponsored Chapelle's relief trip to Austria. When reached out to for comment, he did not provide one.

NINETEEN

MARCH 1957

Pennsylvania

Exile, Dickey thinks, her stomach a churning sea of emotions. On invitation from Jim and Mari Michener, Dickey left Aunt Lutie's place—where Dickey has been staying since her return to the States, took the train to Trenton, New Jersey, and now sits in a taxi for the last thirty miles to Pipersville, Pennsylvania, to the Micheners' house.

Once she was safely home from Hungary, Dickey thought she'd pick up where her life left off and go right back to work. It didn't take long to realize, however, that life had ended.

Leo was ice-cold. He avoided her, broke appointments, gave her no assignments, and kept her from meetings. In the shadow of his disapproval, his anger at what she put them through, and the unwanted publicity for the RIA and IRC, Dickey felt as if she had escaped one prison only to land in another. Stevie tried to keep Dickey from despair, saying it would take time, but when Leo refused to help Ferenc's family and Zoltan, Dickey's pain morphed into fury. She was used to people snubbing her, but she would not stand by and let those who'd helped the United States get slighted, those to whom she had given her word.

With Dr. Faust's assurances, Dickey promised Ferenc the IRC would provide financial support to his family until and after his release, and Zoltan that they'd help get him to the United States. Leo did nothing to heed her requests. Ferenc's wife and Zoltan each wrote to Dickey that they were destitute and losing hope. The more Dickey badgered Leo, the more he shut her out.

She finally reached out to General Donovan's law firm and despaired when they told her he was ill, but her message would be passed along to him. Though he never responded to Dickey directly, within a week not only did Ferenc's family have five hundred dollars—courtesy of the law firm of Donovan, Leisure, Newton, and Irvine—but Zoltan Dienes was flown out on the last transport plane from Europe to the United States, under President Eisenhower's Operation Safe Haven. One of thousands of Hungarian refugees speedily resettled, Zoltan now has a room in a New York City boardinghouse and works at Consolidated Edison.

Once the men were taken care of, Dickey submitted her resignation to Leo and left.

Unemployed, the days stretched as long as those at Fö Street. Her brain remained as foggy as it was from starvation and sleep deprivation, which continued. She awoke constantly from nightmares, anticipating the guards' shouting and cruel marches to the execution courtyard. She still heard the echoes of men's and women's screams. Not only that, but Dickey felt tremendous guilt for being freed while the strong, fierce women of the Hungarian resistance, whose company and care in the holding prison had resurrected her from the hell of Fö Street, might still be languishing there or sent to worse facilities.

Dickey couldn't bear to stay alone in her apartment, but her aunts—feeling increasingly too old to navigate the bustling city—were preparing to return to Milwaukee for the spring, and maybe for good. They encouraged Dickey to go with them, but the thought of returning to the family home, absent her parents and away from the pulsing beat of news and life, filled Dickey with dread, as did Helga's invitation to stay with her and Tony.

Helga called Dickey to tell her how happy she was that Dickey was safe and offer their guest room for her rehabilitation. Incredulous but polite, Dickey refused. While Helga tried to persuade Dickey, Tony grabbed the phone and accused Dickey of purposely getting arrested to get a story, claiming she owed him because it was his letter writing that led to Dickey's release.

"When are you going to realize you can't be some girl reporter, bounding from country to country forever?" he yelled. "You're getting too old for this. And I'm getting too old to keep having to get you outta trouble!"

Helga wrestled the phone back from Tony, sent him back to bed, and confessed in hushed tones to Dickey that Tony was a tyrant, and she could use help taking care of him. That made Dickey laugh out loud before hanging up, though an annoying pang of guilt remained with her ever since.

Finally, Dickey was trying to schedule a meeting with her agent, Marie, but the woman wouldn't return her calls. Dickey didn't know if it was because she left the job at the RIA for which Marie helped her get an interview, or because Marie was Tony's agent, or because Marie never really liked Dickey—likely some combination of the three—but it finally took Dickey stopping by Marie's office for the women to agree to part ways.

The Micheners' invitation was a life ring, but the closer Dickey gets to their home, the more anxious she feels. The sleeplessness, bouts of crying, and painful stomach issues are embarrassing enough to face with family.

Why did I think coming to stay with near strangers was a good idea?

Dickey takes a last drag of her cigarette and tosses it out the taxi window, immediately regretting littering in what looks like Eden. Puffs of new pink buds on cherry trees and patches of slouching daffodils dance in the breeze. The long and winding road on the Michener property follows a meandering stream, is heavily wooded and crossed by walking paths. The home itself is a modest rancher of local wood and stone, in harmony with its surroundings and reminiscent of Frank Lloyd Wright's architecture.

Exile, she again thinks, but this time, the word doesn't feel as heavy.

Exile from Hungary. Exile from the RIA. Exile from the city.

It dawns on her that she has been thinking of exile as banishment, as exile *from* people and places. She must learn to think of it as freedom *from* people and places.

Freedom from Hungary. Freedom from the RIA. Freedom from the city. Freedom from Tony's ever-present shadow. Freedom from the bogeyman.

Once the taxi squeaks to a stop, a yellow retriever runs out the front door. Dickey steps out of the taxi, and the dog bounds to her, leaping up to lick her face and wagging its entire body so happily she has to brace her still-emaciated frame to remain upright. The friendly greeting of the dog, the gentle air, and the tranquility of the estate reassure Dickey, and once Mari and Jim appear with warm smiles and embraces, Dickey is finally able to breathe a sigh of relief.

"Beautiful," says Dickey, admiring every room on the tour.

The facade of the house was deceptively small. The rancher has four bedrooms and four bathrooms, multiple stone fireplaces, natural light from endless floor-to-ceiling windows, and stunning woodland views from every corner of the house. Mari leads Dickey to her room—homey and rustic, with wood-paneled walls and cabinetry—and when Dickey sees what's on the bed, she cries out with joy.

"Oscar! I thought I'd never see you again."

Dickey's stuffed monkey rests against piles of pillows. She hurries over to hug Oscar, not caring that she must look like an oversized child.

"As you know," says Mari, "I had your personal belongings and the gifts you bought for your family sent to your aunt's place, but I wanted to keep the stuffed animal to give to you either on our reunion in Vienna or in the States. I hope you weren't too traumatized, wondering where he'd gone."

"My brain hasn't worked properly since prison. I thought I might have stuffed him in my bag, and he'd been confiscated. Thank you for taking care of my little rabbit's foot. Now you know how strange I am."

Jim and Mari smile warmly at Dickey, then steal glances at each other.

"Oh, you already knew that," Dickey says.

They all have a good laugh.

Mari leads Dickey out to the back terrace overlooking acres of lawn, trees, and a still-covered swimming pool. The afternoon sunlight feels like a gentle incubator. Mari instructs Dickey and Jim to sit at the table and then disappears indoors.

"You'll have to come back in the summer," says Jim. "The pool gets full sunshine all day. The water is like a bath."

"I would love that," says Dickey. "I never want to be cold again. I've vowed to only take assignments in warm climates from now on. I can endure hunger and psychological torture to a high degree, but cold is the thing that threatens to undo me. I have a new appreciation for Admiral Byrd's arctic expeditions."

Chattering chickadees fill the silence that envelops them. Dickey closes her eyes and turns to the sun.

"We were very afraid for you," Jim says.

Dickey opens her eyes and looks at Jim's kindly face. She's moved to see his eyes have a film of tears. She had no idea someone like him could care so much about someone like her. The lump in her throat prevents her from speaking, so she nods and hopes he understands.

Mari returns with a tray of sandwiches and Coca-Cola, and holding a present under her arm, of which Jim relieves her. When Mari places a plate with a peanut butter sandwich in front of Dickey, she exclaims aloud and claps.

"Your favorite," says Mari, taking her seat. "For your thirty-eighth birthday."

"How'd you know?"

"Your Aunt George wrote to thank me for sending your things and mentioned that she and your Aunt Lutie had jars of peanut butter ready for your favorite sandwiches when you returned. And you mentioned your birthday at some point during our time in Vienna."

"Caviar and squab at the Hotel Bristol could not make me happier than this peanut butter sandwich. Thank you."

Mari smiles and motions toward the present.

"Jim, give it to her."

"I'll wait until she's eaten," he says. "You're still very thin, Dickey."

"I know," says Dickey. "It's hard to put on weight when one's stomach is so… tempestuous. Sorry."

"No apologies," says Mari. "It will take time."

Jim slides the present toward Dickey. She unwraps it to find a book.

The Bridge at Andau, by James A. Michener.

"Oh," says Dickey, running her hand over the shining book jacket. The cover image is a dark sketch of an armed resistance man on a white background, with red title lettering. The man on the cover looks as weary as Dickey feels.

"The cover man is meant to be reminiscent of *Time* magazine's January 'Man of the Year' issue," says Jim. "The Hungarian freedom fighter."

"My aunts saved that issue for me."

"You helped bring it about. What you did for the cause."

Dickey is quiet. She still thinks what she did to harm and hinder might have outweighed the helping part.

"Show her," says Mari.

Jim looks from Dickey to the book, where a bookmark holds a page. He opens it and turns it so Dickey can see. She scans the words about the brave photographer who accompanied him on many crossings.

"Carl Hartman?"

"You."

"Me? But it says, 'he.' And I'm not brave. I'm careless, reckless, and foolish."

Jim closes the book and takes Dickey's small cold hand in his large, warm hands.

"You are the bravest person—man or woman—I have ever known. You gave no thought to your own safety. Only to helping. You gave me and all the men courage."

Dickey feels the prick of tears at his generous assessment. His kindness is almost too much for her to bear.

"I felt I had to hide your identity in the book," says Jim. "Because you were lost and feared in prison when this went to print. I didn't know what you told your captors, so I had to be careful."

"How did you get this book out so quickly?"

"My agent thought the pieces I intended to serialize were so complete and narrative in nature that he pitched my publisher. They agreed to a healthy advance and a quick printing."

An agent who works for you, Dickey thinks. *What a novelty.*

"I have instructed that your name should be put in all subsequent printings," says Jim. "If that's okay with you."

"I'd be honored," she says.

Jim releases her hands and pushes the book closer to her. She looks at it in wonder, flipping past his inscription to the page he marked and scanning the text.

"Wait'll Aunt George sees this," says Dickey. "Thank you, Jim, Mari. You can't understand what you've done for my recovery, and I've only been here an hour."

March 25, 1957
Pennsylvania, Michener House

Dearest Aunts George and Lutie,

I'll get the crushing part over with first. I'm sure you've heard by now, Admiral Richard Byrd—hero of my life, man for whom I renamed myself—has died of heart failure, at the age of sixty-eight. I know it will be hard for you to understand the depths of my sorrow, but I feel as broken as I did when Daddy and Marmee passed. Byrd has been my inspiration from the time I was a fat little outcast, to the time I was a skinny old outcast. His writings on his heroic expeditions in places of unholy cold gave me the courage to face frigid temps while escorting refugees, and in my prison cell. He was an honorary chair of the IRC, and I thought we'd meet when I got home. We didn't, and now we'll never be able to, and I regret not sending him a letter telling him all he meant to me.

The rest of this note will only be filled with joy, I promise.

It's a strange place to be in life, happy to put on weight, but here I am, gaining back all I have lost, not only physically but also mentally and spiritually. Mari Michener is an angel from heaven, who won't let me lift a finger, who prepares all my meals—and all those of her husband—with the utmost care. She insists upon doing my laundry and makes sure my coffee cup never runs low. She only asks three things of me:

1. *Make my own bed, which I do with hospital corner–style perfection, since my marine training.*
2. *Write every day, especially about my experience in*

prison. As one who has also been interred, she says that putting it on paper is the way to take the pain out of one's head and keep it out of one's nightmares.

3. *Smoke outdoors.*

All of this, combined with daily walks with Jim and Mari and their dog, along with happy mealtimes, Jim blaring Brahms's Quartets for piano and strings on his record player, and the warming weather, has done wonders for me. I feel reborn, or at least on my way.

We were all thrilled to see the enclosed New York Times *piece on resettled Hungarian refugees from Operation Safe Haven, including some we had helped across the border and interviewed. Featured here is a woman—Maria Marothy—whose tales of prison survival, in spite of torture, helped get me through my own. She is now happily living and working in New Jersey with her family. I hope Zoltan is well. Please keep checking on him until I return to New York, later this month, God willing.*

Finally, enclosed is a signed copy of Jim's new book, The Bridge at Andau. *The pages I've marked are about me. I am the "male photographer" of great courage. Jim protected my identity because he worried exposing me would get me in trouble with the communists, but now that I'm safely home, he'll make sure my real identity is revealed in subsequent printings. I had balked at his praise when I first arrived, but through many deep and healing conversations with Mari and Jim, I have come to believe that I was brave, I do have courage, and I have worth. I don't know if I've ever really believed that to my bones until now.*

You both have been angels telling me such good things my whole life, but you are family, so I never really and truly believed you. I thought you had to say that, or you felt so sorry for me, or you were obliged. Now I know what you said was true, and I thank you. Your love was a light in the darkness that I could feel an ocean away. It helped sustain me during the hell of Fö Street and continues to do so.

The friendship of Jim and Mari also sustains me. Jim was raised in the Quaker faith. Exposure to him and working for the American Friends, I know how much importance they place on one's inner light, the spark of the Divine inside. It is open to all of us, as is our connection with the Divine, and if we allow it, it lights our path and those of others.

Which leads me to what you might consider a little more bad news, though I promised otherwise. I feel ready to again pick up my camera and find the places and the people in the world who need light. It's my calling. I must use my gifts of curiosity, courage, and access to the inner light to go to the darkest places and expose what happens there.

I used to think of myself as a girl reporter, then a war correspondent. Now, however, I see I have to serve as an interpreter of violence. Find it, expose it, name it, exorcise it. That is my task, and I'm ready for my next mission.

Of only one thing can I say surely: It will not be in a cold place. Never again.

All my love,
Dickey Doo Georgie Lou

PART TWO

1958–1960

TWENTY

DECEMBER 1958

Miami, Florida

Dickey revels in the eighty perfect degrees of Florida heat. New York City has already turned windy and frigid. The trees are bare, and the sky is gray. That's not the case in Miami. Dickey is enlivened by the blazing sun and enchanted by everything around her.

Flowers and luscious green trees in winter! What a place!

Dickey heads to the Congress Building. It's a 1920s high-rise of gleaming white glazed terra cotta, done in the Mediterranean revival style. She knows the place well, having worked here in her twenties as an air-show publicist. That job took her to Cuba for the first time, where she'd experienced the dizzy high of falling in love with Havana and the horrific low of witnessing a tragic airplane crash. Now, years later, she's going to return to Cuba, this time for *Reader's Digest*. She's covering an uprising against despot Fulgencio Batista—the dictator of Cuba at the helm of a secret military intelligence service every bit as torturous and barbaric as the Hungarian AVO and the Nazi Gestapo. The uprising against Batista is being led by the young revolutionary lawyer Fidel Castro, his brother Raúl, and a sympathizing Argentinian physician, Ernesto "Che"

Guevara. The men and their guerrilla bands have captured the minds and hearts of the American people as a sort of David collective to the Goliath Cuban dictatorship, but they're selective about the journalists they'll trust to tell their story.

Through Castro sympathizers, who own the grocery store near Dickey's apartment, Dickey was introduced to a network of contacts. She learned Castro will admit her to his lair in the Sierra Maestra—a mountain range in the Oriente Province in southeastern Cuba—because his contacts read how she never gave the names of Hungarian revolutionaries or their supporters while in prison, nor did she betray the location of the Algerians in revolution against the French on her recent assignment there covering their maneuvers and way of life in the desert. *Reader's Digest* is happy to sponsor a trip with such exclusive access.

Once she's inside the Congress Building, passing her old office, the hair on Dickey's arms rises. She can almost see the ghost of her young idealistic self, scurrying in late to work, pencil behind her ear, cigarette hanging out of her mouth. In a wall mirror, she catches a glimpse of herself—late, a pencil behind her ear, a cigarette hanging out of her mouth—and laughs.

I'll never change.

Three doors down from the old office, she knocks. A hatch is opened, and she says the code phrase. She's admitted to the stark, industrial room at odds with the overall building charm, by the head of Castro's underground in Miami, who tells her to call him Doctor. It's her fifth day interviewing refugees who've fled from Batista's reign of horror, and she has to keep shaking off the déjà vu of interviewing refugees in Vienna. Today, she has to turn over her most-beloved possessions if she wants passage to Cuba. Doctor has assured her they will be shipped separately from Dickey so they won't put her guides in danger.

"Both cameras?" Dickey asks.

"I've told you many times—yes," says Doctor. "You'll get it all back."

"Why? If my cover is a tourist, it makes perfect sense that I would have cameras."

"Not these kind. And not two."

"How about I give you one?"

"You'll give me both or you won't go."

With a groan and great reluctance, she places her most precious possessions on the table.

"Aren't you forgetting something?" he asks, pointing at the trench knife at her belt.

"Not this," she says. "It's irreplaceable. It was a gift from a soldier. I'll conceal it beneath the skirt I'll wear to travel."

He shakes his head.

This doesn't feel right, she thinks, an unpleasant roiling in her stomach.

Dickey is aware her instincts have increasingly sent caution flags over the last few days, and she increasingly swats them away. She rationalizes that it's overcaution because of her arrest in Hungary. Then she thinks if she had listened to her instincts there, she never would have been arrested. Then she thinks if she had never been arrested, she never would have gotten the story out about the Hungarian communist prison to the world, and that was worth it. At least, it was worth it to get her new job working for *Reader's Digest*, and the published article—"Nobody Owes Me a Christmas"— from the December 1957 issue that won her a $2,500 prize and that

Billy Graham read aloud on his radio show. She's now a household name and is being called America's first Cold War hero.

"I won't allow an American to transport a weapon into Cuba," Doctor says.

"If you'll recall, America won't allow any more weapons, either. President Eisenhower signed the arms embargo."

"Too little, too late."

"Will you deny me the right to protect myself?"

"You Americans always put yourselves first. The sins of your country have made a hell of ours. No more."

"I thought you said I'd be reunited with all of this."

"You will. On our terms."

Dickey curses under her breath and takes a long time unfastening the knife, before tossing it on the folding table with a clunk.

He smiles, exposing a gold tooth.

The descent over blue-green water as far as the eye can see, into the lush paradise of Santiago de Cuba. makes Dickey swoon. As the plane lands, she's filled with joy.

I have died, she thinks. *And I've made it to heaven, after all.*

While Dickey stands in line at the airport checkpoint, she unbuttons the top of her pale-blue V-necked sleeveless blouse, smooths the front of her navy-blue pencil skirt, and dons the new red harlequin sunglasses she had Stevie pick up in advance of her Cuba trip.

In addition to Stevie's new job working in administration at Bellevue Hospital—across from Dickey's apartment—Dickey employs her as a part-time personal secretary. Stevie employs herself as Dickey's surrogate mother, fussing, worrying, and cautioning Dickey to stop putting herself in harm's way. Dickey ignores all motherly advice, but depends upon Stevie's impeccable taste in feminine clothing, makeup, and accoutrements.

The woman has outdone herself outfitting Dickey as the "typical American tourist visiting her marine beau at Guantánamo." Dickey's cover is complete all the way down to the wallet photo of a marine who'd given Dickey his picture at Camp Pendleton. She had to search through dozens of baby-faced photographs from that time to find a young man who looked like he might shave. Though she found one, she can't remember his name. Dickey pulls out the picture and kisses it, just as she's called forward to the scowling, heavily armed policeman.

"*Pasaporte*," he says.

"Of course," she says.

She places the wallet back in the red pocketbook and retrieves her new passport, fresh and free of stamps, the last one having recently been filled. The timing worked out well, as a typical tourist would not likely have stamps from Austria, Morocco, Turkey, Lebanon, Spain, and Algeria.

"I was distracted by how excited I am to see my husband," she says.

He looks at her left hand.

"Where is your ring?" he asks in Spanish-accented English.

Oops, she thinks. *A detail, overlooked. Think fast, doofus.*

"You know, my *husband*," she says, drawing out the word, raising her eyebrows, and tugging at her top shirt button. She prays her insinuation of a sordid affair between an older woman and a young soldier won't get lost in translation.

He stares, scowling, for a moment, before his face transforms with salacious glee. He winks and licks his lips.

"Ah, your *husband*, yes," he says, passing back her passport.

He motions for her suitcase, which Stevie also lent to Dickey. Dickey feels sweat bead on her upper lip. She took care to cover her combat field pack, boots, and fatigues with lacy panties, bathing suits, and flowery dresses. He lets out a derisive laugh when he finds Oscar the monkey under a pair of black silk pajamas. If he gets to her boots and fatigues at the bottom of the suitcase, there will be no laughter. Her story will be that she's going on a hiking excursion, but she realizes how strange that will sound in the embattled Oriente Province.

The arrival of a truck full of Cuban army officers calls his attention. He pushes the suitcase back to her, and waves her off with a grunt. She hopes he doesn't see how her hands shake when she closes the clasp and nearly trips as she hurries away from his station.

In the twilight, at the restaurant of the Motel Rancho, overlooking Santiago de Cuba, Dickey chews her nails and twirls her earrings. Revolution is coming—fighting is imminent—breathing down the necks of those in the city, yet she's ordering dinner and drinks at a bar, watching an old woman sweep the hallway, and listening to the whoops and cheers of children playing baseball in an empty lot next door. She thinks this city is one of those strange places on the edge of war that hang between time and space.

"It's like in Genesis," Dickey says to Andrew St. George, over a game of gin. He's a strapping *New York Times* reporter, about to leave Cuba just as she's arrived. "Noah warns the people. They tease him while building the ark. They carry on with their lives marrying and working, and then one day it rains. And the next, they are swept away. These people and their way of life is about to be swept away, and while many to most think they'll be glad, they can't be glad at the possibility of destruction."

Those left at the motel are mostly American and mostly in the press. Though life in the city appears to be carrying on as normal, there's a nervous energy in the atmosphere so thick it looks like wiggly heat lines over hot pavement. The tiny waitress with large eyes underlined in dark circles had told Dickey and Andrew, in broken English, this used to be their busy time, but the revolution has driven most tourists away. Dickey couldn't tell if the woman was pleased or displeased by the fact.

"We humans cling so tightly to our routines and our possessions," Dickey continues. "It's good I can live with so little. I think being a war correspondent helps with that."

"Gin," Andrew says.

Dickey falls back in her chair.

"Ugh," she says. "I knew I shouldn't have passed on the ten of diamonds."

"Don't wait, Dickey. Life lesson. You probably waited too long to come here."

"That's me, all right. Late. Scooped. Second. If there is a rendezvous, I'll be sure to pick the wrong time to get there."

"And getting to Castro is no picnic. You have a lot of hiking ahead of you. Overgrown jungle paths. Mosquitoes the size of canaries. Scant provisions. Might you be a little old for this?"

Dickey feels as if he's slapped her. She and Andrew know each other from the Overseas Press Club as acquaintances, at best. That is not something one would say to an acquaintance.

"I'm not even forty," she says, "and I trained with the marines. I could run circles around you, and what are you? Forty-two?"

"Thirty-five," he says, feigning insult.

"It's clearly been a hard thirty-five years," she says.

He laughs.

She stands and walks to the veranda, looking out at the looming forms of the Sierra Maestra.

Andrew joins her.

"When do you go?" he asks.

"Sometime tomorrow afternoon, once my gear is delivered."

A bitter laugh escapes him.

"What?" she asks.

"You will not get your gear."

"What do you mean?" she says, gripped by bowel-churning fear.

"The crooks in Miami will not send your gear. Surely you realized that. I can help connect you to a lead in town to get you a camera of some kind."

Dickey feels as if she's going to hyperventilate. The thought of losing the cameras infuriates her, but losing the trench knife is beyond comprehension.

"We cling so tightly to our possessions," he says, mimicking her earlier statement.

More gut punches from him.

"In all seriousness," he says. "Don't let your guard down for a moment out there."

"I thought you were on the side of the rebels?"

"I am. But that doesn't mean they're perfect. Che Guevara, for example. He says worrisome things."

"Like?"

"Like he told me he was on Hitler's side in the war because he fought British colonialists."

"Oh," says Dickey.

"Yeah, but then you see Che with the poor and he reminds you of Jesus. Until you tell him that and he says the comparison is an insult."

"An insult?"

"Yes, he said he would never let himself get killed by the enemy the way Jesus did."

Dickey feels a wave of nausea.

What am I getting myself into?

She returns to the table, seeking another drink, but there's not a drop left of her El Presidente. Andrew sits down across from her. Just as an anxiety attack threatens to engulf Dickey, the waitress brings the check. She places it in Andrew's hands, and while he searches for his wallet, she flashes a slip of paper in front of Dickey's eyes, rolls it in a ball, and tosses it in Dickey's handbag without Andrew noticing a thing.

She's my guide, thinks Dickey. *No turning back now.*

TWENTY-ONE

DECEMBER 1958

Santiago de Cuba

As Andrew predicted, Dickey's possessions never arrived. The cameras are replaceable, but it's all she can do not to cry over the lost trench knife. Thankfully, Andrew was able to deliver on the camera connection. Now, with her new though inferior camera, buzzing on Cuban coffee, dressed in her fatigues, in the passenger seat of the jeep—waitress from last night in the driver's seat, also in fatigues, wearing a black beret and with a large rifle next to her—Dickey's on her way to rendezvous with Castro and his rebels at their mountain headquarters.

The courier will not give Dickey a name, so Dickey thinks of the young woman as Ladybug. She is even shorter than Dickey, wears the red and black armband of Castro's army, and has big round eyes with full eyelashes. She wears a dozen religious medals and crosses herself every time they pass a Catholic church. Dickey's Spanish is poor, so she asks Ladybug—whose English is poor—to teach Dickey as much as possible.

They pass a gray church with an angel at the roof. Ladybug crosses herself.

"*Católica?*" Ladybug asks.

"No," says Dickey.

Ladybug frowns.

"Christian, though," says Dickey. "*Cristiana.*"

Ladybug nods, the frown softening.

"Padre Nuestro," she says.

The Our Father.

They head north out of Santiago de Cuba, pass a golf course, and the landscape changes quickly to rural. Barefoot children chase chickens through dirt yards, and women who look older than Cuba itself rest their chins on brooms, watching the younger women drive by.

"*Padre nuestro, que estàs en el cielo,*" says Ladybug.

Dickey repeats what Ladybug says in Spanish, thinking the words in English.

Our Father, who art in heaven.

"*Santificado sea Tu nombre,*" says Ladybug.

Hallowed be thy name.

They drive through cane farms and along streams, winding and climbing. Ladybug must have only recently learned to drive, based on how rough the ride is. Dickey can't criticize, however. Her driving is as poor as her flying, and she's never even tried to get a driver's license. A military vehicle, subway, or taxi always takes Dickey where she needs to go.

"Basílica del Cobre," Ladybug says, crossing herself. Then she points. "Hemingway."

"Ernest Hemingway?"

The writer has had a home in Cuba since 1940.

"*Sí. El premio Nobel hay,*" says Ladybug.

"His Nobel Prize is there? For *The Old Man and the Sea*?"

"Sí."

He also won a Pulitzer for that book. It's Dickey's turn to cross herself, the literary shrine as religious to her as the church is to Ladybug. Dickey wonders why the writer would gift his Nobel Prize medal to this Catholic church.

"No, Batista," Ladybug says, as if reading Dickey's thoughts.

To keep it away from Batista.

Dickey nods. They continue on.

The brakes in the truck are slow to respond, and sometimes don't, but Ladybug never looks panicked, only steers off the path into vegetation if she needs to slow. Dickey grows more nauseous by the minute. She's glad they're praying.

"*Venga a nosotros Tu reino; hágase tu voluntad, en la tierra como en el cielo.*"

Thy kingdom come, Thy will be done, on earth as it is in Heaven.

They continue the climb, passing the churches Parrouquia San Joaquin, Sagrada Familia, and Iglesia San Bartolomé.

"*Danos hoy nuestro pan de cada día; perdona nuestras ofensas, como también nosotros perdonamos a los que nos ofenden.*"

Give us this day our daily bread; forgive us our trespasses, as we forgive those who trespass against us.

The "doctor" in Miami said many Cubans cannot forgive Americans their sins against the island. The brothels and casinos and land exploitation—by everyone from American mobsters to the government—have gone on for too long, along with past funding and arming of Batista's military. The only hope will be for the Americans to support Castro and his movement. Popular opinion certainly does so now, but Dickey wants to see for herself so others can.

And I'll be the first American woman journalist to do so.

Three hours after they set out, the jeep stops at a crude gate, guarded by a dozen glowering men with guns. Ladybug nods at the guards and parks, leaving her rifle in the jeep. She and Dickey are patted down, and Dickey's bag is searched before they're escorted onto a dirt path. It narrows the higher they climb, and Dickey's boots slip on the muddy rocks. The air is sweet and fresh, and the whisper of palm trees is soothing. Dickey itches to take pictures but she's under strict instructions to wait until she's in the company of Castro and the rebels. She's been warned, pictures taken along the way could be confiscated by Batista's army and bring danger to the revolution.

At a bend, Ladybug stops and stomps her boot, shooing away a black and green snake. Dickey watches it slither into the undergrowth. She feels the sting of a mosquito and slaps it. It's not even the rainy season, and the bugs are out in full force—something she hadn't considered when making her "no more cold weather" proclamation. Still, this is heaven compared to ice and snow. Her joints are loose and warm, and she has never seen so many orchids or variations of the color green.

Have I found Eden?

They arrive at a crude wooden dwelling. Ladybug crosses herself as if she's at a church.

"*No nos dejes caer en la tentación, y líbranos del mal.*"

And lead us not into temptation but deliver us from evil.

"*Amén,*" the women say together.

The man himself steps out the door.

Fidel Castro.

Fidel is a tsunami, sweeping up all in his path with his enormous breathtaking, noisy, temperamental power. He is a cyclone, a tornado, an earthquake, a volcano. *Mercurial* does not begin to describe the dizzying highs and lows of his moods. His only constant is noise—fighting, laughing, cursing, singing. There is never silence around him. Dickey thinks, if Batista and his army want to find Fidel, they need only be quiet. The cacophony will direct them accordingly.

In the midst of the human noise is radio noise. Broadcasting from a hut at command, Radio Rebelde uses no codes and gives real-time battle updates to the people of Cuba, often announced by Fidel himself.

Carlos Franqui—a short, intense, mustached man—helps with the radio and *Revolución*, the rebel newspaper. He's small and serious. His whole face is transformed when he smiles, but that doesn't happen often.

Fidel's hut is up a long wooden staircase and nestled in trees, and it is forbidden for Dickey to enter. There are rumors he has a refrigerator, but Dickey has not seen it herself. She has seen Ernesto "Che" Guevara, and in spite of being wary of him based on Andrew's caution, Dickey finds Che unsettlingly attractive. He was nicknamed "Che" for the expression meaning "Hey!" that he often uses to get others' attention. His manner is calm, and he looks into the eyes of the one talking. His intensity is both captivating and disturbing. Upon introductions, he tells her to follow him.

"Come, Yanqui," Che says.

Yanqui is a slur for Americans, but he says it with a wink and a grin.

Dickey follows him, readying her camera while she walks,

Ladybug trailing. Che leads Dickey through winding paths that open to a large pit, where dozens of men, hands tied behind them, are guarded by a militia of women. Dickey's emotions catapult from fascination with the armed women to terror at the thought of what she's about to witness with what appears to be prisoners of war. Cold sweat covers her. Having recently been a prisoner under constant threat of execution herself, she does not relish witnessing this. She has to do her job, however. She takes a deep breath and raises her camera to Che in request to photograph the scene. He shakes his head in the negative. For once she does not reprimand herself for asking. She has the feeling she'd be shot dead if she'd taken the picture without his permission.

Che begins his speech. Ladybug translates as best she can. Dickey's face mirrors the prisoners', starting with looks of terror, becoming those of fear, and finally bemusement. In short, Che invites the men to turn coat. He tells them that under Batista they are slaves. With the revolution, they'll be free men. If they accept the invitation, they'll be trained as real soldiers, not as toy soldiers. If they decline, they will be escorted to the Red Cross tent and returned to Batista, no strings attached. They have until the next morning to decide.

The only insult Che gives them is in his confidence that they have no chance against the rebel army. They will continue to either be killed in battle or captured and returned in unmanly disgrace. Che points to the women guarding them.

"Take a good look at the women who helped beat you," he says, "How does that make you feel? That Las Marianas are better soldiers than you are?"

With that, he flashes his wolf grin and leaves.

The next morning, all 242 men are returned to the Red Cross, but every one of them looks over his shoulder at the mountains with longing, seemingly wondering if he should have chosen to stay.

TWENTY-TWO

DECEMBER 1958

Oriente Province, Cuba

In Dickey's wildest marine training dreams, she could never have imagined becoming one of the ranks of a platoon of women, yet here she is.

The Mariana Grajales Platoon is made up of fourteen women who enlisted under Fidel. It's named for the Afro-Cuban mother and medic who bravely gave and lost most of her sons to the nineteenth-century wars of Cuban independence from Spain. Many of the women in the platoon have been active in the anti-Batista resistance since the time Fidel and Raúl were imprisoned for the initial uprising on July 26, 1953. They wear their red and black July 26th armbands and black berets with pride.

These women were couriers and safe-house providers. Their brothers and fiancés had been murdered. Some of the women had been imprisoned, tortured, and raped. It takes weeks for them to trust Dickey but—as she accompanies them on patrol, keeping up, being respectful, and trying to learn the language—they gradually do, telling Dickey the horror of the brutality of Batista's men. They speak in both Spanish and English, Ladybug translating when

Dickey needs it. Some women are comfortable revealing their real names; others—like Ladybug—are not.

"We were gang-raped by all the soldiers at the Manzanillo barracks," says Amelia, pointing at Georgina, a small slight woman with fury in her eyes and who's never without her carbine. The woman cradles her rifle like a baby. She loves her weapon the way Dickey used to love her trench knife, which she still reaches for and mourns a dozen times a day.

"Gang-raped?" Dickey asks, sickened. "By all of them?"

"Dozens," says Georgina, finding her voice. "Sixteen days of unspeakable torture."

"But we never said a word," said Amelia. "No one was betrayed."

"How did you escape?" asks Dickey, almost breathless.

"A relative in a high place in government secured our release. We came right to the mountains. We begged Fidel to fight."

"Some of the men here didn't want us to be soldiers," says Georgina, stroking her rifle. "There aren't enough weapons for them, let alone us. But Fidel said they were lazy and undisciplined, so the women who want to fight get to fight. He trained us himself. We have not had a single casualty."

"Which has earned us the respect of even our toughest opponents. As you have earned ours."

Dickey warms with pleasure. Her yearning for belonging in any form, to any group, has been richly satisfied these weeks. Her hero worship of men—and women—in uniform grows to new levels. She can almost hear Robert's cautions about putting people on pedestals, Tony's reprimands about being more objective and journalistic, and Carl Hartman's admonitions to take herself out of the story. Her passion aflame, Dickey feels powerless to subdue these tendencies.

Doesn't it make the story better when one lives and feels along with one's subjects?

Other bad habits grow like vines.

In the company of Fidel's forces, Dickey's loud voice grows louder. Her patience grows shorter. She performs spectacles of temper whenever Fidel watches because it makes him smile. He says she has *sangre de tigre*—tiger blood—in her veins. She starts wearing her long hair down, in solidarity with the long beards. The longer a rebel's beard, the more respect he has because it shows he has been with the revolution longer, away from the comforts of the city. She starts smoking cigars.

Fascinated by the guerrilla warfare tactics employed by the soldiers of Castro's army, Dickey takes extensive notes. She witnesses firsthand how smart and even psychological battles defeat big guns. Hemingway's Spanish Civil War novel, *For Whom the Bell Tolls*, is never far from Fidel's grasp. He says it has inspired him and the type of warfare he uses. It inspired him to allow female soldiers.

Che is their most effective military leader. When he leads soldiers in the field, their progress against Batista's men is extraordinary. By mid-December, the rebels gain territory, which no one on the outside could have thought possible. When there are losses, they set off Castro's volcanic temper. He drags Dickey by the arm to photograph the faces of his murdered soldiers. Every time one of Batista's bombers—old American B-26s—flies over, wreaking havoc, the days following involve marked setbacks in Dickey's relationships with the rebels. When they're winning, they call her *Americana*. When they lose, she's *Yanqui*.

"How many times must I tell you?" she yells. "The Americans provided those planes years ago for Cuba's defense. They were not sent for use against the people. The United States provides no more to Batista."

Strangely, the louder she fights back with them, the more Fidel, and now his brother Raúl—recently returned from a battle everyone thought would kill him—respect her. They only respond to shows of strength. Fidel especially wants tension. He needs conflict at all times. Dickey has never seen anything like it.

She's constantly surprised by the man, never more so than stumbling upon him in a hammock, talking quietly to his brother and his brother's love, Vilma. With them is Fidel's shadow, Celia, whom they all call their "godmother." Celia is quiet and thoughtful. Though she has a slight and sickly appearance, she keeps up with treks and has fought in battles without complaint. She's most at ease as Fidel's assistant, fetching coffee, serving bread, and sewing uniforms. Dickey cannot tell if Fidel and Celia are lovers, but many assume it's so. To Dickey, their attachment to each other is symbiotic, like a clown fish and an anemone.

Dickey is allowed to document everything. Fidel revels in the coverage. And he has indicated some decisive battles are coming.

Maps are laid out on the ground. Men and women soldiers draw near. Plans are made. The scene before Dickey is comprised not only of both sexes and varying ages, but of differing nationalities and backgrounds. In Cuba, Black men and women have been as discriminated against as those in the United States. The Castros have welcomed Afro-Cubans to the revolution, even promoting them to high ranks. Dickey makes sure the shot includes all the facets of Castro's jewel.

When the meeting concludes, Fidel whistles to Dickey.

"Americana," says Fidel. "Go with him."

Dickey obeys, climbing with her field pack into the passenger seat of the commandeered jeep that has just arrived, driven by Georgi, the mechanic. Georgi has never warmed to her.

This should be interesting.

On the drive, under Dickey's prodding, Georgi finally tells her they're going to the town of Maffo, where the rebels are trying to take a Batistiano stronghold. It takes them well over an hour to reach their destination—and as they get closer and the sun sets, Dickey sees the owl-like whites of many eyes staring out from trees, while bursts of gunfire can be heard in the distance.

"The Maffo townspeople have evacuated," says Georgi, in English.

While Dickey's conversational Spanish is enough to get by, it's a relief not to have the added burden of translation, further exhausting her already tired mind. She hasn't been sleeping well in the company of Fidel, who seems not to need it, calling meetings at all hours of the night. Weeks of this are beginning to wear on her, though she hates the idea of leaving the rebels—who've become like family—in January, the end of her assignment. Las Marianas have started calling Dickey *hermana*. She can't imagine a higher compliment. Las Marianas are not with the caravan for this operation, however. They are with Raúl in Guisa—west of Maffo—where they continue their assault on a Batista garrison there. How she misses the camaraderie of the women.

As they drive on, Dickey's heart hurts to see so many little children sleeping out in the open. She longs to take a photograph of the gaunt, beautiful mother with large eyes nursing an infant in the moonlight, under an almacigo tree.

Maffo Madonna, Dickey thinks.

As in Hungary and Poland, Madonna and Child are everywhere on the faces of the world's refugees. Dickey knows, however, that Georgi won't stop long enough for her to get the lighting right, so the woman and child will have to remain in her memory and her heart.

Dickey glances at her watch and sees it's nearing eleven. Georgi drives onward. They're close enough to the battle that she wonders if stray gunfire might hit them, and is about to ask as much, when all goes quiet. The jeep barrels down the final stretch into town and cruises right through the middle of the square before parking next to the radio building. Across the square, there are men with guns pointed at them from the Batistiano fortress.

Heart racing, she looks at Georgi with wide eyes.

"They agreed on a ceasefire for an hour, at eleven," he says, climbing out of the jeep.

A small knot of tension releases in her, though very small indeed.

"You could have mentioned that earlier," she says, grabbing her field pack and following him into the radio building.

"I don't owe you anything, Yanqui," he says.

He lets the door of the rebel-controlled station slam in her face.

She feels her skin turn hot with a flash of fury. She throws it open and, once inside, grabs Georgi's arm and spins him around to face her. A group of interested young men look on.

"You do owe me to tell your story well," she says. "What do you think Batista's reporters are saying about you? They call you a bunch of communist criminals, bent on anarchy. Boys playing dress-up. I'm here, busting my ass, trying to help you. To tell your story. Those aren't my B-26s, and I didn't make a dime off a single casino or whorehouse here. Above all, your leader trusts me. What do you think he would say if I told him you dared to doubt his judgment?"

The young men in the station look wide-eyed from Georgi to Dickey, like she's their mother reprimanding one of her sons. Georgi—who can't be more than seventeen or eighteen years old—shrinks into himself and lowers his gaze.

The noise of a familiar voice coming loud over a speaker echoes across the square. Dickey pushes past Georgi to find the broadcaster. From an open window, a stout balding man wearing black-framed glasses speaks into a megaphone. He's Captain Luis Orlando, and sometimes broadcasts from Radio Rebelde. From what she can understand, he urges the Batistianos to abandon their posts and fight with the rebels, who will surely take victory. He tells them there will be no penalty if they come now, but he can't promise such leniency if they wait.

Like the Castros, Orlando's speech is loud and long-winded. Men come into the room, leaning against the walls to listen, looking weary and anxious. When he finally finishes, he puts down the megaphone, takes off his glasses, and rubs his eyes. He then looks over at Dickey and motions for her to join him. He moves her gently outside of the frame of the window and takes her hands, holding them in his own.

"We are out of ammunition, Americana," he says. "Get your pictures quickly. You're not safe."

Dickey feels all of her fury drain from her and her heart warm. He has the kindness of a father.

"Felipe," he says, calling the tall lean handsome man who stands in the back of the room. "*Ve, protégela.*"

Protect her.

Orlando gives all the men instructions in rapid Spanish—including some clearly sharp words for Georgi—before again urging Dickey to leave.

"It is a tragedy to fight one's brother," Orlando says. "But we have been forced to this. May it be over soon."

He looks at his watch. Dickey looks at hers. Somehow, it's almost midnight.

"We won't be long behind you," he says. "Go."

Captain Orlando continues pleading with Batista's men to come to the rebels' side as Dickey's crew drives out of Maffo, lights out, as slowly and quietly as they can. Dickey is pressed between Georgi and Felipe in the front seat—her field pack strapped to her chest like a baby—with a lone Black rebel soldier in the back. The rest will follow soon in the commander's truck. They are barely out of town when mortar fire from the Batistianos starts raining around them like fireworks.

Georgi swerves off the road and orders them to take cover. Felipe wraps his arm around Dickey, and they all run to a ditch, where they collapse in the dirt. In a break in the fire, she hears Georgi's laugh.

"Of all things," he says. "An American. Facedown in the dirt with us. You've earned my respect, Yanqui."

"Then stop calling me that, will ya?" says Dickey.

An explosion comes so close that it shudders the ground under them and wipes the smile off Georgi's face.

"We need to keep going," says Felipe.

Georgi nods and the group runs for the jeep. This time, he

throws it into high gear, driving fast enough to take Dickey's breath away. As they veer around turns, he stomps on the brake, but the jeep doesn't respond. Every vehicle they have has been commandeered and is left over from other countries and other wars. It's a miracle it even moves, and this one refuses to stop.

"*Mierda,*" says Georgi.

The sound of rifles comes from the brush around them. Georgi stomps the accelerator. The jeeps slows as they climb a hill, but the terrain quickly shifts, and Dickey's stomach lurches. They start barreling downhill at an alarming speed. Mortar fire continues to rain down around them. She holds her field pack close and prays the Our Father out loud in Spanish. Felipe and the voice of the rebel in the back seat join her. Georgi stomps the brake but still gets no response. There's a turn at the bottom of the hill they'll never be able to make.

Time slows.

The man in the back launches himself, jumping from the jeep. In horror, Dickey realizes her left side goes cold where Georgi sat. He has also jumped from the vehicle. There's no time for her to jump. Felipe doesn't abandon her. He wraps himself around her, and they crouch as low as they can, bracing their shoulders against the dash, trying to secure themselves as much as possible before impact.

The vehicle launches off the side of the road, and there is a breathless, dizzying, prolonged moment of silence as the jeep flips over—tossing Dickey and Felipe loose.

Then all goes black.

TWENTY-THREE

DECEMBER 1958

Maffo, Cuba

There's screaming sounding over and over in the night as Dickey comes to consciousness. It's the hoarse voice of a man in agony.

Dickey can't feel her right leg. She reaches around her and finds her glasses. Miraculously, they're not broken. She tries to sit but sees stars. She tries to crawl, but her leg is deadweight. She collapses on the dirt. When the spinning in her head stops, she pulls herself to sitting. A whimper comes to her through the dark. As her eyes adjust and the silver lines wiggling in her vision clear, she sees Felipe writhing on the ground. She manages to crawl over to him, finding her field pack along the way.

"Felipe," she whispers. "Are you okay. What's hurt?"

He holds his head, grimacing with pain.

A figure creeps toward them.

"I'll get horses," says Georgi.

Dickey and Felipe stare darkly at the driver who abandoned them.

The screaming nearby weakens to a groan. Georgi looks toward the sound.

"He's dying," Georgi says, his voice breaking. "Cut open."

He runs his hand through his hair.

"I'll get horses," he says again.

He starts to run, but then comes back and gets on his knees before Felipe and Dickey.

"I'm sorry," Georgi says.

He jumps to his feet and runs off into the night.

"Sorry," says Felipe, through gritted teeth. "There is no honor in him. Shameful."

After an hour on horseback, in the hospital tent, the numbness in Dickey's right leg has drained out, leaving a throbbing in her knee and searing pain in her swollen ankle. A woman doctor wraps it with torn cloth. She then wraps Felipe's head. That Dickey's camera is not damaged is a miracle. The man from the back seat is not so lucky. The doctor stabs him with morphine and throws the syringe into a box.

"Last one," she says.

There's no more, and the casualties of the battle are only starting to arrive. The floor is slick with blood. Dickey and Felipe are forced to crawl out of the way until they finally settle at the dying man. Felipe holds his hand. Georgi is nowhere to be found. Soon, Captain Orlando arrives. He kneels at the rebel soldier's side and shakes his head.

"He'll die before the sun rises," he says.

Felipe lets go of the man and places his face in his hands.

"You must tell the world, Americana," says Captain Orlando.

There's almost no light in the tent, so a photograph will never take. Dickey will have to describe the dying man. Now that he no longer grimaces in pain, his face has become serene and beautiful, and she can see how very, very young he is. His breath is so slow and shallow; surely it will soon cease.

"Dominican," says Captain Orlando. "Not even Cuban, but a believer in the cause for freedom. He helped us so we could later help him against the dictator Trujillo. Now, he won't even get to fight for his own country."

Dickey has learned that ten percent of the rebels are from other countries in Latin America.

"Come," says Captain Orlando. "Let's get you to the safe house to recuperate."

At the command post in the village of Jiguani, Raúl meets Dickey with the news that Ladybug was killed in battle. He knows how Dickey loved her guide and places his hand on her shoulder.

"I'm sorry," he says. "She fought bravely and with honor. She will be remembered."

"No," Dickey says, her eyes filling.

"The column was victorious," says Raúl. "We now have Guisa. Her death was not in vain."

Raúl's eyes glitter like polished onyx. For Raúl, the cause clearly is bigger than any one member of it. Dickey feels uneasy, but that has been so since the accident. All of them are off-kilter. The overall feeling of victory prevails, but not without losses. The bodies of dead rebels are brought into the command post by the truckload, setting off Fidel's dizzying displays of temper and terror. At his orders, Dickey photographs dozens of dead faces. Dozens of both sexes, varying ages, differing nationalities and backgrounds. There are mass burials and mass funerals. Dickey stays a long time at the grave where they say Ladybug was buried. Dickey places orchids on the dirt and says the Padre Nuestro.

The Castros continue to give long speeches to prisoners of war. There are always invitations to join the rebels.

"We will be merciful now," says Fidel. "But the time for mercy is running out."

Increasingly, there are groups within the rebels who are growing wary, wondering what that means.

"*Comandante*," says Felipe, whom Dickey has befriended in their rehabilitation. He was in Batista's navy but turned coat and joined the revolution last spring. He speaks English fluently, so their communication is easy. "We cannot be brutal like Batista."

"Of course," says Fidel, placing his big hand on Felipe's shoulder. "We are not Batistiano barbarians."

"There will need to be a measure of swift justice for some," says Che. "But only the worst and very quickly. Then we will usher in the utopia."

Utopia.

Felipe's eyes darken. The religious revolutionaries flinch when they hear communist vocabulary. There's been an increase in this kind of talk, especially from Che and Raúl. Fidel avoids such words, but he permits them from others. When the men leave, Felipe turns to Dickey.

"When you write about us," he says, "please be clear. Most of us are not communists."

Dickey and Felipe move to recline on hammocks, smoking cigars, watching the setting sun, while a nearby rebel soldier strums his guitar. Their vantage gives them spectacular views in all directions. A swiftly passing downpour left the colors of the landscape saturated, bold, and rich, like those employed by Cuban artist Antonio Gattorno. Dickey has seen his mural—*Waiting for the Coffee*—outside the Bacardi offices in the Empire State Building. She feels as if she inhabits it.

The fading light flickers through the trembling leaves, bringing to mind lines from Heinrich Heine poems about linden trees and death and peace. She's cocooned in a feeling of well-being and tries to absorb every moment of the time she has left here with people she has grown to love. She hasn't had a nightmare about the bogeyman in weeks. It's astonishing, considering the company she's kept, the things she's learned, and the battles she's faced. Being here, living with these people, has confirmed for her how important it is to embed oneself to get a story. Dipping in and out never gives the same depth of flavor and perspective as one gets in long company with communities.

It's two days before Christmas, one day before Dickey is scheduled to fly from Santiago de Cuba to Havana, and then back to New York in the new year. After all these weeks with her guerrilla family, she will have to swap her boots for heels and tie up her hair. She'll travel from rebel territory to Batista territory, pretending to be impartial in her scheduled interview with the monster Batista himself, arranged by *Reader's Digest* before she'd come. She cannot conceive of how she will make this transition.

"I won't call you communists," Dickey says. "I'll call you revolutionaries."

"Thank you, Americana," says Felipe. "I don't think Fidel will turn communist. He was educated by Jesuits. Even if he is no longer a practicing Catholic, he has the proper respect for the faith in his heart, and we all share a fierce love of Cuba."

Dickey wonders if Fidel does respect the faith. He's tolerant of most belief systems, as long as the believers are earnest and authentic. The exception to this, of course, is anyone who's a fascist.

"Ist," says Dickey.

"Pardon?" asks Felipe.

"Ist. Ists are the problem, yes? Fascists, communists. Nationalists. When one gets into 'ist' territory, there are dangers, no?"

Felipe smiles.

He's a looker, thinks Dickey.

She has started to think seriously again about men. The sting of Tony's abuse is wearing off, and she feels herself awakening, warming to the idea of love, though never again marriage.

"When you leave tomorrow," he says, "my wife will be your guide back to Santiago de Cuba."

Never mind.

"My beautiful Raquel," he says. "She'll take you to the Central Highway and direct you the rest of the way. She should be here any minute."

As if summoned, the woman appears on the path, trailed by two little boys, one about five, the other maybe two. Felipe springs from the hammock and runs to greet them, first embracing and kissing his wife, then crouching down to hug the boys. He lifts the smaller one, throwing him up in the air and catching him over and over. The child's giggles rise in the evening twilight, to where the lights of the fireflies—*cocuyos*—glow like green eyes.

The five-year-old stares up at his papa with such admiration that it brings tears to Dickey's eyes. She thinks of her own dear father. She admires Felipe for the special kind of courage and faith required to support one's family by helping a cause. She thinks, when the government oppresses so harshly, there is nothing left for the people to lose, so even women and children resist. They value the rebellion more than their lives. She wouldn't have understood how this was possible until staying here, until seeing the things she has in war and revolution.

When Felipe puts the little boy down, he catches sight of Dickey and toddles over to her, reaching up to her. Delighted, she gets out of her hammock—bolts of pain still in her knee and ankle—lifts him, and limps him over to the nearest *cocuyo*. He doesn't want to hold the firefly, only to look at it. She teases him, moving him close to the insect until he squirms and shrieks, and then she pulls back quickly, making him giggle. Again and again, they do this until he yawns, and she can no longer stand on her right leg.

That night around the campfire, the boy continues to sit with Dickey, clinging to her like a little monkey. Her heart feels as if it will melt when he starts to fall asleep in the hammock with her. He cries when Raquel lifts him to take him to the hut where the family stays. Dickey asks them to wait a moment. She limps as quickly as she can to her tent, pulls Oscar from her suitcase, and before she thinks too long about it, returns and gives the stuffed monkey to the boy. His joy fills the hole of her own sorrow.

How's that for clinging to possessions, Andrew St. George? she thinks.

It's hard for Dickey to fall asleep without Oscar, but she must, because at two in the morning, a voice awakes her.

"*Tigre,*" whispers Fidel, from the opening of the tent.

She springs to attention, ignoring the twinges in her knee and ankle to join him outside in the moonlight.

"You leave tomorrow for Habana, no?" he says.

"*Sí*. I'll be very sad to go. It's been an honor."

"If you stay in Habana long enough, we will see each other again."

"I'll be there until January ninth."

"We will have victory by then. You'll see the parade."

"I'll be waiting with my camera."

He kisses her on the forehead and leaves her, slipping away into the undergrowth of the jungle.

January 9, 1959
Havana, Cuba

Dearest Aunties,

In spite of the theft of my beloved trench knife and cameras, such horrific mosquito bites I look like a leper, getting in a jeep accident that left me with a sprained ankle and throbbing knee, and getting shot at by B-26s—paid for by my own taxes—on my way to the airport, I made it alive to Havana in time to witness the historic arrival of Fidel Castro and his July 26th Army as they rolled into the city.

The day I was scheduled to interview Batista, I went to the Presidential Palace only to learn he, along with hundreds of his supporters and their families, escaped the night before on planes and boats galore.

There were several days of unrest in the city, during which time I kept my leg up and my head down, filing dispatches from the Hotel Ambos Mundos, detailing the looting, brief bursts of machine-gun fire, and slow but steady takeover by Castro's columns as they arrived in the city. The first thing they did was close the casinos and brothels, and by the time the Bearded One himself arrived, there were no more shots fired. No more fighting. No drunkenness. Every man, woman, and child took to the streets to give the most raucous, joyous welcome of a leader by his citizens anyone could imagine.

During Fidel's (always long) speech, there was a fine bit of theatrics when white doves landed on him. Many of the people gasped, believing God Himself sent the message. Few saw the cages, stage left. It's no matter. Whether Christian, Santerían, or atheist, the doves represent the new age of peace Castro will bring, a welcome and just reward for a people who have suffered too long.

I have not suffered at all. As one of only ten journalists allowed to visit Castro—and the only woman—I feel privileged. Aside from pings in my ankle and knee that improve every day, I feel like a new woman. I am laden with sugarcane sticks and coffee for everyone, a Cuban flag for Slug, and a box of cigars for myself that I might even share with Tony and his son, Ron, who is engaged to be married to his college sweetheart. I'm feeling generous. So generous, in fact, I gave my beloved childhood stuffed monkey, Oscar, to a rebel's toddler who had taken to me. I feel like this marks real growth and maturity in my life.

Once my injuries are healed up, if you need me, I have to get a driver's license to go on a lecture tour through the Midwest, and then I'll be in covering the paratroopers of the 101st Airborne, down south. Before you worry too much, I'm reporting on soldiers learning to jump. It is unlikely they'll let a photojournalist partake in such training—nor will my knee and ankle—but I won't make any promises not to learn if the opportunity arises.

I have one photo left on my camera roll that I intend to use on takeoff, as the plane passes over the new sixty-plus-foot gleaming-white marble statue of Cristo de la Habana, sculpted by Cuban artist Jilma Madera. Batista had a dedication ceremony for it on Christmas Eve. Now he's fled Cuba, his tail between his legs. The statue of Jesus looks like a man of the people and extends His hand in blessing.

There are many wonderful changes on the horizon. I'm leaving a piece of my heart in Cuba and look forward to reuniting with it when I return on some glorious future day.

Happy New Year!
Dickey

TWENTY-FOUR

JANUARY 1959

Shorewood, Wisconsin

At the door of her childhood home, Dickey knocks and hides her face behind an enormous bouquet. When Aunt Lutie opens the door, Dickey holds out the flowers.

"Oh," says Aunt Lutie, taking them.

"Oh!" she says again, louder, when she sees who presented them.

Aunt Lutie hugs Dickey, and they rock back and forth, giggling with delight, until Aunt Lutie shushes Dickey.

"Sorry, dear, Georgie's sleeping," says Lutie.

"Sleeping? At one o'clock in the afternoon?" asks Dickey.

"She's been slow recovering."

"Oh," says Dickey.

She had imagined Aunt George, ten years Lutie's junior, would bounce right back after surgery. Dickey follows Aunt Lutie into the parlor and sees Aunt George asleep in the floral chair by the fireplace, a crocheted blanket over her lap, a book of poetry under her hands. Dickey feels a pang of sadness followed by an explosion of love in her heart for this dear old woman.

Not her, too, Dickey thinks. *Not yet. Please.*

As if sensing her, Aunt George's eyes open. Her face goes from confusion to elation, and she lifts her arms to Dickey.

"Oh, you goose!" Aunt George says. "You tricked us. We thought you were going right from war to jumping out of airplanes."

"I told you I had to heal my knee and ankle first," says Dickey. "What better place to do it than here?"

"What better place, indeed?"

———

Robert and Marion's one-year-old, Hans, toddles around the dinner table. With the aromas of home cooking and Cuban coffee, and the boisterous conversation with her brother, his wife—pregnant with another—and her aunties, Dickey's joy is complete.

"It's heaven seeing you all," she says, placing the coffeepot on the table.

"That smells like heaven," says Marion.

"Tastes like it, too," says Dickey. "And it's pure rocket fuel. It's how I stayed awake with the rebels for night raids."

Dickey has been regaling the family all night with tales from the Cuban Revolution, and they're hanging on her every world. Aunt George is so thrilled she's cheering along, while Aunt Lutie keeps her hand on her chest, shaking her head, nearly apoplectic over Dickey's description of the jeep accident.

"Even women are allowed to be soldiers," says Dickey.

"Really?" asks Marion.

"Yes, they use M1 carbines, which are light."

"Did you join their ranks, fighting? Tell the truth."

"No, I only shoot with my camera," says Dickey. "But it's all very exciting. It's the next best thing to piloting, but my eyes aren't good enough for that."

"Yeah, you almost killed me on a landing once," says Robert, with an edge in his voice.

Dickey doesn't know if his darkening mood is from the beer or her monopolizing the night with her stories, but it's clearly there.

"I had it under control," she says.

"You did not. The wind landed us by slamming us down."

"I guess you're right," she says. "You're lucky to be alive."

The ladies laugh. Robert remains serious.

"No more flying airplanes for me, no sirree," says Dickey. "Scout's honor."

"No, she's just going to jump out of them," says Aunt George.

This sets off a new round of excited discussion for the women. Robert has gone silent. While Aunt Lutie insists on clearing the dishes herself, she sends the rest of them into the parlor for coffee and conversation. While Marion and Aunt George read to Hans, Dickey invites Robert on the back porch for a cigar. As they look up at the stars in the crisp night, Dickey tries to regale her brother with more stories of the "folk hero" Castro and his soldiers.

"You're lucky you didn't end up in prison again," he says. "Those Batistianos sound as bad as Nazis."

"Every bit as bad," she says.

"After Cuba, I hope your thirst for conflict is waning. In all seriousness, you're taking dangerous risks. This Castro is a savior for now, but there are warning signs you might be missing because of hero worship. You've come out okay, but what about the next jeep accident? What about the next time you're being strafed by low-flying aircraft?"

Dickey feels shame and anger in her, warring with each other.

She tries to suppress her temper, to remind herself she's not in the Sierra Maestra, and such fits are no longer looked upon with favor and admiration. She takes a deep breath before speaking.

"This is what I do," she says. "It's who I am."

"Aren't you getting a little old for trekking through war zones with soldiers half your age? You turn forty in less than two months."

Tired of men telling her she's too old to do her job, Dickey feels like tinder struck by a match's flame.

"I don't recall asking your advice," she says, standing and stabbing the air in front of him with her cigar.

"You don't need to attack me," he says, standing up to face her.

"I'm not taking your punches lying down."

"I'm not punching. I'm looking out for you."

"I don't need looking after."

"You're a war junkie."

"How dare you belittle my calling. I resent you making something dark of a vocation."

"For the sake of your family and yourself, I just want you to ask yourself why you're going into these dark places and subjecting yourself to so much danger. It's like you have a death wish."

"I do not have a death wish, though if I die on patrol with soldiers, that's no tragedy."

"It will be to those you leave behind."

This cools the fire in Dickey. She sits and stubs out her cigar.

"I feel with certainty," she says, "that I am called to expose darkness for the world to see. This is the only thing that will eradicate it. My stories and pictures help fight war, poverty, and injustice, and I'm dedicating my life to that, no matter what the cost. With no husband or children of my own, I'm the perfect person to do it."

He sits and is quiet for a few moments.

"Just promise me," he says, "you'll look before you leap. Bravery is one thing. Recklessness is another. They're two sides of the same coin."

"I promise."

―――

Bravery. Recklessness. Bravery. Recklessness.

The words flip back and forth in her mind as she continues to rehabilitate with her aunts. Her ankle and her knee are feeling better, but with each day that passes, Dickey's restlessness grows. Her need for motion spills out of her, making her legs tap. She alternates chewing her fingernails with smoking. She has to force herself off the Cuban coffee and back onto bland, cheap Martinson's.

Brave. Reckless. Brave. Reckless.

Her thinking is stopped in the grocery store checkout line by the face starting at her from *Time* magazine's "Man of the Year" Issue, featuring Fidel Castro.

Brave. Reckless.

Back at the house, Dickey slaps the magazine on the kitchen table, followed by many others, including the *New York Times*, with an article about Castro's military-show trials being held in the Sports City Stadium in front of eighteen thousand people. All weekend, the women pass the papers and magazines around, reading and shaking their heads. Dickey's stomach roils. Stadium trials and mass executions don't give her a good feeling, even if they're against war criminals.

"'Blood will have blood,'" says Aunt George. "*Macbeth*."

It's February, and Dickey's last night in Wisconsin. The three women sit by the fire, light crawling over the walls and making the shadows writhe. Dickey has been down all week from the terrible news of the death of General "Wild Bill" Donovan from vascular dementia. She only knew him briefly, but she respected him enormously, especially for the help he gave her Hungarian friends while the IRC gave her nothing but the cold shoulder. She's sad she couldn't thank him in person but glad she sent him a note.

"I'm afraid you're right," says Dickey. "I've seen enough combat action to know there's something to bloodlust. Like sharks in water. It's a very ugly face of war."

"From what you've told us," says Aunt George, "it sounds like the crimes the Batistianos committed called for justice."

"Justice, yes," says Aunt Lutie. "But sport and spectacle? That's not just. It sounds like the Roman Colosseum. Will they bring in lions?"

"Tigers," says Dickey, her gaze landing on Fidel's face on the cover of *Time*, his visage changing in the flickering firelight. "Tiger blood. That's what Fidel Castro said I had in my veins."

Silence falls heavy over the room. The cuckoo clock sings the ten o'clock hour. No one wants to be the first to break up the last night of rest before Dickey heads out on a short lecture tour arranged by her new speaking agent, Elizabeth Byrd, no connection to Admiral Richard. She also has a new photo agent, Nancy Palmer. Both women are utterly different from her last agent, specifically by encouraging and supporting Dickey and always making time for her. Also, neither has any connection to Tony, so he only learns about Dickey through successful pieces in the papers, about which he continues to write her.

"Aren't we like Shakespeare's three witches," says Aunt George, a little twinkle in her eye. "The Wayward Sisters."

Dickey giggles.

"Speak for yourself," says Aunt Lutie. "Nothing wayward about me, but apt enough to define you two."

"Thank you," says Aunt George. "I take that as the highest compliment."

Dickey reaches for Aunt Lutie's hand. She has taken over with worry where Dickey's mother left off.

"Aunt Lutie," Dickey says. "I've been thinking a lot about some of Robert's cautions, and yours. I *won't* promise not to go into conflicts to report, but I *will* promise not to be reckless."

Aunt Lutie nods, the old woman clearly trying to understand her young niece, so different in makeup from her. Lutie cannot comprehend why anyone would ever want to leave a cozy fireside and the comforts of routine, daily papers, and home-cooked meals. Aunt George understands completely.

"The best thing about being trained with the marines," says Dickey, "is you learn that you only move when your lead moves. There is always a man in front of me. I'm never first in line. If it's time to move, we move. If it's deemed unsafe, we don't."

Aunt Lutie's eyebrows are still pinched together.

"What I'm saying is you don't need to worry about me," Dickey continues. "If not for myself, for you—I promise—I will be careful."

TWENTY-FIVE

APRIL 1959

Washington, DC

Credible Threat of Violence, Cuban Embassy.

The memo subject of the *Classified* sheet Sergeant Bob Morrisey places on Dickey's typewriter shouts almost as loudly as his young daughters, squealing on swings in the backyard. Dickey has an open invitation to stay with her old friends Bob and Mary Jane Morrisey from Camp Pendleton anytime she has to travel to the capital, where Bob is now head of public information for the Marine Corps, under Commandant General Wallace M. Greene Jr.

Dickey slides the memo to the side, finishes the last sentence on her article notes for Fidel Castro's U.S. visit, stubs out her cigarette, and stands.

"You're not going to talk me out of going," she says.

Dickey is on the guest list of a party for the diplomatic corps on Castro's last night in DC, as are many of her peers who so favorably covered the rebels in the Sierra Maestra. She walks to the window and waves down at the Morrisey girls. They wave back and blow Dickey kisses.

"I'm on the guest list as a personal friend of Fidel's," she says, turning back to Bob. "One of a small and elite group who actually lived and fought with him and his rebels."

"Fought?" says Bob.

"You know what I mean," she says.

"Do I?"

Dickey ignores his concerned look.

"I've been in more war zones than you have, Bobby boy," she says. "You don't need to worry about me."

"I watched from a sand bunker on Iwo Jima for a full ten minutes while snipers fired at you, while you took pictures and swatted away bullets you thought were insects. You try to hide it, but you're still limping from that jeep accident. If I don't worry about you, who will?"

"Your concern is very kind, but there are hundreds of our officers in United States law enforcement protecting Castro while he's here. I have full confidence in their ability to keep him and those around him safe."

"Your blind faith in police and military is both admirable and naive."

"Thank you for the compliment."

The grandfather clock chimes in the hallway. Mary Jane peeks her head in the guest room.

"Do you need any help getting ready? Or Bob to drive you tonight?" she asks, her gaze swiftly running over Dickey's fatigues. Dickey can almost hear the woman wondering if this is Dickey's outfit for the night.

"No, thank you," says Dickey. "The Press Corps got a few of us a limousine. It'll be here at six sharp."

Mary Jane raises her eyebrows. It's already four o'clock.

"And don't worry," says Dickey. "I'm not wearing my field gear."

"Why not?" asks Bob, with a chuckle. "Castro will."

———

To the shock of all, Fidel does not wear his field gear, but is turned out in a black suit and tie, his long beard neatly shaped.

"His eyes," swoons a woman on the red carpet. "They're so kind."

Dickey raises her eyebrows at Andrew St. George in the receiving line wrapped around the embassy building. Dickey goes on tiptoe to whisper in his ear.

"I wonder if she'd think him so kind if she saw him at the executions of Batistianos."

"Right," says Andrew. He regards Fidel, just ahead, then looks at Dickey.

"Are you smitten with him?" Andrew asks.

"There's no denying he has a presence that draws one in."

Andrew scoffs.

"Nowhere near as handsome as you, though," says Dickey, nudging Andrew's arm. "You clean up nicely."

"I'll say the same about you," he says. "You are dazzling, Miss Chapelle. Though I have to admit I prefer you in your field gear. Your natural skin."

"That makes two of us."

Dickey can barely breathe or walk in the formfitting, blue-bodiced dress with a white A-line skirt and white stiletto heels. Along with her red clutch purse, the colors match both the Cuban and the American flags. Stevie picked it all out at Saks, and it cost a small fortune. Dickey doesn't mind splurging on outfits for special occasions since her daily garb is so cheap and her standard of living so frugal. The final touch is a sapphire and diamond bracelet Tony bought Dickey years ago but that she's never before had occasion to wear. Mary Jane oohed and ahhed over it while Dickey dressed. If Dickey wasn't so broke all the time and didn't think she might need to hock it someday, she'd give it to Mary Jane.

When they reach Fidel, Andrew stands back to let Dickey go first. She gets a thrill seeing how Fidel's eyes light up when he notices her. He takes her hands in his.

"*Tigre!*" he says. "One of Cuba's dear friends."

"It's good to see you, one of *our* dear friends," she says.

He laughs, though she can't tell if the tone is ironic or not.

"I almost didn't recognize you out of battle dress," she says.

"Nor I, you," he says.

He looks over her clothing, eyes widening at the sparkling bracelet, then narrowing. He returns his gaze to her face, looking stern.

"Such excess in the United States," he says. "When this wasteful pageantry is finished, I hope you'll visit Cuba again soon to see how we seek to build greatness for *all* of our citizens, and not an elite few."

Dickey bristles. She doesn't like being on the receiving end of his negative judgment. She meets his stern gaze with her own, direct and unsmiling.

"You can count on it," she says.

Andrew moves in to greet Fidel, and Dickey continues forward into the lobby. She takes in the grandeur of the foyer, the beautiful wide marble staircase, the stunning stained glass on the ceiling, the ornate moldings, and the gold medallions over the doorways.

Such excess, she thinks, rolling her eyes.

She wonders if Fidel will shun the Presidential Palace, the good seats at sporting events, and the motorcade. Time will tell. For now, he's content to indulge in the comforts of the embassy, though he would say it's because the lodging is free.

There are so many bodies that it's hard to find a space, but Dickey is able to carve one out near the receiving line. Andrew is through and comes to meet her, smiling dumbly.

"*You* look smitten," says Dickey.

"I am. I've never met a man with such a memory and such magnetic concentration."

"His talents and brilliance are not in question. What is in question is how he will use them."

"I'll drink to that," says Andrew. "Let's go find the bar."

"Good idea," she says.

As she walks toward the ballroom, however, the word she overhears from the receiving line stops her short—Andrew running into the back of her.

"*Stoi!*"

Hearing Russian, it's as if all time falls away and she's back in Hungary. Sweat soaks the bodice of her dress and her heart races. She blinks and looks around to see what's happening. A diplomat and his wife are chatting amiably with Castro through interpreters.

"Are you okay?" asks Andrew.

He follows her gaze.

"Mikhail Menshikov," says Andrew. "The Soviet ambassador."

Menshikov and Castro both throw back their heads and laugh at whatever has been said between them.

"I'm fine," she says. "But I do need that drink immediately."

Dickey spends the rest of the evening to which she had been so looking forward trying to calm the waves of panic rolling under her like she's on the deck of a freighter. She reminders herself throughout the night that she is not in Hungary, and that Soviet border guards are not here to take her to prison. The pop of a champagne bottle makes the embattled members of the crowd jump and furthers Dickey's distress. Andrew loses patience with continually having to repeat what he says to her and abandons her to other members of the press. The men look her up and down with disdain or turn their backs on her when she starts toward them.

Dickey longs for her camera. She could point it at them—at Castro, at the Soviets, at everyone—while taking solace behind the lens. Work always steadies her. The best she can do is take out the small pad she put in her clutch and take notes for a future article.

Mikhail M. Castro. Back to Cuba—when?

Once she's reasonably steady, she returns her attention to Castro, trying to get close to him to ask questions. With over a thousand people smushed into the embassy rooms, however—hundreds in the Grand Ballroom alone—there's no chance of that. The closest she gets the rest of the night is when he stands nearby, applauding as the gold medal necklaces are presented to the press corps members who so favorably reported on the rebels. When it's her turn, she's again bathed in sweat. Her ankle and knee are killing her, and she wobbles on the stilettos. On the last stair up to the podium she trips and knows the sniggers coming from the audience are those of her disdainful male peers. It takes an act of will to ignore them and to keep her posture straight.

When it's her turn, she leans down and one of Castro's aides places the necklace over her head, knocking her glasses askew. There are more laughs, and she feels as if she's right back to being fat, little bullied Georgie Lou at primary school. That is, until she meets Fidel's eyes. They glitter, his face attentive and full of pride. He bows to her and starts the applause, and she's able to muster the strength to lift her chin and smile, to remember she has tiger blood in her veins.

July 1959
Fort Campbell, Kentucky

Dear Aunts George and Lutie,

It's official: I am the first woman journalist with certified accreditation as a military parachutist. I have approval from the Pentagon to jump with troops where they are engaged throughout the world. If you had asked little Georgie Lou if she could have ever imagined reaching such dizzying heights of recognition and accomplishment, she would have said...

"Yes!"

I always knew I should be flying, though I couldn't have imagined it would involve leaping from an airplane instead of sitting in the pilot's seat.

I have been training with the 101st Airborne Division of the United States Army—all my marine buddies say I'm cheating on them—and Major Lewis Millett pinned me himself. My certificate is signed by Major General William C. Westmoreland. I will treasure these wings for the rest of my life. From here I'll go jump with the First Special Forces at Fort Bragg in North Carolina. From there, the world's my oyster.

I do hope my first jump over foreign shores will be into Cuba. I'm on call at any point to return, to report on how things are going under Castro. Rumors are dark, but I never believe anything I don't eyeball or overhear myself. I've gotten the green light from my editor at Reader's Digest. We are waiting for Cuban press approval, which I would imagine will come any day now. Castro himself invited me, for Pete's sake. The only question is will I arrive sissy-style, in a plane, or with cojones, paratrooper-style?

*I know what Aunt George's vote would be.
I also know Aunt Lutie's.
One of you will be satisfied.*

*All my love,
Dickey*

TWENTY-SIX

AUGUST 1959

Havana, Cuba

Sissy-style, Dickey thinks, as the plane lands.

Outside the José Martí airport, she hails a taxi and makes her way to the offices of the newspaper *Revolución*, to meet with Carlos Franqui, the short intense man whom she knew from Radio Rebelde. In his correspondence, Carlos was adamant she check in with him to get the proper documents before doing anything else.

Dickey pulls at the buttons on her white sleeveless blouse and leans toward the open taxi window. She's glad she went with the blue and white pedal pushers to hide the sweat. Aside from wiggly lines coming up from the road, everything is still. Where the streets used to bustle with tourists and vendors, they're now empty. There are no lines to get into bars. The brothels and casinos remain shuttered. There are no children anywhere.

It's because it's siesta time, Dickey thinks. *It really is too hot to do anything that involves moving.*

When they pass a church, the words of the Padre Nuestro arrive unbidden.

Padre nuestro, que estás en el cielo.

God rest Ladybug's soul.

The driver doesn't chatter with Dickey, which—based on her last visit to Cuba—is unusual. There are none of the typical exuberant welcomes or queries about her plans, nor are there recommendations of restaurants or places to visit. Her attempts at conversation are ignored most of the ride until a final, gruff *"No inglés"* from the driver quiets her.

As they get nearer downtown, Dickey notices signs hanging in regular intervals along the businesses and residences.

Cuba, sí! Yanqui, no!

Oh boy, she thinks. *The rumors about the growing anti-American sentiment are true.*

What is also true is that Castro has expropriated the internationally owned telephone companies and farmland, nationalizing them. He has also disallowed religious services for prisoners. She intends to question Carlos Franqui about these points and more.

At the newspaper office, when Dickey walks in, the man at the front desk scowls and demands her papers like he's a military checkpoint officer. On the wall behind him, the shape of where a cross used to hang is white on a dingy wall. The words of the Padre Nuestro continue in her thoughts.

Santificado sea Tu nombre.

The man pushes back his chair and heads to the office with *Franqui* on the name plaque, closing the door behind him. Dickey uses a newspaper to fan herself, while looking longingly at the electric fan that isn't plugged in. The desks to the right are filled with sour-faced men and women. After their initial glances her way, they turn back to their typewriters as if Dickey doesn't exist.

Feels just like the press at home, she thinks.

The door to Franqui's office opens and she smiles, expecting to be greeted by her old acquaintance, but it's only the front-desk man. He closes the door, and without a word, he passes her the necessary press paperwork before sitting back at his desk.

"May I speak with Señor Franqui?" Dickey asks.

The man silently regards the notebook in front of him, scribbling notes.

"I have a few questions," she continues, growing irritated. The last time she came here as a member of the American press, they practically rolled out a red carpet. "It will only take a minute."

"We don't need your press anymore, Yanqui."

Dickey feels as if she's been slapped. She imagines she's up in the Sierra Maestra, her temper allowed to vent like a volcano. She leans over the desk and raises her voice.

"Without my press, you'd be rotting in a Batistiano prison, *comrade*, your cojones strapped to a live wire."

The man's mouth hangs open, and the typewriters go silent.

"I'm here on the invitation of Fidel Castro himself," she continues. "I will see him while I'm here, and when I do, I'll be sure to tell him what a little *comemierda* he has on staff at the paper. I don't think it will make him happy."

The door to Carlos Franqui's office opens and the man strides over.

"Chapelle," he says.

"Ah, just the man I was looking for. I have a few questions for you. Your boy here is being very uncivil."

"I don't have time or need to answer your questions," says Carlos. "We are no longer suppressed, so we can make our own publicity. I don't really know why you're here."

"I'm here for the *Reader's Digest* and to tell the American people how things are going for a people we care very much about but who are treating me like an enemy."

"Your publication has one of many foreign-owned plants that has exploited the Cuban worker for years. In fact, the printing plant of your magazine has been nationalized for our purposes."

For the first time in Cuba, Dickey feels a prick of fear. She could not have anticipated this rejection and reprimand would feel so personal. She takes a moment to steady herself, to change tack. She's desperate to get to Fidel, and she sees she's not going to be able to if she's aggressive.

"Señor Franqui," she says, "I am a friend of Cuba. Like Hemingway. I want only the best for you. You and I both have to work in imperfect structures to do the small bits of good we can on the real estate we get. I am here to interview Fidel Castro. If you tell him I'm here, I have every confidence he will meet with me. He knows my intentions are pure."

Carlos considers her words a moment, as his face softens. He nods.

"Where can I reach you if he agrees to meet you?" Carlos asks.

"The Hotel Nacional."

He snorts, his face darkening. Dickey senses that wasn't the best response. The hotel is decadent, but *Reader's Digest* is footing the bill and booked the room.

Carlos pivots, returns to his office, and slams the door.

It's only when Dickey enters the grand lobby of the Hotel Nacional that she's able to get a good breath.

The whole way over she chastised herself for already breaking her promise to Aunt Lutie and to Robert about not being reckless. She vows to do better. It's easier to believe this is possible in the civilized society of the hotel.

The Hotel Nacional is a monument to a decadent time. The blend of Spanish, Moorish, and Roman influence is felt in the massive dual-towered coral stone structure, softened by the large palm trees throughout the property. Inside, brown geometric-tiled floors mirror dark-paneled wooden ceilings, also softened by archways and alcoves.

At check-in, Dickey is relieved the Cuban hospitality industry is still hospitable. Dickey does note that the chandeliers are dark, but it's still daytime. She also notes that the casino is dark. Closing casinos was one of Fidel's first orders of business, because American organized criminals benefited most from them.

Once in her room on the sixth floor, she cranks up the air-conditioning. Citrus fruits and melons overflow from bowls on a wet bar. An ice bucket sweats next to a pitcher of water. She pours a glass, heads to the balcony, and lights a cigarette. She takes in the dazzling views of the Straits of Florida like a queen surveying a kingdom.

Venga a nosotros Tu reino; hágase Tu voluntad, en la tierra como en el cielo.

Thy kingdom come, Thy will be done, on earth as it is in Heaven.

Dickey thinks she should feel bliss over beauty and tropical sun, but she feels mostly guilt. She's not used to luxury, and Fidel certainly wouldn't approve, especially because the hotel is foreign-owned. She wonders how long before he takes over these.

Why did I allow a room to be booked here? I should have stayed in something more modest. These fat Reader's Digest *checks are making me soft.*

Thinking of work reminds her that it usually makes her feel better. She fetches her notepad, lists all she's seen so far, and writes a list of questions for her contacts. When she finishes her cigarette, she goes inside, peels off her clothes, and draws a bath. She wrote to Felipe and his wife, Raquel in advance of the trip, inviting them to dinner at the hotel. They demurred and suggested they meet at El Floridita, and now Dickey thinks she knows why. As head of Castro's navy, Felipe can't be seen in a fancy restaurant at a foreign-owned hotel.

Is this the "freedom" for which the revolutionaries fought?

Two hours later, dressed in the same garb she wore to Castro's diplomatic corps party at the Cuban embassy in DC, she steps out of the pedal cab and walks toward El Floridita. Neon lights announce the name over the pink building. The mambo music spilling out of the open doors lifts her spirits, as does the noisy crowd. She's relieved to see people gathering, smiling, enjoying a cocktail, and eating sandwiches on crusty bread.

Danos hoy nuestro pan de cada día; perdona nuestras ofensas, como también nosotros perdonamos a los que nos ofenden.

Give us this day our daily bread; forgive us our trespasses, as we forgive those who trespass against us.

Dickey spots Felipe and Raquel, who wave to her from a back corner table. Their smiles don't touch their eyes as they rise to embrace Dickey. Felipe is handsome as ever in his uniform, sharp-featured and thin, with intense eyes. Raquel, in a modest brown-and-white polka-dot dress, is soft and feminine with wide dark eyes and pouty lips. When they sit, Felipe keeps one arm around his wife, and she nestles into his side. Their closeness gives Dickey a pang of longing for love that she hasn't felt in a long time, and that she doesn't know if she'll ever again experience.

"Americana," says Felipe. "I almost didn't recognize you. I thought you'd be in battle dress."

"I'm slowly realizing I should have worn that and should've checked into a Cuban-run hotel. My old friends haven't been very friendly."

A bartender arrives to take Dickey's order.

"My fellow Cuban-loving American writer Hemingway inspired the double daiquiri," she says, "but I'll just take a beer."

"No beer," he says.

"Then I'll guess I'll have the Papa Doble, after all."

"I'll drink one of them," says Felipe.

Dickey cranes her neck, staring down the long red bar, eyes passing over hundreds of gleaming cocktail glasses, searching for the writer at his post.

"*Está* Hemingway *aquí?*" asks Dickey.

"*No, Papa está en España,*" says the waiter. "*Corrida.*"

The bullfight.

"*Ah, sí.*"

When the man leaves, Dickey beams at her old friends.

"I'm so happy to see you both," she says. "Is life here all you hoped for after the glorious revolution?"

Raquel and Felipe give each other dark looks. He leans forward, his voice low and serious. "We're making plans to get Raquel and the boys, and my mom and brother, to Miami."

Dickey's smile vanishes. She glances over her shoulder, scanning the faces, seeing no one who'd raise a red flag. She leans in to whisper to Felipe.

"Is it so bad so soon?" she asks. "You love Cuba."

"She no longer loves us. Not with her present governance."

"The rumors about Castro are true."

"*Sí*," says Felipe. "Now, Raúl and Che take no pains to hide their communism, and they have unchecked power."

"I thought they turned Batista's barracks into schools."

"Now it's schools into barracks," says Raquel. "Raúl married Vilma. She's in charge of education. She's making little military training schools, indoctrinating our children."

Raquel moves her hand to her stomach.

Lordy, she's pregnant again, thinks Dickey.

"Sounds like Hitler Youth," she says.

"The other side of the pendulum, but yes," says Felipe.

The drinks arrive. The daiquiri is ice-cold heaven going down, but Dickey drinks too fast, and a stabbing headache moves over her brain. She squints until it passes, then shakes her head.

"They've swapped out the mobsters for Soviets," Felipe says. "Did you see them? Multiplying like cockroaches."

He spits on the floor.

"I didn't see anyone," says Dickey. "It looked like a ghost town when I arrived. I hoped it was because of the heat. The offseason."

"The whole year will soon be an offseason. Mark my words."

The song ends, and in the quiet Dickey takes another look around the restaurant. She listens, imagines raising a radio antenna. She spots a tall fair couple at the bar. She catches the accent. Russian. She shudders.

"They have canceled all religious holidays," says Raquel, her voice quivering. "Soon they'll cancel religion itself. The Assumption is in two days. You will not hear the church bells ring the Angelus. The priests have to look over their shoulders all the time."

Raquel pulls a handkerchief from the pocket on her dress and dabs her eyes.

"And have you heard about the re-education work camps?" says Felipe.

"Jeez, no," says Dickey. "Tell me it's not so."

"Che is organizing one as we speak. On the westernmost point of Cuba, Guanahacabibes. He and the Castros are inspired by Soviet camp models for so-called *asociales*."

"No," she says. "You mean...?"

"Homosexuals. Pacifists. Jehovah's Witnesses. Protestant ministers. Priests."

"Exactly like Nazi concentration camps," says Dickey. The words of a reporter come back to her memory. "One of my peers told me earlier that Che was on Hitler's side for fighting colonialism. I didn't believe him when he said it. I do now."

Felipe waves his hand as if to say, *There you go*.

"We've told our Black Cuban friends they better watch their backs," says Raquel.

"Why? Fidel ended segregation."

"He did, but Che thinks Blacks are inferior to those of Spanish and European descent. He only tolerates them."

Horror-struck, Dickey puts her head in her hands. It's rare she's at a loss for words, but this is beyond imagination. She looks up after a few moments and shakes her head.

"Why?" she says. "Why does power do this? Fidel promised peace. He promised he wasn't a communist. He elevated Black Cubans. He promised he wasn't another dictator."

"He has a few noble attributes," says Felipe. "But he keeps bad company and lied about communism. Many of us are joining a movement against him. The Rosa Blanca. We will not go down without a fight."

It's dizzying to think that men who just fought with Fidel are now going to fight against him.

Is there no end to war?

Despair creeps into the edges of Dickey's consciousness like fog rolling in from the Gulf.

"We have been used," says Dickey. "The American press played right into Fidel's hand."

"You did," says Felipe. "But now you know. And you can tell others. And we can fight evil one man at a time."

After being blocked, given the runaround, and ignored, on Dickey's last night in Cuba, she's finally admitted into Fidel's presence at his new command post: the television station. Under the glare of the lights, he comes alive. Seated like a king at a desk, before a live studio audience, he holds court.

Literally.

Dickey's eyes widen when she sees the white man, handcuffed and being dragged into the studio. The audience boos and hisses as he's pushed into a chair in front of Fidel and his military tribunal.

William Morgan is an American who came to fight with Fidel after saying Batista tortured and fed Morgan's best friend's body to the sharks for smuggling arms to the rebels. From Andrew St. George, Dickey learned Morgan had trained Castro's men and was the only American to make *comandate* in Castro's army. Dickey had not come across Morgan in her time with the rebels, but his bravery was legendary and had earned him the beloved nickname

"El Americano." The audience now spits the slur *Yanqui* at him. His face is unreadable.

Dickey leans toward Carlos Franqui, her escort, and asks why Morgan is on trial. Carlos sighs and rubs his eyes. All of Carlos's earlier rudeness with her has given way to exhaustion.

"He's anticommunist," says Carlos. "And he's accused of smuggling weapons to the Rosa Blanca. You know what that is?"

She nods.

He gives her a long look, then turns back to the spectacle.

In Fidel's typical bluster, his speech is loud and fiery, like a flamethrower. In spite of the glare of the lights, the vulgarity of the public spectacle, and the severity of the charges, Morgan sits up straight, face impassive. When asked how he pleads, he says, "*No culpable.*"

Fidel laughs. He continues his lecture, holding up papers from a file—photographs, raising them in such quick succession, Dickey can hardly see or understand what's going on. She needs no fluency in Spanish, however, to see Fidel has made up his mind, as has the audience. She's tempted to shout out to him that he's a megalomaniac, to ask him what he's allowed himself to become. But that would be reckless, and she has promised not to be reckless.

No nos dejes caer en la tentación.

And lead us not into temptation.

Agonizing hours pass. The heat is unbearable. The obscenity of the spectacle is unimaginable. The devastation of witnessing the corruption of a folk hero is heartbreaking. The embarrassment of being used is nauseating.

A dark, heavy sensation threatens to suffocate Dickey. It only takes her a moment to recognize her old childhood fear, the bogeyman, looming. She's all at once acutely aware that she's in danger, and it's good she is scheduled to leave tomorrow. For the first time visiting Cuba, she can't wait to go home.

"He's being sentenced," whispers Carlos.

Dickey strains her ears to hear, to understand.

"*Culpable*," says Fidel.

She notices another white cross shape on another dingy wall, just over the head of the largest guard. He smiles at the prisoner, showing his sharp canines. He fondles the revolver at his belt.

"*Tu sentencia es la muerte*," says Fidel in a singsong voice.

"Death," whispers Dickey.

Y líbranos del mal.

And deliver us from evil

Amén.

January 1960

Telegram: Franqui to Chapelle

Fidel Castro read the article in *Reader's Digest*. He says if you ever again try to set foot in Cuba, it better be under the guard of the marines, because you'll need it.

January 1960

Telegram: Dickey "Tigre" Chapelle to Franqui

It's a date.

PART THREE

1961–1965

APRIL 1961

NEW YORK CITY

THE JACK PARR SHOW

PARR: Welcome the "bayonet border reporter" as
she's come to be known, the intrepid Miss
Georgette "Dickey" Meyer Chapelle. Dickey was the
valedictorian of her high school and one of the
first women admitted to MIT. She grew up with a
keen desire to be a pilot, which ultimately led
to her leaving college for flight school. Poor
eyesight derailed her dreams of flying herself
but led to publicity for air shows and airlines.
From there, she became one of the first women
photojournalists accredited to the Pacific theater
in World War II, then worked for care organizations
photographing refugees in postwar Europe. Since
then, she has been employed by major periodicals,

going into conflict wherever it takes her, to be the eyes and ears of the American people. Dickey, your passport book must get filled pretty quick. Where have you just come from?

DICKEY: The far side of the moon, with Luna 3.

AUDIENCE: [Laughter.]

DICKEY: Just kidding. I've never attached myself to the Soviets, and I don't intend to start now.

PARR: Yes, I believe you have been banned from two countries under Red influence.

DICKEY: Indeed, I have. Hungary and Cuba. I'm surely the first woman war correspondent to get such an honor.

AUDIENCE: [Laughter.]

PARR: And with all the trouble, I don't see you trying to return to Cuba anytime soon.

DICKEY: Yes, the critical promised air support of the U.S.-sponsored sea invasion of Cuba at the Bay of Pigs never came through. It sure didn't make it easy on the freedom fighters who landed there, who'd been assured they'd have such coverage. I heard Che Guevara sent President Kennedy a thank-you note.

AUDIENCE: [Murmurs.]

PARR: [Nervous laugh.] You're going right for the controversy, aren't you, Dickey?

DICKEY: If truth is controversial, yes. Fidel Castro has stolen all foreign-owned property, closed all religiously affiliated schools and universities, and had those he considers "enemies" executed or interned in re-education camps that bring to mind the Nazi era. Since the U.S. won't buy Cuba's sugar, the USSR has filled the void, and it now pulls Castro's puppet strings. I recently received word Che drains the blood from condemned prisoners to sell before killing them. They get fifty dollars a pint on the black market.

AUDIENCE: [Gasps.]

DICKEY: I guess you have to give the commies credit. They don't waste a thing.

PARR: All right, Dickey, we're live, and that's not going to make the censors happy.

DICKEY: Send me the bill.

PARR: [Nervous laughter.] Now, be a good girl and tell us where you've really been these last few months. And I'm not referring to those endless lecture tours to schools and women's clubs.

DICKEY: When I'm not working on my autobiography—

PARR: Autobiography? What can you tell us about it?

DICKEY: My old pal Brigadier General "Slam" Marshall told me I had the most interesting life of anyone he'd ever met of either sex, and I should write about it. Lo and behold, my agent pitched William Morrow and Company, and they agreed.

PARR: Swell! That will be a page-turner, no doubt.

DICKEY: Thank you. So many of the women I've met across the country have been inspired by my story. It just goes to show, if crazy old Georgie Lou can accomplish just about anything she sets her mind to, anyone can. The book is expected to release in the winter of '62.

PARR: We'll have you back on to discuss it.

DICKEY: I'll be here, God willing. As for the last few months, I was with the sailors of the Seventh Fleet in the Pacific, helping those boys keep an eye on the Reds there. The navy gave me a swell new engraved Zippo lighter as a party favor. Then, I jumped out of airplanes leaving Okinawa for secret landing destinations with our special forces, which got me another set of wings. Then I came home to visit my beloved marines at Parris Island, so they wouldn't feel left out. Next, I'll be in Southeast Asia.

PARR: What, pray tell, will you be doing there?

DICKEY: I'm not yet at liberty to say, but the moment I'm able to, my pictures will tell the story. If they pass the censors, that is.

PARR: And tell the story your pictures do.

You've become one of America's most well-known photographers of either sex. But the rise has not been without its bumps and controversies. Some of your peers say you got yourself thrown into that Hungarian communist prison for the story.

DICKEY: For the record, let me assure you, I did not and would not put myself through that for any story.

PARR: Your ex-husband insinuated his agreement with your peers. The divorce caused quite a scandal in the press. I can only imagine the scandal it has caused at the women's clubs.

DICKEY: There is no scandal at the Overseas Press Club. At least half of my peers are divorced. Being a war correspondent is not exactly conducive to a good marriage. And the women at the clubs have been quite polite, I assure you. Even if you ask my ex's mistress turned wife, she'd be on my side. Wait, I heard she left him for a younger fella.

AUDIENCE: [Laughter.]

DICKEY: Also, for the record, my so-called marriage was annulled because he'd been married to another woman when he married me. So perhaps the press can drop the whole "divorcée" descriptor they love to pair with my name.

PARR: Noted. Now, some of your peers also say you've lost your neutrality as a journalist because you've become such a commie hater. Is that true?

DICKEY: It is not. To be clear, I am a commie hater. Six weeks in their intimate company has a way of doing that to a person.

AUDIENCE: [Laughter.]

DICKEY: But I'm not a McCarthy-style witch-hunter if that's what you mean. I'm against totalitarian rule in all its forms, from fascism to communism.

PARR: That sounds reasonable. Dickey, I have one final charge. There are some who say you're addicted to conflict. Is this true?

DICKEY: Have you been talking to my brother?

AUDIENCE: [Laughter.]

DICKEY: I'm addicted to telling the stories of the

brave men and women who fight to keep the world free. If that's a vice, I'll own it.

PARR: You mention women. Is war any place for a woman?

DICKEY: Absolutely not.

AUDIENCE: [Gasps.]

DICKEY: Nor it is any place for a man. But as long as humans won't get along, it's how it will be. I just hope my pictures reveal what hell war is so it can be stopped.

PARR: For a woman who loves soldiers and whose living depends upon war, you just sounded like a pacifist.

DICKEY: Nothing would make my late mother happier. I do love soldiers, but the more war I see, the more I understand her feelings. I guess I better keep going into war zones to figure this out.

PARR: Is Southeast Asia a war zone?

DICKEY: According to the Geneva Accords and the ceasefire agreement, it shouldn't be, but I'll let you know once I eyeball it.

PARR: If it is, aside from human interest, what is the relevance to the American people?

DICKEY: Ask the families of our soldiers who are rumored to be there.

AUDIENCE: [Murmurs.]

PARR: If we have any men there, we know we can trust you to find them, get to any front there might be, and tell us the hard truth about what's happening. Just keep out of Red prisons, will ya?

DICKEY: I'll certainly try.

PARR: Godspeed, Dickey. We'll see you on the other side.

TWENTY-SEVEN

APRIL 1961

Shorewood, Wisconsin

"Dickey, I was shocked at your candor," says Aunt Lutie.

"I thought it was a scream," says Aunt George.

"Yes, I probably should have left out the bit about Helga leaving Tony for a younger man," says Dickey. "And Che's blood draining, but the ratings were through the roof, and Parr hasn't been fined yet. That's the stuff people want to hear."

"I don't know about that," says Aunt Lutie.

"Well, they need to hear it," says Aunt George.

The women sit on the back porch of the family home, sipping beer and watching the sunset. Dickey is staying with her aunts a few days before heading to Southeast Asia. The sky appears as if in Technicolor. Dickey holds out her hands, framing the scene. She moves her frame until it surrounds the profiles of her aunts—George, younger and frailer, in the rocker closest to Dickey, and Lutie, older and healthier, on the other side of George. The warmth of the sunset gives Aunt George's pale skin false color.

"Tony sure got what was coming to him," says Aunt George.

"He called me, distraught about Helga," says Dickey. "He had the nerve to ask me to come over."

"The man has no shame."

"And yet, I somehow felt sorry for him."

"Don't give into that," says Aunt George. "You know as well as I do that he has other photography students in his Rolodex to tend to his wounds. Didn't you say there's a new one? Katherine?"

"Yes, Kay. She's actually very sweet. When he called, she took the phone to introduce herself to me. She's read many of my articles and is a fan. Tony is harmless to me at this point. He's mostly bedridden and pathetic. At the human level, I feel for him."

"You're a better woman than I am," says Aunt George.

"I don't know about that."

Aunt George coughs, the sound wet and phlegmy.

Has the cancer reached her lungs?

Dickey's heart races with panic. Aunt George has lost a lot of weight very quickly, just like Dickey's mother did at the end. Dickey can't stand the thought of losing Aunt George. Her doctor's appointment is next week, but Dickey will be long gone. She hates to leave when Aunt George is so ill, but Dickey has received her advance and passage to Southeast Asia has been booked. On assignment with *Reader's Digest*, she'll be working between Laos and South Vietnam for an untold length of time, on yet another American Cold War front that's growing hotter by the day.

Dickey reaches for Aunt George's hand, the chilly boniness of it swallowed in Dickey's warmth.

"I hate that I have to leave when you're feeling so rotten," says Dickey.

Expecting Aunt George's usual reassurances, Dickey's more troubled than ever by her aunt's response.

"Well, maybe you can come back here in a few weeks," says Aunt

George. "Maybe you could make this your home base, instead of New York? We all live so well together."

Dickey doesn't have the heart to tell Aunt George that making such an arrangement permanent is unthinkable. From New York, to DC, to Miami, Dickey's home base has to be on the East Coast, where all her press and military contacts are. Wisconsin is a good place for Dickey to regroup, but staying longer than a week makes her go stir-crazy. It's far too quiet.

"I–I won't be stateside until summer at the earliest," says Dickey. "It's a complicated deployment schedule, without easy means to return. I'm one of only a handful of accredited American reporters, the only woman, and the only one allowed to jump with paratroopers."

"Deployment?" asks Aunt Lutie. "Have they decided to make you a marine after all?"

"No, it's how I've come to think of my assignments," Dickey says. "I'll be with the U.S. Special Forces in Laos, where they're training indigenous groups to fight the Reds. Then, I'll head to Saigon for my next assignment, hopefully to a small village at the lowest tip of South Vietnam, called Binh Hung, where an exiled Chinese anti-communist priest and soldier leads a little hamlet of sorts. His men are called the Sea Swallows, for the birds who not only go out great distances to destroy pests, but who always return home, no matter the distance traveled."

"Did you say a priest *and* soldier?" asks Aunt Lutie.

"Yes, Father Hoa, spelled *H-O-A*, pronounced '*Wah*.' One of my contacts at the Pentagon wrote a letter about him that was originally a classified note for President Kennedy. Kennedy was so moved he declassified it, and the letter will appear in next month's *Saturday*

Evening Post. This gives me hope against military censorship. The big guys want this story out, so I'm less likely to be muzzled."

"If that letter's coming out, why do you need to write about the village?" asks Aunt Lutie.

Dickey's editor at *Reader's Digest*, Hobart Lewis, had asked her the same question. She provides the same answer.

"If all goes well," says Dickey, "I'll be granted permission to live among the villagers for at least a month to write an in-depth, extended-form photo piece that will touch the hearts of the America people and might lead to more support for the good work the villagers there are doing to fight communism."

"It's okay," says Aunt George. "It sounds like those people need you to tell their story."

Dickey feels a lump in her throat and the prick of tears. She takes a deep breath, blinks, and finds her smile.

"I could take you with me, Aunt Georgie," says Dickey. "My wingman."

Aunt George smiles and turns her gaze back to the last gasp of sunset.

"I'll strap you to my back," says Dickey. "Or, better, you'll be with some young hunk of a marine. We'll float right into Father Hoa's village. If you're lucky, your cute, young, strapping paratrooper will give you a pat on the rump."

Aunt George giggles.

From her other side, Aunt Lutie leans forward to stare across the profile of her sick sister at Dickey. Lutie shakes her head, but a small smile plays on her lips. It's good to see Aunt George laugh. After a few more minutes of silence, her voice comes to Dickey very quietly.

"How does it feel?" Aunt George asks. "Flying. Parachuting."

Dickey takes a deep breath and closes her eyes.

"It's as much about sound as it is feeling," says Dickey. "You go from where you can't even hear yourself think inside a roaring tube of airplane or helicopter metal, you put your shaking hands on the edge of an ice-cold door frame, and you launch out, like a bird taking flight. You glide through the void in the rush of wind, and then you pull the line, and all is sweet silence. You gently watch the world get closer and think, *My God, thank you! Thank you for this experience quite unlike any other, and for keeping me safe, and for giving me this opportunity to bring light to dark places.* And then you land and hit the ground running."

The wind moves through the leaves on the trees in a rush, bringing the sweet smell of cherry blossoms and damp earth. Aunt George's eyes are closed. She still has a small smile on her lips, but she sleeps.

"My instructor always told me," whispers Dickey, brushing a tendril of hair off Aunt George's forehead. "On the way down—so you don't miss any of the beauty—keep your eyes open. To get the story, to stay safe, to take it all in, always keep your eyes open."

TWENTY-EIGHT

JUNE 1961

Somewhere over Laos

"Keep your eyes open," Dickey shouts over her shoulder to her interpreter.

The young wide-eyed paratrooper of the Royal Lao Army nods. Since she arrived, he's scarcely been able to take his eyes off Dickey—a woman old enough to be his mother, dressed like a soldier, about to jump out of a helicopter. She hopes he can concentrate, or he'll be toast.

The other men are as young and wide-eyed as he is. Dickey feels a maternal pang in her heart for these boys from Laos and Cambodia, but she prefers being with American paratroopers. To keep fear at bay, Americans joke around even when bullets start flying. These young Asian men are silent and serious.

Dickey steps up to the opening behind Sergeant Nelson West, the U.S. Marine adviser to the paratroopers. A tall, dark, and handsome Texan with heavily lashed eyes, West is the coldest marine she's yet met. Dickey senses she'll need to prove herself to him before he welcomes her. She knows she's up for the challenge.

As Nelson jumps, however, Dickey is hit with a feeling of dread. She never can quite believe she'll be able to make herself leap out of a working aircraft, but she hasn't yet choked. He has gone so she must follow. She takes a deep breath, puts her hands on the metal opening of the helicopter, and launches herself into the void.

It's bliss breaking free from the noisy H-34 chopper, one of four flying in tandem from the CIA's Air America fleet. The choppers each have at least one soldier from the MAAG—the Military Assistance Advisory Group, across all branches of the U.S. military—who have been training and also fighting beside the men of the Royal Lao Army, in defense against the Soviet-backed communist Pathet Lao Army. Dickey has very much eyeballed armed conflict in violation of the ceasefire agreement, and she has very much observed American men engaged in the conflict.

Dickey tries not to think about putting her life on the line to be dropped fifty miles into enemy territory for pictures that might not pass military censors. She has resigned herself to knowing they can at least be used in military briefings, a reality that happens more and more with her work. Also, with the backing of strong military contacts, periodicals continue to send her out for assignments.

Dickey looks down in awe at the endless green of the jungle-covered mountains, a swirling, writhing mass far below her. She falls between clouds, passing through them while their water droplets touch her face like dewfall. When the count is right, she pulls the cord of her parachute pack, and sweet silence envelops her.

It's just me and You, she prays, looking up toward heaven. *Thank You for protecting me. For protecting the men. Please keep doing so. Help me find the story and tell it. Help me bring light to the darkness. And please keep Aunt George well until my return. Amen.*

It's Dickey's sixth jump with the Royal Lao paratroopers. She has been living in crude conditions with the men, and she's covered in the most vicious bug bites imaginable. She dons a new bush hat like the soldiers wear, one that automatically puts a $25,000 bounty on her head. Still, she was thriving until she received yesterday's letter from Aunt Lutie.

Aunt George is fading fast. She's asking for you. Is there any way you can come home?

Dickey began trying to plan what it would take to get her from the forward war zone of Laos to Wisconsin and back to Laos, but the thought of organizing and funding such a trip was making her so frantic that she gave up and turned her attention back to the men in her group.

"This is why combat reporters should be islands," she told Henri Huet, a kind, earnest photojournalist with the AP, when they were both filing dispatches. He'd come to Laos last week to see if anticommunist forces really were losing ground, as the rumors had suggested, and to persuade Dickey to come to Saigon earlier than she'd planned, where he predicted all the big action was to come.

"I know," Henri said in French-accented English. "It's very hard for our loved ones."

Over drinks—beer for Dickey, orange soda for Henri, who did not drink alcohol—Henri revealed he had an estranged wife and two little children. It broke his heart to live apart from them, but he would not leave his duties as a war correspondent. Many would question how a father could essentially abandon his family to work in such dangerous conditions. No one but a fellow combat reporter could understand the calling. Dickey could barely understand it herself. Hearing his agony over leaving children made her very glad not to have any of her own.

Henri's father was French and his mother Vietnamese. Henri's fluent in all the languages of the region and in English. He's also been a generous peer, happy to show Dickey the ropes. With him, there's none of the usual judgment or meanness she so often experiences from other men in the field. She told Henri she'd meet him in Saigon next week.

The sound of tracer fire erupts, shocking lines of light darting back and forth below her.

"Shit," she says.

If I make it to next week.

The ground, which had looked far away, suddenly comes fast to meet her boots. She pulls up her knees to brace for impact. On impact, she feels the familiar sting in her right knee and ankle.

"Cover!" yells Nelson.

Dickey crawls, chute still attached, toward the brush from where her order came. When she arrives, Nelson lunges forward to drag her by the arms the last few feet. Mouth full of dirt, she's unable to properly thank him. She spits and curses while pulling off her chute. Her interpreter soon follows, eyes wide and hands shaking. She nods at him, and as she reaches toward her bag to pull out her camera, the sound of an explosion causes all of them to gaze upward. They watch in horror as a helicopter from their fleet falls like a flaming boulder from five hundred feet. Once it hits the mountainside, it becomes a pyre for all onboard.

Dickey feels a stabbing pain in her chest as the men around her groan. She has lived with these soldiers for weeks. Men from Laos and the United States. Men with wives and children and families. Men dying at the hands of communists violating an agreement that the press can't even reveal because the United States and the Soviet Union aren't supposed to be fighting a proxy war here.

As soon as her camera is ready, Nelson orders her to follow him to the rendezvous point, a tiny hamlet of huts, heavily guarded and surrounded by barbed wire. They reach a patrol of barefoot Royal Lao soldiers and proceed en masse toward the forward area. Dickey follows Nelson, camera poised. There's a heavy and terrible quiet for a moment before a blast destroys the silence. The point man trips a wire and sets off an explosion that throws him twenty feet in the air, tossing him like a bloody rag doll.

So close to the compound, she thinks with a shudder.

The guerrillas of the Pathet Lao got close enough to camp to set booby traps, and no one heard them. The communists here have learned how to make themselves ghosts.

Bogeymen.

The group recedes to the rendezvous point to regroup, as others from the jumpers join them. One bloody Laotian comes in staggering and mumbling. The interpreter rushes to him. The man survived the helicopter crash because he jumped as soon as they were hit. No one else has made it.

Dickey photographs the bloody survivor. She photographs the jungle around them, more terrifying in its silence than when it was noisy with gunfire. Then she takes a picture of the body of the young man blown from the booby trap, wrapped in a parachute, blood seeping through where his eyes are, watching like the bogeyman. As night falls, she photographs the machine-gun warning fire. There will be no sleep.

The region is as good as lost. The Ho Chi Minh Trail—the ever-shifting network of roads and waterways supplying weapons to North Vietnamese communist guerrillas known to the United States as the Viet Cong, or VC—grows by the day. The communists are winning Laos. All Dickey can imagine are jungle cats prowling, waiting. Does she see a flash of light reflecting in their eyes?

The next morning, as the sun rises, the sound of the Air America helicopter landing on the pad behind them is a welcome noise. She doesn't argue when ordered to be among the first evacuated. As they fly out amid a fresh spray of gunfire, the bullets hit the side of the chopper with pings. The roar is too loud and the tension too great to speak, so it isn't until Dickey arrives back in Wattay Airport in Vientiane, Laos's capital, that she learns there are dozens of Americans wounded, four captured, and the death count has reached nineteen.

She feels lightheaded and like she's about to faint. As she turns to go, Nelson grabs her arm.

"You did well out there, soldier," he says in his Texas drawl.

Nelson's approval is a relief and gives her the fuel she needs to make it back to the Constellation Hotel. It's a concrete structure where everyone from covert officers to reporters to opium dealers congregates. The man at the front desk has to call her name twice to get her attention. Her ears still ring from the helicopter noise and explosives.

Dickey walks on trembling legs and aching knees to the desk and raises her eyebrows in question. She can't imagine how filthy and strange she must look, but he has seen her come back from battle more than once, though never in this condition. He passes her the cable. Her body goes cold from head to toe, as if ice-cold water is being poured over her.

No, she thinks. *Not today. Please not today.*

Dickey doesn't look at the cable, only shoves it deep in her pocket and leaves the man at the desk without a word.

In her room, she removes her clothing, leaving it in a pile on the floor. She draws a bath and climbs in as the ice-cold stream slowly turns to warm and then to hot. In the layers, her legs are freezing, and her neck is boiling. She dunks herself and scrubs at her skin until the water is all one temperature and cloudy with grime. She pulls the plug and lets it drain, turning the cold on again to rinse the residual dirt from her skin. She puts the plug back in the tub.

Shivering, she climbs out of the bath and grabs a towel, still damp from leaving it in a ball on the floor yesterday, and wraps it around her. She stares at her filthy pants and thinks of the cable in the pocket.

Please no.

Hands shaking, she lights a cigarette and retrieves the cable. She still doesn't look at it, only sets it on the table and then places her filthy fatigues in the tub for washing. When the tub is full, she turns off the water and stubs out her cigarette. She sits at the table, takes a deep breath, and only then allows herself to open the envelope and read, confirmation of her deepest fears being realized with every word.

June 4, 1961
Cable: Aunt Lutie to Dickey

Aunt George passed peacefully this morning. She sent her love to you on her dying breath. She said she'll always be your wingman.

June 4, 1961
Cable: Dickey to Aunt Lutie

Brokenhearted. So sorry not to have been there. So sorry.

August 1961
Saigon, Hotel Majestic

Dear Stevie,

For the first time in my life, I feel all forty-two years of my age. My body is betraying me. Everything hurts. The curse has become unbearable.

Back in WWII, when I was a cocky little pissant, and the army PR officer in charge of my accreditation had stammered his way through telling me there were no women's facilities in the field, I'd assured him that the Fourteenth Infantry had tackled much bigger issues and would no doubt again rise to the occasion. I don't know if the Fourteenth could handle this now.

Instead of one week, my cycle lasts two. Then I get two weeks off and start the whole damned thing over again. It's hard as hell hiding it from the men, but it's easier now that I'm in Saigon, holed up in a hotel—writing, instead of sharing tents with soldiers in Laotian jungles.

This big stud of a fella, Nelson—before you ask, he's married—was transferred to Saigon and got me transferred right along with him. It was a miracle, because it took about six drops and me nearly getting killed at least twice for Nelson to get past his reservations about a woman in the field. If he found out about my lady issues, it would be a setback in our relationship.

My reporter friend Henri—before you ask, he's married—got me established with the press in Saigon. I'm almost finished my Laos article for the Digest, *and I can't wait for my editor, Hobart—before you ask, he's married—to see it. The pictures I took there are my best work yet. I believe I'll finally win an award. It's not just my ego that longs for decoration, though that could sure use a boost. An award* means high-paying assignments with snazzy publications, and maybe even the respect of my peers, though I won't hold my breath on that one.

Since you told me about Tony's bankruptcy, I've been in a cold sweat. Thank goodness for the annulment. My bank account is healthy now, but I need to start saving. Like you're fond of telling me, these knees and this body aren't going to be combat ready forever. I'm starting to believe you.

I'm also working on my autobiography. Wouldn't it be nice if that became a bestseller? All sales from it, and payment for my lecture tour, will go right into the bank. Maybe I'll make enough so you can join me on the tour. The lecture bureau will provide me with a car. (Don't tell them I don't technically have a driver's license yet.) We'll ask for a convertible, and only tour in warm states, and we'll wear kerchiefs, and smoke cigarettes, and wear red lipstick, and we'll be so damned glamorous crowds will stop and take our picture and wonder who the starlets are.

In all seriousness, writing the story of my life so far is bringing me healing. I've been incredible places and met wonderful people—like you—and some not so wonderful people, but that's helped me learn just as much. This book has given me time to reflect upon how I've grown from a flighty girl reporter to a seasoned combat correspondent, and that fills me with pride.

All my love,
Dickey

PS: I just heard my late Aunt George's voice in my head, saying, "Oh, come on, Dickey. You're still flighty. And may you always be so."

PPS: Golly, I miss her.

August 1961

Cable: Hobart Lewis to Dickey Chapelle

Regret to inform you, *Reader's Digest* will not publish the Laos piece. Letter to come with full explanation but don't waste any more time there. Concentrate on South Vietnam.

TWENTY-NINE

AUGUST 1961

Saigon, South Vietnam

D ickey crumples Hobart's letter in a ball and throws it in the wastebasket.

Was nearly getting killed in Laos for nothing? Was missing my last chance to see Aunt George for nothing?

Dickey curses, pacing in her hotel room. It's not even the government censoring her this time, but her own editor. Hobart says Dickey's too critical of the government for not adequately supporting the U.S. fighting men—just as she was in the articles about lack of U.S. support for the Bay of Pigs invasion—and too revelatory about classified positions. The latter is nonsense. The government wanted that information out there for the American public in order to garner support for an expanding effort in Southeast Asia. The former is the problem, but she refuses to water down the truth, and for that she's being punished. The crack that started in her relationship with the *Digest* over U.S. policy in Cuba is growing to a chasm. She doesn't know how much longer she can work with them.

After a bath that cools her skin and her temper, Dickey heads to the rooftop bar of the Hotel Majestic. She waits for the contact her Pentagon connections and the *Digest* helped arrange for her.

She takes a deep breath and gazes out over the city. Reflected in the Saigon River, lights dance to the music of a piano player—a handsome young Filipino singing American songs. Rain pours as if from a faucet—saturating cabs, cyclos, and people splashing through several inches of water. A lone slender Vietnamese woman holding a dainty umbrella walks along the boulevard as if untroubled by the fact that she wades up to her ankles. It's the rainy season, and it will be for months.

At least it isn't cold, Dickey thinks.

It's quite the opposite. The heat and humidity make a lush greenhouse of the region, reminding her of the Sierra Maestra. She feels a pang of longing for Cuba, made stronger and sharper because she's been banned. She thinks with sorrow of Ernest Hemingway's suicide last month. Dickey wonders if he did it because of despair over forced exile from his beloved Cuban home. She wonders if Fidel feels responsible in any way for the loss of a man he claimed to admire, a man he called a friend of Cuba to the end.

Probably not. Fidel has lost his heart.

If Dickey ever returns to Cuba, she'll have a price on her head. Just like she does in Laos. Just like she does in Hungary. She hopes her luck will change in Vietnam, but the signs don't look good.

What does look good is you, Dickey can almost hear Aunt George say.

The thought brings a sad smile to Dickey's face. She feels as if her aunt still encourages her when she most needs it. It's one of the good voices that have embedded themselves in Dickey's consciousness. She thankful not to hear one of the bad, especially having been in such a dark place these past couple of months.

Fit and tan, Dickey is dressed up for the evening's soiree in another Stevie purchase: a black-and-gold sleeveless cocktail dress with a matching short-sleeved jacket. Stevie had bought it on behalf of Dickey before she'd left and, when she delivered it, begged Dickey to make this her last assignment.

"You're not getting younger," said Stevie. "And there's plenty going on stateside that needs coverage. My goodness, civil rights? Your Cuban exile friends. Miami has planeloads of kids arriving by the day. You told me yourself that Castro's closing of religious schools and threatening to indoctrinate kids in the Soviet Union has desperate Cuban parents shipping their kids to the U.S. How are you not covering this?"

"If I could be in two places at once, I would," said Dickey. "But I'm making serious headway in Laos, and my reports are being used in actual military briefings. It's more than just articles; it's intelligence. I need to see this through."

"I don't have a good feeling about Southeast Asia."

"I do," said Dickey.

But that's no longer true. Aunt George's death and Hobart's rejection of the Laos article have crushed Dickey and made her question why she's still here. There remains a feeling deep inside her that she should be, and she prays tonight's meeting will affirm that.

Dickey pulls her Zippo lighter out of her small black pocketbook, but after a few flicks, the damp cigarette won't catch and she's out of fluid. A hand appears, placing a lighter before her. She leans toward the flame, taking three long draws to get the cigarette burning before looking at the face of the one helping her.

An elegantly dressed Chinese man of about forty smiles at her. In her briefing, she'd seen his picture and file: General Bernard Yoh, formerly of the Chinese Nationalist Army, leader in the "Shanghai

Net" WWII American airmen rescue operation, anticommunist, Catholic, and guest conductor of the Shanghai Philharmonic Orchestra. Working with the United States Senior Liaison Office in Saigon, Yoh is an adviser to South Vietnamese President Ngo Dinh Diem, and an intermediary to Father Augustine Nguyen Lac Hoa, leader of the hamlet of Binh Hung.

"Miss Chapelle?"

"General Yoh," she says, extending her hand.

"Call me Bernie," he says, shaking it.

"Pleased to meet you, Bernie."

"Welcome to the Pearl of the Orient. I hope your stay has been relaxing so far."

"Saigon and its people are marvelous, and I'm comfortable in the hotel, but I'm ready to get back out in the field."

His eyes sparkle with approval, and he extends his arm

"Come, it's time for your next assignment," he says.

They leave the bar, take the elevator down to the lobby, walk under ornate chandeliers, across a gleaming marble floor, and out to where a sleek black car idles. Bernie holds the door for Dickey, and she slides in across the smooth tan leather, Bernie following. The car pulls into traffic, rainwater pounding the roof and splashing under the tires.

"The late great Wild Bill told me about you long before I met you," says Bernie, his English strong.

Dickey smiles for what feels like the first time in weeks.

"The fearless lady reporter," Bernie continues. "Foe of communists. Enough courage for an army. A survivor. Loyal to the end."

"These are high compliments coming from a man I greatly admired," she says. "Thank you. Bill Donovan was an inspiration to me. He also knew how to stir up quite a bit of trouble, a trait with which I can identify."

"He might have mentioned that about you, too," Bernie says, with a smile. "But he said you were rock solid, never giving up the ship. Never betraying those still operational, even under torture and duress. The tip of the spear."

Not for the first time, Dickey thinks how astonishing it is that what happened to her in the Hungarian communist prison is what has made rebels from Algeria to Cuba to South Vietnam trust her, no matter their political affiliation. It reaffirms in her that good can come from dark times, and she'd endure all her sufferings again for the relationships and travels that have resulted.

"Donovan established the American Friends of Vietnam," says Bernie, "and helped lay a foundation to fight communism in the East. His work and the work of others inspires Father Hoa and his army, the Hai Yen, or Sea Swallows. Their success depends upon American support."

"I hope to get even more of it through my photo pieces."

If they pass censor, she thinks.

"I think you will," he says.

Dickey looks out the car window at the passing city, the rainy scene like a blurred watercolor. An old woman sits in a doorway, smoking a pipe, watching their car pass. At a thatched-roof shack, a naked, barefoot toddler splashes in a puddle while his tired father looks on, unsmiling. Young men play dice on the side of the road, cheering and jeering at one another. They are beautiful to Dickey and lodge themselves in her heart. She feels her photo trigger finger twitch, but she left her cameras in her room. She'll go out early tomorrow to photograph the people and the city at sunrise.

They soon reach the St. Francis Xavier Catholic Church in Cho Lon—the Chinatown of Saigon—where a party is being held in the meetinghouse. All at once, the rain stops as suddenly as it began. It's the same in Laos. It pours full blast or not at all, and circumstances change as quickly as one can blink. The driver comes around to open the door and, after Bernie climbs out, helps Dickey out of the car. Bernie motions toward a triple-gated entrance to the church courtyard.

"In the East, entranceways are typically arranged as three-gate structures, representing various passageways to liberation, or Nirvana. In Catholic Christianity, we see the love of the Trinity as paramount to our understanding of true liberation. Our paths to God can be through wisdom, compassion, or usefulness." He points to each gate. "Which passage will you choose?"

"Do I choose what I am or to what I aspire?"

"Wherever the Spirit moves you."

Dickey looks between each gate, weighing what she most desires. Practicality wins, and she walks through the gate of usefulness. Bernie passes through wisdom. Dickey looks back over her shoulder, feeling a strange sadness at the thought there was no one to walk through compassion.

"I'm quite sure Father Hoa took the middle gate," says Bernie.

As they enter, the bells of the church ring. Dickey feels a knot of tension release. Bernie leads her past a pagoda, glowing with lanterns, where a statue of Mary watches in the shadows. The mother's gaze is a comfort to Dickey. The church has a facade painted saffron with white accents, a large clock with golden Roman numerals, and a bell tower. To the left, there's a white boardinghouse, like a motel, where a line of bedraggled men leads to an open door burning with a white light.

"Who are they?" Dickey asks.

"They are here to sign up for the Sea Swallows. When Father Hoa's in town, we can barely keep up with the recruits."

As she was with the American fighting men in Laos and the rebels in Cuba, Dickey is struck by the courage of soldier volunteers. The length of the line is a testament to Father Hoa's leadership. She again laments leaving her cameras at the hotel.

At the church, they turn right and enter the meetinghouse, where the sounds of chatter and the aroma of Chinese food draw them into a room packed with men and women from all over the globe. The first familiar face she spots is Nelson's. He nods at her—raising his eyebrows to show his approval of her dress—and she returns the look, drawing forth one of his rare smiles. Standing with Nelson is Father Hoa. She recognizes the soldier-priest from the *Saturday Evening Post* article.

Just over fifty years old, Father Hoa is about six feet tall and broad-shouldered, with a crew cut and smile lines reaching beyond his glasses. When their eyes meet, both faces burst into smiles. He must recognize her because she's with Bernie.

Father Hoa holds out his hands and walks toward Dickey while she does the same. They meet and grasp each other. It's as if they've been waiting for each other for a long time. She feels the full warmth of certainty that she's where she should be.

"Daughter," he says in heavily accented English, looking down at her. "Welcome home."

THIRTY

SEPTEMBER 1961

Binh Hung, South Vietnam

Sissy-style, again, Dickey thinks, as the helicopter touches down on the landing area.

Children wait off to the side, bouncing like jumping beans. When Dickey hops out, they run toward her, bear-hugging her, Father Hoa, Bernie, and Nelson. Lines of soldiers salute them, as do more village children, melting Dickey's heart. Their trust and adoration sparkle in their eyes, and she hasn't even earned it yet.

Not being a mother to anyone makes Dickey, in a way, a mother to all. She and Father Hoa had discussed this form of parenthood that night at the party, along with many other deep subjects. The freedom from responsibility to a few allows for an enormous amount of affection and patience for multitudes, and Father Hoa is clearly the father of hundreds, if not thousands.

"Binh Hung," he says, holding up his hand. "I gave the hamlet this name because it means 'to clear obstacles.'"

English is a struggle for him, but he has clearly practiced this introduction. Bernie does the translating for her and Nelson. Father Hoa and Dickey are also conversant in French. The languages weave in and out of one another like silk in a tapestry.

The sun breaks through the clouds and shines in shafts along the canals. Gentle breezes ripple through the grasses and make the water sparkle. Dickey's camera is ready, so as Father Hoa starts his tour, she snaps pictures.

The hamlet is essentially a military installation, with a base, a church, a school, and community buildings at its center. Houses for soldiers' families are arranged in neat rows on either side of a canal, where chickens and small children roam the banks. Cows—gifts from the United States—graze in a field manned by old men. Women and men in an open-air building sit at stations with sewing machines, making clothes. The villagers are dressed well, in silk clothing sets that look like pajamas. The children wear short-sleeved button-down shirts and shorts, and are barefoot. Some adults are, too, but most wear thongs with thick platformed soles to keep their feet high above the clay and mud.

Through briefings, Dickey learned the nearly uninhabitable swampland gifted by President Diem in 1958 to one hundred refugee families fleeing communist China, has now grown to a community of roughly a thousand people. Their leader, Father Hoa, was ordained in 1935. He was conscripted to fight the Japanese during WWII, as part of a guerrilla unit in the Chinese Nationalist Army. Bernie's unit was in Shanghai for the surrender of the Japanese, in 1945, but when China faced civil war, he emigrated to the United States and continued his work with American media and intelligence, and Father Hoa fought the communists until Mao Zedong's triumph in 1949. From that point on, communist persecution of Catholics began in earnest. Father Hoa returned to the priesthood but was imprisoned twice and told his death and that of his congregation was imminent if they didn't abandon their faith. He fled with the people.

After years of hard travels, President Diem gave Father Hoa and his refugees a tract of land—the Ca Mau Peninsula—at the southernmost tip of Vietnam as a refuge. Not only have the families cleared and cultivated this swampland into a thriving village, but the vigilante force of Sea Swallows has been engaging bands of VC and winning. Battle by battle, the borders have expanded outward to envelop many more hamlets in the Mekong River Delta.

"We are the safest hamlet in South Vietnam," Father Hoa says, pointing out the sandbag, barbed-wire, and mud-wall borders.

Dickey feels another knot of tension release. It feels like a cocoon to be here, protected and guarded by vigilant watchmen. She might even be able to sleep at night. She was told she'll have a cot in the barracks of the American fighting men and some of the Sea Swallows, divided by a partition, and she can use a bathroom at a family home nearby. She's happy with this arrangement. For Dickey, there is no medicine like camaraderie, the esprit de corps.

"We go on patrol," Hoa continues, "fight and defend if necessary, and once the areas are secure, expand and guard our new lands. And more land is necessary, with the number of hamlets and families who have joined us."

"Vietnamese families?"

"Yes, including many who had been under the thumb of the communists until we liberated them. Many of the villagers only supported the VC because they harass, threaten, and intimidate them. We don't threaten anyone, including our prisoners. We sentence them to six months of manual labor, while inviting them to observe our way of life. At the end of that time, they are free to either join us or leave. So far, of the hundreds we've released, only four have gone back to fight with the VC. Most join us and bring their families."

"This is how it has to be done," says Bernie. "One settlement at a time. It's a battle for the minds and hearts of the people, and it is best won through dialogue and education. Fighting must always be a last resort."

"Are priests even allowed to fight in wars?" asks Dickey.

"I do more leading and planning now than fighting. The name I took in seminary was Augustine, for the Bishop of Hippo, whose writings are the foundation for determining if a war is just."

"And those conditions are?" she asks.

"The damage from the aggressor must be profound and long-lasting. All other means of negotiation have been tried. There must be a good chance of success. And the use of weaponry and tactics must be proportionate to what was inflicted, not creating a greater evil."

"Great progress would be made in the world if all abided by these conditions," says Dickey.

"I'll second that," says Nelson.

"What better place to start than Binh Hung?" says Father Hoa.

When they reach the prison, Dickey stops, her heart racing. She's mortified how her breath comes in quick gasps, and she can't proceed. She thought she was past the trauma of her internment at Fö Street. Observing her distress, Father Hoa takes her arm and leads her inside. There's only one prisoner, in a solitary cell. The rest are out working. The man spits when he sees them. Dickey looks around her, and as she takes in the humane conditions, her heartbeat and breathing return to normal.

"You have been in prison," Father Hoa says.

"Yes, a communist prison in Hungary," she says.

"I was in a communist prison in China. The experience never leaves one."

She nods, grateful for his validation.

"Our prisoners have a different experience," he says. "All have a bed, a clean blanket, and a mosquito net. He or she is fed three meals a day."

"She?" asks Dickey.

"Yes. The women's building is next door. There are sometimes children with them who acted as couriers or even fighters for the VC. We have the prisoners work at farming, home building, and land clearing but no more than six hours a day. Each evening there's time to bathe and dress in clean clothes for dinner and sleep. Most of the prisoners leave here healthier than when they arrived."

Dickey looks out through the bars of the low building along one of the canals that act as roadways through the village. From the prison, one can see the family homes, the schoolhouse, the marketplace, the church, and the town square. The prisoners can observe that the villagers are happy, well-dressed, and well-fed. The children are fluent in Chinese, Vietnamese, and English. The people work and worship and play, their lives revolving around the church at its heart—Our Lady of Victory—where most gather for daily mass with Father Hoa.

After a few moments, he leads the group out of the building to stand at the canal bank, where a boat with baskets full of fish moves slowly by them.

"I can see why so many prisoners convert," she says. "It's idyllic. I could live here."

"And you will. You are. For the next couple of months. But the patrols, they are not idyllic. War is very much going on, just a few kilometers away. It's an ambush war, and it is deadly."

Dickey strains her eyes toward where he points. It's hard to imagine, but she knows it's true.

The church bell rings. Dickey raises her face to the sky, closing her eyes and taking a deep breath. She feels peace settle over her like a mantle. She feels as if she has come home.

"Your mission is blessed," says Bernie.

"I think so," she says, opening her eyes and looking around her.

A young woman with a baby strapped to her crosses a narrow bridge. A line of schoolchildren walks to a group of picnic tables laid with bowls of soup. In the distance, a group of male soldiers in training do exercises. A group of uniformed women joins them.

"Women soldiers?" asks Dickey.

"Yes," says Bernie. "The Home Guard. They don't patrol, but they are armed and trained to defend the village in case of attack."

Dickey smiles and waves at the women, who return her greeting. They are young and bright-eyed and pretty with the flush of youth and health. They remind her of Las Marianas. Dickey feels an ache in her heart thinking of how Aunt George would have loved to see all this.

"I think I'm falling in love with Binh Hung," Dickey says.

"It already loves you," says Father Hoa. "And your country, who has given us so much support. Through the grace of God."

"And the grace of Bernie," says Dickey.

They share a laugh. Bernie is clearly a force and a favorite of not only the Americans and the Chinese, but also the South Vietnamese.

"But we are in debt," says Bernie, his face growing serious. "We need more. So much more. Your pictures will help us."

Father Hoa continues the tour, leading Dickey to his home, a modest dwelling just off the church, where two Doberman pinchers wag their tails. There's a radio room where Father Hoa can contact Saigon or even men in the field directly, and the main living space is full of maps, where Father Hoa meets with his staff to plan campaigns. Bernie told Dickey that Father Hoa only sleeps about three hours a night.

"Meet Bullet and Jesse," says Father Hoa, petting the dogs. "My most faithful companions. Gifts from Sergeant West."

Dickey smiles up at Nelson, who nods. She wishes she'd brought a gift. Nelson's rapport with and affection for Father Hoa instill the kind of trust and loyalty that will make everyone more successful. Father Hoa and the villagers look up to Nelson like a beacon of hope, and it fills Dickey with pride to be a part of the country doing what it can to support such a place and a people.

The Dobermans are friendly, jumping and licking Dickey while she fawns over them. Father Hoa gently scolds them. He shoos them away and sighs, shaking his head.

"I'm too soft on them," he says. "They have no discipline."

"You save that for the Sea Swallows," says Nelson.

"Oh yes," says Father Hoa. "I am not soft on them."

THIRTY-ONE

SEPTEMBER 1961

Binh Hung, South Vietnam

Dickey leans forward in the boat, straining to scan the vegetation closing in on the canal around them.

Anyone could be hiding in there, she thinks, touching her new trench knife.

When Nelson gave it to her, it felt like she'd had a lost limb reattached. She won't let anyone take this one.

A shiver in the leaves brings forth a burst of sweat on Dickey. Father Hoa had explained that in an ambush war, VC move like snakes through the brush. They surround from all sides in their attacks, so backtracking only leads to ensnarement. At the first sound of bullets, soldiers must push forward at the greatest speed possible, mowing down the enemy.

In the briefing with Captain Chuong Quay, Father Hoa's second-in-command, Dickey learned today's mission is to go to the northernmost hamlet in the district. Intelligence reached them that VC are in the region, trying to take back some of the land and people the Sea Swallows won. From Father Hoa's and Bernie's backgrounds in irregular warfare, they make great use of spies from their village in the markets of others. Their contacts told them they would be ambushed.

Dickey had felt the thrill and terror of what was to come. But now, like a sitting duck along the canal, there is only terror. Dickey feels a hand on her arm and jumps.

"We're still safe," says Tien, her interpreter. He's eighteen years old, has high cheekbones, and wears his thick black hair slicked back like Elvis Presley. "This area is clear."

She sighs and drops her shoulders. They'd been up by her ears.

"I'll tell you when we are in enemy territory," he says. "But even then, you will be safe."

"How's that?"

"Because you are with the Hai Yen."

Dickey grins. Young men all over the world are the same.

When they had set out from the village, there had been a young woman waving to Tien from the banks, dabbing her eyes, with one arm around a girl of about ten, who also had Tien's high cheekbones. The young woman's face had turned red when Tien blew her a kiss.

"My betrothed, Anh," Tien had said, nodding toward the young woman. "And my little sister, Lai."

Anh had a broad face and voluptuous lips. She looked like she could be a statue of the Chinese goddess Guanyin, the patron of sailors, fishermen, and mercy. There are many statues of Guanyin in the huts in Binh Hung. Though most of the villagers are Catholic, there are some who are from other traditions, or who hold some tension between those of their ancestors' geography and the Christianity to which they have converted. It reminds her of the Santeríans and the Catholics in Cuba.

"We marry next month," Tien had said. "Anh is a serious girl. She will make a good wife."

"Are you in love?" Dickey asked.

He'd looked down, little circles of red forming on his cheeks.

"Good," said Dickey.

I hope he makes it until then, Dickey thinks.

The vegetation opens around them to rice paddies. In the distance, there are watchtowers and barbed wire.

"Is that the end of the safe zone?" she asks.

Tien nods, his face growing dark and shadowed. As they get closer, Dickey sees a crude cross with writing on it, erected by a watchtower. An assortment of flags, candles, and statues are under the cross.

"Where Anh's cousin, Ah, was murdered," Tien says. "He was eleven. The VC crucified him on that cross."

Dickey gasps.

A child. Murdered!

"When?" she stammers.

"In 1959, when we first arrived," says Tien. "There were elections in a nearby village. All the adults went to vote, leaving the children in the care of the teenagers. I was on lookout at the east gate. Ah was on lookout here. The VC made this cross and killed him in a mockery of our faith. They left a note that they would do this to all the children in Binh Hung if our parents did not abandon the faith and become communists."

Dickey feels sick. The stakes are so high. Americans can't comprehend it.

I'll make them understand.

"That very night," says Father Hoa from the bow of the boat, "we formed the Hai Yen. And we have been fighting and protecting and winning ever since."

He touches the insignia patch on his uniform, with the sea swallow over the water and a gold branch to the side. Dickey longs for one of her own. She's honored to be among them.

The moment they pass into no-man's-land, guns point outward from every man onboard. Tien nods at her. Dickey points her camera. She swallows, but her mouth is dry. Mosquitoes swarm. It's all Dickey can do not to slap at them, but that would make noise and shake the boat. The engines are cut, soldiers rowing the final stretch to where they'll disembark for foot patrol.

After what feels like an eternity, the boats bump land on opposite sides of the canal. Scouts slide out, carrying weapons from old wars—French and American—and fanning in every direction. After a whistling sound, Father Hoa orders the soldiers out of his boat. Dickey follows Tien, tripping up the embankment and falling into forward march. Limbs stiff from crouching for so long, knee protesting, Dickey is still able to keep up as the patrol moves at a shockingly fast clip in lines that would make the marines proud. They run through waist-high reeds and come to streams where the men don't stop but plow forward, always forward, waiting for the ambush.

Dickey's socks and pants to her knees are wet from the many streams they've crossed. As they approach the next one, she anticipates the same foot or so depth of the last but is shocked when she sinks to her chin. She yanks up her camera, but it's too late. It's soaked. Cursing inwardly, she consoles herself that there's another back in the village, and that she has already changed out one roll of film that should be dry in its case. Though it's probably hopeless, she lifts the camera above the water. She crawls through the shin-deep mud on the bank and is relieved to reach dry land until the telltale ping of bullets whizzes around them.

"Down!" Father Hoa yells.

Dickey hits the ground as the men around her press forward, guns blasting in a sharp, terrifying eruption. A grenade explodes close enough to her and Father Hoa that a spray of dirt falls over them. She's breathing so fast she inhales some of it and has a coughing fit. The sound is drowned in gunfire.

Just like Laos, she thinks.

"Forward," shouts Tien, translating Captain Quay's order.

Dickey scrambles to her feet and runs like her life depends upon it, because it does.

Gunfire crackles around them. Her position is central, guarded on all sides by Sea Swallows. They are surrounded by VC, but they plow forward, guns facing out in all directions like a star. None of them have yet fallen.

The star soon opens wider. Dickey is left alone with Father Hoa and two Sea Swallows. The gunfire diminishes. Captain Quay's voice comes with a word that must indicate all is clear.

The remaining men disperse and soon return with three prisoners and six dead VC. Father Hoa prays first over those killed, followed by the prisoners—a pack of heaving, scowling, scrawny, filthy men with blank eyes. Dickey looks at the Sea Swallows and wonders how many were once on the other side. She longs to photograph them and could cry over her wet camera.

"Daughter," says Father Hoa. "You did well. I see why so many recommended you."

His praise lifts her spirits, until she realizes Tien is not with them. Her heart pounds as she looks around, scanning the area, wondering if he was killed. A moment later he emerges from the brush, flashes a grin, and throws her a balled-up cloth. She catches and opens it, revealing a VC flag.

"War prize," Tien says.

"Don't you want it?" Dickey asks.

"Nah," he says, sounding like an American. "I have dozens."

Tien's cocky smile looks like that of a thousand servicemen she's seen before. It makes her swoon. It makes her happy.

It makes her feel like she's home.

THIRTY-TWO

OCTOBER 1961

Binh Hung, South Vietnam

Dickey climbs into the tower, scowling, trying not flinch over her aching knee. She's been put on watch with Tien, instead of being allowed on night patrol, and she's angry.

"I've been on seven patrols with the Sea Swallows," she argued with Bernie and Father Hoa. "Each more dangerous than the next. I've proven myself. You've just decorated me, for Pete's sake!"

Dickey ran her hand over the beloved Sea Swallow patch Father Hoa had just given her. He said she was the first non-Asian to be awarded such an honor. She bawled like a baby to receive it. Now she feels like bawling to be denied a position on night patrol.

"The VC in the region are particularly lethal," Bernie said. "They are well organized and well funded."

"I was on Iwo Jima, for crying out loud. You think I don't know well-organized and well-funded enemies?"

"On Iwo Jima, you had a strong knee," Father Hoa said. "And stronger eyes."

"My parts are working just fine. I—"

"Enough," Father Hoa said sharply. His inflection made clear the discussion was over.

It was the first time his sternness was directed at Dickey, and it stung like a slap. She ignored the voice in her head telling her he was right.

In the watchtower, Dickey takes deep, steadying breaths, releasing her fury. Tien climbs up behind her, joining her at the railing.

"He's a father in every sense," says Tien. "A good father."

He winks at her. She narrows her eyes at Tien but does not argue.

Dickey reaches for the cigarette pack in her breast pocket and sighs when she sees there's only one left. She's going through these things at a rate that will leave her broke and with a worse cough than she's already got if she's not careful. She lights the cigarette and passes it to Tien, who takes a long drag before passing it back to her and leaning against her shoulder. In the quiet of the moment, with her friend, under a million stars, she forgets herself and surrenders. It's then she can fully take in the unutterably beauty of the landscape. A full moon glows over the delta, illuminating the waterways, and a low wind whispers through the yellowed stalks of the rice paddies.

Shhhh. Shhhh.

"No picture could do this justice," Dickey says, framing the scene with her hands. "If it weren't for the mosquitoes, I'd think I'm in heaven."

The bell of Our Lady of Victory rings as if in confirmation.

"'All is well,'" Dickey whisper-sings.

It's a hymn from her youth. She passes Tien the cigarette. He inhales and passes it back, singing the next line.

We are from places a universe apart, Dickey thinks. *Yet we sing a common song. Is there anything more beautiful than this coming together?*

THE LAST ASSIGNMENT

When they finish their song and cigarette, Tien points to Dickey's Sea Swallow patch.

"You are one of us," he says. "Hai Yen."

Dickey beams. Along with her paratrooper wings, this patch is a most-beloved treasure.

"It almost makes me wish I had a child," she says, "so I'd have someone to inherit it when I die. Maybe I'll give it to Lai, my little shadow."

"You are her hero-saint," he says. "Her Joan of Arc."

"I can't imagine a better compliment. Though I'll try not to get burned on a stake."

As soon as the words leave Dickey's mouth, she regrets them. They have seen villagers burned. Tien has seen a child on a stake.

The crack of a reed interrupts Dickey's shameful moment. She and Tien turn to face the sound—Tien's gun drawn—and are relieved to see Father Hoa climbing into the watchtower, followed by Lai. Her eyes are puffy, like she's been crying.

The presence of two others in the small wooden blind makes a sardine can of them. Lai burrows into the front of where Dickey stands. She drapes her arms over Lai, who clings to Dickey like a life raft as they stare out over the delta.

"Lai longs to be of service," says Father Hoa, in slow English. "It burns in her heart and stirs her passions. Refusal makes a caged tiger of her."

She has tiger blood, Dickey thinks. *Like me.*

"I thought you'd understand, Miss Dickey," says Father Hoa. "Do you have wisdom for the girl who is not yet a woman but so dearly wants to be?"

Dickey thinks the wisdom by which she has lived her life—*be first, ask forgiveness instead of permission, keep your eyes open*—doesn't feel quite appropriate for this girl in this place at this time. Dickey settles for one of the few Bible verses she knows.

"'Trust in the Lord with all your heart,'" she says. "'And lean not on your own understanding.' Proverbs."

"Is that wisdom for you or for Lai?" says Father Hoa.

"It's for all of us," Dickey says, nudging Father Hoa. "Cheeky."

He smiles, the moonlight reflecting on his glasses making him look like an owl. Dickey realizes she looks the same, and understands she would have been a danger to men on night patrol while wearing such reflectors.

"A white dragon," Lai says, pointing.

To the east, the moonlit curl of a meandering stream does indeed look like the tail of a white dragon. White is a color of mourning and death in many Asian cultures. Dragons of course symbolize China. For Dickey, here, they're the bogeyman, the relentless shadow form always over her shoulder, pursuing. Lai reminds Dickey of the evil lurking, so hard to believe in a hamlet of such beauty and tranquility.

"You are safe here, now, child," says Father Hoa. "The head of the snake has already been crushed. Good wins. The story is done. We are just living in it, year after year, until the last year."

"On we fight," says Dickey. "The older I get, the harder it is for me to comprehend war."

"You can't comprehend war?" asks Father Hoa. "A chronicler of six conflicts?"

"Seven, including Vietnam."

"Seven is a number of totality. Completeness. Perhaps this war will be your last. Perhaps, as you told me, on the night we met, you will make the picture to end all wars."

"From your mouth to God's ears."

Dickey realizes, with some surprise, she means it.

In Binh Hung, she has finally found home. She has found peace. If she wants to, she knows Father Hoa would welcome her to live here, not just during conflict, but forever. And Dickey thinks she might just make a formal request soon. These knees don't have much landing and patrolling life in them, especially in such thick clay-mud. This is the only place in the world she can imagine putting down roots.

A breeze moves low over the land, rustling the reeds in a whisper. She shakes her head.

"How could anyone assault a peace like this?" she whispers.

"Because of the war in our hearts," says Father Hoa. "In your heart. In Lai's. In Tien's. In mine. It spills over."

Dickey thinks of all the bitterness and anger she has stoked in her heart. What starts as justifiable frustration or hurt, with tending, becomes fiery fury, a desire for revenge, and sin. Dickey's anger against Marmee, for always trying to tame and remake her daughter. Against Tony, for his betrayal, and Helga, for hers. Marie Rodell, for not making Dickey a priority. Countless peers and editors and bosses. Communist prison guards. Military censors. Fidel Castro. Raúl. Che. Hell, even Bernie and Father Hoa telling her no, for her own good and the good of others, gave rise to her fury. Dickey imagines anger as a stone dropped in water, its ripples expanding ever outward.

You can't have peace in a Manhattan apartment, and you expect the world to be at peace?

Dickey realizes, with exhaustion, that echoes of Marie's words, spoken so callously in a bar in New York are just as applicable to

Dickey's life years later in a hamlet in South Vietnam. It's hard to know that one plants the seeds of world war in the garden of one's own heart. It has been that way since the first humans walked the earth, and likely will be until the end of time.

"So, what do we do to stop it?" Dickey asks.

"Forgive from the heart," says Father Hoa. "Start by forgiving yourself. Then you'll be able to forgive others. Even those who don't seek or deserve it."

Dickey thinks of all the places of shame in her own heart that she needs to forgive, but that feels too daunting. She looks outward.

"How do you forgive those who've exiled you from your home?" she asks.

Father Hoa sighs. He switches to Chinese. Tien translates.

"It is the work of every day, every hour of my life. I have heard, through prayer, that I must transform my anger into sorrow. When I'm angry, I'm thinking about how I have been wronged. It's selfish. I should think about the Lord. How my sins and the sins of those who've hurt me have caused us both to be separated from the light. How He longs for all of us to be healed and with Him in the light. Thinking of how sin pains Him turns my anger to sorrow, and allows me to hope for the best, even for my enemies."

Love is a stone dropped in water, Dickey thinks, *its ripples expanding ever outward.*

"That's a hard teaching," says Tien.

"The hardest," said Father Hoa, again in English. "We must invite God in and ask for His grace to do the work in us. We cannot do it ourselves. But nobody said becoming a saint was easy."

"I think you'll be a saint," says Lai, looking up at Dickey, with adoration in her eyes. "Or an angel. The angel of Binh Hung."

Me, an angel.

Dickey, looks down at Lai's sweet face with gratitude, and then at Tien's and at Father Hoa's.

Father Hoa is the first to crack over the absurdity of the foul-mouthed, chain-smoking American war correspondent being called a saint or an angel. He makes a snorting noise that sets off Tien, and finally hits Dickey and then Lai. The group on watch in the tower tries to stifle their laughter. They have to crouch down low and press their hands over their mouths to contain it.

THIRTY-THREE

OCTOBER 1961

Binh Hung, South Vietnam

It's Dickey's last patrol with the Sea Swallows. Her budget has run out and her article will be due soon. She can barely breathe every time she thinks about departing from Binh Hung, so she pushes the thought way down and leans deeply into whatever moment is before her. She's running out of moments.

This particular moment is like a parade. Amid raucous fanfare, Dickey and the newest graduating class of Sea Swallows are being blessed and cheered for along the canal as the soldiers raise their rifles in celebration and depart for their first mission. The new boys are from China, Cambodia, and Vietnam. They're mostly Catholic, but they're also Buddhists and some who've grown up Cao Dai—a fusion of Catholicism and Buddhism, with sprinklings of Taoism and Confucianism.

Father Hoa is welcoming of all faiths as long as all are respectful of his. Unfortunately, the same cannot be said for Catholic South Vietnamese President Diem, whose younger brother and closest adviser, Ngo Dinh Nhu, is growing more intolerant by the day of all non-Catholics, including Buddhists. Dickey's friends at the

Pentagon say the United States has an uneasy relationship with President Diem, but from their view he's the best they have.

So was Castro, at one time.

Today's mission is to protect Father Hoa as he says mass in Tan Hung Tay, a hamlet in the northern region of the district. The village has been plagued by VC spies and terrorists, and the people live in a constant state of fear. The village radioman contacted Binh Hung the night before and said VC had snuck in the town square in the middle of the night and nailed a paper on the hut that served as a church. It said the villagers would be ambushed if they participated in mass. The Sea Swallows will make sure that doesn't happen.

At the front of the boat, Father Hoa sits in full uniform, his vestments and mass accoutrements in the rucksack at his feet. He smokes a cigarette and looks as calm as if he were heading out to go fishing instead of saying mass in a volatile, communist-infested village at the edge of the borderlands. When Dickey raises her camera, he gives her that warm, fatherly look she has grown to love. How she adores him. Also looking up at Father Hoa with unmasked adoration is Tien's eighteen-year-old cousin, Ming. His parents and uncles and aunts were so proud of the young man when he was given the patch making him an official member of the Sea Swallows.

How does one send a son off to war? Dickey thought at the graduation ceremony. *Then again, in these circumstances, how does one not?*

As the boats pass the cross in the village, Tien, Lai, and the rest of their siblings wave furiously, including the youngest of the boys, the giggliest little fellow Dickey has ever met, four-year-old Vinh, whom she calls Vinnie. She's old enough to be all their mothers, and their own mother, Buu, is younger than Dickey by a few years.

They have adopted Dickey, and she loves them like her own family. She feels a pang of uneasiness that Tien won't accompany her, but it's a big day for him.

Tien holds up his arm and points to his watch.

"I won't be late," Dickey calls. "I promise."

She hopes that's true. Tonight, Tien marries Anh.

Buu lent Dickey a lovely lavender qipao dress. It makes Dickey smile to think of the looks on all their faces when they'll see her out of her usual bush hat, olive drabs, and muddy boots. She can't wait.

The cheers and celebration fade quieter and quieter behind them. As soon as they pass out of the borders, mud walls and barbed wire behind them, the mood sobers. The clouds are so low that it looks as if she can reach up and touch them. The temperature is in the seventies, but the humidity makes it feel hotter. The rice fields are open, making for good visibility in all directions, but the closer they get to Tan Hung Tay, the more the vegetation thickens. Guns and her camera point in all directions. Dickey barely breathes until they reach the crude dry dock that leads to the overgrown footpath to the village.

The scouts go first and fan out. In a few minutes, since no warning is issued, the rest disembark. Dickey jumps out and sinks to midboot. She notes the many barefoot soldiers—the restrictions on dress are loose because of a lack of supplies for all the new recruits—and understands the wisdom of not wearing heavy shoes in these parts. Of course, she's seen enough snake bites to err on the side of boots, but they do make squelching noises, which isn't optimal. How Ming, also in boots, manages to glide so quietly is beyond Dickey's comprehension.

They creep forward through an abandoned French colonial

coconut plantation. Dickey notices a clump of palms shivering, yet there isn't a hint of breeze. She touches Father Hoa's arm and motions to the disturbance just as a terrible thump before them draws their eyes to a grenade on the sand. Ming lunges forward, picks it up, and flings it back toward the palms. It explodes midair just as the ambush starts.

VC drop from trees like snakes, but the Sea Swallows counterattack with force. Dickey finds cover behind an ancient stairway leading to nowhere, snapping photos while making sure she doesn't come into the line of fire. She spots one of the VC jumping from an old outbuilding, scurrying away like a rat.

"VC!" she yells to the nearest Sea Swallow, who promptly chases and overcomes the man in seconds.

The shooting and scuffling continue around them, gradually growing quieter until all that can be heard is heavy breathing. When they rise to search and clear, the mood and bravado of the new men grows with each empty building. Dickey follows them, laughing with them and snapping pictures along the way.

As always, she's struck by the wild beauty of Vietnam that she hasn't fully been able to capture with her photographs. The VC camp is in an abandoned French villa, a place of crumbling, moldy, mossy stone beauty. Archways hang with vines. Curved staircases and iron balconies lead to stunning views of mountains. Dickey wanders among the towering palms and lofty architecture, taking pictures of the light slicing in, illuminating the vegetation and haunted halls like a cathedral, until a horror stops her. Dickey gasps and drops her camera on its strap. As the men hurry to her, curses in many languages are uttered. Father Hoa soon arrives and goes pale.

The bodies of two Sea Swallows are impaled by poisoned stakes, hidden in the understory. The dead men's backs are to the group, blooms of blood around the stakes jutting through them.

Some of the men with machetes clear around the bodies revealing an entire row of stakes. This could have been any of them. If she'd been running, it could have been her. Dickey feels a wave of nausea at the thought of the bodily pain of charging into such a trap, and how thin the line is between life and death.

The men pull the dead Sea Swallows off the stakes, and there, on the first day he started as a soldier—the warmth of his father's blessing still on his shoulders—is Ming. His young, clear eyes stare lifeless at the canopy until Father Hoa reaches down and closes them.

He weeps.

It's the only time Dickey has seen the soldier-priest cry. It's a brief burst like a summer storm, and then it's over.

The soldiers look at their leader for direction.

"Mass is in one hour," he says. "Clear the area."

If they thought they were going to abandon the mission, they were wrong.

Dickey takes a deep breath and follows the men through the remaining buildings. Underground, she finds a VC bunker of sorts. When she sees what's in it, she again stops short. In addition to Ho Chi Minh's picture and the North Vietnamese flag hanging on the wall, is a sight that makes her blood run cold. She calls for Father Hoa. When he enters, his face darkens.

The Soviet flag.

Stoi!

It was one thing to suspect that, in addition to the Chinese, the Soviets were supplying the VC here. It's another to have such explicit evidence. Of course, Dickey can't pretend to be fully surprised. After all, the United States supplies the South Vietnamese. She rips the Soviet flag from the wall, followed by the VC flag, and carries both out to show the men. They wrinkle their noses in disgust.

"Keep them," says Father Hoa. "Show the Americans."

Dickey balls them up with as little respect as possible and stuffs them in her field pack back at the boat.

The bodies of their dead are wrapped in sheets by the time she returns. She says a silent prayer of thanks that Tien was not on patrol that day. It could have been him instead of his cousin. Then she feels guilty for the prayer.

They leave the prisoners under guard and interrogation by four Sea Swallows back at the bunker and proceed into town, where the people have to have their doors knocked on to be assured the area is clear and covered, and they can attend mass safely.

While Dickey watches the mass though her lens and takes pictures, everything starts to look blurry and strange. It's during the consecration that she realizes her glassy eyes and sweating feel like a fever, coming on like a brush fire. There is a young man who looks like Tien to her. She has to keep blinking to reassure herself that he's not there. Then another looks like Ming. She has to remind herself that he's dead.

After mass, on the boat ride back to Binh Hung, Father Hoa touches Dickey's arm. She can see his lips moving but she can't understand his words. She thinks he's inquiring after her health. She nods as if she's all right, but she isn't.

One of the boat engines stalls before they make it into the safety of Binh Hung, and they have to sit baking in the sun, which has emerged while the mechanic works. The water in Dickey's canteen runs out. Her tongue sticks to the roof of her mouth.

They get back just in time for Father Hoa to put his vestments back on, break the news to Ming's parents and family, and start the wedding. Because of the time it took to fight the ambush, to manage broken boats and broken hearts, and to get the bodies home with dignity, Dickey isn't able to change out of her filthy fatigues. She doesn't have the energy anyway. Though she burns with fever, she gives everything she has to taking pictures.

Tears of mourning and tears of joy fall. Tears of the bride flow the heaviest, as it is custom for Chinese daughters to weep over leaving their families of birth. Anh's tears flow like the stream, filling her parents with pride and revealing what a good and loving wife and mother she will be to her new family.

Anh weeping. Tien nervous and hopeful. His parents, proud. Lai, wide-eyed. The Sea Swallows, at various turns raucous and joyous, then serious and mournful. Children smiling. Vinnie giggling. The tension of everything coming together in blessing and sorrow at the strange and vivid darkness and lightness of living.

There's a young pretty girl—one of the Home Guard—who becomes quietly drunk. She vomits in the canal. Lai tells Dickey the girl was Ming's betrothed. Ming's parents sit and watch the celebration, still as stone figures. They will not be kept from their obligations by communists. They only go home once dancing begins, when they might have anyway, as elders. They will cry in private.

Dickey is so feverish that the figures in Binh Hung became like those at her own wedding. Delirium is setting in. When she can take no more, she bids Lai a good night and starts back to the barracks. Along the way, the dark looming jungle around Binh Hung becomes the Sierra Maestra. When she passes the prison, the venomous stares of the new captures become those of the Hungarian prison guards. Dickey stumbles, but strong hands help her up and to bed.

"Father," she says.

The priest sits by Dickey, makes her drink, and places a wet cloth over her forehead. He becomes her birth father. He becomes Aunt George. For two days, Dickey mumbles in an incoherent fog, talking to her beloved dead and the people of Binh Hung. She thinks she would rather die here than have to leave. In moments of lucidity, she's thankful that, though stuck in a fever dream, at least it extends her stay in one of the only places on earth that has ever felt like home.

November 1961
Saigon, Hotel Majestic

Dear Aunt Lutie,

My bank account just got $12,000 richer, thanks to Aunt George. She's still trying to take care of me, even after she's gone. I promise I will save what she willed to me as a nest egg to maybe buy a future place in the States, a home of my own where I might put down roots when I retire, and eventually become a wedding photographer.

It made me laugh out loud to write that. I hope it did you, too.

In all seriousness, one of my beloved Sea Swallows married a village girl, and though I was sick with mosquito-borne plague, it was one of the most joyous, beautiful events I've ever had the privilege of photographing. It's hard for me to express how dear the people of Binh Hung have become to me. Please pray for their success. If the ripples of their freedom and tranquility continue to expand outward into secure hamlets at the rate they have, in no time at all Vietnam will be a land of democracy. Then Cambodia, then China. A welcome domino effect. Can you imagine?

I'm working to get back to Binh Hung as soon as possible. The American people need to know about this place, to lend a helping hand, and the people of the village need to know they are supported.

My piece on the "Fighting Priest of South Vietnam" is one of which I'm most proud. If the *Digest* can stop censoring me, it will run early next year, and will hopefully help garner American support for Father Hoa and Binh Hung. The *New York Times Magazine* has also bought one of my photos for the February 1962 cover. I'll be sure to save you a copy once it hits stands.

I'm in Saigon now, working on pass pages for my autobiography. I'm burning again, not with fever, but with anger. These silly editors are desperate to feminize my book. They want me to cut the scenes that are "too graphic, too dirty, too bloody..." They think only flighty women clutching smelling salts will read it and are catering to the audience they've created in their minds. If any of these ninnies had seen the women of the Binh Hung Home Guard, Las Marianas of Cuba, or the ladies of the Hungarian freedom fighters in prison with me, they'd realize how small their vision of women really is, but since William Morrow's paying that bill, they pull the strings. I'm working to find something we can all live with.

On a sweeter note, South Vietnam has lodged itself in my heart. I'm making some good press friends here, including Henri Huet, and some enemies not worth naming, the usual jealous Joes too afraid to go out on patrol and embarrassed and resentful that I'm not. Though I have to leave to debrief my DC pals about all I've seen, I'll be pitching more pieces to the biggies, to get back to Vietnam ASAP. This time I'm aiming for National Geographic *to foot the bill. Send luck!*

> *All my love, still with all my limbs and digits, though desperate for a sniper to take out my uterus,*
> *Georgie Lou*

November 1961
New York City

Dear General Lansdale,

I was sorry to miss you in DC, too, but General Wallace Greene took good care of me. He assured me the materials from my briefing would make it to President Kennedy, via you, in the days to come, and would be returned to me shortly thereafter. It was the thrill of my life meeting the commandant of the corps, especially when General Greene called me "a good marine." His commendation along with yours—"a good girl guerrilla"—means I can now die happy.

Regarding Cuba, I was angry, though unsurprised, to hear about Castro's mass expulsion of Catholic clergy to Spain. The pope issued a notice that declared it was grounds for excommunication. Though I'm not a Catholic, I sure would like to see Pontifex follow through with that. Some of my Catholic friends would, too.

I'm relieved to hear Felipe, Raquel, and the boys—among others Castro calls "criminal defectors"—are safely settled in Miami. Refugee payments should help them get on their feet, and Felipe's loyalty to the cause of democracy is without question, though he can't feel too good about Uncle Sam after the Bay of Pigs situation. If you need a liaison, I'm your gal. Felipe trusts me, and since I'm a journalist, and in a constant state of movement, I am at your and the agency's disposal if needed.

In January, I'm heading out on a lecture tour for my autobiography. I wanted to call the book With My Eyes Wide Open but the d*mned editors insisted on What's a Woman Doing Here? I'll be disparaging the publisher and telling the real name for the book—along with all *the juicy and violent parts they made me cut—in women's clubs from coast to coast. I have several events in Florida, so please do let me know if you need me to establish a line of contact with Felipe and his circles while I'm there. Your service fighting communism—from Cuba to Southeast Asia—is good and noble and I'm honored if my work can shed light or help in any way.*

I hope our paths cross soon in either DC or Saigon.

Until next time,
Dickey Chapelle

THIRTY-FOUR

APRIL 1962

New York City

Used to being on the other side of the camera, Dickey is taken aback when the flashbulb goes off.

"Oh!" says Aunt Lutie, her arm threaded through one of Dickey's while Stevie is on the other side.

"Stop and show 'em your choppers," says Dickey, flashing her smile.

The women beam at the collection of press photographers outside the Waldorf Astoria before proceeding into the hotel. Dickey can't remember the last time she felt so glamorous. Stevie helped her pick out the ball gown with a marine-green velvet bodice and a shimmery white-and-gold floor-length skirt, complete with long white gloves. On the matching green velvet purse, Dickey had pinned her parachutist wings. Her outfit was topped off by a real splurge. Every dime of the five-hundred-dollar cash portion of the Overseas Press Club's prestigious George Polk Award she would receive at the dinner that night was spent on dangly gold Tiffany earrings.

Though it feels strange not wearing her pearls, since the windfall from Aunt George and the payout from the *Digest*, Dickey has no guilt over indulging herself. For the first time in her life, she's on good financial footing.

After the requisite pictures, she leads her aunt and her best friend into the lobby of the Waldorf Astoria. Art deco surroundings, bronze details, elevated ceilings, fat columns, palm trees, and the two-ton 1893 World's Fair clock make the hotel a beacon of luxury. Dickey parades the ladies down Peacock Alley, glancing up at the curved marble stairs, hoping to catch sight of Cole Porter, who has lived at the hotel for almost thirty years. Orchestra music from the Grand Ballroom beckons—the rich, jazzy sound of "Autumn Leaves," always in season. When the women reach the ballroom doors, they stop and marvel over the twinkling lights hanging from the soaring ceiling, a red-velvet-curtained stage, and hundreds of circular tables dressed to the nines hosting over a thousand members of the Overseas Press Club.

"Dickey Chapelle!"

The moment she enters the ballroom, she hears her name from her old pal and Hungarian Revolution partner Carl Hartman. They embrace, exchange kisses on cheeks, and remark over how swell they each look.

"I hardly recognized you," says Carl. "So glamorous and svelte!"

"Gee, thanks, Carl."

"Aw, come on, you know you're more comfortable in field gear," he says. "Hell, I thought you'd be wearing something made from a parachute. Heard you're the first woman correspondent to jump out of an aircraft into combat. Well done!"

"Thank you, sir. Indeed, I am, and I highly recommend it. It gets you much closer to the front much faster."

Dickey introduces Aunt Lutie and Stevie, and after pleasantries, the ladies excuse themselves to find their table and put down their bags. They're seated all the way at the front of the room, closest to the podium and the dance floor.

"For it being Friday the thirteenth, I sure feel lucky," says Dickey.

"Don't look now, but your luck has run out," says Stevie.

Dickey turns to where her friend points and sees Tony and his new wife, Kay, coming toward them. Kay fits the type—petite, blonde, far prettier than the man escorting her but too innocent to know better. Though Dickey feels a splash of cold seeing Tony, she arranges her posture to stand tall. She knows she's successful; she looks as good as she ever has, and she's about to be given the top award of the OPC. More than that, she's delighted that she's not the abused caregiver of the aging, gluttonous, greasy-haired boor waddling toward the group. For that, Dickey's smile is genuine.

"Look at you," says Tony, arms open wide. "From the foxhole to foxy!"

Aunt Lutie huffs in disapproval. Stevie rolls her eyes.

"Tony," says Dickey, not going in for the hug she knows he wants. She does, however, take Kay's hands and kiss her on both cheeks.

"Dickey," says Kay, "I've read your book twice now and it's just tremendous. I could never imagine anyone being so brave. Let alone a dame. And here you are, getting honored tonight! I'm so proud to know you."

"I taught her everything she knows," says Tony.

"I somehow don't remember you being at boot camp or paratrooper school," says Dickey, "but you sure did teach me how to go over budget on assignment."

"Oh, ha-ha," he says. "If you wanna forget all the good I did, fine."

"Hard to remember after the gun-wielding incident," Stevie mumbles in Dickey's ear.

"You know," says Tony, "you're not the only one with a book-publishing credit this year. I have a recipe in the *OPC Cookbook*. Persian chicken. Remember when we ate that under a starlit night in a desert tent?"

He winks at her.

He's so inappropriate.

Dickey grimaces for Kay's sake and shudders for her own.

"How are Ron and his wife doing?" Dickey asks. "Judy, yes?"

"Yes," says Tony. "Judy's a good girl. They're a perfect couple."

"I'm glad to hear it," says Dickey. "And he's in the air force. I'm so proud of him. Please give him my best."

"We sure will," says Kay. "He talks about you all the time. You're his hero."

Dickey feels a pang that she hasn't made more time for Ron. He's a sweet young man and managed so well in school in spite of having a father like Tony. She hopes the good guys clean up Vietnam before Ron and other young soldiers might have to go.

"Dickey!"

She turns to see her old Cuba buddy Andrew St. George.

"If you'll excuse us," says Dickey. "So nice to see you, Kay. Tony."

As Dickey turns to leave, she feels Tony's big mitt on her arm, but the pressure is gentle instead of harsh. She looks at his eyes, drooping and sad like an old basset hound, and she's able to muster enough pity not to yank her arm out of his grasp.

"I'm real proud, kid," he says. "You've done well for yourself."

Moved by his earnest compliment, and pleased that it's doing nothing more to her than filling her with the appropriate level of gratitude, she places her hand on his.

"Thank you, Tony. You did get me started in photography, and for that I'm forever grateful. It has taken me to the four corners of the world."

Tony's eyes become watery with unshed tears. He mumbles a thank-you and she leaves him. In this moment, she feels a knot untie itself, followed by a peaceful release. She thinks of wars and truces and of Father Hoa, and how she can't wait to get back to him to tell him she's making progress in her own little conflicts and is hopeful their ripples will extend outward as far as the eye can see.

The evening passes so quickly that Dickey longs to photograph it, to freeze time, to linger over the delicious food, the luxurious surroundings, the good cheer, and being passed from one correspondent's arms to the next, dancing to the excellent music of Ben Cutler and His Orchestra. When Tony tries to cut in on Andrew St. George, Dickey makes a beeline for Aunt Lutie and Stevie. The younger ladies coax Aunt Lutie on the dance floor for "The Twist" and after her initial protests, she consents and finishes the dance in a fit of giggles.

"You girls are too much," says Aunt Lutie. "I can't believe you made me do that."

"If only I got a picture of us," says Dickey.

"It's okay for some experiences to live only in our memories, dear. For you to be fully present."

Dickey ponders this. She knows the camera is a kind of safety blanket for her, a veil between herself and the world. She doesn't know if that's healthy but she's not about to change course now. She hardly knows what to do with herself when her camera isn't hanging around her neck.

Dickey finishes her champagne and is rooting through her purse to powder her nose before the awards begin, when she feels Aunt Lutie's hand on her arm.

"I hate to bring this up again, but were you able to change your tickets?"

Aunt Lutie has been hounding Dickey about moving her upcoming trip to South Vietnam from May to later that summer. Dickey has a hysterectomy scheduled next week, and both the doctor and Aunt Lutie don't want her back in the field so soon after the operation. She has assured them that she'll take it easy and that if things don't go well following surgery, she'll cancel the trip. Of course, she has no intention of doing either and they all know it.

"As I told you," says Dickey, "I will reassess the trip plans after surgery."

"It's no use," says Stevie. "You know Dickey won't be deterred. If anything, you should encourage her to go, and then maybe she'll stay."

Dickey narrows her eyes at Stevie.

"I appreciate your love and concern," says Dickey. "Both of yours, but I'm in the best shape of my life and the doc doesn't expect any complications. Not to mention the fact that in the village of Binh Hung I have more aunties and surrogate mothers to take care of me, should I require it, than I do here. And that's saying something."

"You'll leave your birth auntie for an auntie oceans away," says Aunt Lutie. "I'll never understand it."

Dickey feels a stab of guilt and is about to apologize when the speaker of the night takes the podium. Edward R. Murrow, long-time broadcaster appointed by President Kennedy as director of the U.S. Information Agency, begins a speech about freedom of the press that stirs every heart from every political leaning in the room. Murrow is followed by Black comedian Dick Gregory, who does the same, though in a different way.

"America is such a great country," Dick says. "Where else could a guy like me make several thousand a week to joke about having to sit in the back of a bus and take my kids to segregated schools?"

There's dark laughter at the gallows humor. A feeling of nausea follows for Dickey, however. She thinks about what Stevie has said about covering the fight for civil rights at home. She'll think harder about it on the other side of Vietnam.

Dickey's award comes next, and she doesn't know how she'll follow either man. While she's being introduced, she takes a deep breath and imagines she'll be talking to a company of marines or a gathering of families in Binh Hung. That sets her heart at ease.

"Reporter George Polk, a protégé of Mr. Murrow," says Bill Lawrence, president of the OPC, "was killed in Greece, while pursuing—*for* pursuing—the truth about corrupt governments and regimes. Every year, the OPC honors one of our own who courageously pursues truth, even in the face of danger. The winner of this year's prestigious George Polk Award has been in solitary confinement in a Hungarian communist prison, has taken photos over the shoulder of Fidel Castro's revolutionaries while they were engaged in battle, has allowed themselves to be 'kidnapped' by Algerian rebels in order to live with them in the desert, and now jumps out of perfectly working aircraft behind enemy lines in

Southeast Asia, all because while many of us are content to stay at the bar sipping Pernod and taking notes from returning soldiers for our articles, this correspondent insists on only writing about those things personally 'eyeballed.' Did I mention the person of whom I speak barely crosses the five-foot mark and is a lady?"

There are gasps throughout the ballroom.

"For a lifetime of exceptional courage and enterprise covering combat, most recently in Vietnam, I'm honored to present this award to the second woman in history to win it..."

"Second," whispers Dickey to Stevie. "Blech."

Stevie nudges her friend. "Oh, shush."

"Paratrooper and photojournalist Georgette 'Dickey' Meyer Chapelle."

The roar of cheering and applause from the room takes Dickey so aback that she's surprised to feel tears spring to her eyes. She had no idea she would be celebrated like this. Most of the people she knows in the room have discouraged, disparaged, and disdained her for the length of her career. The very eyes that have rolled and the backs that have turned and the lips that have sneered are now gazing on her with smiles reaching from their mouths to their eyes, their enthusiasm genuine. Aunt Lutie passes Dickey her handkerchief, and Dickey dabs her eyes, takes a deep breath, and moves as gracefully as she's able to receive her award.

Don't trip like you're apt to do, she coaches herself, forcing herself to move slowly. Doing so both keeps her upright and extends the thunderous applause that she thinks might be healing about four decades of bully wounds. When she reaches the podium, Bill passes her the certificate and plaque, points to where the photographer stands, and instructs her to smile. The flash temporarily blinds her.

Dickey looks out at the sea of faces coming into form and feels the heat of the room and the thrill of victory. Then, unbidden, follows a strange longing inside her for a thatched hut, the whisper of wind in bamboo, an Asian flute, a lookout stand squeezed with people from a faraway place, looking up at stars and laughing over absurdities. This longing to be somewhere else is not what she anticipated from what she would have thought was a pinnacle moment of her career.

The audience takes their seats, and Dickey takes a deep breath.

"Thank you, Bill. Ladies and gentlemen of the OPC, your long-suffering spouses."

Knowing laughter moves through the crowd.

"It's hard to follow Mr. Murrow and Mr. Lawrence, let alone Dick Gregory, a man who like so many faces battles at home on U.S. soil that I'll never understand. I salute you, sir."

Dick—from where he stands along the wall, not even given a seat at a table—places his hands in prayer and bows to her. She nods back at him.

"This award is the honor of my career," says Dickey. "And I'm grateful. If I had only received it earlier, maybe I could have spared myself time in solitary and a few wars."

More laughter titters around the room.

"But as many of you know, once you've gone as close to the front as you can, it's hard to imagine living anywhere but on the edge of freedom. Everything is sharpest and in highest, most vivid color there, sadly making everything else look like the black-and-white scenes from *The Wizard of Oz*."

She sees knowing nods in affirmation.

"My editor in WWII gave me a directive," says Dickey, "and I've been trying to live up to it ever since. He said, 'Dickey, as a woman in a male-dominated field, you have to *be first* to distinguish yourself. *First.*' As you heard Bill say, I'm the second woman to win this award. But one thing I'm consistently first at is disappointing my editors and underwhelming them with my performance."

The audience again responds with laughter. They are still looking at Dickey with affection, the way people look at naughty puppies during moments of good behavior, when the promise of their adulthood can be glimpsed.

"Of one thing you can be sure: I'll continue to push the boundaries until my dying breath, seeking the one thing I know I'll never attain but for which I'll forever hope and strive. Before I get to my last assignment, I want to get the picture to end all wars."

The faces before her are serious and rapt. Her Aunt Lutie and Stevie beam with pride. She winks at them.

"Before I go, I want to give special thanks to the two women here with me tonight. My best friend in the world, the reason I'm not wearing olive drabs and boots right now, and—though she's about my age—my surrogate Jewish mother, Stevie Blick. She is a voice of constant caution and reason that I always ignore but who loves and supports me just the same. And finally, my dear, loving, warm-hearted, sweet Aunt Louise. She is another surrogate mother, since I lost my own, and her prayers are what have surely kept me alive to be here tonight to accept this award. Thank you. All of you. Good night."

THIRTY-FIVE

MAY 1962

Binh Hung, South Vietnam

Dickey's heart could explode with joy to be back in Binh Hung, and this time for *National Geographic*.

Sayonara, Digest, *on to greener pastures!*

Dickey ruffles Vinnie's hair, salutes Lai, and waves at the cheering, jumping lines of children seeing them off. The helo rises and sets its course, and soon they pass over the tranquil rice paddies, cross the borderlands, and swoop over jungles.

Dickey stares across the company of Sea Swallows at Sergeant Nelson West, where he looks down at the ground, five hundred feet below them. Helicopter blades from a fleet of four chop loudly over the metal can carrying them over what is now VC-infested jungle. Captain Quay, West's South Vietnamese fighting force counterpart, sits at his right. His men covering the space between them are armed with carbines from WWII and riding in such an old helicopter that it requires twelve hours of maintenance to make a one-hour patrol, but they're glad to have anything the United States will give them—man or machine. Dickey's photographs and articles have been a big help with that.

"Old weapons from old wars," Dickey had said to Nelson when they loaded up the chopper. "Relics, like me."

"Not old," he'd said. "Tried and true. Like you."

Marines always knew how to build Dickey up, and she needed it. Her posthysterectomy bleeding was so heavy it required a second surgery, where they discovered her bladder had been nicked. Luckily, things improved after that. Since the pathology on the nasty little fibroids that had been causing her so much trouble was clear, she took it as a rubber stamp of approval for the trip. Her doctor, Aunt Lutie, and Stevie couldn't disagree more. But ultimately, none of them could stop Dickey. She promised she'd take it easy, and she had.

Mostly.

Though she's sad not to be with Tien and the Sea Swallows—she's not yet up for multiday foot patrol through mud and mangrove—she likes being with Nelson and the helo fleet, including men from the ever-growing South Vietnamese Army. Not only is Nelson a great leader, but he's easy on the eyes. Further enhancing his attractiveness is his devotion to his family. He carries a photograph of his pretty red-haired wife and their two little kiddies everywhere. Every time he goes out for battle, Dickey catches him touching the pocket over his heart where he keeps the picture.

Dickey longs to photograph Nelson and the men in this chopper. The image would win awards. It would show a United States Marine fighting shoulder to shoulder with the South Vietnamese for their freedom. Aside from its poignancy, such a photograph would counter the communist lie plastered on propaganda that Americans would never degrade themselves by putting themselves on the line for Asians. The helo in which they travel, however, shakes so violently that the picture would be nothing but a blur. Yet again, Dickey thinks her best work will be forever censored by man or circumstance.

Returning to Vietnam—to Binh Hung—she felt as if she were coming home. She could never have predicted a hamlet in Southeast Asia could give her so much of what she'd always been searching for and had never fully found: career success, belonging, family, and camaraderie, all in one place.

Aunt Lutie frets that Dickey doesn't have a man, but Dickey assures her she never wants to marry again. She doesn't feel lonely. She has the kind of love about which Father Hoa has preached. It's the brotherly love the apostles spoke of in their letters that they knew so deeply from their teacher. It's a love of equals in generous, self-giving support of the other and with a common goal. It's laying down one's life for one's friends. Dickey doesn't need anything more.

Last night, Dickey and Nelson threw a dance party for the villagers. They put on Chubby Checker and taught Vinnie and Lai and all of them the twist and how to pony. All that boogety shooing made Vinnie hysterical with laughter. He might have wet his pants.

Hell, I might have wet mine.

Dickey had recently sent Aunt Lutie a picture of giggly little Vinnie and herself and said he was the only man Dickey needed in her life, the kind who kept her laughing and whom she could throw over her shoulder and put in time-out when he misbehaved. In her next letter, Dickey will write to Aunt Lutie about the dance party and send pictures of herself with the children in the school, and the women of the Home Guard, and the men of the Sea Swallows. She hopes it, and her assurances of good health, will settle Aunt Lutie's worries.

The green jungle opens below them. Beyond the brown-puddled rice paddies, the village of their destination appears: Vinh Quoi. It's one of the satellite villages the Sea Swallows engulfed and hoped to have made safe. Dickey's heart sinks as she sees confirmation of what they feared. Bright-orange fires burn in all the structures that aren't already leveled. There's not a living soul in sight. She takes a picture out the window and hopes it won't be too blurry.

Binh Hung lost radio contact with Vinh Quoi two days ago—never a good sign. Shortly after, a teenager from the village came, having run and swam and waded all the way, to report an ambush. Most of the families were now missing their fathers; some were missing mothers and some children. Tien's group set out by canal and land, and Dickey and the helo team set out for air coverage to clear the area, search for survivors, and bury the dead. She prays all the VC vermin have scattered, but the threat remains.

After the chopper's 360-degree check around the village borders, the pilot starts to take them down. Suddenly, all goes silent.

The engine stalls.

Dickey's breath and heart do, too. Luckily, her mind jumps into action. While they aren't vibrating, she snaps the photograph she wanted when the engine worked. If her camera survives the fall, the picture could still win an award for her, even though she'll be dead. Just as the helo begins to pitch, God must hear someone's prayer because the engine coughs back to life, and they steady. Wide eyes all around soften with relief.

While Dickey's heart returns to normal time, the pilot continues to take them down as if on an elevator. They keep their gazes scanning in every direction, searching for movement. There's nothing below, save the smoke of a dozen smoldering fires. On touchdown,

Captain Quay orders everyone out—his men first, then him, then Nelson, then Dickey. U.S. advisers train and lead, but orders to soldiers fighting for South Vietnam come from their own people.

Dickey makes a mental note to tell Aunt Lutie in her next letter that she let Nelson help her out of the helo instead of jumping herself. She had to tell him about the surgery and was relieved he still thinks the world of her, a woman he once didn't want in the field with him.

While two companies scatter to the borders of the village, the rest of them search the homes and buildings. The dead lie everywhere. Most were shot, some were stabbed, and some burnt. Some lie without discernible wounds, eyes closed, looking peaceful as sleepers. One of them is a child of about two, lodged half under his mother. She clearly moved in front of him as a shield, and the bullet that went through her heart must have also passed through his.

Dickey takes deep breaths to steady her emotions and lifts her camera to take what will surely be a picture to end all wars. Suddenly, her view is blocked by an old Vietnamese man with a long wispy beard. He stands in front of her and shakes his head, his eyes red with tears. An interpreter comes over and tells Dickey it's the man's daughter and grandson, and he cannot stand for Dickey to photograph them. She's about to argue—she longs to explain to him that without the photo, their deaths might be for nothing—but the old man's anguish is too great to disturb further.

Sickened by the murder of the innocent, the grief of old men, and censorship, Dickey moves away and photographs the other dead, the burning huts, and the damaged buildings. Coming around the corner of one, she finds survivors—a man with two small children on his lap. Dickey snaps their photograph. The baby boy looks at her in silent curiosity, but the little girl stares blankly in the distance. The interpreter catches up to Dickey and reveals these were related to the dead woman and the boy. Dickey's heart aches for them.

Will humanity ever get off this wheel of war and retaliation? If children continue to see their parents slaughtered by enemies—and the seeds for vengeance are planted—it's unlikely.

The members of the patrol carry the dead, lining them up inside a building and covering them with tarps, sheets, or whatever can be found. Rows of singed, battered, and desecrated bodies grow.

A shout, followed by scuffling sounds, draws Dickey and Nelson to a concrete building. Inside a young barefoot woman dressed in black pajama-type clothing is pinned to the ground, struggling under a South Vietnamese fighter who works to tie her hands behind her back. Her gaze meets Dickey's, and though there's a flare of curiosity, her face quickly blanks. Once the prisoner is bound and subdued, she turns away from them and refuses to speak. Dickey's interpreter tells her the young woman was with the enemy.

Why did she align herself with the VC? Was it fear or belief?

The body of the child under his mother assaults Dickey's senses. Her lip curls in disgust. She spits at the prisoner's feet and leaves her. On the way out, Dickey's interpreter stops her.

"Don't do that," he says.

"Why? She's part of the VC scum who massacred women and children."

"How do you expect to win the heart and mind of the enemy if you spit at her? She has a warrior's heart, like you, but she's misguided. Bring her to your side, or there will be no hope for the future."

"You can bring her to your side. My eyes are still seared from the dead kid."

War in my heart. War in her heart. There is no end to war.

Uneasy, Dickey walks away from the building. She sees the jungle's edge where the men patrolling are on high alert. Survivors creep back to the village by the dozen, mostly women, children, and the elderly. Mothers carry babies strapped to their chests and backs. Toddlers and young kids follow like lambs. Many of them cry, but just as many are in shock. There are ten or so wounded lying in the dirt, at various stages of hurt. Dickey snaps pictures of them, then a woman with blood on her arms and a man with blood running down his face.

A young woman holding a baby calls for help. Her husband lies before her in the dirt in a mess of blood. The medic runs over and checks for a pulse. He looks up with sorrow at the woman, mumbling that her husband is gone. She begins to cry, wailing like a siren. She pushes her baby toward Dickey. Dickey swings her camera behind her neck and takes the child, trying to envelop him in love and security if only for a moment. His sweet little face is just inches from Dickey's. He reaches for her glasses, but his mother's distress distracts him. He twists toward her, seeking her arms now wrapped around his dead father. Dickey rocks the baby while he squirms, and the blessed boy doesn't cry. His mother has enough tears for them both.

In Dickey's savage heart, she indulges a wish for vengeance. She thinks if she had a gun instead of a camera, she might shoot that girl VC. Dickey hates herself for thinking of such violence. She must shoot with her camera instead, so she might preserve and bring life instead of taking it.

Triage. Transport. Refugees.

Motherless. Fatherless. Childless.

A fleet of choppers.

New villagers in Binh Hung. Women who need husbands. Children who need fathers. One man who needs a wife. A new prisoner.

Grief like a storm cloud is heavier when Father Hoa and Bernie greet them in Binh Hung. Dickey thinks their faces are serious because the radioman briefed them about Vinh Quoi and what was coming, but Father Hoa has his own bad news. Tien's patrol was ambushed, likely by the same VC cell that had destroyed Vinh Quoi.

"Tien?" Dickey asks, horrified.

"He survived, but we lost thirty."

"Thirteen?"

"Thirty."

Dickey breaks, no longer able to hold back her tears. She has the irrational thought that if she had been with Tien's group, this wouldn't have happened. She was their lucky rabbit's foot. The tiger to fight the dragon.

"Show me," she says.

Father Hoa leads her to the briefing building, where all the dead are laid, already interred in rows of ornate black-and-gold coffins the village had made years ago anticipating heavy casualties but which they'd rarely had to use until now. Mourners sit by the dead, burning incense and candles, placing their hands and heads over the coffins, wailing and praying. Dickey sees Anh in the distance, crying over someone she loved. Everyone here is related by blood, theirs or Christ's.

Thank God it wasn't Tien.

As if conjured, Dickey feels Tien's hand on her shoulder. His eyes are red and all the easy confidence he used to carry is gone. He has dark circles under his eyes and his shoulders are slumped. War has aged him. Dickey wraps her arms around him and feels the small shudders that reveal his crying.

"The funeral mass will be this evening at six o'clock," says Father Hoa.

Dickey pulls back from Tien and nods at Father Hoa. She wants to get cleaned up for this service.

Dickey uses the shower newly installed at the barracks for the women of the Home Guard. Burning from the heat and horror of the day, she keeps the water ice cold and scrubs her nails, face, and skin clean, while crying out as much as she can. After toweling off, she returns to her area and dresses in what Buu had lent her months ago for the wedding. Dickey takes care with her hair and makeup. She pins her paratrooper wings and Sea Swallows patch to her dress and wraps her waist with her trench-knife belt.

Nowhere is safe, not even Binh Hung. I will never again lie to myself about that.

In the bunker community room, Nelson and some men are seated, talking quietly and smoking, wearing clean uniforms. When Dickey walks in, they stand, their eyes open wide. Their admiration gives Dickey no pleasure as it would have under other circumstances. They proceed wordlessly to the church.

Because of the weeping from the congregation, Dickey can barely hear Father Hoa or Bernie's whispered translation of the mass eulogy. Her own grief has grown too great for tears—not only for the dead and those who mourn them, but for herself. She feels suffocated. She knows, as usual, she idealized what was happening here. She has even romanticized it. She allowed herself to think Binh Hung was a new and impenetrable Eden where all were safe. But on this earth, there exists no such place. Even the usually confident Bernie looks deflated. The serpent has triumphed in the garden, and they will get no rest from it. Dickey feels empty and aged and almost without hope, until the end of the service.

The lights are put out and the back doors of the church are opened. The headlights from a transport truck shine in and Tien's sister, Lai, strides forward and stands before the altar facing the congregation. She wears traditional Chinese dress and carries a sword. Dickey is struck by how—even in the short time she was gone—Lai has grown taller, leaner, and fiercer. She holds the weapon straight out and looks down at it like it's a baby. The light from the headlights illuminates her face. Flute music begins from the back of the church, and Lai begins to dance.

At first her movements are quiet and mournful, graceful and slow, honoring the dead and their souls. Then, a drum starts. Lai's face hardens into the mask of a warrior. Her movements grow brisk, athletic, and powerful. All are held captive in her thrall. Dickey is dazzled by how striking Lai is. With the music, Dickey's heart beats faster, as if she's being pursued. Lai draws the sword and spars with an invisible enemy, the bogeyman, and one can feel her gaining ground. The music becomes faster and louder, and with a battle cry Lai makes a final thrust and then raises the sword in victory. The headlights again illuminate her eyes.

Dickey has the presence of mind to snap a picture.

Lai saved my life with that dance. She gave me hope. She gave it to us all.

Dickey prays the ripples of Lai's symbolic victory and the new confidence it produces in all of them will extend outward, healing the world.

Later, after Dickey develops the picture, she puts it in her breast pocket to carry near her heart into battle, to remind her for whom she fights, now and forever.

July 1962
Pennsylvania, Michener House

Dear Stevie,

What a whirlwind this time has been. Vietnam. A stateside return. Reunion with my beloved friend Bob Morrisey and his beautiful family in DC. Briefings at the Pentagon. Lecture tours for the book. (Sad we couldn't make that convertible happen.) Mike Wallace's show. Endless women's clubs. I'm busier than I've ever been, and I'm glad.

The Micheners are taking good care of me, and tomorrow I'll attend the nearby reunion of the U.S. Marine Corps Combat Correspondents and Photographers Association.

Much to Mari's dismay, Jim is running for Congress. He was inspired after working on President Kennedy's campaign. Jim is still cranking out books like a machine, though. Mari worries he moves too fast and works too hard.

Jim is still in tight with **Reader's Digest** but knows my relationship with them is strained. I can no longer pretend everything is hunky-dory with the government's handling of cold and hot wars. I don't know how much longer we'll be able to work together.

My new partner, National Geographic—who took me on because of the Polk award—is just as prestigious anyway, and I have big news. **Nat Geo** is not only paying me a bundle for a multipage spread for my piece, "Helicopter War in Vietnam," but they are giving me...drum roll...

THE COVER!

They are using my aerial shot of the VC burnt village of Vinh Quoi on the cover. Inside includes one of the best photos I've ever taken: a *helo shot of my buddy U.S. Marine Sgt. Nelson West—that big stud of a fella I wrote you about—surrounded by South Vietnamese fighters. The only reason I was able to capture the picture was because our engine had stalled, and the vibrating stopped for a moment. I thought the picture would be published posthumously, but the pilot was able to regain control. Dickey's guardian angel comes to the rescue again.*

After a short spell in NY, I'm heading back to DC for more Pentagon meetings in late summer and early fall.

> *See you soon,*
> *The Angel of Binh Hung*
> *(What my village daughter, Lai, calls me. Hilarious!)*

March 1963

Dear Aunt Lutie,

I'm sorry I'm not able to visit to celebrate my birthday with you. I've been pulled back into the Cuba situation. I cannot put pen to paper about it to say more than that. But please know I'd prefer to be with you over the hot, smoky, smelly briefing rooms where I've been learning things I want to unlearn.

On a lighter note, I've enclosed the National Geographic with my cover and story in case you don't already have it. I've never been prouder of a long-form piece, and I hope you'll see—through the faces from Binh Hung to Vinh Quoi—just why I'm so often called back to that land of my heart.

I've also enclosed the press release for my latest award. The shot of a U.S. fighting man and the South Vietnamese men in the helo got me the National Press Photographers Association Picture of the Year. As it is the pinnacle of my career so far, I wish we could have celebrated in person, but I was too busy getting the runaround all over India about the reported pressure from Chinese communists at the border there, and the reported American weapons in the hands of Indian military. I never got close enough to the action to see anything of the sort. The most significant thing I got to eyeball in India was a men's bathroom. Because of my preferred olive drabs, slicked-back hair under my bush hat, and lack of makeup, an Indian security guard thought I was a man in the ladies' room. He dragged me out of the women's bathroom and tossed me in with the men. My press pals and I got the laugh of a lifetime from it. Never a dull moment with Dickey.

I'm heading to New York to dump my dead houseplants, air out the apartment, and organize my files. I have such a robust historic archive, and no more space in my flat, so I'm donating my files to the Historical Society at the University of Wisconsin. Then it's off to give the keynote at the Girl Scouts' Annual Conference. I'm going to tell those young women they can do anything they want as long as they are willing to sacrifice absolutely everything to do it. It's true for my life, and I choose this life every day. I know it's hard for my loved ones to understand, which gives me sorrow, but it's impossible to explain unless you have the call. It feels a little like the priesthood, though I'm a far unworthier vessel than any priests I know, and I don't know that I've saved a single soul. Working on my own is hard enough.

The crown jewel of my New York trip will be receiving an award from the International Rescue Committee for my work with refugees. Stevie will be my date at a small luncheon at the Overseas Press Club. I wonder if Mr. Cherne will be there to present the award to me, but I won't hold my breath. He did sign the letter announcing my award and thanking me for all I've done for world refugees, particularly those displaced by communist governments. It gives me peace closing that chapter of my life, which is a big deal.

After that, my next mission will be underground. Communication will be sparse. Stevie has the number of a contact in Washington whom you can reach out to in case of emergency. Do not worry for one moment. I will be based in the States, though I'll be deployed on missions over foreign waters. I'll be far safer than I've been in Laos, and as safe as I've been in Binh Hung. Less than if I took up wedding photography, but if my knees continue to ache at the rate they're going, your prayers for that will be answered sooner rather than later.

All my love,
Dickey

THIRTY-SIX

JUNE 1963

Miami, Florida

"The Angel of Hialeah."

Dickey stubs out her cigarette, stands from the high table at the bar, and tries to hide a coughing fit under laughter.

"People keep calling me 'angel,'" she says. "Utter nonsense. How the hell are you, Felipe?"

Dickey's old pal from Cuba wraps her up tightly in his arms.

"I've been better," he says.

Felipe looks as if he hasn't slept in weeks, and he reeks of alcohol. His hair is cut short and gelled smooth, so in spite of the haggard face he's still as attractive as ever.

Somehow, more so.

His wife peeks out from behind him, her enormous, pregnant belly reaching Dickey before Raquel's embrace. She's adorable as ever, though she too has dark circles under her eyes.

"Oh, sweet *mamacita*," says Dickey.

"Maybe a girl this time?" Raquel says.

"Girl or boy, another soldier for your growing army."

"Hey, we're navy," jokes Felipe, pulling out a chair for his wife and taking his own.

They meet at the Copa Lounge in Little Havana. The bar is a shadow of its former self. It used to be the famous Ball and Chain, where Black artists Ella Fitzgerald, Billie Holiday, Count Basie, and more performed. A lawsuit from Count Basie for insufficient payment, however, along with the bar's criminal founders racking up debt, made it change hands. It's still packed, though its patrons look tired, and the music comes from a jukebox instead of an instrument.

Dickey is on what might be her last assignment for *Reader's Digest*. They wouldn't send her to Binh Hung or anywhere in Vietnam but advanced her a thousand dollars for a picture story on Castro's former revolutionaries, now fighting him with all they've got from American shores. Dickey had been gobsmacked to learn members numbering in the thousands—including some of Castro's highest-ranking men, like Captain Orlando from Radio Rebelde—are now part of the anti-Castro movement. Hobart Lewis instructed Dickey that this piece needs to be as journalistic as possible.

"It's not about you," Hobart said.

"*National Geographic* doesn't share your view," said Dickey. "I was all over that award-winning picture story."

"You know what I mean," he said.

Dickey had more clout since her awards started coming, but Hobart still wanted to control her. He didn't think readers wanted her inserted in the story. She believed he was wrong, but she didn't push hard, not if they would finance the anti-Castro coverage. *National Geographic* wanted her in Cambodia, but she couldn't bear to start new relationships with new people outside of Vietnam. She was working every angle to get sponsorship to return, but until that date, it was back to Miami and maybe Cuba, if she could get onboard a raid boat.

Felipe orders daiquiris for Dickey and himself. Raquel sticks to water and watches her husband with every sip, her face a mask of worry.

"Your guys sure are fickle," says Felipe, getting right down to business. "First they finance our ops, then they pull out the rug."

"Yeah, getting that close to Armageddon scared everyone," says Dickey.

After the Cuban Missile Crisis, which almost led to nuclear war between the United States and the Soviet Union, both countries backed down from hastening the end of the world. The United States said agencies from the FBI to the coast guard would prevent Cuba raids originating from U.S. soil if Soviets promised to decrease the number of soldiers in Cuba. From that point on, Commandos L, for Liberty—as the anti-Castro guerrillas were known—no longer received financing from the CIA, and they resented it. They'd started calling themselves Commandos X.

"If Kennedy had ordered air support for the Bay of Pigs invasion," says Felipe, his voice a growl, "and Castro could have been overthrown, we'd never have gotten to that place. Thousands of Cuban kids were shipped here by parents who thought they'd soon be reunited once Castro was deposed. Now there are a bunch of unaccompanied children stuffed in group and foster homes all over the States, and parents risking their lives on old rafts and single-engine skiffs trying to escape across the Straits of Florida to get to them. He doesn't have a lot of fans in our corner."

"I'm careful not to judge those at the top when I've never sat at their desks."

"Their desks are very far indeed from where little people like you and me have to live."

"I'll drink to that."

They do.

"So, when will you take me to the men?" she asks.

"I have a favor to ask."

"Fire away."

"We need a house. A headquarters. The FBI is all over us, so we can't rent without raising suspicion. But you can."

"You want me to rent a place to act as a guerrilla command center for a group Kennedy has blocked and whose chances of beating Castro are almost nil."

Dickey thinks of Aunt Lutie, of Stevie and her reporter friends. They would all tell her this is a terrible idea. She thinks of Hobart Lewis not wanting her inserting herself in the story. She thinks of Robert telling her she's too old for this nonsense.

Raquel reaches across the table and takes Dickey's hands.

"My sons deserve to return to the land that is their home," says Raquel. "Free to worship in church, get an education free from indoctrination, and choose their paths forward rather than being forced into slave military service under communist commanders who drain the blood of prisoners before execution to sell to the North Vietnamese. Our parents deserve to live out their final days in freedom, praying in the churches they built with their own hands. And it's not just Catholics being persecuted. Three Protestant ministers were just executed. Please, Miss Dickey. Help us."

Dickey thinks of the refugees scattered throughout the world because of totalitarianism. She thinks of the award Leo Cherne just gave her for her work with refugees. He was so kind in his remarks about her—praising her for going behind enemy lines like no one he'd met before—that she forgave him for the way he'd left her dangling all those years ago. She thinks of Father Hoa and Bernie. The futures of Tien and Lai and Vinnie. She thinks of the Hungarians, Zoltan and Ferenc and his baby girl. She thinks of Maria Marothy. Castro's roundup of all the priests and bishops, expelled to Spain. The Cuban people, who fought so hard to get out of fascist control only to land under the hammer and sickle of communists. The Cuban families desperate to be reunited.

Bernie told her, in China there is a saying.

If you don't go into the lair of the tiger, how will you retrieve its cub?

She thinks of Fidel.

Sangre de tigre. *Tiger blood.*

"I'll do it," Dickey says.

THIRTY-SEVEN

JUNE 1963

Miami, Florida

From the outside, no one would guess the little yellow two-bedroom with a sunroom and grapefruit trees, at the end of a cul-de-sac in the largely Cuban-immigrant-populated Hialeah, is acting as a barracks, safe house, and explosives factory for anti-Castro guerrillas.

Dickey had to laugh when she signed the six-month lease for 1261 SE 8th Court under the name she hadn't used in a long time: Georgette Meyer.

Marmee would be turning over in her grave.

Only later did Dickey reflect that might be for good reason.

The advance she and her agent negotiated from *Reader's Digest* was so generous that Dickey was able to not only rent the house, but also upgrade the motors on one of the speedboats used by Commandos X. She would love to ride along on a boat raid mission and take another award-winning picture, especially in support of old friends like Felipe. She considers it goodwill on behalf of the United States, who couldn't openly support the missions to exchange weapons and refugees but who'd surely turn a blind eye, if not cheer from the shadows.

At the house, while *son cubano* music plays on the radio, Dickey, Felipe, and a revolving door of men from the anti-Castro underground assemble bombs. They take breaks to smoke outside, far away from fuses and flammables. It's a motley crew of pirates, from the United States and Cuba, moving between Miami and the Florida Keys, training in weaponry and preparing for raids and refugee rescue missions.

Often Felipe meets Dickey's gaze over the arsenal, stewing with resentment. He resents the Castro family and revolutionaries for hire, like Che, who've forced this life upon men like Felipe. Guerrilla units attract mercenaries—shady types in search of money and adventure, who leech onto earnest men trying desperately to free the home they love from the clutches of the dragon. Felipe's tension and paranoia are palpable. Her old friend is growing dangerously dark of heart.

A moving truck was parked across from the house a few days ago and hasn't budged since. It has raised suspicion in the group and puts Felipe on edge even more. Dickey takes a picture of the truck out the window to show her DC contacts. She hopes it's one of them, and not one of Castro's spies, who are thought be crawling all over Miami.

"This is what we've been reduced to," Felipe tells her, swatting at mosquitoes in the mangroves of No Name Key. "Working with men like him."

Felipe refers to the six-foot-eight, twenty-six-year-old ex–U.S. Marine and paratrooper Gerry Hemming, helping train Commandos X in guerrilla warfare. After leaving the military, Gerry fought with Castro's revolutionaries, but when communism reared its ugly head, Gerry vacated the island and has been anti-Castro ever since. He's a character no one quite trusts in spite of the quantity of weapons he's been able to procure for the group. There's something off about him, and he's always glaring at Dickey.

"Fire him," says Dickey. "As a long observer of guerrilla warfare, I could train the men. There's not one thing Gerry has taught that I couldn't have. Except maybe weapons. But you'd have that covered."

Dickey thinks the mercenaries are like the male reporters who resent her for having the courage to go to the front when they won't. There are always men who resent a woman working with them, a woman who knows more about bomb assembly and guerrilla tactics than they do. Most of Felipe's men, however, have welcomed her, so she keeps her eyes on them. As much as possible, she avoids Gerry—who lurks, leers, and sneers at her like a grade school bully, and the two young ex-air-force men he's brought on, whom she knows only as Hargraves and Collins. She doesn't trust the American mercenaries farther than she could throw them. But Gerry has a pipeline for weapons and says he's committed to overthrowing Castro at any cost, so they have no choice but to trust him.

Dickey takes time each week to call General Lansdale at the Pentagon from a tap-free line. She's been keeping him up to date on her dealings. At first, he was supportive, but as the months pass, his tone changes.

"It's time to start disentangling," he says.

Dickey thinks of the arsenal they've assembled. Of the hundreds of bombs. Of the plans being made for the upcoming boat trip across the Straits of Florida to drop off weapons for the Rosa Blanca Cuban resistance and collect refugee parents desperate to be reunited with their children.

"Negative, sir," she says. "I'm in too deep. I won't let Felipe and the Cuban freedom fighters down."

"Be very careful with him."

"Felipe? Don't you mean Gerry Hemming?"

"Hemming, of course. But Felipe...there are some red flags. You're in a little over your head, Dickey, and I care for your safety."

"Felipe is an old friend. He's as suspicious of the mercenary types as I am."

"Yes, but some of his associations in the name of the ends justifying the means with Castro are causing increasing alarm. He might be losing his head."

"No, sir. He's as clearheaded and clear-hearted as always," she says, feeling a tinge of guilt for misrepresenting the truth. "He fights for his land. For his children and his family to enjoy the fruits of a free and democratic Cuba. He'll lay down his life for the cause."

"I have no doubt," says Lansdale. "But his wish for vengeance is growing. FBI men think he's tangling with dangerous people for financing. Be careful. Keep your eyes open. Listen to your instincts. When they tell you to bail, do it fast and without a second thought."

"I appreciate your concern and promise to be careful."

After the call, Dickey tries to watch Felipe with as much detachment as she does the rest of the men. Unfortunately, she can only see him in light of his family, dinners around the table at their little place on the Miami River, where the boys—already fluent in English and adjusting to their new home—are happy, even if their parents have a perpetual shadow hanging over them. She sees him in the adoring eyes of the refugees he risks his life to transport across the Straits of Florida, parents and grandparents who look at him with admiration and respect, and some who call him their savior.

Felipe has started storing bombs and weapons aboard the boat docked at his house so they don't lose everything if Dickey's place gets raided. The temperature grows every day, and not just on the thermometer.

One steamy night in September, Felipe comes over to where Dickey and a small group of Cuban members of Commandos X make plans for a boat weapons and refugee exchange in Cuba. After hurrying through the secret knock, Felipe enters sweating and shaking his head.

"What's wrong?" asks Dickey.

"The damned feds," Felipe says, sitting heavily. "Tracking me night and day. I had to get a taxi to a safe house to a café, where I just got another taxi to come here. Yesterday I asked the suits in the black car across from my place if they'd like to give me a ride, so we all didn't have to waste gas. They laughed and said they were just doing their jobs. They're the kind of Joes you'd like to smoke a cigar with if they weren't willing to haul you off to prison."

"I know," she says. "It's awful how they're cracking down, but they aren't moving in. It's for show."

"Not for long," says Felipe. "I can feel it. It makes me sick how they've turned on us. How we're forced to finance the fight for democracy they have every bit the stake in that we do, with any dirty money we can get our hands on. We work all hours of the day and night to provide for our families and finance a war. Kennedy's damned shiny-toothed mug is everywhere. Everyone thinks he's some saint when his dealings are dirtier than ours. And you've heard he's tiptoeing around withdrawing American military aid in Vietnam. He's trying to bail out on them the same way he did with us."

Dickey's eyes open wide. Being underground and so focused on the story and cause here, she's been paying little attention to the world. Her heart races at the thought of support for the South Vietnamese being pulled. She'll ask Lansdale the moment she's able to talk to him.

Felipe continues to rant, his mood, speech, and eyes growing darker by the second. Lansdale's caution rings in her ears.

Should I bail? she wonders.

"Some days I feel like a damned prostitute," Felipe says.

Dickey's *Digest* advance has run out, and she's dipping into savings just to eat at this point, but she has great pictures and copy. Once she gets photos onboard a raid boat the story will be solid gold, and the American people will have awareness of the courage and bravery of the freedom fighters. Support might return to them.

Dickey snaps to attention. Sirens outside are growing louder. Felipe stops talking and the men and Dickey look at each other, listening. Suddenly, lights flood the house.

"*Mierda!*" says Felipe.

The men spring to action. Dickey directs them to clear the refrigerator of the nitroglycerin and rush it to the back bedroom where the arsenal is kept. They do so, throw sheets over the bed, and lock the closet and bedroom doors. She shoos them toward the back door, but there's banging at the back and the front.

"Customs, open up!"

"We're done," says Felipe.

"Go to the living room and put on the TV," says Dickey. "I'll handle this."

The men obey, and once they're seated, Dickey opens the front door.

"Jeezy peezy, are you rude," she says. "I was in the bathroom."

The men, taken aback to see the angry little American woman scolding them, lower their guns. The one in the front removes his hat.

"Miss, you know as well as I do why we're here. Now let us in so we don't have to destroy property."

"I most certainly do not know why you're here."

The man in front stares past Dickey and points at the refrigerator, where the hastily slammed door has slowly opened. She looks over her shoulder, and when she sees, she groans. In the door shelves, labeled clearly, is the nitroglycerin they missed. She turns back to the feds.

"I don't know how you sleep at night," she says. "Working for Castro like you do."

THIRTY-EIGHT

NOVEMBER 1963

Miami, Florida

The explosives and weapons were confiscated, but neither the rebels nor Dickey were charged. While the government said it could no longer support or promote U.S.-launched anti-Castro raids, they would not prosecute. They did say next time they would not be as forgiving, and the Cuban immigrants were slapped with legal orders not to leave Miami-Dade County.

This directive is ignored, and a month later, while Felipe is traveling to raise money, Dickey joins the remaining Commandos X on a four-boat mission to a remote portion of Cuba to drop arms and collect refugees. The moment their vessels break out into the Atlantic from Biscayne Bay, the coast guard charges. They were waiting. The boats are stopped and boarded, and every single weapon of their forty-thousand-dollar arsenal is confiscated.

The following day, one of the Cuban men of Commandos X calls a press conference near the marina, where some of their confiscated boats used to be docked. He gives an impassioned speech about how the United States is letting down not only the Cuban people, whom they'd promised to support in the work of freedom, but also the entire free world threatened by communism. Dickey is proud to stand at the sides of Commandos X and nod along. When they finish, and the crowd disperses, reporter Andrew St. George finds her. He, too, has been covering the anti-Castro underground.

"Don't you dare accuse me of being too old for this," she says.

"I was going to say *I'm* getting too old for this."

Dickey looks at the man, four years her junior, and thinks he does look older than she does. The Florida sun and guerrilla training are keeping her in shape. He looks bloated and sunburned, obviously in over his head with the anti-Castro commandos. Dickey swats away the thought that she might be, too.

They walk out to the pier. The night under a waxing crescent moon is gentle, with a friendly breeze bringing the brine to them. The old reporter friends light cigarettes and lean on the railing. They are quiet for a long while until Dickey breaks the silence.

"Do you worry sometimes our guys are mixing with the wrong sort?" she asks, looking over her shoulder. "I mean, I know the enemy of my enemy is my friend, but there are rumors of former Batistianos in the mix, mercenaries, and general ne'er-do-wells that are raising my caution flags. Not only that, but anger in these exiled Cubans is growing to a storm. They hate Kennedy. They hate the CIA. They resent the rug being pulled out from under them. I feel like they're becoming part of the arsenal they try to amass. One spark and *boom*."

"First, they're not *our* guys," Andrew says. "We are reporting on them. You have to stop getting so personally involved. Second, when you get in with subversive underground types, it's to be expected."

"I know. I get all tangled up," she says. "There's no hope of that ever changing because I can't write about things unless I live them and feel for my subjects. I have to embed myself in their lives to understand. And they have a point, you know. They've been done wrong. But it's all so complicated. With the Soviets prowling, one does have to tread with caution."

"Fascinating. I never thought I'd hear you use that word."

"I'm growing up. Becoming a woman of wisdom and maturity."

He laughs.

"Anyway," she says, "I'm getting a little tired of watching people with the side-eye. I like to work with the good guys. Where things are black and white, clean and simple. This feels very gray."

"Dickey, don't be naive. Who among us is a good guy, clean and simple?"

Dickey mulls this cynical point of view. Father Hoa's face comes to mind. He's a good guy. His people have pure motives and honorable procedures. Binh Hung is one of the last places on earth that is purely good.

"There is a place. A people," she says. "In Binh Hung, South Vietnam. The first chance I get, I'm going back. Want to join me?"

"No, I'm in it too deep here, and in Central and South America. I don't want to involve myself with a whole other cast of characters and criminals. I've got my hands full. You will, too. President Diem and his brother assassinated? You're going to return to a different Vietnam than you left."

General Lansdale had shocked Dickey on their last call when he told her about the assassination. The Diem brothers had tried to claim a kind of sanctuary at St. Francis Xavier Church, in Cho Lon, but they'd been dragged outside, thrown in a van, and shot en route to prison. Diem's brother's persecution of Buddhists had led to immolations, monks burning themselves in protest. Now the Diem brothers are dead.

Did Kennedy authorize the assassinations? What would this mean for South Vietnam? How about Father Hoa and Binh Hung, who had received so much support from President Diem?

Dickey's mind has been spinning ever since.

She can only work in the here and now, however, so she turns her attention back to her present situation. She needs to return to Felipe and Raquel's place to help with bedtime, now that there's another baby boy in the house. She stubs out her cigarette and pats Andrew's shoulder.

"Well, until next time," she says.

He nods. As she starts to walk away, he calls to her.

"Be careful," he says.

"I just told you I'm being careful."

"No, you said your caution flags are up. But I know Dickey Chapelle, and warning flags have never once stopped her from moving toward danger. In fact, I think she looks for them as guideposts, showing her where to go next."

Dickey starts to argue but then grins and raises her hands in surrender.

NOVEMBER 23, 1963
NEW YORK TIMES
KENNEDY KILLED BY SNIPER IN DALLAS;
JOHNSON SWORN IN ON PLANE

November 24, 1963

Dear Slug,

Thank you for sending the explosives handbooks and for your guidance. Also, thank you for not asking questions. I know you must disapprove of what you imagine I'm doing—and you are not entirely wrong in that judgment—but I appreciated your concern for my safety, trumping any of said disapproval. I promise I will be as careful as one possibly can be when working with explosives and revolutionaries.

The assassination of the president has spun my circles in wildly varying directions. I am, of course, heartbroken for the destruction of human life and the representative of the American Dream. I also know that our new president Johnson understands the threat of communism, and this gives hope to those on the front lines all over the globe working against it.

Where I am currently stationed is getting hot. Too hot to handle much longer. I have one more mission, and then I'll return to New York, and maybe for a visit in Milwaukee.

Until then, kiss the kiddies for me. I've enclosed Christmas presents for everyone, since I don't think I'll make it home by then. Enjoy the cigars!

All my love,
Big Sis

THIRTY-NINE

JANUARY 1964

Miami, Florida

It's Dickey's last mission with the Cuban exiles. She has been living with Felipe's family since her lease ended. She's not willing to sink in any more personal funds and wants nothing more to do with the rebels' money sources. Her lecture tour agent has her booked on a dozen stops, starting next month, and Dickey's looking forward to returning to the circuit.

As a gal who's been ignored, shushed, and talked over most of her life, I can't resist a rapt audience.

The world feels even more unsteady than usual. Kennedy's assassination in the United States and President Diem and his brother's in South Vietnam continue to send shock waves throughout the world. Dickey obsesses about what Diem's killing will mean for Father Hoa and Binh Hung, who received much economic and military support through Diem's channels. The instability will make wary villagers all over susceptible to communist propaganda. It will shake trust.

Then, there's Miami.

Felipe has become a silent man. Dickey understands his pain, but she no longer feels as if she can be of real help to him. Her picture story will be dynamite and will honor the cause, but it has reached its end. It's time to bail. She'll include no photographs of the American mercenaries, Gerry Hemming and his men. They have sullied the cause for her. Besides, they can barely stand to be around each other, she and Gerry each suspecting the other of being a plant by a government intelligence organization.

After a dinner of rice and beans, Dickey helps Raquel put the older boys to bed so she can attend to the infant. The three older boys share a room—two in bunk beds and one on a trundle—and the baby sleeps in a cradle in his parents' room. Dickey has been sleeping on the couch, which is quite cozy, and they all share a bathroom. The family is delighted by the hot running water, something they hadn't experienced since before the revolution. The place is tiny but it's bursting with love and vitality, and Dickey will miss it when she leaves.

"I'm sneaking Oscar in my field pack when I leave," says Dickey, teasing Felipe's eight-year-old son, who was just a toddler when she gave him the stuffed monkey. She'd been delighted to see he still had her childhood toy.

The boy giggles, shouting no—as he does every night—and races her to the bed. Dickey lunges at the stuffed animal, but the boy beats her to it and wraps himself around it. She tickles him, telling him to give up Oscar, but he won't relent.

"Fine," she finally says. "I suppose you've taken good care of him. Keep it up."

Dickey kisses the boy on the head, tucks him and his brothers in, and heads back outside, where the men load the boats with weapons and fuel drums for the journey to Cuba. Their mission is still getting weapons to Cuban freedom fighters, bringing refugees to the States, and—while the exchange takes place—for Hargraves and Collins to try to get pictures of the cache of nuclear weapons from the caves where Soviets are allegedly hiding them.

Dickey helps load the remaining fuel drums on the boats, then heads back inside the house to pick up her camera pack. She stops at the door, arrested by beauty.

In the candlelight, Raquel nurses her baby. An icon of la Virgen de la Caridad del Cobre—Our Lady of Charity, the patroness of Cuba—hangs on the wall next to Raquel. During the 1868 fight for Cuban independence from Spain, the image was the uniting symbol. Now Castro defiles it. His militiamen shot seventeen-year-old Arnaldo Socorro Sanchez on the steps of Our Lady of Charity Church in Havana, while he carried the image in a procession, in defiance of the regime trying to stop religious demonstrations.

If only someone had gotten a picture, maybe the world would do more to help the oppressed people of Cuba.

Dickey pulls out her camera, and after getting Raquel's nod of consent takes the shot.

"You're like the Virgen de la Caridad del Cobre," says Dickey.

Raquel smiles, weary, and shakes her head.

"I wish," she says. "But you will be forever known in our circles as the Angel of Hialeah."

"Still absurd. But thank you."

"It's true," says Felipe, entering the house. "It means more than you can know to have a *yanqui* helping us."

Dickey smiles. It's the first kind word he's said in weeks.

When Felipe sees his wife and newborn son, his face softens. He kneels before Raquel and looks up, adoring. She puts her hands on his head and whispers a blessing. They look like the Holy Family.

The intimacy of the moment is almost too much for Dickey to bear. She takes a picture and then leaves them.

In a few minutes, Felipe climbs aboard his boat with Dickey. He nods at Hargraves, who fires up the motors of the other boat. Hargraves winks at Dickey, but she looks away. He and Collins are even shadier than Gerry, but since they got the boats for Felipe, she's putting up with them.

Yes, indeed, I'll be glad to wash my hands of all of them, she thinks as they pull out of their slips in the quiet of the night and start their journey.

Dickey has a bad feeling. She can almost see the bogeyman looming in every shadow, in every doorway and dock along the river. It feels like a miracle when they hit the Atlantic unscathed and start the journey south for Cuba. The seas grow rougher and choppier by the moment, and the boat rides low and slow from the gasoline drums and weapons. They're pleased with their progress, however, and by the fact that the coast guard has not yet intercepted them. At the first glow of sunrise, the seas lie down and Dickey's shoulders relax.

There's only water in all directions, miles and miles of the most glorious blue-green water and cloudless sky she's ever seen. As the light grows, she snaps pictures: a silhouette of Felipe at the helm, Hargraves and Collins in their boat, a pod of dolphins hopping playfully along. Dying for a cigarette, she holds up her pack and asks Felipe. He looks back over his shoulder at the gasoline drums, frowns, and shakes his head at her.

"There's water everywhere," she argues.

"And gasoline," he says. "And an arsenal. And sharks. And I didn't bring my swimming trunks."

She groans.

"On the way back, you can smoke," he says. "Once we've had success, and when there is far less gasoline."

"You're right," she says. "Okay."

Dickey puts her cigarettes back in her field pack and searches around until she finds the peanut butter sandwiches she made. She holds one out to Felipe, but he grimaces and shakes his head.

"Fine, more for me," she says with a shrug.

The seas pick up again, and every time a large wave comes at them, a deluge of water spills into the boat. Soon, there's a puddle growing in the stern. Dickey finishes her sandwich, places her camera in the bag, zips it up tight, and heads to the back to bail out with the bucket placed there for just such a task. With her full belly, the gorgeous pictures she knows she's taken, and her belief in the mission, her spirits are high. She starts singing "Day-O" while she works, and soon even Felipe cracks a smile. He shakes his head again.

"I never thought I'd have a *yanqui* lady as a crew member," he says.

"Lucky you," she says.

"Yes, we've been really *lucky*," he says, voice dripping with sarcasm.

"It's all about to change," she says. "I can feel it."

Like sun breaking through clouds, Felipe's smile beams forth at her. It's like he's the old Felipe from the Sierra Maestra, full of hope, integrity, and purpose. Her heart warms. She hadn't realized how much she missed the old Felipe.

Then Dickey hears a sound—a pop and a crackle. The word

spark comes to mind followed by a feeling of panic. Suddenly, an enormous blast hits her and knocks her backward, stumbling toward the gunwale. The heat on her skin feels strangely, icily cold. It's fire, and it is burning her.

"Water," she hears herself say.

Then she falls backward, overboard, and all goes black.

JANUARY 6, 1964
THE MIAMI NEWS
WRITER INJURED IN BOAT EXPLOSION

Freelance photographer and war correspondent Dickey Chapelle, 45, was thrown from a boat twenty miles off the coast of Miami after the engine sparked and the full gas drums onboard exploded. She suffered serious burns on her hands and face, was rescued by Felipe Vidal Santiago, 37, and taken by another nearby boat piloted by Americans Roy Hargraves, 28, and Ed Collins, 28, to Jackson Hospital. Chapelle—whose house was raided last year for storing weapons for exiled anti-Castro Cuban commandos—is expected to make a full recovery, though her uninsured camera equipment (worth over $1,500) and what she called the "Pulitzer Prize winners on its film" are forever lost to the sea. When asked to summarize the experience she said it was quite a "blast."

January 1964

Telegram: Dickey to Stevie

Coming home next week, after hospital discharge. Lecture tour starts next month. Need outfits with long sleeves to cover the burns.

APRIL 28, 1964
NEW YORK TIMES
FIGHTING PRIEST REPLACED

Father Augustine Nguyen Lac Hoa, 56, has been relieved of his command. The beloved military and spiritual leader of the hamlet of Binh Hung and borders beyond has been replaced by Major Chuong Quay. Father Hoa made several trips to Saigon to negotiate with Premier Nguyen Khanh and the new government, hoping to keep his command—of which Hoa said he'd been assured—but he later learned of Quay's appointment. Now Hoa thinks leaving Vietnam might be his only choice. American leaders who have been working with Hoa think this change was motivated by jealousy, and fear that removing Father Hoa will mean the inevitable fall of Binh Hung and the surrounding hamlets to the communists.

MAY 30, 1964
THE MIAMI NEWS

WIDOW MOURNS SLAIN CUBAN PATRIOT

Former Lieutenant Commander in Cuba's Navy turned Castro revolutionary, turned anti-Castro commando Felipe Vidal Santiago was executed by Castro's regime, by firing squad—along with three other Cuban exiles—at Havana's La Cabaña Fortress Prison. Santiago had been held there since March and was accused by Castro of working for the United States Central Intelligence Agency, a charge which Santiago denied. The men were trying to smuggle weapons in to anti-Castro resistance and take refugees back to Florida. Santiago's loss will be mourned deeply by the community, including his widow, Raquel, and their four young sons, the oldest eleven years old and the youngest six months.

August 1964
New York City

Dear Aunt Lutie,

It feels as if the world is ending.
   Reader's Digest *and I are done. Nine months of my life underground, wasted. They rejected my long-form photo piece on Cuban exile commandos, and when they shelved my eulogy piece on a dear friend and freedom fighter executed by Castro's regime, I wrote them off forever. I'm gutted.*
   Then, there's Vietnam.
   My beloved Father Hoa has been removed from his command leadership of Binh Hung. He was the only hope for stability in a region plagued with communists. It's inevitable now that it will fall, and probably before the close of the year. If the region falls, the domino effect will be profound.
   President Johnson signing the Gulf of Tonkin Resolution is essentially a declaration of war. Our men believe China's Mao ordered, or at least encouraged, the attack on our destroyers in the Gulf. Johnson wants us drawn into open war in his backyard, where we've been hiding in plain sight for years. I hope the American military machine lets the guerrillas fight as surgically as they've been doing, but it looks unlikely. The hawks like to bring in big guns and that won't work there. I feel so hopeless.
   As for me, I'm finally out of the hospital, following my kneecap surgery. I'm just starting to feel up to my old self, before becoming a paratrooper, though I'm not happy about the weight I've gained. The doctor assures me I'll get back to marine shape in no time, but he

doesn't understand who he's dealing with: a gal who can't sit still for one minute without going bats, let alone weeks.

I'm sorry to be so negative. Switching to good news, for me, that is. It will probably be more bad news for you.

National Geographic *is sending me back to Southeast Asia, and they're paying me handsomely to go. They'll advance me two grand, guarantee over a thousand a month for living, then pay $2,500 for words and $200 per color picture for the article. I'll be there through the New Year; then I promise I'll make my return flight to you in Wisconsin.*

Vietnam has been calling me back for a long time, and I should have known better than to go anywhere else. I ship out to Saigon on September 15, and from there I'll satellite out on missions chronicling our guys trying to cut off the commie supply line—the Ho Chi Minh Trail—from jungle paths to rice paddy canals, from Laos to Vietnam. I'll be covering the waterways with our U.S. and South Vietnamese Navy men. (No jumping out of planes for a bit while recovering from knee surgery.) I'll also try get back to Binh Hung, to see how Father Hoa and the Sea Swallows and all my sweeties—especially that little Vinnie—are doing. I pray Hoa at least stays in Binh Hung to be the spiritual leader of the people, even if he can't lead them in battle.

I know you are already worrying, and I must assure you that I will be in the greatest, safest hands. I'm much more cautious in my old age. I'll practically be a tourist, drinking Pernod while watching sunsets, taking lovely pictures for my scrapbook, picking and pressing tropical flowers in my journal, and gliding through rivers and canals like a Venetian.

Blowing kisses until I can give you the real thing in the New Year.

All my love,
Dickey

FORTY

NOVEMBER 1964

Vinh Long, South Vietnam

"There!" says Dickey, pointing to the line coming from the brush and firing a warning shot from her automatic carbine.

Since she refused the flak jacket, Lieutenant Harold Meyerkord—U.S. Navy adviser to the South Vietnamese Navy—insisted she carry the weapon. He told her the VC now treat all journalists as spies, so she must be armed and, if she spots them, fire warning shots into the air. It felt strange at first to Dickey, adding a gun to her load, but she assimilated fast. She also added a new uniform to her rotation: tiger-striped camo.

When she arrived in Saigon, Bernie was there, meeting with American officials. He gave her the new uniform. It was the same one he wore—the one worn by an ever-growing number of U.S. Special Forces—but tailored to her petite frame. He worried that other units could not protect her the way the Sea Swallows did, so he wanted to do what little he could to help her, even if that was only with her clothing. The tiger uniform had a silvery green base, overlaid with black stripes, like the coats of those felines native to the jungles of South Vietnam. When Bernie presented it to her, she ran her hands over the material.

"*Sangre de tigre,*" Dickey said, in a whisper.

"What's that?" asked Bernie.

"Tiger blood. Fidel Castro, of all people, said I had tiger blood in my veins."

"No matter the side, the soldier can recognize and respect greatness."

"Thanks, Bernie. Speaking of, how is Father Hoa?"

Bernie was quiet a long time. Finally, he answered.

"He's heartbroken. We all are. The war is growing to a machine. Machines chop and pillage and operate without precision. Machines don't try to win hearts and minds; they destroy bodies. Machines cannot look a man or woman in the eye to see if they are the enemy or not. Machines kill widely and make new enemies."

Bernie's words haunted her all the way to Vinh Long, where she was assigned for her first stop for *National Geographic*. Her mind wouldn't stop spinning.

Am I joining the war machine? Am I coming into a new group to grow an attachment that will be yanked away from me? I won't get attached. I won't romanticize this. I will be an objective reporter.

Dickey wears her tiger camo, and it's a good thing. The jungle here is thick, concealing predators in its fat waxy leaves and deep heavy shadows. Dickey hasn't felt a level of terror in battle like this since World War II when the hospital ship on which she traveled was attacked by Japanese planes. Then, however, she could see the enemy and his approach, and adjust herself accordingly. Here, she's one of a flock of sitting ducks, tense and ready to spring. She touches her breast pocket, where she keeps the photograph of Lai from the sword dance.

This evening's mission is to find and destroy a hut on an old

French sugar plantation, where villager intelligence has warned them that land and river mines are being assembled. On the way, Dickey feels as if eyes watch from every fern and palm. Worse, the VC have put out a directive to kill on sight any American with the South Vietnamese, and U.S. Navy casualties here are growing by the day, up to forty percent of soldiers so far.

Forty percent.

A moment after Dickey's warning shot, the VC she spotted holding the line attached to the water mine pulls it. A geyser erupts mere yards ahead of their leader boat. The Twenty-Third River Assault Group, with which she travels, is a fleet of gunboats patrolling thousands of miles of waterways through three provinces. In the Mekong River Delta region, whatever highways might have once existed have been destroyed by the VC, and roads are mere cart and footpaths. Traveling on sampans and junks on rivers and canals is the way to get around, but it leaves one vulnerable to ambush. The way they continue to fight, however, consoles her. It's still surgical. This is no war machine.

Dickey and the men lie on their stomachs on the boat. While they shoot with guns, she shoots pictures, watching the brush shiver and close around the VC slipping away, silent as ghosts. Soon, all is quiet.

Harold orders his men to beach the boats and start foot patrol—half on the east bank, half on the west. Foot patrol here is equally terrifying as river patrol, with the jungle so dense around them, night falling fast, and the VC disappearing into the landscape like camouflaged snakes.

"Where are you walking?" Harold asks Dickey as they disembark.

"Behind the broad wall of your shoulders," she jokes.

She sees his blue eyes crinkle at the corners and feels a surge of warmth for this tall young blond fighting man.

Do not romanticize him, she thinks. *Do not become attached.*

They start patrol.

In the blackness, Dickey's eyes soon adjust to the surroundings. Clearings are a relief, and she holds her breath between them. They stop and listen. The VC make birdcalls to communicate with each other in the dark. Dickey has been taught the difference between the sounds of the native night birds of Vietnam and the calls the VC make.

All is silent.

They soon reach the outbuildings of the plantation. This is where a new level of terror rises. They must search and clear each building. They rotate who goes first and cover the rest. It's a game of Russian roulette. Dickey knows she can only enter a building once it has been cleared. She holds her breath with each search, the cycle of tension and relief taking an exhausting toll.

Most huts and buildings are empty, but in a small hut along the jungle's edge, the soldiers are surprised to find an old woman crouching in the corner. She holds up her hands. One of the South Vietnamese men moves toward her and quickly searches her. Once he's sure she's not armed, he questions her. They exchange a few quiet words and then the solider turns to Harold.

"The mine building is ahead. The storage barn."

"Thank her," says Harold.

The soldier speaks to the woman, then tries to pass her money. She refuses. The soldier turns back to Harold.

"She is on our side," he says.

Dickey smiles and holds up the camera to see if the woman will allow a picture. She shakes her head no. She's too afraid. Dickey respects the woman's wishes and follows Harold and the men toward the barn.

As they creep toward the building, weapons ready—Dickey's too—she has the strange feeling that they have become one being, one entity. Their hearts pound in unison. Their eyes and ears are fixed together on the same destination, watching and listening. Their mission is the same. They will cover one another. They will protect one another. They will lay down their lives for one another if necessary.

It's Harold's turn to enter first. He takes a deep breath, then pushes open the door.

Too soon, she thinks, sucking in her breath.

Harold slips into the building, followed by one man, then another, then another. In less than a minute, Dickey is waved to come into the barn. She exhales and obeys. The men are safe, and as the old woman had said, there's a cache of mine supplies inside, under an old tarp.

Dickey has a sudden, vivid vision of the men of Commandos X gathered around the table at the Miami house she rented for them. She can see Felipe flash his handsome grin at her. She can't believe he's dead. She thinks back to that awful night the guards in the Hungarian prison threated her with execution. To think of Felipe on a wall, having to order his own murder—as is the custom in Cuba—makes her sick to her stomach. Poor Raquel and the boys. A stab of grief punctures Dickey's heart.

The sound of shots calls her forth from her memory. The men race outside, Dickey following. They run toward the canal, from where the sound originated. Through the dark night, on the western bank, a line of fire climbs the side of a thatched hut, followed by an explosion that turns the sky orange. She snaps a picture of the silhouettes of the men of the River Assault Group, black against the conflagration. VC pour out of the hut, and more gunshots ring out. Her men are soon victorious and have suffered no casualties. Three VC are dead, and their mine cache has been found, confiscated, or destroyed. After the last of the undetonated arsenal is loaded, the men and Dickey move out, back to headquarters.

They glide home in the water. When they break free of the heavily forested canals, Dickey's chest opens and her heartbeat returns to normal cadence. The fleet motors toward a rim of light that has started on the horizon. Birds lift from the mist, the air is cool and damp, and as Dickey and Harold smoke, she thinks she might be perfectly happy.

She's aware how strange it would be for most people to feel content, and even elated, in war zones with strangers, where one can feel the breath of death on one's neck, but perhaps it's because the bogeyman looms so heavily that one can fully immerse oneself in the joy and the gift of life, nature, and camaraderie. In war, where one constantly vacillates between fear and euphoria, one knows the goodness of relying on one's fellow man, gratitude for moments of peace, and the joy of every cigarette, every drink, every meal, and every sunrise as if it is one's last.

It's how we're meant to live, she thinks. *And I am doing it. So, no day is lived in vain.*

"Hey," says Harold, nudging Dickey. "I know when I go, it will be here in the Mekong Delta."

Harold gestures like a showman at the glorious stage around him. His voice is not sad or filled with any false bravado. It's only matter of fact. His death in the field is something he has accepted and will do for mankind. He is a volunteer soldier—one with a vocation—and he will lay down everything, even his life, if necessary, to answer the call to preserve freedom. His sacrifice will allow others to live in safety and comfort, from here to a world away, even if he cannot, even if they do not support him.

"But today's not that day," Harold says. "I didn't see the VC hiding in the jungle. He would have gotten me, you, and a maybe a few others with that mine. I confess, when I heard a woman would be on our boat, I wasn't exactly excited. But you are a soldier. And I owe you my life. So, thank you."

He whispers to his South Vietnamese counterpart sitting behind him. The man reaches in his rucksack and passes something to Harold, who gives it to Dickey. It's the silver twin-sail insignia of the South Vietnamese Navy. Dickey's face warms.

"It's my honor," she says, running her finger over the patch, thinking how glorious it will be to add this to her hat with the others she's earned over the years. The one she most covets is the insignia of the U.S. Marines—the eagle, globe, and anchor. Maybe someday soon she'll have it.

Harold pulls a picture from his breast pocket and hands it to her. From the photograph, a pretty blonde holds a towheaded toddler girl of about two.

"My girls thank you, too," he says.

The faces of his wife and daughter blur in the tears that spring to Dickey's eyes. She doesn't know if she's glad she's seen Harold's family or not. She can't imagine the agony his wife must experience, knowing how dangerous her husband's job is, and being alone raising a baby while he is on the other side of the world. Families serve every bit as much as their soldiers.

Poor Raquel.

Dickey nods, thinks of Lai's photograph in her breast pocket, swallows the lump in her throat, and passes Harold's picture back to him.

"You will make it to February," she says, feeling certain. "When is your tour over?"

"July," he says.

She cannot assure him of that date. She looks away and back at the horizon.

Dickey's stomach churns with anxiety at the thought of how the casualty rate climbs. Then, at the idea of a draft forcing men to fight. When WWII started, every able-bodied, of-age man—and even those who were not—rushed to enlist. There are many now who don't believe America should be fighting in Vietnam. The protests make her angry because she believes those people, in their fat American comforts, don't understand how dangerous any form of totalitarian rule is anywhere, how innocent men and women suffer, and how every small victory of the communists adds gasoline to their fire.

She longs to change minds and hearts, the way Father Hoa does with his prisoners. Conscripted soldiers do not fight the way volunteers do. President Johnson promised that he wouldn't ship American boys off to the jungles of Southeast Asia without their consent, but with the Gulf of Tonkin Resolution, it looks like he'll do just that. Eighty percent of Americans currently support the war effort, but that number is dropping fast. Dickey believes men should want to fight for their country, but she doesn't think they should be forced to do so against their wills.

Binh Hung comes to Dickey's mind. She thinks it's better there, where the soldiers are volunteers, where the wives and children can have their men with them every day until they cannot. There, if the worst happens, the families can touch the bodies before they've grown cold and bury them quickly and know that they were given every possible moment together. There, the men don't go to bars and brothels and accumulate rot on their souls trying to forget the ambushes and remind themselves of what they're missing back at home. In Binh Hung and places like it, the reminder of who and what the men fight for waves them off to battle every day and is there to welcome them into loving arms when they come home.

Dickey knows she's romanticizing but she can't help it. The villagers themselves romanticize it, so is it fiction?

The longing to return to Binh Hung rises in her like aching hunger.

FORTY-ONE

DECEMBER 1964

Saigon, South Vietnam

For a large man, Dickey thinks, Father Hoa looks very small. He sits on the left side of St. Francis Xavier Church gazing up at the crucifix.

When Dickey arrived in Saigon and told Bernie she wanted to visit Binh Hung, he told her Father Hoa was coming to town and to wait for him. She spent two weeks at the Hotel Rex, where the press folks stayed these days, and finished her article for *National Geographic*. It turned out beautifully, with so many vivid, colorful pictures from which to choose that she knew they'd have trouble, which was good for both her bank account and the faces portrayed in the photos. The picture she loved most was of the laughing children playing along a canal. It was strange to see their smiling faces not far from where she'd just returned from a gun battle, but such was life in Vietnam and in so many places around the globe.

When he came to tell her that Father Hoa had arrived in Saigon, Bernie looked more serious than ever.

"More casualties?" she asked.

Bernie nodded.

"Tien?"

"No, he's alive. Anh is expecting."

"That's good to hear. I can't wait to see all of them again."

Dickey expected to see a smile on Bernie's face, but it remained serious. She couldn't penetrate his thoughts.

"I'm not going back, am I?" she asked.

He didn't answer, which was an answer.

Bernie now leads Dickey up the center aisle of the church, their boots thumping in unison along the tiled floor. When she reaches Father Hoa's row, Bernie motions for her to go in and sit next to the priest. Bernie genuflects and follows, slipping past her and Father Hoa to the priest's other side, sandwiching him between them.

The three of them sit in silence for many moments, and in the quiet, Dickey finds herself praying. She prays for Harold, and for his wife and daughter, for Tien and Anh and their baby, and for Lai and Vinnie. She prays for Felipe's soul and for Raquel and their sons. She wonders if it's inevitable that the children of those killed in war or grow up with it continue the cycle. It's all they know, and vengeance is planted deep in the marrow of their bones. As she often thinks, if a child sees his parents killed, how can he or she not want to avenge that death? A dark feeling of hopelessness rises in Dickey. She looks to the altar, to the stained glass, to the candles and the cross to keep it at bay.

"Miss Dickey, I have a lot to say," says Father Hoa. "I will speak in my native tongue and ask Bernie to translate."

Father Hoa speaks in Chinese, Bernie's translations running alongside like a path he clears by a river she cannot traverse. Somehow, as usual, all the words blend together, making her feel as if she understands Chinese. The merging of words and worlds is hypnotic.

"Do you remember where you were during the Great Aurora of 1938?" asks Father Hoa.

Dickey has spent enough time with Father Hoa to know he brings his non sequiturs around to present relevance. She answers in English, Bernie translating back to Chinese.

"Of course," she says. "That was back when I was a nineteen-year-old airfield rat, chomping at the bit because the planes were grounded from the solar storms. My brother and I went outside with our family and watched each night. It was extraordinary—deep reds, blues, and oranges, churning like flames. The papers said Europe was in hysteria. England thought it was a great fire. France thought it was war. Germany thought the red lights were a trick of the communists. But it was just a geomagnetic storm. A really, really big one. What about it?"

"I was thirty years old," says Father Hoa. "I had just been ordained to a parish in my home, in Guangdong, South China. The river pirate who ruled the region hated Catholics and wanted to kill me. Much to the worry of my family, I went to the pirate's home, introduced myself, and offered to educate his five sons in schooling and in jujitsu. He accepted, and we became close. I was able to start three schools in the village, and over time the area became peaceful and prosperous."

"That doesn't surprise me one bit," says Dickey.

"The night of January twenty-fifth, 1938," says Father Hoa, "the old pirate and I and all his sons watched the sky, marveling at the red flame display—the way your family did—and the faint crackles and hisses we heard in the air. Many people were afraid, but it was a wondrous sight, the kind that inspires fear—yes—but fear as awe of God and His power and His creation."

Dickey nods, knowing exactly what he means.

"We were also told it was a geomagnetic storm," says Father Hoa. "But it had felt like a warning. Five days later, Hitler was appointed chancellor. Two months later he annexed Austria. China was sucked into war with the Japanese. I had to exchange my cassock for a military uniform. It was only later still that—scientific explanation or not—we learned the aurora *was* a warning. It was predicted. And we are still living the consequences because the warning came with a directive that was not obeyed."

"Predicted?" asks Dickey. "By whom?"

Father Hoa is quiet again for a moment, then he sighs.

"Mary," he says, in English.

"Mary who?"

"Jesus's mother. On behalf of her Son."

"What do you mean?"

He removes his glasses, sets them in his lap, and rubs his eyes.

"This is going to be a lot for you to hear," he says.

"I beg your pardon, but after all I've seen and lived, there is nothing left in this world to surprise me."

"If it doesn't surprise you, it's because you'll think I'm crazy."

"I do think you're crazy. In the best possible way. If you haven't noticed, I am too. Don't even get me started on Bernie here."

Smiles flash across Bernie's and Father Hoa's faces but disappear as quickly as they arrived. Father Hoa resumes his talking in Chinese.

"In 1917, Mary appeared to three young children in Fatima, Portugal. One is still alive, and she is a nun, Sister Lucia. Mary told Lucia that one day she would need to tell the pope and his bishops to consecrate Russia to Mary's heart, to stop the spread of Russia's errors throughout the world. If the warning was not heeded, and her instructions were not followed, Mary said a worse war than the last would break out. We would know that war was imminent by a great light in the sky. Mary came back to Lucia in 1929 and said it was time to complete the consecration. For unknown reasons—maybe disbelief of a humble woman, maybe what he thought was diplomacy with the Soviets—Pope Pius the Ninth did not do it."

"So, you believe…" Dickey says.

"The Great Aurora was the warning."

For one of only a few times in her life, Dickey doesn't know what to say. Nor does she know what to think, but she respects Father Hoa. She doesn't want him to feel ashamed or frustrated for speaking these things, especially not when he's in such a fraught time. He saves her by continuing.

"Portugal's bishops enacted the consecration of their country in 1931 and in 1938, and as you know, Portugal was spared the horrors of both the Spanish Civil War and World War Two. During World War Two, Pope Pius the Twelfth tried to do it twice, but he wouldn't name Russia specifically during the consecration—he only said 'the world'—for fear of rattling the tiger's cage, and it was not done in conjunction with all the bishops. In 1952, he tried again, but again, no proclamation of 'Russia.' No bishops. Last month, Pope Paul the Sixth tried, but he said 'the *people* of Russia' instead of the whole country, and again, not with all the bishops, so again, Sister Lucia said it did not meet Mary's requirement. So, I'm afraid, Dickey, that communism isn't going anywhere for a long time or maybe ever until the end of linear time, and for that reason, I no longer want to lead people into battles they cannot ultimately win."

Father Hoa's confession of his personal defeat feels enormous. Darkness returns to Dickey. Whether what he says is real or not, Father Hoa's fear and loss of hope is real enough to spread. Morale is everything. There is no esprit de corps without courage, faith, and confidence. The war might as well be over just as it has begun on the large scale.

"We can't roll over and give up," she says.

"We can detach," says Father Hoa. "We can focus sharply on our personal lives, on the people within arm's reach."

He takes her hand in his.

"We can make sure we reconcile with those in our homes, our parishes, and our communities and pray the ripples move outward. As Jesus was dying, He left us His mother. Before Jesus ascended into heaven, He left us His peace."

I leave you peace. My peace I leave to you.

"His mother always points to Him," continues Father Hoa. "It is never about her. And He would have us live in peace. We each have that flame of peace within us. Sometimes we are called to use it for bonfires, but mostly, daily, for candles. Candle to candle until the whole world glows with peace and light."

Dickey's eyes blur with tears. She looks at Bernie. He takes Father Hoa's other hand.

The three of them sit there in the quiet church, holding on to each other as if for dear life. They all know without saying it aloud that they will never again see each other. Dickey will return soon to the United States for her lecture tour. Bernie will settle his family in Washington, DC, to continue his work with American intelligence agencies. Father Hoa will go to Taiwan, where he will wait and pray that whatever must happen to end communism will, and maybe someday he'll be able to return like a sea swallow to his beloved home in China.

Dickey thinks back to the first night she met Bernie and Father Hoa—at the entrance through the three gates of wisdom, compassion, and usefulness—when Bernie asked her which she'd choose. Here they are now, all these years later, still on the paths they've chosen, yet somehow bearing the fruits of those the others chose because they continue to walk together. That is the flame of hope that remains like a pilot light in Dickey, and she will carry it on, always, until her last assignment.

MARCH 1965
THE ST. LOUIS POST-DISPATCH

Lieutenant Harold Meyerkord, 27, of the Twenty-Third River Assault Group was the first officer of the United States Navy to be killed in combat in Vietnam. A fearless leader of thirty operations, he was known for his courage under pressure. After being shot in ambush, he continued to fight until succumbing to a mortal wound. He leaves behind a wife and daughter and will be awarded the Navy Cross posthumously.

FORTY-TWO

APRIL 1965

Madison, Wisconsin

Dickey's eyes are still bloodshot from crying through Harold Meyerkord's Navy Cross ceremony in Missouri, days ago. His brokenhearted wife and parents, and his little daughter who is so young she won't remember him—for better or worse—will be forever in Dickey's own broken heart. The accumulation of losses is starting to weigh too much.

All the peace she'd had in church with Father Hoa is gone. She feels unmoored. She hates that Father Hoa has been forced out of Binh Hung. Hates how the war is changing. Hates the dissention it's creating in the United States. To remember how unifying World War II was, contrasted with how divisive Vietnam is becoming, is agonizing.

Stranger still, there's the growing war for civil rights going on in the States. Two months ago, a state trooper shot a young Black man, Jimmie Lee Jackson, during a voting rights demonstration in Alabama while Jackson was trying to protect his mother, who was being struck by police. Last month, there was horrific violence against Martin Luther King Jr. and the marchers on Selma. Dickey loves her country so much it breaks her heart to see it being ripped apart. She wonders if she should stay home to cover this war here.

When will the world not be plagued by war? When will people learn to sit around a table and talk things out? When will people learn, it's better to walk up to the river pirate's door and offer him an olive branch as the first line of defense rather than beat him, hose him, shoot him into submission.

A sign, shoved in Dickey's face, startles her. She leaps back, having to shake off the thought that she's being ambushed by VC and remind herself she's at the University of Wisconsin, Madison. Dickey's hand moves on instinct to the belt where she normally keeps her trench knife, but thankfully, she left that back in her room at her brother's house. The Vietnamese face in her memory dissolves into the face of the young red-haired white woman in front of Dickey. The student shoves her protest sign in Dickey's way, and screams, "Hawk!"

A swarm of protestors crowd Dickey and those leaving the teach-in, where she just engaged in a debate about American involvement in Vietnam. At the start, Dickey felt that her unique perspective and wisdom would enlighten protestors to at least stop villainizing American soldiers, but emotions ran high, and the debate became a shouting match. She felt as if she were speaking another language. She listened to arguments against colonialism and American involvement where it isn't warranted and tried to explain the Sea Swallows and special forces operations and only ended up sounding like a fool. By the time it ended, she was so flustered and hot and desperate for a cigarette—she'd smoked the only pack with her throughout the teach-in—that she practically ran out of the back of the auditorium.

"Fascist!" a young man yells at Dickey, so close to her his spittle lands on her glasses.

Before she can quell it, white-hot fury erupts.

"You don't even know what a fascist is," Dickey says. "I was being strafed by Japanese fascists at Iwo Jima when you were wetting your bed, you coward."

"Puppet!" yells another young man, hair down to his shoulders.

"Go ahead and burn your draft card," says Dickey. "You're not fit to wear the uniform anyway."

"Hawk," the redheaded woman again yells.

"It's easy to be critical from your nice comfy room here. How about I set you up with a little raw eel and muddy water and see how you fare. Or go live in a VC-controlled hamlet. You wouldn't have enough paper to wipe your ass, let alone the opportunity for literacy and supplies to make a poster."

The shouts of students flare up behind Dickey as she stumbles toward the gate. She'd run all the way to her brother's house if she weren't wearing pumps. She thinks she should have worn her boots and tiger-striped camo. Maybe then they would have understood how all this started, even if that wasn't where it was going.

An arm wraps around her shoulders. She flinches, ready to fight.

"Sis," says Robert. "Come on, let's get you out of here."

Dickey's head pounds. Her heart races. She can barely breathe. It's only when they get to his tree-lined street and the eaves of his pretty red house come into view, gardens bursting with spring flowers, that she's able to speak.

"I'm sorry," Dickey says. "I don't know what came over me. I mean, I do. American men are dying for the protestors' rights to free speech and democracy, and they're vilifying them. I'm sorry if I made trouble for you at your place of work."

"Don't worry about me," he says. "Everybody knows you march to the beat of your own drum."

When they arrive at the house, Marion is out picking up the kids from school. Dickey stumbles up to her room, changes out her heels for the rubber shower shoes she picked up in Laos, and walks out to the flagstone patio, overlooking a koi pond. She plops down on the pillows of the settee, lights a cigarette with a shaking hand, and inhales deeply. Robert soon joins her, placing two glasses of water on the wrought-iron table between them, and sits at a chair on the other side.

"Got anything stronger?" she asks.

"Not until you calm down," he says.

Dickey puts her face in her hands.

"I can't even keep *myself* from making war," she says. "How will the world ever stop?"

"It won't."

"Maybe I'll become a Buddhist."

"They make war on themselves. I can't go to sleep at night without thinking of the immolations."

"Why, Slug? Why?"

"This is why our parents were pacifists. They came from a continent of war. They understood the consequences."

Dickey laughs until a wet cough rattles her chest. She shakes her head.

"I might be a pacifist, too," she says. "After all these years. I had to go to seven wars to learn what they tried to tell me."

Dickey stands up and calls into the backyard. "Do you hear me, Marmee? You were right! I'm a pacifist!"

She plops back down on the swing.

"No, you're not," says Robert. "Your love of the fighting man would never make space for pacifism."

"I don't cover the fighting man because I enjoy watching him fight. I cover him so his fighting is not in vain. And to prevent his children from having to fight. Your children. Clearly, I'm not doing a good job."

The door bangs and the sounds of little voices reach them. Martha and Hans, running, pounding toward them, launch themselves into Aunt Dickey's lap and beg her to play dice and cards and show them again how to fall into a forward roll by jumping down the hall stairs.

Dickey tickles Martha, the little girl squirming and squealing until she extracts herself and runs back to the house, asking when dinner will be ready. Her brother follows, and Marion peeks out her head.

"How was the teach-in?"

"Don't ask," says Dickey.

"That good, huh?"

"Disastrous." Dickey rises and walks toward Marion. "I'll cook tonight. I want a shot at a real kitchen before it's back to campfires and C-rations."

"We've got it," says Robert. "After the day you've had. Stay here."

"Was it that bad?" asks Marion.

"If I could just sit at a bar with the protestors," says Dickey. "If we could talk face-to-face, and I could show them my photographs, I could make them understand."

"Dickey," says Marion. "This war is a lot different from the way it was when you first went. Surely you can understand why students don't want to fight this. Why mothers don't want to send their boys overseas."

"I understand that mothers now coddle their kids. They hover over them. They try to make the path smooth before them. Present company excluded, of course."

Marion smiles.

"Life is too easy now," says Dickey. "When we were growing up, we didn't have time for navel-gazing and philosophy. We had to roll up our sleeves and help our families earn a buck."

"You sound like an old woman," says Bob.

"Not that again," says Dickey.

"You need a break."

"That's what I'm doing here. Taking R and R."

"You are not resting or relaxing. You've lost two men close to you in a very short time and countless others. Your Camelot at Binh Hung has been dissolved. You need to grieve, and grief needs space and time, or it will get stuck in you."

She quiets, knowing what he says is right.

"Look at your arms," he says.

Dickey runs her eyes over the burns and scars, her skin splotchy.

"I'm becoming quite the weathered old soldier, aren't I?" she asks. "Forget leatherneck; I'm leather skinned."

"You don't look a day over one hundred."

Dickey throws a pillow at her brother.

"I thought you were going to stop making war in your personal life," he says with a laugh.

"I'll start tomorrow."

FORTY-THREE

AUGUST 1965

New York City

The longtime head bartender at St. Regis Hotel's King Cole Bar, with tightly cut salt-and-pepper hair and wire-rimmed spectacles, nods at Dickey when she arrives. By the time she makes her way over to her favorite seat, stopping to say hello to the regulars along the way, her drink is waiting.

"Thanks for the Red Snapper," she says.

"Bloody Mary," he says with a wink.

It's funny how things change, she thinks.

It feels like just yesterday Dickey was broke, trying to extract herself from an abusive marriage, being insulted by an agent, unable to get a story with any of the big publications. She still doesn't exactly have a nest egg, but she's doing well enough, and the rest has sorted itself out. The decorations—military and journalistic—bring her healthy satisfaction, especially because she realized along the way they were not the goal. It was the life moments and relationships and the fulfillment of purpose getting the pictures that brought her true satisfaction, and she'll do that until the day she dies, awards or not.

Stevie walks in, brightening when she sees Dickey. Dickey's eyes mist over seeing her happy friend, who always has a bounce in her step, and by the time Stevie wraps her in a big warm hug, Dickey's tears break free.

"What's this all about?" asks Stevie, her New York accent becoming more profound every year. She passes Dickey a monogrammed hankie. "Just like your first day at the RIA."

Dickey laughs.

"I'm getting sentimental in my old age," she says.

"Finally! You're acknowledging your years. Time to retire."

The bartender brings Stevie's Red Snapper, and she blows him a kiss.

"How was the Dominican Republic?" Stevie asks.

"It was good to get back to parachuting. My knees feel great. The marines were as swoony as ever. I was able to connect with the rebel force leader—an old Cuba friend I met the day of the jeep accident. It's a miracle the guy survived. He was as good as dead the last time I saw him. Anyhoo, President Johnson was worried the revolutionaries in the Dominican Republic would go commie after deposing the fascist in charge, but they won't. At least, my old friend assured me so. Hopefully his assurances aren't like Castro's."

Stevie shakes her head.

"I'd love for the world to know you are at the forefront of intelligence gathering," she says.

"They'd never believe it."

"Cheers to that."

The women clink glasses and take a long drink. The piano plays soft jazz. It feels as if they are in a womb of luxury and comfort. Dickey revels in it like a warm bath before her next deployment.

"So, can you get back to Binh Hung?" asks Stevie.

"Not this time. I couldn't get *Nat Geo* or *Reader's Digest* to send me back, so I'm off to DC next week to try to get the *National Observer* to at least send me to Vietnam to cover action somewhere else. My Pentagon buddy is going to put in a good word for me."

"Why won't the other magazines send you back?"

Dickey takes a drink and looks at the piano player.

"They think it's too dangerous," Stevie says, answering her own question. "They don't want your blood on their hands."

Dickey lights a cigarette.

"Do you have some kind of death wish?" says Stevie.

"No," says Dickey. "I have a calling. And if I go while fulfilling that mission, that's no tragedy. Dying slowly of cancer or heart disease or boredom—no, thank you. When I go, it will be a blaze of glory."

Stevie shakes her head.

"I'll never understand you," she says. "But I do love you."

"I love you, too."

The bartender comes over and asks if the ladies want another.

"Just a beer, please," says Dickey.

"Martini, please," says Stevie.

When he leaves them, Dickey leans close to Stevie.

"Changing subject," Dickey says, "I've got most of my files organized to donate to the Historical Society at the University of Wisconsin. I have half my pictures and my photo agent has the rest, so she'll box those up to send. I'm happy the Historical Society will still take it all after the pushback I got from protestors at the teach-in."

"It is getting hot at home," says Stevie. "Doesn't it seem like the time to start covering wars here?"

"If my body ever does prevent me from keeping up in the field, I'll consider it."

"Good. Then I'll be praying for the complete breakdown of your knees and your ankles."

Dickey pushes Stevie on the shoulder.

"Seriously, when do you think you'll go?" asks Stevie.

"The fall. October. Barry Farber at WOR Radio gave me a tape recorder to pack. He wants live recordings from the field. So, I'll have to navigate carrying that, my cameras, my field pack, and my carbine."

"Carbine?"

"Yep. A necessity, these days."

Stevie shakes her head.

"Will I get to see you before you leave?" she asks.

"Yes, I'll make a point of it. Breakfast or lunch, depending on the flight I can get. I'm also hoping to visit the Micheners in Pennsylvania before I go."

"Swell."

The women sit and listen to music for a while, nursing their drinks. Dickey lights cigarette after cigarette, happy with every flash of the military-issue Zippo. Tony's fancy gold lighter used to embarrass her. She's much more suited to the industrial over the decorative.

"Oh," says Dickey. "I have a gift for you."

She pulls the Tiffany box with the dangly gold earrings, cleaned and shined, out of her pocketbook and passes it to Stevie. She opens it and then promptly closes it, shakes her head and tries to pass it back to Dickey.

"No way," says Stevie.

"Yes."

"I couldn't."

"I had you pick them out, so I knew you'd like them. I won't wear them again. It's only my pearls from here on out."

"It's too much," says Stevie.

"It's not enough. You've done so much for me over the years. I can't thank you enough."

Stevie opens the box and runs her fingers over the shining gold. After a moment, she puts them on and shakes her head, making the dangles dance.

"Beautiful," she says.

Stevie hugs Dickey.

"It's too much," Stevie says, "but I love them."

"I'm glad," says Dickey, "You'll be unhappy to hear I stopped by Tony and Kay's place to give him back his gold Dunhill lighter, some old ephemera from our travels, and an early draft of my memoir to Kay, who so sweetly tells me she rereads it all the time."

"He doesn't deserve your kindness."

"Maybe not, but Father Hoa says we can stop world war by reconciling in our own little lives, and that's what I'm trying to do from here on out. If someone doesn't swallow the darkness instead of shoving it back from where it came, the game can never end. I failed with one set of protestors but was able to do it with the next. I'll keep trying one day at a time."

"You're a better woman than I am."

"I couldn't disagree more."

The bartender hovers. He looks as if he wants to ask Dickey something but can't decide when to do so.

"What's up, Buttercup?" asks Dickey.

His face colors.

"First, I want to apologize for how rude I was to you the first time I met you," he says.

"Apology accepted. Don't feel too badly. In case you haven't noticed, I can be a little ...much."

He grins.

"What's second?" she asks.

He rings his hands, then gathers the courage for his request. He ducks down and pulls an issue of *National Geographic* from under the bar. It's the issue with the picture that won her the National Press Photo of the Year award, of Nelson in the helo.

"Could you sign it?" he asks.

"Delighted to," she says.

Dickey takes the magazine, thumbing through it until she finds her article. She smiles when she sees the familiar faces. The bartender passes Dickey a pen and she signs next to Father Hoa's picture.

Peace, Dickey Chapelle.

Peace, she thinks. *Peace, I leave you. My peace I give to you.*

She hands the bartender back the magazine.

Dickey feels all at once very tired. She asks for the check, but Stevie paid without Dickey noticing. Dickey thanks her.

"Ready?" Stevie asks, holding out her arm to Dickey.

"Ready."

September 1965
New York City

Dear Mari and Jim,

I'm sorry to hear about Jim's heart attack, but so very glad to hear the prognosis is good and he is in such excellent care. More long walks, more healthy eating, lots of rest, and he'll be back up to snuff in no time. I'll try to visit next year, once I'm back from Vietnam. Maybe for my birthday, like when the cherry trees and daffodils, and your tender care, brought me back to life after that old commie prison.

I was thrilled to receive a signed copy of The Source, though Mari said that novel nearly killed you, Jim. I'll read it on the very long plane and boat and helicopter rides to Da Nang.

You suggested I might gather notes during my world travels for books in the style of Jim's. I could never make up characters—I have no imagination. But I am considering another memoir. I've lived many lives since the last, and maybe this time I'll be able to tell my own story on my own terms without censorship or feminization. A soldier can dream.

Take good care of each other.

Until we meet again,

All my love,
Dickey

FORTY-FOUR

SEPTEMBER 1965

Washington, DC

G eneral Lansdale got it all for me," says Dickey. "Full accreditation, a visa to South Vietnam, and a commission with the *National Observer*."

Dickey walks down a hallway in the Pentagon with Bob Morrisey. They just left a briefing meeting with General Lansdale and now head to the office of Bob's boss, U.S. Marine Corps Commandant General Wallace M. Greene Jr.

"Who knew an air force general and agency guy would make such a great literary and photo agent?" says Bob. "Will you have to pay Lansdale commission?"

"Only in intelligence," Dickey says, with a wink. "I'll be traveling with and covering the ops of marine recruits from California to Da Nang. While they're searchin' and clearin', I'll be shootin'. Hopefully, only with a camera. And hopefully I'll be the one targeting, and not getting targeted."

"You should be safer on the beaches and on foot patrol than you were on those canals. You were a damned sitting duck. Lucky as hell you didn't get sniped. Just like Iwo."

"Don't I know it."

A brief painful memory of Harold comes to mind. She crosses herself.

"I didn't know you were Catholic," says Bob.

"I'm not, but my papist friends are rubbing off on me."

Bob laughs and they continue, passing men in crisp starched uniforms from all branches of the armed services. Every time Dickey sees a salute, she stands taller. She's glad she cleaned and pressed her fitted tiger stripes today and polished her boots. The Pentagon is not the jungle, and she likes to look the part. She still carries her old battered field pack, and as they near Greene's office Dickey pauses, remembering the gift she brought for Bob's wife. She stops, fishes through her field pack, and passes Bob the black box with the sapphire and diamond bracelet Tony gave her ages ago. Bob opens it and looks at Dickey with a question in his eyes.

"For Mary Jane," Dickey says.

"Not for me? Darn."

Dickey slaps Bob's shoulder.

"Mary Jane admired it that time I wore it to the Cuban embassy," says Dickey. "With all the officers' wives' balls she has, she'll use it more than I ever will."

"It's too much, Dickey. This thing must have cost a fortune."

"My ex bought it. I don't want it, and it suits MJ's beauty. I'm more of a pearl and patch girl than a diamond girl. Now, put it away before one of the criminals around here steals it."

He smiles and places it in his pocket.

"Are you sure you don't want to hock this when you get back?" he asks.

"Nah," she says.

Bob looks at her a long moment, then continues leading her to

General Greene's office. The silence that has fallen over them feels heavy. Dickey chatters to fill it.

"I will say the one decoration I've always wanted and never gotten is the good ol' eagle, globe, and anchor insignia. As much training as I've had with you marines, I should have that by now."

"You sure are one of us, Dickey."

Bob knocks at the door and a deep voice barks him in. When they enter, Dickey feels strangely bashful. She removes her bush hat and twirls it in her hands while Bob announces her. She has met Greene before and has long admired and corresponded with him, but now that he's a four-star general and such a highly decorated leader, he's like a superhero to her. When he sees Dickey, he stands and his stern face breaks into a huge smile. She salutes him.

"Chapelle," he says. "I've been looking forward to seeing you again."

Dickey's mouth pops open like a striped bass.

"Sir, you took the words out of my mouth," she says.

"Your reports from all over the globe on irregular warfare have been invaluable."

"Thank you, sir. It's my honor."

"You've got brass balls, which is more than I can say for any other correspondent I've met. I do have one question, though."

"Thank you, sir. Yes, sir?"

"Why are you returning to Vietnam for a fifth time?"

She dreads this question from him, because he's one of the only people on earth who is asking it as a military leader and not a family member or friend. Her answer, however, remains the same.

"The marines are my men," she says, "and I have been accompanying them in the field since Iwo Jima. I'm not about to stop now."

He stares at her so long she breaks eye contact and looks down at her boots.

"Chapelle," he finally says. "You have the training of a marine and the heart of a marine. But you are missing something."

He unpins the gleaming gold eagle, globe, and anchor insignia from his own uniform and walks up to her.

"May I?" he asks.

She struggles to hold in the tears and nods.

"This is all I've ever wanted," she says, once she finds her voice. "Now I can die happy, sir."

"You are not to die. That is an order."

"Yes, sir."

"And you won't because you'll be with the marines. Not like those Army Airborners. No wonder you had to have surgery on that knee. Jumping with the likes of them."

Dickey and Bob laugh.

"I look forward to your dispatches, Chapelle," says Greene. "You are dismissed."

"Thank you, sir."

Dickey and Bob salute and turn to leave. As Dickey walks out the door, Greene calls her name. She stops and looks back at him.

"Be sure to keep your head down out there," he says.

"I will, sir. If for no other reason, I won't be able to take my eyes off my shiny new pin."

FORTY-FIVE

OCTOBER 1965

Wisconsin

After leaving the rest of her papers at the University of Wisconsin and saying her goodbyes to Robert, Marion, and the kids, Dickey takes the bus to Milwaukee. Aunt Lutie picks her up from the station and drives her to Shorewood—to the old family home—for her last night before deployment. Tomorrow Dickey will fly to San Diego and join the recruits at the U.S. Marine Corps Air Station in El Toro. Then, it's off to Vietnam.

Dickey still feels guilty for canceling lunch with Stevie before leaving New York, but packing and arranging transport of the files took Dickey longer and was more of an ordeal than she'd anticipated. With an earlier flight than she initially thought, she had to bow out. Her friend was sad but understanding.

"I'm used to it," Stevie said over the phone. "I'm like your long-suffering wife."

Dickey laughed and thanked Stevie for her endless patience, but Stevie's words haunted Dickey.

"Don't go," Stevie said. "We aren't winning. *You* told me that."

"It might be different."

"It will be different. It will be worse."

"You know I have to see it for myself."

Dickey did, but knowing Father Hoa wouldn't be there, thinking about a superhero like Harold Meyerkord getting killed, did give Dickey pause. She promised herself she would tread more carefully than ever. If the tide had turned and it was as Bernie had feared—that the Americans could not protect her the way the Sea Swallows and those native to the land could—then this would be her last assignment in Vietnam.

"When will you be back in New York?" Stevie had asked.

"Christmas. We'll take a carriage ride through Central Park and catch a show and get drinks at Bemelmans. Is it a date?"

"It's a date," said Stevie. "Love you, Dickey."

"Love you, too, ol' pal."

Dickey was glad for the time at the university, this time without protestors, and with Robert and his family. Now being with Aunt Lutie is the perfect last night send-off.

Aunt Lutie makes Dickey a wonderful dinner of sausage, sauerkraut, and potatoes, and the women talk over current events, solving the world's problems, and end up in stitches over the memory of doing the twist with Stevie at the ball.

"Oh, Aunt Georgie would have loved that," says Dickey.

Mentioning Aunt George sobers them. Aunt Lutie looks more and more old. She's an orphan and the last left of her generation, all her sisters and their husbands gone before her. She has no children of her own. Dickey takes a moment to really look at her aunt and process how lonely she must be. Dickey feels that old familiar guilt creeping over her, but also knows it's never enough to fix her in one place. She reaches for Lutie's hand.

"Should we visit Aunt George?" Dickey asks. "All of them?"

Aunt Lutie nods.

After cleaning up dinner, Dickey and Aunt Lutie drive to the cemetery. In the evening sun, they stand, arm in arm, looking down at the gravestones of their loved ones. A wind gust brings a flurry of leaves falling around them like colored snow. When a red willow-oak leaf lands on Aunt George's grave, Dickey smiles and picks it up.

"It looks like red lips," she says. "Aunt George sends her kisses."

Aunt Lutie smiles and dabs at her eyes with a handkerchief.

Dickey puts her arm around her aunt.

"It's hard being the last," says Dickey. "You bear it well."

Aunt Lutie puts her head on Dickey's shoulder.

"I won't ask you not to go," says Aunt Lutie. "But can this be your last assignment?"

"While that is unlikely, if I deem the situation unwinnable, I will certainly consider your request."

"Goodness!" says Aunt Lutie, pulling away and facing Dickey. "You've never said anything like that before. It gives me hope."

"What, that I'll come home and start that wedding photography business?"

"Yes, starting with your own nuptials. Why don't you find a nice marine finishing a tour? You do love them so. You wouldn't have to travel around the globe following him. He'd be right in your own home."

"I'm old enough to be the mother of the boys I'm shipping out with."

Aunt Lutie shrugs and raises her eyebrows, giving Dickey a naughty smile.

"What's wrong with that?" says Aunt Lutie.

Their flutters of laughter are almost visible to Dickey, rising up over the cemetery and into the sunset like sea swallows.

THE LAST ASSIGNMENT 383

OCTOBER 11, 1965
SAIGON, SOUTH VIETNAM

TAPE RECORDING, FOR WOR

DICKEY: Is this thing on?

[Tap. Tap.]

Barry Farber, you're the only person in the world for whom I'd project my old, gravelly, smoker's voice into a tape recorder for a radio audience to hear. You aren't even paying me. Good thing the *Observer* is, but we'll need to negotiate some perks later, and not just the honor of appearing on your show. Okay, starting now.

[Clears throat, coughs.]

This is Dickey Chapelle, reporting to you live from Saigon. October eleventh, nineteen sixty-five. I'm on my fifth trip back to a land that has stolen my heart, but oh my, has the land changed. I fear there are some in power who have wrestled the conflict from the hands of those trying to liberate themselves surgically and strategically, starting with the hearts and minds of the enemy, and are moving in the big, impersonal, imprecise war machines. More will be revealed. What I can see with my own eyes and feel in every cell in my body is how Saigon has changed since my last visit just months ago. The tension is so potent, it buzzes like electrical wires. Along the once lovely, scenic Saigon River are hundreds of threadbare tents as far as the eye can see, populated with gaunt, frightened, hungry, dirty refugees who have been forced from their homes by the communists and the fighting.

The American conscripted soldiers now match the numbers of volunteers, and I'm sorry to report, in the ranks of the new and the very young the worst of America is on display. Many of the soldiers are loud and drunk. They fight. They're crass and vulgar, and come spilling out of brothels and opium dens at all hours of the night. Every time I flick open my Zippo to light a cigarette I wonder if it will somehow reach the tinder smoldering in the air of this city and take the whole place down in flames.

One spot of light: yesterday an Italian envoy arrived with a statue of Our Lady of Fatima to display at Saigon's Notre-Dame Cathedral Basilica and take throughout South Vietnam's hamlets—all the way down to Binh Hung—promoting the message of God's mercy and peace. Children dressed like angels and ranks of nuns and priests that looked like the army of Heaven's Hosts paraded with the lovely lady of Father Hoa's fascination. When the sun set and the night rose, young women carried lanterns as

THE LAST ASSIGNMENT   385

the parade continued. It was a dramatic and moving display of beauty and peace in a place badly in need of it. If only Father Hoa were still here to see this. It might give him hope.

My old friend and fellow reporter, Henri Huet, is with me. While he was also moved by the parade, he's despaired by the pervasive atmospheric changes in Saigon and the country at large. His mother is Vietnamese, so everything here is personal for him. But he keeps his dignity while I have fits of temper, revealing I too am one of the crass and vulgar Americans. Without Father Hoa to keep me steady, I'm lucky to have Henri. One gentle word from him brings me back from the brink. I'm glad he'll be my traveling companion.

We'll helo out to Da Nang next week. I pray it's better there.

Signing off.

OCTOBER 19, 1965
DA NANG, SOUTH VIETNAM

TAPE RECORDING, FOR WOR

DICKEY: Mustering at oh six hundred, I look at the faces of the First Platoon of F Company, Second Battalion, 3rd Marine Regiment, waiting to board the choppers to Da Nang, memorizing them. It's my first time in an American-only platoon in Vietnam, and their first time with a press member of either sex. Until boot camp, most of them had never been outside their hometowns, let alone the country. Here, they might as well be on another planet. Most are taller than I am by a foot, and I am indeed old enough to be most of their mothers.

In the letter I compose in my head to my dear Aunt Lutie—desperate for me to settle down and take a husband—I tell her I've zeroed in on two six-footers. One is blond and one brunet, both are brown eyed, both single, both dimpled, both with ages that round up to thirty, and both have already proposed to me. I tell the men it depends upon their courage under fire before I finalize my choice. More to come.

Signing off.

———

DICKEY: Oh seven hundred.

A VC sniper finalized my choice for me.

The blond didn't survive our helo fleet transport to Camp Merrell, China Beach.

I can't breathe.

Signing off.

OCTOBER 23, 1965
DA NANG, SOUTH VIETNAM

TAPE RECORDING, FOR WOR

DICKEY: Today was Operation Red Snapper.

Yep, they let me name it. Yep, I did it for the drink at King Cole's bar. Yep, I also suggested Bloody Mary, but they thought that was too vulgar for a war zone.

Ooh-rah.

Henri Huet covered a parallel op. He says the press must spread itself out, in case of disaster, so someone will survive to tell the story. There's no point in being here if we can't tell the story. A good policy.

I didn't feel like lugging the tape recorder in the field, so this recap before supper will have to suffice.

My boys and I fell out at oh six hundred from Camp Merrell—named, as I learned, for the first marine killed there, Corporal Lowell H. Merrell.

Company F—mine—went by land. Company G proceeded via watercraft in the South China Sea. Our mission was to search and clear along Route 1, a vital road including bridges connecting Da Nang to Phu Bai. It was a relief to me that two South Vietnamese battalions from the ARVN—the Army of the Republic of Vietnam—joined the operation. The implication of Bernie's words—that Americans couldn't protect me as well as those born in Asia—stayed with me. With so many drafted boys, it was good to see men fighting for their homes, or at least their continents.

If one looked out at the South China Sea from the dunes, it was hard to believe we were at war, but the quick bursts of gunfire and the lightning-fast switch from quiet to shouting dispelled any thoughts of relaxation. I kept my head down between photo and gunshots and in the end, we had success. The ARVN killed seven VC and captured five. Our company killed one. Our boys seized four weapons and ninety pounds of TNT. With no American casualties, it was a good day, but the boys were disappointed they hadn't ferreted out more VC. I explained that first, it was Day One, and there were plenty of days left in their tour for action. Second, the more VC they ferret out, the more casualties we tend to suffer, so to thank God for the quieter days. They received my wisdom as well as young men who feel invincible can.

Much to what will be Aunt Lutie's dismay, they mostly think of me as their den mother. But maybe I'll find that husband yet.

On a more serious note, I never can get used to the body counts, and the picture I got of the VC the marines killed—riddled with bullet holes and being dragged across the beach for burial—was gruesome. There's not a publication in sight that'll take that picture. It's the kind of photograph that the military keeps for its bloody vaults or maybe the kind they don't even want, so it will go to my personal catalog, a requiem for a man who probably doesn't want prayers because he doesn't believe in God.

On the way back to Camp Merrell, one of the boys blared a radio, a GI station for the Americans playing "California Girls," by the Beach Boys. Little by little we joined in, and soon we were all singing at the tops of our lungs, riding along the shore—me on the top of the tank, the dimpled brunet named Al with his head poking out—with the wind in our faces and the joy of success, or at least not failure. I got that feeling again, of being where I should be, of belonging, of the esprit de corps. I welcomed it. It had been gone from me a long time.

I'll put that in letters to Aunt Lutie and to Stevie and to Slug, to set their hearts at ease.

I'll remind myself when the bogeyman plagues me at night.

Signing off.

OCTOBER 25, 1965

DA NANG, SOUTH VIETNAM

TAPE RECORDING, FOR WOR

DICKEY: I've been putting off today's report because it has disturbed me to my core.

Here goes.

At camp, the afternoon sun blazed, relentless, making a brick oven of the brick building where the VC prisoners were kept under lock and armed guard. I'd witnessed no food or water being brought in and I was beginning to feel unsettled. Even the communists in Hungary fed and watered me while I was jailed.

Henri and I smoked outside the mess hall, the interior growing too rowdy for us old war correspondents. I nodded toward the prison building.

"You think they're gonna cook 'em or ship 'em somewhere?" I asked.

Henri said the ARVN would probably ship them to one of their prisons, either on the island of Phu Quoc or Con Son. He said Con Son was also known as "Devil's Island."

All at once my skin was hot and soaked with sweat. It had been almost a decade since I'd been in the Hungarian prison, yet I still at times heard the clink of the metal gates, the screams, and the gunshots as clearly as if they were happening live.

Henri continued, telling me Con Son was built by French colonists, and that they locked up, tortured, and starved Vietnamese prisoners.

While we were talking, another truck of prisoners arrived. A trio of boys who looked like my third-grade bullies ordered the VC down but instead of leading them to the building, took them to the beach. The youngest VC prisoner cried like a baby, and he wasn't much older than one. This seemed to enrage the marines.

All the while, Henri's voice continued, telling me about what are called tiger cages at Con Son. Dugouts with bars on the ceiling. No shade from the sun. The only water for prisoners some days, the rain that falls.

I felt like I was having some kind of flashback of my own prison experience, blending with Fidel Castro's voice whispering in my ear the nickname he gave me. *Sangre de tigre.* Tiger blood.

While trying to haul myself out of my memories, I watched the marines wrap the crying VC prisoner's hands and feet in barbed wire, the blood making red tracks down the dirt and sand on his legs. He shook violently.

My temper exploded.

I threw my cigarette on the ground and ran toward them, thinking not only of myself as an innocent prisoner—which these prisoners may very well not be—but of the way Father Hoa treated all prisoners.

As I got closer, I could hear the taunts, the

foul, racist names the marines called the crier. They spit on him and alternated laughing with screaming at him. The sneering face of my old vampire guard came into my mind. I launched myself at the nearest marine.

"What the hell is wrong with you?" I said. "This is a human rights violation."

"A human rights violation?" he said. "This little bastard was wrapping punji steaks in poison and human shit as a booby trap when I found him. Act like an animal, get treated like one."

"Torture is a savage behavior," I said. "You are a savage if you engage in it. If you start to mimic the enemy, you will become him. Abusing prisoners of war makes you a prisoner of war."

"Who let the bitch in here?" said another marine.

Anger exploded in me like an aneurysm, but almost as quickly as it arrived, I felt a hand on my shoulder, like the gentle pressure of Father Hoa's grip. I looked behind me, half expecting him to be there, but he was not, at least not in form. There was no one.

Take a picture, I thought, the words coming from outside of me. *Make the picture to end all wars, one picture at a time. Make a quilt of pictures. A legacy. A requiem.*

I felt my heart rate slowing, my skin cooling. I readied my camera, pointed it, and shot.

As I clicked, the guns pointing at the prisoner slowly lowered, the spit and racist comments stopped flying. The mouths grew silent, until all that could be heard was the crying of the prisoner, until even he stopped.

An image, an action, a line from an ancient story came to my mind. I crouched down and drew a line in the sand.

Let he who is without sin cast the first stone.

I stood and glared every solider in the eye, staring each one down until all looked at their boots.

I left the men and returned to Henri.

Soon I saw the prisoner, hands and feet cut free. Water was dribbled over his wounds and then into his mouth from a U.S. Marine canteen.

Signing off.

NOVEMBER 3, 1965

DA NANG, SOUTH VIETNAM

TAPE RECORDING, FOR WOR

DICKEY: Though I hate to admit it, I'm starting to like the tape recorder, Barry Farber. I can riff a little, and record dialogue and feelings. I can record in the moment or after the moment, and then type it all up the way I like later, without having to mine my aging memory or read scribbly handwriting. And I always have liked hearing myself talk. As much as I pushed back when you handed me this thing, you clearly knew me better than I know myself, so thank you.

Pleasantries aside, here's tonight's retrospective.

A funny thing happened to me earlier. On my way into the officers' mess with Henri, where we were invited to dine with General Lewis Walt, I was intercepted by three young marines.

"Miss Dickey Chapelle?" they asked.

I hesitated in responding. Since the incident with the prisoner, many of the men kept a wide berth. These young soldiers however had hopeful and excited faces, as if they were looking at a celebrity. And let's face it, as the only female at camp, not only was I kind of a celebrity, but I could not deny who I was.

"All five-foot-nothing of her, yes," I said.

They pulled out their own cameras, asking me to pose for pictures.

"For whom?" I asked.

"Our dads."

"Are they reporters?"

"No, ma'am, soldiers. You were with our fathers at Iwo Jima."

A sharp feeling came over me, like a splash of cold water. I realized I was on my second generation of soldiers in war.

I consented.

My smiles for their pictures didn't reach my eyes. When they left me, chattering with excitement over the letters they'd write their fathers, I was happy to enter the officers' mess with those of my generation and older. Henri asked me if I was okay.

"I think so," I said. "The passage of time, though. Mutability. What a trip."

General Walt spotted us and folded us right into his company at the table.

We ate well on fresh local food—fish and rice and vegetables—and smoked and told stories all night. General Walt had been handpicked by General Greene to lead here, and Greene had written kindly of me. Walt was a big stocky guy with a great big smile he rarely had for those under his command but had in spades for me.

Time passed too quickly, the way it always did in enjoyable circumstances, especially in war. Henri looked at his field watch and told me it was time to turn in since we had to muster early. General Walt said he'd join us and walked us outside, the lights of a thousand stars pulsing over us in the black night sky. I thanked Henri for looking out for me. Otherwise, I would have stayed up all night talking.

"Somebody has to," Henri said.

"My guardian angel begs your pardon," I said. "He's been keeping me safe for forty-six years."

"And he's exhausted."

"True, true," I said. "Same with yours."

Henri shook his head.

"Your platoon was the one fired on?" asked General Walt of Henri.

"Yes, sir," said Henri. "Dickey and I had a bet on who would get it first. She lost."

"It's my turn tomorrow," I said.

General Walt took my arm to stop me from walking. He asked me if I wore a flak vest.

"Negative," I said. "Too heavy for little ol' me."

He frowned and told me to make sure I had guys in front of me and to keep my head down.

I assured him General Greene told me the same thing, and I would certainly obey both generals' orders.

Then I told him what I'll tell you, Barry, for your listeners, and for my family and friends, and even for my enemies.

If something happens to me out there, it's no tragedy. I'm where I belong, with whom I belong. And when my time's up, there's nowhere I'd rather be than on patrol with the marines.

Signing off.

NOVEMBER 4, 1965
CHU LAI, SOUTH VIETNAM

TAPE RECORDING, FOR WOR

DICKEY: Real-time reporting this morning, since we're

heading out for a multiday mission, and the action isn't expected early on.

You can hear the morning in my voice, the bird calls ringing out behind it, like sea swallows. I woke up in a state of euphoria, certain my boots belong here. My head is clear.

Last night, I had a dream that I was back at the family plot at the cemetery with my Aunt Lutie, and she asked if this could be my last assignment. We laughed about me finding a young marine to marry and settle down with, and then the bogeyman appeared, a shadowy form standing at the edge of the graves. I'm so used to him haunting me all over the world, I didn't even feel afraid. We watched each other for a few moments, and then he turned and walked away. I waved him off and felt a lightness like I have not in years, maybe ever. Have I finally made peace with him?

My favorite marine, Al, met me with coffee this morning. We'd slept together—not that way, in a friendly way—in the dugout, whispering late into the night. He told me all his plans and dreams and I could see his future like a runway lit for takeoff, long before him. I don't know if I got a moment of shut-eye, but I'm buzzing like a live wire now, energized and ready to go. My thoughts are pouring out too quickly to write or type or maybe even speak. Bear with me. I'm using stream of consciousness like a Beat poet, but it won't be as poetic. I will shape this into prose later, but for now, I'll let the thoughts and memories come as they will.

It feels safe at camp here, like Binh Hung did. There's a good secure perimeter. There are fighting men everywhere. A chaplain—Father McNamara—a priest like Father Hoa, but American, is a kindly father figure praying over all of us. He waves to me from his tent, where he stands with Henri. When my company gets back, we'll dine together. Father McNamara wants to hear all about Father Hoa and Binh Hung, having read my piece on them and having been inspired by it.

Al walks with me to muster. Our mission today is to search and clear the mountains outside of Chu Lai. We are a pebble thrown in a lake, ripples of safety and freedom spreading outward. May we proceed as gently as possible.

The wind moves through the linden trees, and I think of the lines about lindens from the poems in the Hungarian prison, and the linden I saw in the Rorschach ink blot test for the RIA. Did I have a premonition of this place at this time? I take a picture of the trees, and then of the line of men before me. Al turns back, and motions for me to look at the sky. I look up to where he points and see the long curved graceful arc of a rainbow, shimmering in the morning sunrise. It feels like a good sign, a promise.

THE LAST ASSIGNMENT

Will today be the day I make the picture to end all wars?

It's a day of high color, saturated. The world looks like a poem. I feel both here and in a dream. On earth and in heaven.

How I talk nonsense.

A bell rings the all clear at camp, like the bell at Binh Hung, like St. Patrick's. It's like the beginning of a new mission, blessed. A benediction.

We start the march. Words come like poetry in the cadence of our steps. Names, places, prayers.

Angel of Hialeah. Angel of Binh Hung. Angel of Chu Lai.

I touch my breast pocket, where the photo of Lai is tucked.

Guardian angel, keep me safe. Keep her safe. Make the world safe for the children.

Not my will, but His be done. On earth as it is in heaven.

En la tierra como en el cielo.

I could be in Vietnam or in Cuba. Ladybug's sweet face fills my memories, followed by Felipe's, then Harold's. I'm flooded with a film of all the faces and peoples and languages and places that have woven the rich tapestry of my life. I think of the sisterhood that sustained me. From the prison women of the Hungarian freedom fighters, to Las Marianas of Cuba, to the Home Guard of Binh Hung. From my beloved Stevie to my aunts George and Lutie. Then

I think of the brotherhoods on four continents and countless platoons and regiments that have welcomed me. U.S. Army, Navy, Air Force, Marines. Hungarian rebels, Cuban rebels, anti-Castro rebels.

They all feel like a blessing, including my enemies, because of what they taught me about the world and myself, and how they forced me to grow. We are all connected in spirit and in life. In blood. In the blood is the life.

Tiger blood.

As we forgive those who trespass against us.

A pebble dropped in water.

And lead us not into temptation but deliver us from evil.

Peace, I leave. My peace I leave with you.

Hans and Martha, may you have peace. Lai and Vinnie, Felipe's sons, may you have peace. Second generation of marines I'm covering, may the third have peace.

It's so beautiful here I could cry. My insignia flashes in the light. I look down at it.

Keep your head down.

Semper Fi.

Before leaving the cocoon of camp safety, I lift my head back up for one last look at the rainbow.

There's a staggering light. A pulse of sun. A bright glow, engulfing me, bearing me up into it.

Amen.

THE EPILOGUE I'VE
BEEN DREADING...

On that fateful morning, setting off on patrol, one of the men ahead of Dickey accidentally set off the trip wire of a booby trap. The VC had set it within five feet of where marines had slept. Dickey's throat was slit by a shard of shrapnel. Father McNamara saw the blast and ran to administer last rights to Dickey, while Henri Huet snapped the photograph as he thought she would have wanted him to do. It was reported that as she died very quickly—within minutes—her last discernible words were, "Well, I guess that was bound to happen."

She was Dickey, fully and completely, until her last breath. Sadly, she was the worst kind of first—the first American woman war correspondent killed in action. There are photographs and videos of the moment online for those who wish to see. Maybe if enough people see the image, it will be the picture to help end all wars.

Sergeant Albert P. Milville accompanied Dickey's body back to the States and was an honorary pallbearer at her funeral at the Forest Home Cemetery in Milwaukee. She was buried at the family plot with full marine honors, including the playing of *Taps* by U.S. Marine Sergeant James Folk. Bob Morrisey was among the attendees of the funeral. Albert Milville went right back to war, and I could not find what became of him.

Donations raised by CARE and by Dickey's brother, Robert, through the University of Wisconsin came pouring in and went to fund a field hospital for children in Chu Lai. One year after her death, upon its opening, General Lewis Walt presided over a dedication ceremony for the Dickey Chapelle Memorial Dispensary. The plaque there read:

> "TO THE MEMORY OF DICKEY CHAPELLE
> WAR CORRESPONDENT KILLED IN ACTION
> NEAR HERE 4 NOV 1965
> SHE WAS ONE OF US AND WE WILL MISS HER."

AUTHOR'S NOTES

- Dickey covered dozens of countries and territories on four continents. It was not possible to plumb the depth and breadth to which she went. I hope the regions and conflicts I chose best honored her work and revealed her character.

- I encourage all readers to visit Dickey's online photo archive at the Wisconsin Historical Society, where many of the pictures covered in the book can be found. Her work was a guide for me in terms of both plot and theme. Particularly moving is the photo of the village girl in Binh Hung doing the warrior dance. I've also put together a Pinterest page highlighting key figures and photos from Dickey's life.

- The novel is interspersed with letters, diary entries, telegrams, and radio and television show transcripts that I fictionalized based on and inspired by real documents, appearances, and recordings.

- At the Hungarian border crossing, there were other reporters, and the groupings weren't always the trio of Jim, Carl, and

Dickey, as I wrote, but I wanted to keep the characters as tight as possible while conveying the reality. Since Carl Hartman was at Dickey's trial and wrote the article about her release, I carried him through.

- While Sergeant Bob Morrisey was at Iwo Jima the same time Dickey was, I do not have confirmation that they met at that time. It is within the realm of possibility, so I made it so to suit the story and to consolidate characters, especially because she and Bob stayed in close contact the rest of her life.

- After Tony, Dickey's love life was not a primary or even secondary focus for her. There were rumors of and insinuations about relationships with various men from the writing world and the military world, but nothing notable, life-changing, or documented enough to warrant treatment in the novel.

- Dickey met Stevie Blick when she worked as a secretary for Tony's cardiologist before eventually doing personal secretarial work for Dickey. I placed Stevie with Dickey at the RIA because the time periods overlapped, and it made for simplicity of story.

- Dickey met Fidel Castro later in her 1958 trip to Cuba than I recorded. I condensed the action for more fluidity in the narrative.

- There are conflicting reports over whether Dickey met Felipe Santiago and his family in Cuba or later in Miami. I chose to make it in Cuba to keep his thread moving through the story. There are also conflicting reports as to whether she was riding in Felipe's boat or with the Americans when the explosion occurred, but all accounts state that Felipe saved her life.

- The mercenaries with whom Felipe and Commandos X began to associate themselves were not always men of integrity or morals. They are all suspected of involvement in the assassination of JFK. For a short time, Dickey was also investigated because of her association with the men, but she was cleared, and her file has since been declassified.

- Henri Huet was also killed in Vietnam, six years after Dickey, when the helicopter in which he traveled was shot down over the Ho Chi Minh Trail in Laos.

- Father Hoa and many of his people returned to Taiwan. He died there in 1993.

- Tien, Anh, and their family moved to the United States in 1979. They had seven children and many grandchildren, and were married for fifty-one years before Anh died in 2014. Tien died in 2019.

- Bernie Yoh settled in the United States. An accomplished musician and lecturer, he continued work with American intelligence and media throughout his life, including teaching psychological warfare and special ops at various military academies. He died in 1995, leaving a wife, five children, and many grandchildren.

- I was able to find out little to nothing about Sergeant Nelson West from Dickey's award-winning helicopter photo. For ease of story and fewer characters to wrestle, I placed him with Dickey starting at Laos and moving throughout her time in Vietnam. While not impossible, it would be unlikely to have such an arrangement. She was mostly with the Green Berets in Laos, and West likely would not have been with her the entire time. I do hope his characterization honored his service, and the thousands of men and women in the shadows of war history.

- The conversation with the three young marines who told Dickey their dads were with her at Iwo Jima happened in Vietnam in 1962, but I put it as part of her last mission in 1965 to serve the story.

- Before her last trip to Vietnam, Dickey made arrangements with the Historical Society at the University of Wisconsin to archive her papers. She left the bulk of her papers, however, in the care of her photo agent, Nancy Palmer, who eventually sent the files well after Dickey's death. I had Dickey do some of the transporting of boxes herself for purposes of story.

- In 1981, Pope John Paul II performed the full and valid consecration of the world and Russia. In 1985, Mikhail Gorbachev became secretary general of the USSR and started the reform regime. In 1989, the Berlin Wall came down, communism ended in Poland, and Soviet tanks left Hungary, among other countries and states. On Christmas Day, 1991, Gorbachev resigned, and the hammer and sickle flag came down, marking the official collapse of the Soviet Bloc.

ACKNOWLEDGMENTS

First and always to God, for revealing this story to me.

To my editor, Shana Drehs, for her insight and encouragement. It's a joy to work with you.

To my agent, Kevan Lyon, whose partnership for over a decade has meant the world to me.

To my team at Sourcebooks, including Dominique Raccah, Molly Waxman, Beth Sochacki, Cristina Arreola, Kate Riley, Sarah Brody, Diane Dannenfeldt, and Jessica Thelander, for all your hard work and support.

To Emily Noffke and Lisa Marine at the Wisconsin Historical Society. Your help with Dickey's archive was invaluable, and I'm grateful for your permission to use the epigraph quote from Dickey's autobiography, *What's a Woman Doing Here?*

To David and Dorie Thompson, and Frank and Sheri Damico, dear and supportive friends.

To Connor, Kelly, and Isabella Swegle: Thank you for the many hours you let me ramble on about this story on your pier.

To Kirk Regina, U.S. Army veteran and Apache pilot. I'm grateful for your consultation on helicopters and for allowing me to use your family Christmas tree farm name for the stand Dickey visits in New York. Thank you for your service.

To my in-laws, Richard and Patricia Robuck, to whom the book is dedicated. Thank you for your service, the artifacts from Vietnam, and all your love and support.

To my father, Robert Shephard, who remains my greatest cheerleader.

Finally, to my greatest blessings: my sons, Jake, Joe, and John, who inspire me every day, and my husband, Scott, for early and ongoing encouragement of this project, and for over three decades of love.

SUGGESTIONS FOR FURTHER READING

Chapelle, Dickey. *What's a Woman Doing Here: A Reporter's Report on Herself.* New York: William Morrow and Company, 1962.

Edwards, Julia. *Women of the World.* New York: Houghton Mifflin Co., 1988.

Fabian, Dr. Bela. *Notes on Cardinal Mindszenty: The Story of a Modern Martyr.* Chicago: Arcole Publishing, 2017.

Feldman, Andrew. *Ernesto: The Untold Story of Hemingway in Revolutionary Cuba.* Brooklyn: Melville House, 2019.

Greene, Graham. *The Quiet American.* New York: Penguin Books, 1977.

Hoffman, Joyce. *On Their Own: Women Journalists and the American Experience in Vietnam.* Cambridge, MA: Da Capo Press, 2008.

McGurn, Barrett. *Decade in Europe.* New York: Dutton, 1959.

Michener, James. *Bridge at Andau.* New York: Random House, 1957.

Ostroff, Roberta. *Fire in the Wind: The Life of Dickey Chapelle.* Annapolis: Blue Jacket Books, 1992.

Rinehart, Lorissa. *First to the Front: The Untold Story of Dickey*

Chapelle, Trailblazing Female War Correspondent. New York: St. Martin's, 2023.

Smith, Andrew F. *Rescuing the World: The Life and Times of Leo Cherne.* Albany: State University of New York Press, 2002.

Szabo, Father John. *I Was in Prison with Cardinal Mindszenty.* London: Muriwai Books, 2017.

READING GROUP GUIDE

1. Dickey's career (among other things) makes many personal relationships difficult, including her marriage. Has your career ever interfered with your relationships? Do you believe a career should take precedence over a relationship?

2. Do you like to travel light, or do you prefer to bring everything with you, just in case? Would you prefer a tent or a hotel room, or something in between?

3. Do you believe there is power in photography and photos? Do you believe newer technologies, such as deep fakes and AI, harm the credibility and intended effect of images we see on the internet or in the news?

4. Will war continue to be inevitable? Why or why not? Is there one single thing (such as a photograph) that could end all wars?

5. Consider the ethics of photojournalism. Where do you believe the balance is between reporting on traumatic events and

retaining the integrity and respect of the people being photographed? Should you always ask permission before taking a photo of someone?

6. Is there a hero or idol you look to when you're going through difficult times? Who is it and why?

7. Mari recommends Dickey write about her experiences in prison to work through her trauma. What do you believe are the best methods of coping with trauma or difficulties? Would writing about such things help you?

8. Do you have any possessions that are irreplaceable to you? What makes them so? In general, do you believe people nowadays place too much stock in their possessions?

9. Is there a place you feel truly at home, where you believe you could live out the rest of your life? Is it where you're living currently? Why or why not?

10. Dickey has very strong opinions about whom she's fighting with and whom she fights against. Do you agree with her opinions? Why is it that one often believes the side they are fighting for is the "correct" side of a conflict?

11. What were your main takeaways from Dickey's story? Was there anything you learned about the Cold War you didn't know before or that you're interested in learning more about?

A CONVERSATION WITH THE AUTHOR

How did you come to learn about Dickey and her story, and why did you choose to write about her specifically?

I came across Dickey while researching Virginia Hall and American women involved in global conflict. For a long time, I had stayed away from Dickey's story because of its tragic ending. But she haunted me, and eventually I knew it was time. I was assured throughout the writing process that Dickey did not consider dying in the field, doing what she felt she was called to do, was in any way tragic. I'm so glad I finally wrote her story.

This novel mentions Dickey writing her own autobiography. *Is* that version of her story censored, as she complains?

Yes, Dickey was frustrated by how censored and edited she was. She did not appreciate having to "feminize" her story, taking away the roughest, darkest places. Still, she was able to speak on nationwide lecture tours, so the experience was overall a highlight in her work life. For anyone who loves Dickey, I highly recommend reading it. Her voice is delightfully entertaining.

What is your writing process like?

I research for about six months, culminating with a novel timeline. Then I begin to write the first draft, which usually takes about nine months. It feels very gestational. I work five days a week, in the morning, for four to five hours—writing, editing, and revising—and stop once my brain gives out. Then, after a quick lunch, I walk, jog, or hike outdoors, in all weather. During exercise, I send myself a half dozen emails working out problems to fix the next writing morning. Then I start again the next day. Saturday mornings I tend to address ongoing research questions. Sundays are a day of rest.

How was writing this story different from writing your most recent historical fiction, *The Last Twelve Miles***?**

Writing *The Last Assignment* was more challenging because of the expanded timeline—covering many years, locations, and characters—instead of a short timeline with a small cast. From WWII through Vietnam, Dickey covered seven conflicts. Deciding which of those to write into the action of the novel took a lot of planning and discernment. My favorite part of the historical novel process is research, however, so I was deeply engaged in learning about the 1950s and 1960s, which I had never before studied in such detail. It felt fresh to me, as I hope it does to readers. And doing it all with a "guide" like Dickey was a tremendous joy. I adore her.

What would you like readers to take away from Dickey's story?

I would like readers to see that finding one's vocation and doing what we are made to do brings peace and joy. In spite of harrowing circumstances, Dickey knew she was living her calling and was doing so—in spite of mistakes along the way—with integrity. She always had hope, and that hope was for peace. It is my deepest prayer for the world.

THE LAST TWELVE MILES

Two real, brilliant women on opposite sides of the law, in a deadly game of cat and mouse...

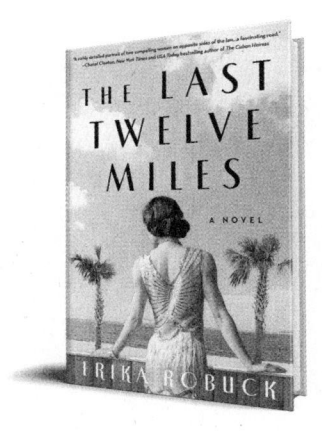

In 1926 Washington, DC, the coast guard is losing the Prohibition Rum War, but they have a new secret weapon to crack smuggler codes, intercept traffic, and destroy the rum trade one skiff at a time. That secret weapon is a five-foot-two-inch mastermind in heels, who also happens to be a wife and mother: Mrs. Elizebeth Smith Friedman, one half of the husband-and-wife pair who invented cryptanalysis.

Meanwhile, in the Bahamas, Cleo Lythogoe, the Bahama Queen, announces her retirement while regaling the thugs at the bar with tales of murder and mayhem on the high seas. Marie Waite, listening in, knows an opportunity when she hears it, and she wants the crown for herself so badly she can taste it. So begins Marie's plan to rise as rumrunner royalty long enough to get her family in the black. But the more sophisticated her operation grows, the more she appears on the radar of the feds.

Meanwhile, Elizebeth is the only codebreaker battling scores of smugglers. Despite the strain of solving thousands of intercepted messages, traveling the country, and testifying in court, Elizebeth's work becomes personal—especially when she discovers the identity of her premier adversary is the notorious Marie Waite.

From the glamorous world of DC intelligence to the sultry shores of the Straits of Florida, *The Last Twelve Miles* is based on the true story of two women masterminds trying to outwit each other in a dangerous and fascinating high-stakes game.

"A fascinating read!"

—Chanel Cleeton, *New York Times* bestselling author of *The Cuban Heiress*

For more Erika Robuck, visit: sourcebooks.com

ONE

MARQUESAS KEYS

Elizabeth

No matter how many jokes Elizabeth cracks, she can't make the coastguardsmen on patrol relax. Especially now that they've got the suspect's three-masted schooner in their sights.

"Special Agent Friedman, I beg you to go belowdecks," says Commander Jack Wilson. "This could get dangerous."

Jack is a gentle giant of a man, who's probably not much older than Elizabeth's thirty-four years but weathered far beyond. They're both a decade older than any of the crew onboard this brand-new seventy-five-foot patrol boat—*CG-249*—and Elizabeth is the only female in sight, a reality that she lives daily in her profession. Jack has been fretting all morning about the fact that he's responsible for her safety, especially since their first stop involved the empty, blood-splattered boat they found adrift and are now towing.

Jack would have a stroke if he knew it wasn't only me that he had to worry about, she thinks, touching her stomach.

"If anything happens," she says, "I promise you won't be held accountable. I signed a waiver. Besides, they wouldn't dare shoot a lady. Well, probably not, with so many witnesses."

The commander and his crew look at Elizabeth with unmasked horror. Until she arrived at base at sunrise, the coastguardsmen of Sector Key West hadn't known Special Agent Friedman—the one who solved a two-year backlog of intercepted messages in just three months, bringing an increase in the coast guard budget, allowing for shiny new boats like the one they're on—was a *she*. Her husband, William, would have laughed aloud to have seen their faces. Their bulging eyes and gaping mouths made them appear like a school of grouper on ice.

In addition to the shock of her womanhood, Elizabeth also showed up wearing linen trousers and a sleeveless white top, an outfit a Key West shop owner assured her was all the rage in women's nautical fashion. It has proven to be an unfortunate distraction. The coastguardsmen look from her bare arms to her trousers to each other in wonderment—as if she's a rare new marine species—when they think she's not paying attention.

I always pay attention, Elizabeth thinks.

"The rummy in charge could very well *be* a lady," says Jack, "and let me assure you, if it's one of the so-called ladies who run these operations, she has no conscience about whom she shoots."

Elizabeth motions to Boatswain Harvey Parry—the lanky fellow with big lips, whom the others call "Two-Gun"—for his field glasses. She lifts them to her eyes, and when she sees the vessel's name, passes back the glasses.

"This schooner does not have a lady onboard," Elizabeth says. "It's the *Betty*, captained by Robert Peltz, a so-called gentleman rumrunner. Based in Nassau, he has no record of violence, only extreme craftiness. It will be interesting to see why he's chosen to anchor within American waters, but no doubt he'll have a good explanation, and if we're in luck, the cargo that will land him in prison. I have good intelligence that his live well doesn't hold only bait."

Jack's great shoulders slump. Beaten, he commands the helmsman to steer closer and a boatswain to raise the pendant and the ensign.

Elizebeth inhales a deep breath of briny air. She can't believe this is her life.

The youngest child of nine, she endured half a lifetime of midwestern winters, lost her beloved mother too young, and had to work jobs she hated to pay back her father's loan for her college tuition at six percent interest because he didn't think women had any business in higher learning. Years ago, if she was asked if she could ever imagine she and her husband would be among the most highly sought-after minds of American military intelligence, traveling on work trips to places like this, Elizebeth would have laughed.

I have it all, she thinks.

Elizebeth is too busy to examine the reasons why her stomach constantly rumbles, why her sleep is so fitful, and why she often finds herself holding her breath. The perpetual shadow of unease is only quelled when she's codebreaking. At work, when she immerses herself in the letters and numbers, her mind takes an elevator that lifts her above her daily cares. Coming down from that headspace into wifehood and motherhood, however, is another story. It isn't a gradual ride, but a drop, like the plunge of a coast guard patrol boat on rough waves.

A flare shoots high, drawing her out of her mind. The crew watches, tense, but no one can be seen onboard the *Betty*. They increase their speed, and as the patrol boat slips in the crosscurrents,

Elizebeth loses her footing and grasps the railing for balance. An easterly wind picks up, blowing strands of her hair in her eyes. If only she remembered to buy new sunglasses. Her two-year-old daughter, Barbara, snapped Elizebeth's while she was packing for the trip. Elizebeth leans forward, scanning the scene before her, straining to catch a glimpse of Peltz.

Robert Peltz came on Elizebeth's radar last month. A coast guard patrol intercepted a group of messages in alphabetic codes from Nassau via radio. The coastguardsmen at Sector Key West and Base Six, in Fort Lauderdale, couldn't make heads or tails of them, so the messages were sent to Elizebeth, in Washington, DC. At first run, the letter groupings didn't point to any known codebooks, like *Bentley's*, so Elizebeth thought they might represent a book cipher, where a common text was agreed upon between supplier and runner.

Working the marks methodically, hour after hour, pencil on graph paper, Elizebeth found the telltale letter pairings that gradually revealed words, including *Nassau* and *Friday*, which, while possibly referring to a day of the week, also—because of her English degree—called to mind Robinson Crusoe and his man Friday. Further, she intuited this meant a smuggler had a Black man as a mate, likely Bahamian. Searching *Robinson Crusoe* as the codebook quickly brought success. As she broke the code to find the pages, lines, and positions of words, more started to come.

Peltz, Betty, Turtles.

Elizebeth's knowledge of the patrol region and fluency in the Spanish language brought to mind the translation of turtles—*tortugas*—which indicated the Dry Tortugas, which were close by. The other word of note was *Lunar*, but since it didn't come with any comment on the phase of the moon, she would consider it extraneous information until it wasn't. A call to the American Consul in Nassau revealed the date the *Betty* was registered at harbor and when she left. The ship manifest listed fish—canned and fresh—but omitted what was likely *under* the fish and the ice.

There can be no high like codebreaking, Elizebeth thinks.

This kind of high lasts and requires no loss of self and no inebriation. It's better than all the whisky they're about to confiscate. Better than the opium on the West Coast freighters she's intercepted. It's the thrill of hunting, of catching one's prey—of power—and she will never tire of it.

Something winks in the sun. A hastily thrown sailcloth fails to fully conceal the submachine gun bolted to the bow of the *Betty*. Elizebeth nudges Jack and motions with her head. At his word, Harvey "Two-Gun" and the portside crew point their weapons at the schooner. Elizebeth swallows. She longs for a glass of water, but now's not the time to ask.

"Fire a shot across the stern," says Jack to Harvey, "but do *not* hit the vessel."

Harvey's frown reveals his disappointment, but he obeys. The blast causes hysteria among the gulls bobbing on the surface of the water, and Elizebeth feels it in every cell of her body. A moment later, there's another sound, like the prolongation of a gull's cry. Hearing it causes the hair on Elizebeth's neck to rise, and her hand to move to her stomach.

"Is that...?" she asks.

The *Betty* comes to life. There's a stirring from inside the cabin, and a man dressed in white, from his hat to his boat shoes, strides out and throws up his arms. His shouts, alternating with what is now clearly a baby's cry, reach them on the wind gusts.

Jack's shirt is soaked through. His Adam's apple bobs as he swallows and tells his men to stand down.

Though the coast guard, and all who enforce Prohibition, are technically the "good guys," public opinion in the Rum War runs against them. Eleven million gallons of illegal liquor a year have created a booming smuggling economy, and the majority of Americans resent the liquor laws and sympathize with the rumrunners over the feds. The press feeds the division, characterizing smugglers as Robin Hood figures.

If they only understood the depths of the depravity of the illegal booze industry, Elizebeth often thinks, *they'd think twice about their contributions to it.*

As someone who's always been able to take or leave alcohol, Elizebeth doesn't find the country going dry to be a trial. She believes in the rule of law, believes that criminals should not profit at the country's loss, and has an insider's view into the horrors of the culture of violence that dominates smuggling. Women and children—particularly the poor—suffer the worst from it. Those who scoff at the law for a night of fun refuse to allow themselves to see the dark underbelly of the industry, and the papers don't want to run those stories, especially when it comes to mobsters, who think nothing of offing journalists.

Popular or not, Elizebeth and the agencies fighting the Rum War have pledged to uphold the law, but that doesn't make bad publicity easy to stomach. If the newspapers get wind of coastguardsmen firing on a schooner with a baby onboard, there will be no end to the trouble.

Elizebeth grips the railing. The metallic smell of her sweating hands on the steel bar puts an unpleasant tang in the air, and she wonders if the sudden rise of nausea is more from pregnancy, seasickness, or shame. She was so sure of herself about the boat and its function, and so intent on showing these men that she was capable. If she's wrong about the purpose of the schooner, she will not only embarrass herself, but also feed the inherent prejudice against her, as a woman in a field populated almost exclusively by men. Not to mention putting a baby—*or two*, she thinks—in harm's way.

No. Baby or not, she's certain: Peltz is a criminal. He might also be a father, but that doesn't change the fact that he's breaking the law. She'll be angry with herself if she missed a detail that should have alerted her to a baby onboard, but until then, she'll only be angry with Peltz.

A Black man emerges from the *Betty*'s cabin, tips his wide-brimmed straw hat at them, and hurries to raise a white flag. Once Peltz sees the lowered guns, he dips down and picks up the squalling infant, who has crawled out of the cabin door. He lifts her and plants a kiss on her fat cheek. Her halo of blonde ringlets is the same color as little Barbara's, and the girl wears only a tiny pair of pink gingham breeches, dirty at the knees. When she points at the cannons, Peltz says, "Boom! Boom!" until she giggles. The laugh triggers a physical ache in Elizebeth to hold Barbara, followed by an impulse to slap this man who's raising his baby like a pirate.

"*Betty*, ahoy!" calls Jack.

A boatswain throws Peltz's mate a line, and he catches it and pulls them in with ease, slipping bumpers between the boats so they don't smash against each other in the currents.

When the tanned, tall Peltz notices Elizebeth, she can see his surprise and pleasure. He flashes a white-toothed grin that she's mortified to realize draws forth a blush, though he could never tell. Her skin was already flaming red from the sun.

"Look, Betty," Peltz says. "A lady, on a coast guard patrol boat. What a novelty."

Betty, Elizabeth thinks. *A boat name and a baby name.*

"See, daughter," Peltz continues. "You can do anything you set your mind to."

Peltz's sentiment and his good looks are an irresistible package but Elizabeth can't allow herself to be charmed.

"Permission to come aboard, Captain?" she asks.

Jack whips his head around to look at Elizabeth as if she's gone mad.

"Only if you promise to leave your weapons behind," says Peltz, with a wink.

My only weapon is my brain, and that's coming with me, she thinks.

To Peltz's amusement, and the coastguardsmen's continued astonishment, Elizabeth makes a show of emptying the pockets of her trousers. A moment later, Peltz passes Betty to his mate and holds out his hand as if expecting Elizabeth to climb over, like a capuchin monkey, from one railing to another.

"I can't advise this," says Jack, intercepting. "It's not protocol."

Elizabeth can see that Jack is flailing and feels as if he has lost control of his ship. She doesn't want to undermine his authority in front of his subordinates.

Lord knows, I've felt the sting of that, she thinks.

"I agree," says Elizabeth. "But I want to get my hands on that sweet baby, and I can't do it from over here."

She looks up at Jack and widens her eyes, hoping to convey to him she can help them gather intelligence, which is, after all, why she's along for the ride. When he sighs, she knows he's going to let her. He's not a fighter. She can see that Jack went into the coast guard to rescue people, not enforce smuggling laws.

Though that enforcement, in many cases, she thinks, *is arguably a kind of rescue.*

"At least board safely," Jack says.

Elizabeth acquiesces, allowing him to escort her to the stern, where a side door opens that allows her to step down onto the *Betty*, rather than scamper from one railing to another. Peltz is there, hand out, and she takes it, noting his hand is even sweatier than hers, and that his blue eyes shift away when she looks up into them at close range. He's a head taller than she is, and so ripe she has to hold her breath. Her eyes sweep the decks, noting an empty crate on its side, a line of fishing poles with rusty reels, and a tangle of dry-rotted lines. There's a border of grime on the boat's edge, and several empty sardine tins in a bucket, revealing this ship is not shipshape.

Concern for the child's welfare rises, but when Elizabeth sees Betty's easy attachment to both her father and the mate, and how they soften and smile when the sunbeams of her attention hit them, Elizabeth is reassured. Though in need of a bath, the baby is clearly happy and well fed, and her skin is tanned, but not burned.

Peltz takes Betty from his mate, and she gazes at Elizabeth with frank curiosity. Elizabeth smiles and holds out her arms, which Betty looks at for a moment before turning to her father with a question in her eyes. When he nods, Betty consents, and Elizabeth's arms are filled with the very heavy infant.

"How old is Betty?" asks Elizabeth.

"Eleven months, but she's about to outweigh me," Peltz says.

"She looks wonderful."

"It's a good life on the sea," he says. "Are you a mother?"

Elizebeth doesn't answer. She tries never to give personal information. Increasingly, Elizebeth needs a security detail when appearing as an expert at trials. There are many criminals who would love to "take her for a ride."

"Pardon my curiosity," she says, "but is Betty's mother onboard?"

Elizebeth notes the tightening of Peltz's jaw.

"No, she prefers dry land," he says. "Thousands of miles away."

Elizebeth burns to ask more, but senses that subject is closed. Instead, she walks the baby around the deck, pointing at objects and seeing if Betty can name them. The child parrots Elizebeth and soon points out things on her own for Elizebeth to mimic. The baby is so heavy that Elizebeth has to put her down and hold her hands to walk her.

"Po,'" the baby says, passing a fishing pole.

"Pole," says Elizebeth. She steers the baby toward the live well, while pretending to allow her to lead.

"Wa wa," the baby says, stomping in the puddle by the well's hatch.

"Water," says Elizebeth.

Suddenly, looking in the well, Elizebeth hopes there's no illegal contraband on this boat. It will bring her no joy to see a father hauled into jail. She no longer feels like a happy hunter, no longer cares about proving herself to these coastguardsmen. She realizes that going in the field makes her targets human, which—while valuable from an intelligence-gathering standpoint—makes them sympathetic.

"Eith," says Betty, with a lisp.

"Ice," says Elizabeth.

"Sish," says Betty as they look down at fish covered in ice.

"Fish," says Elizabeth, her heartbeat quickening.

Peltz walks over and scoops up Betty, taking her to the railing.

He's trying to divert me.

"Pelicans," he says, pointing at the flock bobbing in the current.

"Pecansth," says Betty.

They laugh at her pronunciation, releasing the tension.

From the patrol boat, Jack has been moving parallel to Elizabeth the entire time, and now clears his throat.

"As you are within the twelve-mile zone," Jack says. "We are within our rights to board and search. We prefer to do so peacefully."

The United States has signed treaties with dozens of countries recognizing their authority over an increased area in offshore waters from three to twelve miles. This has made it harder for rumrunners to race the last twelve miles of their journeys from the islands and the floating offshore liquor warehouses—known as Rum Row—to the coasts. However, the change has also made it harder for the coast guard, whose patrol area has expanded exponentially.

"A squall put us off course," says Peltz. "We thought we'd camp here before we got back to fishing. You're welcome onboard. If you want to waste your time."

Jack nods at Harvey, who leads the crew as they climb onboard. Because of Peltz's cooperation, the coastguardsmen must search more cleanly than if they had been opposed, allowing the mate to open doors and hatches instead of breaking them down themselves. Elizabeth can see Harvey's unrestrained disappointment. Stiff and shifty-eyed, he looks like a coil about to pop. Jack, however, looks more at ease, glad not to have a contentious captain or a battle on their hands, only an interesting story to take home to the bars of Key West.

So far.

"Ba ba," says Betty, pointing to an empty bottle.

"Bottle," says Elizebeth.

She leans down to pick up the empty, label-free bottle. Making eye contact with Peltz, she brings the bottle to her nose and inhales at the opening. It smells only of the sea.

"You must be a reporter," Peltz says.

Elizebeth passes the bottle to him. He sits baby Betty down and gives her the bottle, where she proceeds to spin it around on the wooden decking.

"She keeps us honest," says Peltz. "No curse words when Betty's onboard. Which is always."

He gives Elizebeth a pointed look before turning his attention to the coastguardsmen, who inspect the live well.

Please, don't let there be any booze in there, she thinks.

Elizebeth moves away from Peltz, continuing to scan the ship, ending up at the helm. There's a radio in the dash, and a map is laid out on the stand behind the steering wheel. Her eyes dart left and right, up and down. She can feel the words on the map of the Marquesas Keys impressing themselves in her mind, sliding into one of the endless file cabinets contained there.

Mangrove, Mooney, Gull, Key, Harbor, Shoal.

She gets a thrill when she sees the spine of a book peeking out from under a map.

Robinson Crusoe.

Feeling Peltz's eyes on her, she walks over to the starboard side, which faces the uninhabited island, and notes the lowered straps, grazing the waves, where a dory is meant to hang. She realizes there have to be more than two people onboard to man a schooner this size. As if conjured, the small craft emerges from the mangroves, six onboard, on course for the *Betty*. The coastguardsmen haven't noticed. They're questioning the mate about the submachine gun.

Is the dory dropping off or picking up? she thinks.

Peltz joins her at the railing.

"I'm all Betty's got," he says.

Elizebeth continues to watch the dory, trying to make out its cargo, and opens the Peltz file in her brain. There has not yet been any tie between Peltz and a larger crime syndicate, so he's likely operating alone, both in his business and in his family. He has indicated that Betty's mother has abandoned them both.

Betty crawls over to Peltz. He lifts her, pressing his nose into the baby's cheek.

Elizebeth looks back at Harvey and the men, who still haven't noticed the dory. Peltz's crew, however, has noticed them and works to row back into the mangroves. They're lucky the wind, waves, and gulls are so lively. The noise hides the splashing sounds of their oars on the sea. They're soon swallowed by the vegetation. Peltz exhales.

"Thank you," he says.

For a moment, Elizebeth doesn't respond. She doesn't feel good about what she's done. Or rather, not done. She thinks she shouldn't have come out on patrol. It made the waters too murky, too gray. She prefers black and white. Pencil and paper. She can't wait to get back to her desk in her home library, and back to her husband and baby.

"I'm trying to be a better father," Peltz says. "Every day. For Betty."

The coastguardsmen complete their search and return to their patrol boat. Jack whistles and motions for Elizebeth to join them. Before she goes, she turns to Peltz.

"I hope so," she says. "Next time, we won't turn a blind eye."

"We?" he asks. "I thought you were a reporter."

"You said that. I didn't."

ABOUT THE AUTHOR

© Nick Woodall

Erika Robuck is a national bestselling author of historical fiction, including *The Last Twelve Miles*, *The Invisible Woman*, and *Hemingway's Girl*. Her articles have appeared in Writer Unboxed, CrimeReads, and *Writer's Digest*, and in 2024, she was named a Maryland Writer's Association Notable Writer and won the Anne Arundel County Arts Council Literary Award. A boating enthusiast, amateur historian, and teacher, she resides in Annapolis with her husband and three sons.